PRAISE FOR DHARMA KELLEHER

"Shea Stevens is just about the most interesting and sympathetic criminal you'll meet."

— PAULA BERINSTEIN, AUTHOR OF THE AMANDA LESTER DETECTIVE SERIES

"A thrilling ride that will have you turning pages into the wee hours of the morning!"

— RENEE JAMES, AUTHOR OF SEVEN SUSPECTS

"Dharma Kelleher breaks new ground and breaths new life into a great genre. The best thing to happen to crime fiction since V. I. Warshawski."

— GREG BARTH, AUTHOR OF SELENA

SNITCH

SNITCH

A SHEA STEVENS THRILLER

DHARMA KELLEHER

ACKNOWLEDGMENTS

Thanks so much to everyone who helped make this second installment of the Shea Stevens thriller series possible, starting with the members of the various writer groups I'm a part of, including FF7, Sisters in Crime Desert Sleuths Chapter, the West Valley Critique Group, and the West Valley Writers Workshop. Your honest feedback, your wonderful suggestions, and your never-ending support are fuel to my engines.

Super duper thanks to my agent Sharon Pelletier of Dystel, Goderich & Bourret. You are a master deal maker, advisor, therapist, and friend. I am beyond grateful for all you do.

And last, but not least, the amazing team at Red Adept Editing and Damonza.com who helped me re-release this novel. You all have repeatedly gone above and beyond. Thank you for believing in me and in Shea.

1

———

Terror gripped Genette Abrams. *What's wrong with me? Can't breathe.*

Earlier in the evening, Ironwood's Downtown District had pulsed with Central Arizona University students. Genette had been having such a good time at the Trip Hop Lounge, dancing and rolling on a drug called hex, a mix of heroin and ecstasy, that she told her sorority sisters to go home without her.

But at eleven thirty, her stomach had begun to cramp. She'd stepped outside, hoping some fresh air would help make her feel better. It hadn't. The stomach cramps worsened until she hurled next to an ironwood tree planted along the sidewalk. She would have been embarrassed had anyone seen her. But on a Monday night finals just a week away, the streets were all but abandoned.

As she walked away from the club, her legs and chest stiffened, making walking and breathing difficult. Her four-inch heel slipped off the sidewalk. She tumbled into the cold, dark street and lay shivering on the pavement. Above her, the red and green lights of a holiday decoration affixed to a streetlamp glowed cheerily.

As quickly as it came, the bizarre tightening of muscles released. Using a small ironwood tree planted along the sidewalk to pull herself up, she hobbled against a nearby building and took a breath. *I'll be okay. Just need to find my car and get home.* She managed a smile, as the bass beat of the club's house music lingered in her drug-lubricated mind. *Where the hell'd I park, anyway?*

A second wave of stiffness battered her, more intense this time. Hands trembled. Jaw tightened. Leg muscles seized. Her chest muscles constricted and squeezed the air out of her lungs. Genette cried out in agony through gritted teeth as she collapsed. "Grrrngh . . ."

What's happening to me? Please, God, don't let me die.

Moments before she blacked out, the tightness and pain eased up again. She took deep, gulping breaths. A gust of icy November wind blew across her bare legs. *Gotta get out of the wind.*

Holding on to a wall to steady herself, and inched along the steep sidewalk into an alley. It wasn't much warmer, but at least it cut the wind screaming down the street.

Gotta call Sarah. She'll help me.

She reached for the phone in her purse. With clumsy fingers, she dialed her roommate's phone. Another wave of cramps and tremors hit her.

"Hello?" asked a gravelly, irritated voice.

"Su . . . muh . . . heh . . ." The words would not come out.

"Genette, is that you?"

"Brah . . . nee . . ." With a squeal, her jaw clamped shut and refused to open.

"Dammit, girl! I told you before—don't be drunk dialing me this late. I'll talk to you in the morning."

"Ughnnn . . ." Her lungs burned for air. Her chest tightened. Her pulse thrummed in her ears, like taiko drums from a horror movie soundtrack. A foamy liquid in her throat choked off her breathing. Panic and confusion gripped her. She collapsed on the ground. The phone clattered onto the sidewalk next to her.

"Shut the fuck up!" came a voice farther down the alley. "Some of us is trying to sleep!""

A woman bundled up in a coat with a hoodie loomed over her, illuminated by the dim light spilling from the street. "Jesus H. Christ. Can't you find someplace else to make noise?"

Genette reached out, her eyes bulging in their sockets. "Mmrrnngh ..."

"Fucking drunk college kids ain't got nothing better to do than interrupt my sleep. Shit." The woman disappeared from view, followed by the rhythmic squeaking of a grocery cart wheel.

Genette collapsed as her muscles no longer responded. *No, don't leave. Please. Help.*

Her body arched backward in crushing waves of pain, twisting and contorting. The cold deepened. Genette's mind went dark. Dead eyes stared sightless into the night.

Twenty miles to the south, in the town of Sycamore Springs, Shea Stevens and three of her employees at Iron Goddess Custom Cycles were rushing to finish the one-off bagger. It was nearly midnight. The new owner was scheduled to pick it up in the morning.

The scarred-over gunshot wound on Shea's lower back burned as she tightened the leads on the motorcycle battery. The ache in her recently healed collarbone wasn't helping either.

Three months earlier, two sheriff's deputies had attempted to silence her after she learned they were running a heroin-trafficking ring. Sergeant Willie Foster had run her bike off the road with his car, breaking her collarbone. After she killed Foster with a shot to the head, his cohort, Detective Edelman, had put a bullet in her back. Had it not been for Edelman's assigned partner Detective Rios, Shea would have been dead.

But Shea didn't have time to worry about old wounds. If they didn't deliver the bike on time, the shop would incur expensive penalties. Shea didn't care so much, but Terrance Douglas, her business partner, would have a shit fit if they missed the deadline.

"Okay, folks, let's bring this baby to life." Shea inserted the key and pressed the starter button.

The engine went *rurr-rurr-rurr,* but didn't catch. A series of frustrated glances passed between Shea and her crew. She tried again, holding the starter a few seconds longer. It refused to turn over.

"We did put gas in the tank, right?" Shea asked.

Lakota, an Oglala Sioux woman who served as the shop's mechanical engineer, inspected the bike. "Full tank. Battery's fully charged. Oil pan's filled. Air intake looks fine. It should start."

"Maybe it's the wiring," suggested Kyle Flores, Shea's newest hire. Despite being just under four feet tall, he still managed to ride a standard-size motorcycle and had turned out to be a decent motorcycle mechanic.

Switch, the shop's electronics specialist, stared at the bike. "It's not the wiring," she said firmly.

"If we got air and we got fuel, problem's gotta be electrical." Shea rubbed the scar on her back. "No offense, Switch, but I think something's miswired"

"I didn't miswire it. I did everything right. I always do everything right."

Shea caught a cautionary look from Lakota that said, *Don't set her off.*

Outside the closed garage bay doors, the throaty growl of a Harley from the back parking lot caught everyone's attention. A moment later someone pounded on the back door with such force it made everyone jump.

"Who could that be?" asked Lakota.

"I'll deal with this bozo." Shea grabbed a large deadblow hammer and marched toward the door. "Y'all figure out why this bike won't start."

Whoever was knocking was probably not someone she wanted to talk to. A tweaker looking to rob the place. A cop looking for her or one of her team of second-chancers. An ex-girlfriend making a late-night booty call.

"We ain't open yet," Shea yelled through the closed door. "Come back at eight."

More pounding followed by a familiar voice. "Shea-Shea? Open up. It's Monster." He sounded drunk.

Anger rippled up her back and into her fists. *Like I ain't got enough shit to deal with.*

Shea kicked open the door, nearly knocking the heavyset biker off his feet. "What the hell you doing here? It's late and I'm busy."

Monster sported a halo of snowy hair and longish slush-colored beard tied with a rubber band. His leather vest, known as a cut, identified him as a member of the Confederate Thunder Motorcycle Club. "Easy, girl. Saw the lights on. I left you messages, but you never called back."

"I ain't got nothing to say to you, old man."

"Now, Shea . . ." Monster reached out to put a hand on Shea's shoulder, but Shea backed away, warding him off with the hammer.

"Keep your fucking paws off me. I don't want nothing to do with you or the Thunder ever again. You got me?"

"Shea, darling, I just wanna see my grandbaby."

"Annie ain't your grandbaby."

"Like hell she ain't. I raised your sister Wendy since she was seven years old. I was there when she gave birth to Annie. I'm the closest thing to a grandpa Annie knows."

"Wendy's dead because of her involvement with the Thunder. I ain't gonna let that happen to Annie."

"Aw, that's horseshit and you know it. That no-good cop's the one shot Wendy. She'd still be alive if you two had stayed at the clubhouse like y'alls supposed to."

Shea swung at him but he caught the hammer and pulled her close.

"Wendy's dead cause the Thunder are the biggest crank dealers in the county," she said. "I'm the one who rescued Annie from the kidnapper. I'm her guardian now. And I say you ain't getting nowhere near her."

"Shea, I know you're angry. Hell, I'm angry, too. It can't be easy raising Annie by yourself. I'm here 'cause Julia and me wanna help."

"Me and my girlfriend are doing just fine without you."

"The girl needs a father figure in her life. She ain't getting it having two mommies."

"Get the fuck outta here, Monster, 'fore I call the cops."

"Shea, please. Julia cries every night she don't see Annie. We lost Wendy. Least you could do is let us see our grandbaby."

Shea studied Monster's face. "As long as you're a member of that drug-dealing, murderous band of misogynists you call a motorcycle club, you and Julia ain't stepping anywhere near Annie."

Monster scoffed. "You been hanging around them femi-Nazis in the Athena Sisterhood?"

The Athena Sisterhood was a women's motorcycle club that frequently staged protests and rallies for feminist causes. There were rumors that the local chapter had fire-bombed a state senator's office and a strip club. Shea had avoided them because the chapter was run by an ex-girl-friend of hers.

"None of your business who I hang with."

Monster's face changed from pleading to threatening. "You best stay clear of them Barbie bikers, if'n you know what's good for ya."

"Tell me, old man. Is the Thunder still using the old stash house to store drugs and guns? Be a shame if the cops busted the place."

His eyes narrowed. "Shea, talk like that could get you hurt. Your daddy mighta been the Thunder president once upon a time, but that won't protect you if you go snitchin'."

"This conversation's over." Shea tried again to close the door, but Monster stopped it with his boot.

"I'm gonna see my grandbaby, Shea. Ain't no reason to be stubborn about it."

She smashed Monster's boot with the dead-blow hammer. He fell back cursing and holding his foot.

"Stay away from my family, or I'll put a bullet in your brain." She slammed the door and locked it.

Monster pounded on the door. "This ain't over," he yelled in a strained voice. A moment later the roar of his bike filled the air, then faded into the night.

Shea trudged back to her crew and their work in progress. Kyle and Lakota were staring at her. Switch had unbolted the tank and propped it out of the way as she worked with the bike's ignition system.

"You okay, Shea?" asked Lakota.

"Just peachy. What's the story with the bike?"

"Spark plugs were bad out of the box. Switch is

replacing them now." Lakota leaned close to Shea. "Who was that guy?"

"A member of the Confederate Thunder I used to know."

"Should we be worried? Last time they showed up here, they shot up the place."

"Nah," Shea said, hoping to convince herself as much as anyone.

2

———

AT HOME, Shea pulled off her motorcycle gloves and helmet and rubbed her deeply scarred face, a memento of a childhood dog attack. Overwhelmed with fatigue and a growling stomach, she dragged herself through her garage —navigating around her personal collection of custom bikes—and into her house.

The kitchen was dark, but the aroma of cooked meat and spices lingered in the air. Shea deposited her keys in the blue enameled dish on the breakfast bar, which separated the kitchen from the living room.

Jessica, her girlfriend, sat on the love seat, twirling and untwirling an ebony braid around a finger and staring at her laptop. Their black cat, Ninja, lay curled up next to her. She looked up as Shea closed the door to the garage and tossed her armored hoodie onto one of the mismatched recliners.

"Hey, babe! I was getting worried. It's after one o'clock." Jess stretched and nudged Ninja to the floor. The cat meowed in protest but retreated to the quiet of the master bedroom.

"Sorry. I shoulda called." Shea plopped down beside Jessica and gave her a quick peck on the lips. "Damn bike wouldn't start. Practically took the whole thing apart looking for the problem."

"Well, I'm glad you're home safe." Jessica rubbed Shea's shoulder. "Your collarbone giving you any problems?"

Shea groaned with pleasure at Jessica's touch. "Not at all," she said, wishing it was true. "Annie get to sleep okay?"

"Yeah." A frown creased Jessica's face. "Kid at school was teasing her about the scar on her ear."

"Damn. Ain't enough that fucking kidnapper cut her ear off. Now some snot-nosed brat is making fun of her? What the hell's wrong with people?"

"Her teacher's going to talk to the parents." Jessica said. "Want me to heat you up some leftovers?"

"No, thanks. I'm too tired to eat. I do wanna check in on Annie."

"Don't wake her."

Shea crept into Annie's room and sat on the edge of her bed. The eight-year-old's cherubic face was highlighted in the glow of a nightlight. The scar where the surgeons had reattached her left ear was still visible. What wasn't visible was the emotional trauma from her kidnapping and the death of her parents. But Shea knew it was there, having witnessed her own mother's murder at the hands of her outlaw biker father.

"Kids are resilient," the social worker had said after Shea gained custody of Annie.

Shea wasn't so sure. She only had to look in the mirror to know that some scars lasted a lifetime. And it was this shared trauma that left Shea uncertain what to do. Being around the girl brought up memories Shea had spent years trying to bury.

"I'll take care of you, Doodlebug," she whispered.

Annie stirred but remained asleep. Shea walked out, closing the door behind her.

"Annie still asleep?"

Shea nodded and collapsed next to Jessica, resting her head on Jess's shoulder.

"Shea, I'm worried about Annie. She's so young to have gone through what she did. Seems like every night she has nightmares. More than a few times she even wet the bed. And now kids at school are picking on her. I think we should take her back to the therapist."

"She already went three times."

"She clearly needs more. It takes time to heal. Not just time, but quality time. Now that you're back at work, you're hardly ever around."

"I'm catching up after being out for three months."

"I know you're busy, but it feels like . . ." Jess's face clouded over and she turned away.

Shea tilted Jessica's chin back until their eyes met. "What?"

Jess sighed. "Feels like you're avoiding her."

"Don't be ridiculous. I just sat for ten minutes in her room."

"While she's asleep."

"You want me to wake her up?"

"No, it's just . . . I don't know. I guess I'm also worried about you, too."

"Me? I'm fine."

"When was the last time you really talked to someone about what happened?" Jess placed her hand on the center of Shea's chest.

"Whaddya mean what happened?"

"Your sister getting killed. You getting shot." Jess paused, then whispered, "You killing Annie's dad."

"Who'm I supposed to talk to about that? A shrink? They'd arrest me for murder."

"Not if it was self-defense."

"What's a shrink know about what I been through, anyway? Not a goddamn thing, that's what. All they got is theories and book learning. 'Tell me your feelings,'" said Shea in a mocking voice. "It's bullshit. I know what I fucking feel. Don't change nothing."

"Doesn't have to be a therapist. There's a group of women I know. They call themselves the Garden Club."

"Garden Club? I ain't got time to be planting tomatoes and orchids and shit."

"They're not a gardening group. They're women who get together and discuss things going on in their lives. Not just things, but emotions, struggles, trauma. I hear it's very spiritually enlightening."

"Sounds a little touchy-feely, woo-woo."

"So what if it is? Maybe that's what you need."

Shea shook her head. "This girl don't do touchy-feely."

"Okay, maybe not them. What about that feminist biker group you mentioned a while back?"

"The Athena Sisterhood?" Shea asked incredulously. "My ex is their president. Remember?"

"Oh. Definitely not them, then. But you need somebody to talk to about what happened."

"Ain't nobody wanna hear that shit." Shea sighed and their foreheads touched. "Besides, I got you to talk to. Ain't that enough?"

"Might help to talk with someone you're not sleeping with."

"I'll consider it." Shea nuzzled the side of Jessica's face with her own. "Right now I just want to spend time with you. In bed."

Shea and Jessica ambled to the bedroom in a flurry of

kisses and gentle caresses. Waves of arousal pushed out the haunting darkness in Shea. She cupped Jessica's delicate face in her hand, drawn in by the openness and vulnerability in Jess's eyes. "I really love you, you know."

"I know." Jessica pulled off Shea's shirt and grazed her nails across Shea's back, causing her to groan. "I love you, too."

Shea reached under Jessica's shirt, unhooking her bra. Her girlfriend's skin was like the softest silk, her body so feminine. Her scent filled Shea's senses with notes of cinnamon and rose petals, transporting her to a world of safety and nurturing. A place to let down her guard.

Shea covered Jessica's chest with kisses, each one a tiny, tender expression of gratitude. Her hand explored farther down, causing Jessica to gasp with pleasure. Jess pressed her pelvis against Shea's hand as arousal became need.

A high-pitched scream from the other room jolted Shea back into reality. Shields slammed back into place. Shea tensed with frustration, mixed with a need to protect. "Damn."

"Nooooooo . . . please. Mommy, help me!"

Shea shimmied back into her shirt and jeans and ran into Annie's room. "It's okay. You're safe."

"Mommy, it hurts." Annie's choked cries ripped open Shea's heart.

She flicked on the bedroom light. Annie's eyes were still closed, her face flushed and wet with tears.

"Annie, sweetie, wake up. It's Aunt Shea. You're home. You're safe."

Annie's eye's fluttered and took a moment to focus on Shea's face. "Aunt Shea?"

"Yeah, Doodlebug. It's me."

Annie wrapped her trembling arms around Shea's neck. "I dreamed they came and got me again."

"I know, baby. I'm so sorry." Shea sniffled, struggling to control her own feelings. *What good am I to Annie if I get all emotional?*

"I wish Mommy was still here."

"Yeah, me, too."

"She really in Heaven looking down on me?"

"Of course." Shea wished she believed it herself.

"Daddy, too?"

No, your Daddy's in hell, where he belongs, Shea wanted to say. "Yeah, him, too."

"I'm glad I got you." Annie's eyes locked with Shea's.

Shea held the girl's gaze as long as she could stand before looking away, afraid Annie might see how not-so-strong she was. "I'm glad I got you, too, Doodlebug."

"Aunt Shea?"

"Yeah?"

"Can we see Grampa Monster and Gramma Julia sometime?"

Shea grimaced. "Why you wanna see them?"

"I miss them."

"Not sure that's such a good idea."

"Why? Monster calls me his little princess. And Julia always made me cookies when I came over."

"Let me think about it, okay?"

"Okay."

"Now get some sleep and try to dream about something fun."

"Like what?"

Shea searched her tired mind for something to say. "I dunno, like unicorns and fairies."

"And riding motorcycles?"

Shea's smile returned. "Yeah, and riding motorcycles." She tucked Annie in and stood up.

"Don't go."

"You want me to stay here all night?"

"Uh-huh."

"I gotta sleep in my own bed with Jessica."

"Please . . ."

"Tell ya what. I'll stay here till ya fall asleep."

Annie pouted. "Okay."

A few minutes later Annie was snoring softly. Shea turned out the light and snuck out.

Jessica was curled up in bed when Shea got undressed and climbed in beside her.

Jess turned over. "How's Annie?"

"She wants to see Monster and Julia. But I don't want any member of the Confederate Thunder or their old ladies near Annie. This is her chance to get clear of the violence and bigotry of outlaw biker culture. She deserves better."

"She'll be disappointed. What are you going to tell her?"

"I'll figure something out. For now, I just want to sleep."

"We're going to have to do something about her nightmares. We can't go on like this."

"She'll grow out of it. I did." Shea turned over and let her consciousness dissolve into her pillow.

3

———

CRIME SCENE TAPE stretched between traffic barricades at the alley between the First Arizona Bank and the Manila Grill. Two deputies sipped coffee by one of the barricades, redirecting the occasional pedestrian away from the scene.

Detective Toni Rios stepped from her warm car into the frigid morning air. She tightened the belt on her black wool coat and shielded her eyes against the rising sun, which had painted the buildings of downtown Ironwood in golden light.

"Morning, deputies." Rios nodded as she approached. "Coffee smells good."

Graham, the older deputy, wiped his mustache. "It's hot. That's all I care about. I moved from Detroit to get away from the cold and here I am still freezing my ass off in twenty-eight-degree weather. I thought Arizona was supposed to be warm."

Rios smirked. "You want warm, you should have headed farther south to Phoenix."

Graham harrumphed. "Now ya tell me."

"Coffee and doughnuts are on the front seat of the coroner's van, if you're interested." Cruz, the younger deputy, stuffed his free hand under his other armpit. His breath billowed in a cloud of water vapor. "Dr. Crawford stopped on her way in."

Rios' nose wrinkled in distaste. "Not sure I want to eat or drink anything from the coroner's van." Her gaze turned down the alley. "What do we got down there?"

"Deceased white female," said Cruz. "Looks like she had some kind of seizure. Detective Johnson's canvassing the neighborhood for possible witnesses."

Graham scoffed. "My money's on an overdose. These dumb kids are snorting and shooting all kinds of weird shit. What's that new drug making the rounds?"

"Hex, sometimes called magic molly," said Rios.

"Yeah, that's it. Heroin mixed with ecstasy. I ask ya, how stupid ya gotta be to put shit like that in your body? A wonder more of these kids don't end up in the morgue."

"It's a tragedy." The scene evoked memories of Rios' heroin-addicted sister, threatening to unleash emotions she didn't need to deal with when she had a job to do. "Stay warm, guys."

A uniformed deputy with a shaved head and beefy build emerged the alley.

"Aguilar," she mumbled.

"Fuck you, traitor." Aguilar bumped Rios' shoulder with his elbow, nearly knocking her off her feet.

A few months earlier, Rios had been forced to kill her former partner, Detective Edelman, to protect Shea Stevens. Edelman and their boss, Sergeant Foster, had killed several people and kidnapped Stevens' niece while running an illegal heroin operation.

After Rios learned of Foster's involvement, she'd reported him to Internal Affairs. When he and Edelman tried to murder Stevens, Rios had intervened. Since then,

Aguilar and others had treated her as an outcast for crossing the blue line.

"Shut the hell up, Aguilar!" Rios shouted at his back. "Foster and Edelman were dirty. Maybe you know a bit more about that than you've been saying?"

Aguilar turned on her like a roaring puma. "If they were dirty, you should've arrested them instead of gunning them down like dogs."

"I acted to protect an innocent civilian from being executed. It was a good shoot."

"Good shoot, my ass. Your little girlfriend was caught with a weapon tied to several murders and was fleeing a gangland shooting when Foster tracked her down."

"Shea Stevens isn't my girlfriend," said Rios, her nostrils flaring. "And all charges against her were dismissed."

"Such bullshit. You turned on your own so you could tap that skanky biker bitch's ass. Everybody knows that."

"It's a goddamn lie." Rios stepped into Aguilar's personal space, her nose inches from his chin. "I know you've been spreading rumors about me to people in my unit. That stops now."

"And if it doesn't, what? You going to shoot me, too?"

"No, Deputy, I'll have your badge." She held his gaze, refusing to flinch. "Do I make myself clear?"

After a long, tense moment, Aguilar turned on his heel. "Watch your back, Detective," he said over his shoulder.

Rios took a deep breath to let go of her frustration. *Hell with him,* she told herself. *You got a job to do here.*

At the end of the alley, the stench of vomit and feces made Rios doubly glad she hadn't eaten one of the coroner's doughnuts. Two evidence techs placed yellow numbered markers by potential evidence. A third snapped photographs of the scene.

The victim lay on her side, body arched unnaturally backward. Fists were balled and held against her chest. Champagne blond hair partially obscured the woman's ivory face. White foam coated her mouth, which appeared to be grinning.

Vomit dappled her emerald spaghetti-strap blouse. Black, four-inch heels clung to her feet, the left one with a broken heel. A few feet from the body, a black leather purse lay on the ground, the main zippered compartment wide open.

Winslow, a deputy with a boyish face and a pear-shaped body, hovered over the dead woman. Despite being Aguilar's partner, Winslow had always been nice to her, even after Foster and Edelman were killed.

A tall woman in a Cortes County Medical Examiner's coat crouched next to Winslow, studying the victim. She stood as Rios approached. "Good morning, Toni. If you'd like some coffee, I got some in the van. Doughnuts, too, if you're interested."

"Maybe later, Dr. Crawford." Rios covered her nose with the inside of her arm. "What do we know?"

"Victim appears to be in her early twenties, dead approximately six hours. No lacerations aside from a scraped knee, no bruising or other indications of physical trauma. Hyperextension of the body, combined with the frothing at the mouth and a risus sardonicus grin suggests either tetanus or strychnine poisoning."

Rios pulled out a notebook and wrote down Dr. Crawford's findings. "Anything else?"

"The back of her hand bears an ink stamp of the letters THL."

"Trip Hop Lounge."

"That would be my guess."

Winslow reached down and lifted a plastic bag

containing a few dark pills from the victim's purse. "We found these."

Rios took the bag from him. Each of the four pills was stamped with a pentagram. "Could this be another hex overdose?"

"We won't know for sure until the tox report comes back, but it is strikingly similar to two recent hex-related deaths."

Rios shook her head. "I don't get it. Hex has circulated in the clubs for months now. Why are people dropping dead all of a sudden?"

Crawford crossed her arms. "Drugs like heroin are cut multiple times before they hit the street. Usually with something inert like cornstarch, but that dilutes the potency. Cutting it with strychnine, which is cheaper than heroin, still gives a bit of a high. But too much can lead to stomach cramps, convulsions, and death."

Rios turned to the deputy. "We got an ID, Winslow?"

"Not yet." The young deputy pointed the open purse. "Her wallet is missing. We found a cell phone but the battery was dead and the screen cracked. We also found a partial footprint not matching the victim's heels. I'd guess a boot, either military or motorcycle. Also got some finger-prints off the purse. Might lead us to whoever took the wallet."

"Detective Rios!" At the entrance to the alley, Ebony Johnson, a young female detective, held the arm of a person clinging to a grocery cart full of belongings.

"Good work. I look forward to your autopsy report, Doctor," Rios said to Crawford before jogging back to the street to talk with Johnson. "What's up, Detective?"

Johnson gestured toward the person holding on to the grocery cart. "Detective Rios, meet Miss Luz Escobar."

"Sergeant Escobar! I ain't no miss. I'm a goddamned

marine." The husky woman wore an olive drab utility jacket over a gray hoodie. Her face was grimy and she smelled of body odor, garbage, and alcohol. It was hard to tell under the rough exterior, but Rios estimated the woman's age to be late thirties, maybe early forties.

"Sorry, this is *Sergeant* Escobar. She witnessed the victim having a seizure."

Rios gave Johnson a knowing look, then turned back to Escobar. "Sergeant, you hungry by chance?"

Some of the fire went out of the veteran's eyes. "Yeah, maybe."

"Deputy, could you bring the sergeant a couple of doughnuts and a cup of coffee from the van?"

"Yes, ma'am." Johnson hustled off to the coroner's van.

Rios gestured toward a bench along the wall in front of the Manila Grill. "Why don't you and me have a seat, Sergeant?"

Escobar eyed Rios suspiciously, but shuffled to the bench without a word. One of the wheels of the grocery cart clacked over the seams in the sidewalk.

Johnson returned a moment later and handed the woman a couple of doughnuts and a steaming cup of coffee. "Anything else, Detective?"

"No, thanks." Rios took a seat beside the homeless veteran.

Escobar set the doughnuts in the front basket of the cart, then sniffed the cup before taking a long slurp of coffee.

"You serve overseas?"

"Two tours in Afghanistan driving a Humvee till I got my ass blown up. Took three pieces of shrapnel in the *cabeza*." The woman pulled back her nest of dusty brown-black hair to reveal an indentation near her temple the size of a quarter.

"Sorry to hear that. How'd you end up on the streets?"

"Got arrested for kicking some butter bar's ass after he got handsy with me. Corps kicked me out for assault and insubordination. Dishonorable discharge. Can't get no job, especially with this PTSD fucking with my head. So here I am."

"You deserve better after your service." Rios met her gaze. "You see what happened to the woman in the alley?"

Escobar rubbed her face and peered at Rios over the rim of her coffee cup. "I mighta seen something."

Rios let the silence hang heavy between them, waiting for the veteran to continue. The minutes dragged. Escobar scarfed down a doughnut, chased it down with coffee, then inhaled the other, glancing periodically at Rios.

"Fine, that junkie bitch woke me up stumbling down my alley, moaning and shit. Looked like she was tripping on something."

"What time was that?"

"Hell if I know. I don't have a watch."

"What did you do when she entered the alley?" Rios eyed the grocery cart, wondering if the victim's wallet was in Escobar's pile of belongings. All she could see clearly was a worn olive drab duffel bag underneath a dusty bedroll.

"I told her to shut the fuck up. She just moaned louder, like she was having some sorta fit. So I bugged out. Got no time to waste on junkies."

"You didn't try to help her?"

"Do I look like a goddamn doctor?" Escobar downed the last of her coffee, crumpled the cup, and tossed it into a nearby bin.

"Where'd you go?"

"Up a few blocks to Waldorf Park to sleep on a bench."

"What happened to the victim's wallet?"

"You think I stole it? I ain't no thief." Escobar shoved her cart toward Rios. "Search it if you don't believe me."

Rios studied Escobar's face, then smiled. "That's okay. I believe you. Did the victim say anything while she was still alive?"

"Naw, just made a lotta weird grunting noises, like she was trying to talk but forgot how."

"Anyone else around?"

"Nope, just the junkie."

"Tell me something. Why sleep in the alley? Why not in the Samaritan Shelter on Pinetop Street?"

"You ever stay at the Samaritan Shelter?" asked Escobar.

"Can't say I have. Stayed in a group home for a while as a kid. Beat sleeping on the streets."

"Trust me, the Samaritan Shelter ain't no place for a decent person. Full of junkies, dealers, and hoes. Last time I stayed there, some bitch tried to cut me for my shoes. And don't get me started about them bedbugs. Ugh! I do not need that kind of aggravation."

"Can't say I blame you. Still, must be hard when it gets cold like this."

"Afghanistan was a helluva lot colder than this."

"I suppose you're right." Rios pulled a twenty out of her wallet and held it out for Escobar to see. "Anything else you can tell me about who this woman was or how she died?"

"Ain't no more to tell."

Rios handed the woman the twenty. "Thanks for your help, Sergeant."

Escobar pocketed the money and wandered off pushing the cart.

Johnson caught up to Rios as she returned to the crime scene.

"Get anything from her?" asked Johnson.

Rios shook her head. "She only confirmed what Dr. Crawford's telling us. The victim died from a seizure, most likely due to strychnine-laced hex. But we still don't have an ID."

"So what now?"

"Contact the media and give them a physical description of the victim. Maybe we can get a lead from someone who knows her." Rios checked the time on her phone. "Trip Hop Lounge probably won't open for a few hours yet. When they do, we can check their security feed. If she paid for drinks with a credit card, maybe we can locate the transaction and put a name with the face."

4

THE MOMENT SHEA walked in the back door of Iron Goddess, her ears were assaulted with the sounds of a forties-style crooner singing so loud her vision blurred. With her hands over her ears, she rushed over to Lakota, who was installing a lowering kit on a BMW K1300. "What the hell is that?"

"What?" Lakota slipped off her ear protection.

"The fucking music."

Lakota smirked and gestured toward Switch, working on the wiring of another bike ten feet away, her bushy hair looking more out-of-control than usual. "She's taken a sudden liking to Perry Como."

Shea buried her face in her palm. "My ears are bleeding."

"She had a rough night last night," Lakota explained. "I was at her place until three calming her down."

A bad night for Switch was something Shea didn't want to imagine. When Switch was a kid, the Department of Child Safety had found her naked and chained to a pipe in her sadistic parents' laundry room. Shea had a soft spot in her heart for the young woman, but she also had a shop to run. "At least turn the volume down!"

Lakota hurried over to the sound system and dropped the volume to a more reasonable level.

"Thank you!" Shea cocked her jaw to equalize the pressure in her ears. "And if you can do it without triggering Switch, change it to something from this century. That crooner shit makes me want to strangle someone."

Lakota nodded with a shrug. "You're the boss."

"Yes. Yes, I am." Shea rubbed her temples, warding off a headache that was forming.

Kyle approached and cocked his head at an angle. "Dude, we gotta talk."

"What's up, Kyle?"

"Look, I know I'm new here. And I'm really grateful for this job. But, dude . . ." He frowned; an embarrassed look darkened his face. "I got to talk to you about Switch."

"Come on back." Shea led him down a short hallway to the shop's office.

Terrance Douglas, her business partner and the shop's operations manager, was sitting behind his desk talking on the phone. His trim, full beard and tidy afro gave the burly man a warm, fatherly look.

Shea took a seat behind her own desk and gestured for Kyle to grab one of the chairs in front. "So what's up?"

He hopped onto the chair and flipped open a pocket-size notebook. "In the past week, Switch has called me midget, squirt, half-pint, hobbit, Keebler, and man-baby. I may be an ex-con, but I shouldn't have to put up with that crap."

Shea rubbed her throbbing temples. "Agreed."

"People act like Switch can do whatever she wants."

"Well, when she gets upset, things tend to get broken."

"All due respect, boss, but that's bullshit. I shouldn't have to be insulted just because she's batshit crazy."

"I'll take care of it."

"Thanks, dude. I appreciate it." Kyle hopped down from the chair and ambled back to the workshop. Terrance hung up the phone.

"Trouble in the ranks?" Terrance asked.

"Switch being Switch. How was your date last night?"

Terrance broke into a goofy grin. "It was good. Jake's coming over for dinner tomorrow night."

"Wow, two nights in a row. Sounds serious."

"I'm hoping."

"He know you're trans?"

"Yes, I told him before he first asked me out. It's a nonissue."

"Glad to hear it. 'Bout time you found someone. What's your son think of him?"

"They only met briefly when Jake picked me up. But I think Elon likes him. I figure if he hated him, he would have let me know." Terrance picked up a folder from the side of his desk. "I see the Wexler bike is finished. Nice job. How late were you here?"

"Too late." Shea poured herself a cup of coffee and settled behind her own desk, rubbing the sleep out of her eyes. "But it was due this morning."

"Oh. Ms. Wexler called yesterday and said she can't pick it up for another week or so. I thought I told you."

"Apparently not."

Terrance gave an apologetic look. "Sorry."

"Oh well, now we can show it off at the Women's Bike Night event on Thursday."

"Good idea. Kokopelli Café agreed to do the catering. One of the DJs from HausMusik will be providing the music." Terrance handed Shea a piece of paper from his desk. "Oh, and before I forget, we may have another order for a custom bike."

"Another one? I was hoping to build a show bike for the Tucson Bike Expo." Shea's expression darkened as she examined the quote sheet.

"The expo's a gamble. This custom job is money in the bank. This bike should be our first priority."

Shea rolled her eyes. "Whatever." She looked name on the sheet. "When is this Chlöe Stansbury supposed to be here?"

"Early afternoon."

"Great." Shea noticed a pink message note on her desk. "What's this?"

"A woman came in asking for you. She was wearing an Athena Sisterhood cut," he said referring to the leather vest that members of biker clubs wore. "After I informed her we don't allow gang colors here, she left her name and number. Didn't say what it was about."

The name on the note read 'Debbie Raymond'. Shea didn't need Terrance to tell her what her ex-girlfriend wanted. It was another invitation to join the Athena Sisterhood. But Shea had no desire to spend another minute with Debbie, much less become a prospect.

Shea tossed the message in the trash, and stood up. "Until Ms. Chlöe Stansbury gets here, I'm going to be welding together a fucking motorcycle frame."

5

RIOS SAT at her desk examining the overdose victim's purse and phone. A single crack traversed the phone's screen. It was also out of juice.

She opened her bottom desk drawer and sorted through a tangle of cords until she found a charger that fit the phone and plugged it in. With a little luck, it would lead her to the victim's identity and, more important, to whoever sold the drugs that killed her.

Detective Johnson, who shared a cubicle with Rios, walked into the Violent Crimes Division and set an evidence bag on Rios' desk containing a black Louis Vuitton wallet. "Good news. We caught a woman using your Jane Doe's credit card."

"Who had it?"

"A woman named Tracy Phillips. A clerk at a convenience store asked for ID when she tried to buy a case of beer. Phillips panicked and tried to run with the beer. A uniformed deputy happened to be in there and nabbed her. She's down in interview two."

"Who's our Jane Doe?"

"Genette Abrams."

"How did Phillips get the wallet?"

"Claims she walking down the street when she spotted Ms. Abrams' body in the alley around two in the morning."

"Walking down the street an hour after the bars closed? This Phillips woman have any priors?"

"A few. Solicitation, shoplifting, and possession—marijuana, less than an ounce. You want to interview her?"

"Yeah. Maybe she knows who's dealing hex at the clubs." As Rios stood up, a blue battery icon appeared on the cracked phone screen. "Thank goodness for small miracles."

Rios entered the interview room carrying her case folder. At the far side of the table, a woman wearing a lot of makeup and a low-cut tank top leaned back in a chair with her arms crossed. Her flowery perfume hit Rios like a cloud of kerosene vapor.

A man in a chocolate-brown suit sat next to the woman. His hands rested on a black leather binder in front of him.

"Tracy Phillips?" Rios sat opposite the woman.

"Yeah."

The brown-suited man extended his hand. "And I'm Richard Velasquez, Ms. Phillips' attorney." The droop of his right eyelid became more prominent as he spoke.

Rios shook his offered hand. "I'm Detective Rios with the Violent Crimes Division. I'm investigating the death of Genette Abrams." She pulled out a photo of Abrams' body and slid it over to Velasquez and his client. Ms. Phillips stared at the far wall without a glance at the photo.

"My client had nothing to do with this woman's death."

"The victim's wallet was found in Ms. Phillips' possession after she attempted to use Ms. Abrams' credit cards to purchase beer."

"That junkie bitch was dead when I found the wallet," said Phillips. "Ain't like she was gonna need it no more."

Velasquez tried to hush her. "Detective Rios, based on what my client has told me, the victim died of some kind of poisoning. Is that correct?"

"We are still investigating cause of death. Why?"

"My client witnessed the deceased buying drugs that quite possibly killed her. What would that be worth to you?"

"If your client can ID the dealer, I can talk to the DA about a reduced sentence on the credit card fraud, theft, and shoplifting charges."

Velasquez consulted with his client in whispers, then sat up again. "My client is willing to share what she knows in exchange for immunity from all charges."

"Immunity? Your client has a record. Her information better be rock solid. Otherwise, she's facing at least six months in jail, plus an additional year of probation."

Velasquez nodded to Phillips.

"Fine," said Phillips, rolling her eyes. "Last night I saw some chick at HausMusik dealing something in the ladies' room."

Rios perked up. "*Some* chick dealing *something*? You're going to have to do better than that. What'd this chick look like?"

"White and kinda skinny."

"Could you be more specific? Any distinguishing features? Hair color? Age? Clothing?"

"Didn't pay that much attention to her, to be quite honest. Brown hair, maybe. Or was it blond? I don't know." Phillips picked at a scab on her arm. "She wore a leather vest with some patches on it; that I do remember."

"What did the patches look like?"

"The patches on top and bottom had pink lettering and

curved around a big one in the middle that looked like an owl."

Rios recalled seeing a patch like that, but couldn't place it. "What did the ones with the lettering say?"

"The one on bottom just said Arizona. There was a little one in the middle that just had the letters MC. Top one said *something* Sisterhood."

A lightbulb went on in Rios' mind. "Athena Sisterhood?"

"Yeah, that sounds right."

"What else?"

"I don't know what else." Phillips shrugged. "Like I said, I didn't hardly notice her. I was just in there to pee."

"And you saw this woman in the biker vest sell drugs to the deceased?"

"Yeah. It was the dead chick. I remember I liked her lacy green top."

"And her designer wallet, apparently." Rios looked at Velasquez and crossed her arms. "Hardly the rock-sold information I was looking for."

"Come on, Detective. She told you what she knows."

"What she knows will not get me a conviction."

"No, but it's a lead. You know it's one of those biker chicks selling the dope. Now how about that deal?"

"I'll leave that up to the folks in the Property Crimes Division." Rios stood up with her case folder and left.

After giving the detective in Property Crimes an update, she returned to the Violent Crimes Division. Lieutenant Dennis Goodman, a man with thinning white hair, intercepted her on her way to her desk.

Permanent creases extended down from the corners of his frown, giving him the look of a ventriloquist doll. "Detective, I'd like to see you in my office." He beckoned with his finger. Rios followed him into his office. Goodman closed the door.

Rios took a seat. Her pulse quickened. "What's up, Lieutenant?"

"You missed roll call this morning. I want to know where you are with the two strychnine poisoning cases. The media's crawling up my ass claiming someone's poisoning college coeds."

"It's three now."

"Three? Jesus Christ on a cracker!"

"As of this morning. But I think we've caught a break," explained Rios. "A witness claims she saw the latest victim buying drugs at the Trip Hop Lounge. Didn't get a very detailed description, but the dealer was wearing an Athena Sisterhood biker vest."

Goodman let out a harsh breath. "Can't say I'm surprised."

"Why's that, sir?"

"These women are fanatics, attacking anyone perceived to be sexist. Property Crimes Division is liking them for a couple of fire bombings at sites where they've held protest rallies."

"I heard about the one at that strip club a few weeks ago."

"And before that it was Senator Braeburn's office. He's a family man, for God's sake. And that church run by that Reverend What's-His-Name."

"Reverend Phillips." Rios was all too familiar with the preacher and his "kill the gays" rants. She wasn't sorry to see his church burned to the ground. "Has anyone in the Athena Sisterhood been charged with any of these arson cases?"

"Not yet. But now that they're killing people with rat poison, it's in my wheelhouse." He leaned over the desk, his face dark and brooding. "I want them shut down, Detective."

"I have an informant who can probably get inside."

"Make that happen. You close these cases, you'll be that much closer to making sergeant."

"Yes, sir."

Goodman leaned back. "Dismissed."

"What was that about?" asked Johnson as Rios returned to her desk.

"Goodman wants this new women's motorcycle club shut down, especially now that it looks like they're connected to these strychnine deaths." Rios retrieved the victim's wallet from the evidence bag. "According to her ID, latest victim's name is Genette Abrams, twenty-two. Lives at 2416 North Shadow Hills Road, unit D-209."

"That's in the Desert Vistas condominium complex," said Johnson. "Six-figure luxury lofts. I'm surprised they'd let a druggie live there."

"Drugs don't care who you are." Rios flipped through some of the cards in the wallet. "Besides, she has a university ID. Insurance card for a 2015 Mercedes C320. I'm guessing her wealthy parents were bankrolling her."

"So, what's our next move?"

"Check with the university's Admissions Department. See if you can get the contact info for her family. I'll get a search warrant for her condo. I'm also going to set up a meeting with one of my confidential informants. If we can get her inside the Athena Sisterhood, maybe we can locate our dealer."

6

―――

SHEA PEERED through her welding goggles at the join between the pieces of aluminum that were coming together to form the frame of a new custom motorcycle. *Who cares if our last show bike didn't sell well? We're building a reputation here. It's an investment. Why doesn't Terrance see that?*

She pulled the trigger on the TIG welder. The aroma of ozone and carbon filled the air. Sparks exploded from the welder tip with an angry sizzle as aluminum glowed and softened, two pieces of metal melding into one.

Shea flipped up the mask and inspected her work. Her finger drew a line across the warm surface, brainstorming ideas for creating an agile bike with a Gothic biomechanical style. Despite the nagging ache in her collarbone, she was pleased she could still do the work she was so passionate about.

Her phone's old-fashioned ringtone interrupted her inspection of the work in progress.

"Iron Goddess Custom Cycles. This is Shea."

"Miss Stevens, this is Detective Rios with the Cortes County Sheriff's Office."

Shea tensed. She was never fond of talking to cops, least of all Detective Rios, who had forced her to sign a confidential informant agreement months after she was shot. "What do you want?"

"How's your recovery going?" The compassion in the detective's voice almost sounded genuine.

"My recovery?" She scoffed as bile burned her throat. "You mean after your fucking boss gunned down my sister in the street *after* he kidnapped her daughter?"

"Shea, I—"

"Or you talking about the broken collarbone I got when he ran me off the road?" It felt good to let it out after three months of simmering.

"Listen—"

"No, wait, you must mean my recovery from when your asshole of a partner shot me in the back."

"I saved your life, Shea. I think a little gratitude is in order."

"Fuck gratitude. I risked my neck to save my niece from you drug-trafficking cops. And that's the thanks *I* got. A dead sister, a broken collarbone, and a goddamned bullet in the back. And since you asked, it all *still fucking hurts!*"

"Sergeant Foster and Detective Edelman were bad apples. I grant you that. And I am truly sorry for what you went through. I know how painful it is to lose a sister."

"Bullshit, you ain't lost no sister."

A moment of silence passed and Shea hoped the call had dropped. No such luck.

"Shea, I need your help with a case."

"I ain't got time to help you, Rios. You're the detective. Solve your own damn cases. I build bikes for a living, in case you forgot."

"You also signed an agreement to be a confidential

informant in exchange for us dropping those weapons charges. In case you'd forgotten."

"Those weapons charges were bogus, and you know it. So, you can stick that agreement where the sun don't shine."

"I would really hate to send you back to prison. But if you refuse to—"

"Do what you gotta do, lady. I *ain't* gonna be your snitch."

"People are dying, Shea. Women are dying."

Shea stopped for a second, processing what Rios had said. "What the hell you talking about?"

"I don't want to discuss it over the phone. You know where the Black Rock Mine is?"

"'Bout halfway between Ironwood and Bradshaw City. What the hell's that got to do with anything?"

"Meet me there in an hour."

"The mine's closed."

"Yes, the county seized it a while back for safety violations and unpaid taxes."

"Yeah, right. Sounds like Buzzkill wanted his own gold mine," Shea said, referring to Sheriff Buzz Keeler.

"Half an hour, Shea. The gate will be unlocked."

"And if I don't go?"

"I'll have Deputy Aguilar pick you up. You're at Iron Goddess, judging by the sounds in the background. Am I right?"

"Fuck," Shea whispered under her breath.

"What'll it be, Ms. Stevens?"

"Fine. I'll meet you at the goddamn mine."

Shea hung up and tossed the welding torch onto the rack. She felt like pounding something with a hammer. "As if I ain't got enough shit to deal with."

She traipsed into the office and snatched her hoodie off

the coatrack so hard it fell over with a loud clang. "God-damn fuckity fuck."

Terrance glanced up at her. "Everything all right?"

"Everything's fucking fine."

"'Cause you just assaulted a perfectly innocent coatrack."

"Detective Rios wants me to meet with her about something."

"Uh-oh. What trouble you get yourself into now? You doing burnouts in front of the Tastee-Freez again?" He grinned, no doubt attempting to lighten her mood. It wasn't working.

"Funny. It's that fucking confidential informant agreement she forced me to sign when I was in the hospital doped up on painkillers."

"What does she want you to do?"

"No idea."

"Maybe she just wants you to keep your ears open for illegal activity."

"I doubt it. She wants to meet with me at the old Black Rock Mine."

"Really? Why there?"

"Prolly so nobody sees me meeting with her. Such bull-shit. I'll be back in a while."

She stormed out to the back parking lot, slipped on her Shoei helmet, and threw a leg over Sweet Betsy, a black cruiser, low and mean, with a high performance 750cc engine that could outrun a Harley twice its size.

The motorcycle peeled out of the Iron Goddess parking lot and turned north onto Sycamore Springs' Main Street. The quaint, tourist-driven shops of Olde Towne Sycamore Springs blurred past, replaced by rolling hills of prairie grass dotted with juniper.

The crisp morning air and bright blue sky took the edge off her anger. Wind therapy, Shea called it.

BLACK ROCK HAD BEEN a gold mining town back in the 1800s. The recent spike in gold prices had inspired some opportunistic businessmen to make another go of it. At least until Buzzkill shut them down. No doubt to put some coin into his next election campaign.

Now there was nothing left of the town but a faded welcome sign, a feed store, and the shuttered gold mine.

Just past the feed store, Shea pulled onto a gravel drive and stopped at a ten-foot chain-link gate topped with razor wire and bearing a sign that read CORTES COUNTY PROPERTY. TRESPASSERS WILL BE PROSECUTED. A steel chain dangled from the adjoining fence.

With a nudge from the bike's front tire, the gate swung open. She drove through without closing the gate and followed the gravel road around a wide turn and down a steep hill. Half-buried rocks and sand-filled ruts made driving tricky, adding to the tension Shea felt about this meeting.

At the bottom, the road opened into a gravel lot with a rusting yellow excavator and an enormous blood-red wash plant at one end. Several fifteen-foot-tall mounds of tailings bordered the edge of the lot.

At the other, a blue Honda Accord parked beside a wooden building the size of a double-wide. The place felt empty and lonely, like a community wiped out by a flood. Dreams had died here. Fortunes lost. Hope shattered.

She steered Sweet Betsy toward the building and crunched to a stop beside the Honda. No sign of Rios in the car. Shea shut off the bike and let her side stand sink into the soft ground.

A wooden sign identifying the building as the mine office hung from hooks and clacked in the breeze. Shea found herself staring at the doorknob. Her shoulder throbbed. Her hand balled into a tight fist and pounded on the door.

"Come in," said an all-too-familiar voice.

The overhead lights were off. Sunlight from the window filtered through a haze of dust motes. Rios sat behind a battered metal desk. A green shaking table for separating gold from concentrates stood at the far end of the room.

Shea plopped down in a metal folding chair and stared at Rios. "Why the hell am I here?"

Rios opened a manila case folder on the desk and spread out three eight-by-ten crime scene photos.

Shea picked one up and felt her stomach sour at the image of a woman's ashen face contorted in pain, eyes bulging, and foaming at the mouth. The other two photos were equally gruesome. "Jesus Christ, what the fuck happened to these women?"

"Hex laced with strychnine. It's a brutal way to die. Muscle seizures. Agonizing pain. Victims die from a lack of oxygen because their lungs quit working."

"What's this got to do with me? I don't deal drugs."

"We have evidence that someone in the Athena Sisterhood Motorcycle Club is dealing the strychnine-laced hex," said Rios. "We need your help to find out who it is so we can keep anyone else from dying such a horrible death."

"I ain't involved with the Sisterhood."

Rios leaned forward, a slight smile curling the corner of her mouth. "You're about to be."

Shea clinched her jaw, remembering Jessica's pleading to spend more time with her and with Annie. "Why me?"

"You're a perfect fit. You grew up around a motorcycle club. You're a woman involved in the biker community. You support feminist causes. And the local chapter president is a close friend of yours."

"Debbie Raymond?" Shea winced. "We broke up years ago. We are definitely *not* friends."

"You don't have to date her. But given your history, I suspect she'd be more inclined to open up to you than anyone we could send in undercover."

"Why are you looking at the Sisterhood for this? The only ones dealing that kinda shit are the Confederate Thunder and the Jaguars street gang."

Rios shook her head. "What's left of the Jaguars relocated to Phoenix."

"And the Thunder? They stole a ton of hex from the Jags. How do you know they're not behind these deaths?"

"A woman wearing an Athena Sisterhood vest was seen dealing drugs to the latest victim at the Trip Hop Lounge."

"Why would the Athena Sisterhood kill other women? It don't make sense."

"That's what we need you to find out."

"Junkies overdose all the time. Why is the Violent Crimes Division investigating?"

"These aren't overdoses. Someone is *deliberately* putting rat poison in hex. That's murder."

Shea ran a hand through her hair while eyeing the photos. The thought of being a snitch sickened her. But something about the women in the photos tugged at her conscience. "What d'you expect me to do? I ain't no detective."

"Have you heard from Ms. Raymond?"

"Couple months ago, she invited me to become a prospect. Told her I wasn't interested."

Rios inched the photos closer to Shea. "Call her back and tell her you've changed your mind."

Shea stared at her. "Do you have any idea the time commitment required to be a prospect for an MC? I'd be at their beck and call twenty-four-seven. I got too much on my plate as it is."

"I'm not saying you have to become a prospect, Shea. Just hang out with them. Get them talking. Maybe they'll tell you something that can help me nail whoever's dealing."

"They ain't gonna tell me shit. I'm an outsider."

"Hardly. You're one hundred percent USDA prime Athena Sisterhood material. And you're resourceful."

"I got other priorities right now."

"Such as?"

"Raising my niece, for one, since the sheriff's office made an orphan outta her."

Rios' face hardened, all traces of politeness gone. "Shea, if youf violate your CI contract, I'll have the DA press charges against you. You go back to prison. Annie ends up in the foster care system. Is that what you want?"

In a fit of fury, Shea kicked the desk, leaving a dent in the beige metal back. Rios backed up, her hand hovering over the gun at her hip. "Are we going to have a problem here?"

"You're a real bitch, ya know that?"

"I'm trying to save some lives here. If that makes me a bitch, so be it. But you have a choice to make."

Shea weighed her options. She wanted so much to tell Rios to fuck off. But she couldn't risk Annie getting put into the system. Or worse, into the care of Monster and his old lady. "I can't guarantee they'll tell me who's dealing."

"I have faith in you," Rios replied.

Shea stood up, arms wrapped around her chest, and

stared blankly out the dust-covered window. "Fucking cold in here."

"So, I can count on you?"

Shea let out a harsh breath. No way should she do this. Jessica was already complaining Shea didn't spend enough time taking care of Annie. And to top it off, Shea would be hanging out with Debbie, the manipulative bitch from hell. All to save a few junkies.

But the disturbing images of the dead women had burned themselves into her mind. No one should have to die like that. *What if Deb really is behind this? Wouldn't it be sweet to send her to prison after all the crap she put me through? That alone might make it worth the trouble.*

"All right, I'll do it." Shea stormed out the door without waiting on Rios' response.

She threw a leg over her bike and yanked on her gloves and helmet. Memories of her fucked-up relationship with Deb twisted her insides. The passion. The love. The sex. The mind games. The fights.

At the main road, her front tire hit a deep pothole. The bike pitched left. Shea planted her foot and strained to keep the bike upright.

"Fuck! Get your head straight, girl," Shea mumbled. Condensation from her heavy breathing fogged the inside of her visor.

Rios pulled up alongside her in the Honda and rolled down a window. "You okay? Need some help?"

Shea flipped her off, sending up a rooster tail of gravel as she tore off down the highway.

7

───────

WHEN SHEA RETURNED to Iron Goddess, Terrance was out at lunch. Shea spent ten minutes locating Deb's office number on the Central Arizona University website. It rang several times and then switched to voicemail.

"You've reached Professor Raymond."

The sound of Deb's voice set Shea's teeth on edge. She resisted the urge to hang up.

"My office hours are Tuesday and Thursday afternoons from three until five. Please sign up via the sheet on my door. All other business, please leave a message."

"Hey, Deb, it's Shea." She struggled for words. Didn't want to seem too eager. "I wanna talk to you again about the Athena Sisterhood. Gimme a call."

A knock on the office door startled Shea. "What?"

Monica, the shop's salesperson, stood in the doorframe wearing a tight Iron Goddess T-shirt that accentuated the curves of her chest. "Customer up front wants to order a custom bike. Chlöe somebody. Says she's got an appointment."

"Yeah, I'll be right there."

Shea felt like a rag doll being ripped apart in all directions. Jessica. Annie. Rios. And now a custom job postponing a project that could get them on the cover of some motorcycle glossies. It was all too much. She grabbed the bottle of Bushmills from her bottom desk drawer, took a long pull, then marched to the showroom with a blank custom job folder in her hand.

In the customer waiting area, a willowy woman sat sipping a bottle of water and thumbing through an issue of *Motorcyclist* magazine. Wearing a fuchsia business suit and a perfume with smelled of lilac and orchid, the woman was a bit more corporate than Shea's usual clientele—less leather, more lace.

Maybe it was just the foul mood Shea was in, but something about this lady drew her ire. She'd met executive types in biker groups before. Most were more interested in showing off their wealth and drinking overpriced cocktails than in going on rides or participating in real biker culture. The kind that couldn't tell a spark plug from a piston.

"You Chlöe Stansbury?" Shea asked the woman sitting on one of a half dozen stackable chairs in the customer waiting area, each upholstered in worn burnt orange tweed. A small TV mounted near the ceiling played a muted video of the Isle of Man TT Race on a loop.

"I am." The woman stood, her black three-inch heels raising her to about five and half feet tall. Her smile was pleasant, but with an air of sophisticated authority. "Shea Stevens?"

Shea extended a hand that was relatively grease free. "Yeah."

Her grip was delicate and brief. "I liked what you did with the Pink Trinkets' bikes."

"You listen to the Trinks?"

Chlöe chuckled. "I suppose I don't look like a punk rocker, but I do have a rebellious side."

"Of course," Shea said with a forced smile. *Probably just buying a motorcycle to show off to her friends at the country club. Oh, look at you! You're so rebellious.*

"I was hoping you could build me something equally spectacular."

"How long you been riding?" Shea asked.

"Almost a year. After I turned forty, I decided to start checking off items on my bucket list."

"What are you riding now?"

"A V Star 250. It's a good beginner bike, but I'm ready for something with a bit more power. And a lot more pizzazz."

"Have you looked at our production bikes?"

Chlöe glanced at the display of bikes on the showroom floor and frowned. "I did, but nothing really spoke to me. I want something built just for me."

"We can do that. How much you looking to spend?"

"Under fifty grand preferably."

Shea choked to hide a chuckle. "Uh, well, you can have one of our production bikes for that, but if you want something custom, it's going to run more in the seventy-five to a hundred range."

Chlöe cast a scolding glance. "Oh, I'm sure you can do better than that. I can give you some great exposure with the circles I travel in. Bankers, real estate developers, local celebrities. You'd have more business than you'd know what to do with."

Shea's jaw tightened. *I already do.* The more Stansbury haggled, the more Shea dug in her heels, half hoping the woman would just walk away. "Sorry, no can do. You want a custom bike, that's what it'll cost ya."

"Oh, very well," Stansbury said with a sigh. "Can't blame a girl for trying. Let's do this thing."

Damn. "What style bike you want?"

"Well, I just love pink, don't you?"

Shea snorted. "Not really a pink kinda gal myself, but hey, it's your bike. You like pink? We'll paint it pink. You looking for a cruiser? A sport bike? A standard? Café racer?"

Chlöe knitted her brow. "Honestly, I don't know the difference."

Of course, you don't. "Follow me and I'll school ya." Shea gave Chlöe a tour of the production bikes, pointing out the different styles, riding positions, and unique features of each one. They stopped next to a café racer with a checkered racing flag painted on the tank.

"You know, I really like this café racer. It's very retro."

"It's a popular style."

"I think I heard there's a café racer owners' group somewhere in the area."

"I believe there is." *And you'd fit in like a turd in a punch bowl.*

"How exciting. I love the checkered styling on the fuel tank. Very fifties chic. Although I would want mine—"

"Pink."

Chlöe beamed. "It's like you can read my mind."

"Let me start by getting some measurements." Shea took out a tape measure and began measuring her client's height, inseam, arms, and legs.

"It's like getting measured for a bespoke suit," Chlöe said with a smile.

"A bit. You from around here originally?"

"Oh no. I've always been a bit of a vagabond, never staying in one place more than a few years. My father was in the army, so I've lived all over the world. I've been in

Ironwood for four years, which is the longest I've ever spent in one place."

"What do you do for a living?"

"I'm the CEO at Optimus."

"Optimus?"

"Optimus Rehabilitative Services. We're a state-of-the-art chemical dependency treatment facility."

"How'd you end up in that line of work? Are you an addict yourself?" Shea scribbled down the measurements on a sheet from the client file.

"Oh, nothing so crass as that!" Chlöe's nose crinkled at the suggestion. "I started out with a BA in chemistry and couldn't find a job. So, I earned my MBA and started Optimus."

She pulled a business card from a pocket and offered it to Shea with a condescending look. "And if you'll forgive me for saying, I can't help smelling the alcohol on your breath. I think we can help you. Alcoholism can destroy your life."

Shea examined the card, smirked, and handed it back to her. "Oh yeah, I hearda you. One of my former employees went through your rehab center in Bradshaw City."

"Oh really? How wonderful. How're they doing?"

"He relapsed. I fired him."

"Oh." Chlöe frowned. "I'm sorry to hear that. Drug abuse has reached epidemic proportions. Just this morning a girl in Ironwood was found dead from a suspected hex overdose. College student and a member of a sorority. Such a waste."

Shea perked up, wondering if her new client might know something that could make spending time with the Athena Sisterhood unnecessary. "I heard someone spiked the hex she took with rat poison."

"Dealers put all kinds of awful stuff in drugs—strychnine, Fentanyl, even ground glass, if you can believe it. Maybe it's a good thing she died."

"How could dying be a good thing?"

"Oh no, not good for the dead girl, of course. But if such a tragedy encourages addicts to come in for treatment, then maybe more lives will be saved in the long run. Kind of a scared-straight sort of thing."

"That's one way to look at it." Shea took some final measurements. "With all the addicts you work with at the clinic, any idea who's dealing hex around here?"

"It was that Mexican drug gang. What were they called?"

"The Jaguars."

"Yes, that's right, though I hear they've moved south."

Not before the Confederate Thunder raided their stash, thought Shea. "So, who took their place on the local drug scene?"

"I hear rumors, but they're just that. At Optimus, we focus on helping addicts get clean. We're less concerned about who their supplier was when they were using."

"I see. Well, I've got all the measurements I need." Shea closed the job folder as Terrance breezed through the showroom to the office.

"Wonderful! What's the next step?"

"Me and my crew will customize one of our stock frames to fit your measurements. We'll modify the fuel tank as needed, fabricate fenders, and other parts. Once everything's painted, we put it all together and let you take it for a test ride."

"How long does the whole process take?"

"Two to three months."

"That long? That would put us into January. Couldn't

you squeeze it down to one month? I'd love to show it off at my New Year's soiree."

"We can rush it, but that doubles the price." Shea hoped that would dissuade her. With all the other shit Shea had going, the last thing she needed was to be working overtime to please some stuffed shirt.

"Double? An extra ten grand, I can understand. Maybe. But double? Can't you cut me a deal?"

"Nope." Shea sat there, stone faced. *Just cancel, lady! I don't wanna work on your dumb pink bike anyway.*

After a few moments, Stansbury huffed. "Oh fine. Double it is. What's the bottom line?"

Shit. "Terrance, our business manager, can give you the final numbers, and write up your contract."

Shea led Chlöe down the hallway to the office. "Terrance, this is Chlöe Stansbury."

Terrance stood and shook her hand. "Yes, we spoke on the phone."

"We're building her a café racer on a one-month rush job." Shea handed him the folder with the details.

"Thank you, Shea," said Stansbury with a smile that did not reach her eyes. "A pleasure to meet a fellow biker woman. I look forward to what you'll create." She offered Shea the business card again. "And in case you change your mind."

"I got your number, but thanks." Shea's phone rang. "Sorry, gotta take this call."

She stepped out of the office, relieved to be away from Stansbury, and pressed the call button. "This is Shea."

"Hey, sexy! Long time, no see," said a gleeful, smoky voice that sent Shea's heart pounding.

"Uh, hi, Deb." The scar from Shea's bullet wound twinged. "Thanks for calling me back. About your invite to join the Athena Sisterhood . . ."

"Ha! I knew you'd come around sooner or later."

"Well, I am giving it some thought."

"Meet me tomorrow morning around seven at LezBeans. I'll tell you all about it."

What will Deb do if she figures out I'm snitching for the cops? Shea wondered. For all her craziness, Deb always had a good bullshit detector.

"Yeah, LezBeans at seven. I'll see you then."

8

———

RIOS PULLED up to the black iron security gate of the Desert Vistas condominium complex. Detective Johnson sat in the passenger seat reviewing the files on the other hex-related deaths.

A twenty-foot-tall, three-tiered water fountain rose from a stucco retaining wall on their right. To their left stood the guard shack—a small reclaimed-brick building with taupe geometric accents reminiscent of Frank Lloyd Wright.

The guard stepped out. He had a squarish jaw, capped teeth, and a name tag that read Doug. "How may I help you ladies today?"

Rios flashed her detective shield and held up a warrant. "We're here to search Unit D-209."

Doug raised an eyebrow. "Are you expected?"

"I'm afraid the owner, Genette Abrams, died this morning."

Doug's eyes widened. "Oh dear. Is Ms. Cohen okay?"

"Who is Ms. Cohen?"

"Sarah Cohen, her roommate."

"I wasn't aware Ms. Abrams had a roommate. We'll

need to speak with her as well." *Perhaps the roommate will know who the dealer is,* thought Rios.

"Let me give her a call." Doug stepped back into the guard shack.

"I'd rather you didn't."

"Well, I can't just let you in unannounced. It's against policy."

Rios held up the search warrant. "This search warrant says you can."

He squirmed. "I should still call Ms. Cohen to let her know you're on your way."

"Jake, ever been charged with interfering with a murder investigation?"

"What? Of course not!"

"Well, if you want to keep it that way then I suggest you let us through without giving the roommate a heads-up."

"Very well." He pressed a button and the gate swung open.

Rios flashed him a smile. "Thank you for your cooperation."

She pulled through and turned right at the first of several three-story buildings that shared the geometric structure, reclaimed-brick walls, and taupe concrete accents as the guard shack. Porches with privacy walls ran along the first buildings' ground-floor units, while covered balconies extended out from the third floor.

"Would you really have arrested him?" asked Johnson.

"Probably not. But if the roommate's involved somehow, I don't need her flushing evidence down the toilet while we're looking for a parking space. Keep an eye out for building D."

Rios cruised along the parking lot surrounding the complex. Courtyards with fountains and cobblestone paths stretched between the buildings.

"There it is. Building D."

Rios squinted. "Where? I don't . . . oh there, it is. Good eye. I swear they hide those signs on purpose."

She parked and the two of them approached the building, looking for unit 209.

"Can you believe these condos go for $150 to $200 grand each?" asked Johnson.

Rios shook her head. "That's more than I paid for my whole house."

"Lifestyles of the rich and pampered."

"No doubt. Looks like her unit is up on the second floor, number 209." They climbed a concrete staircase and Rios knocked on the door. A brass mezuzah featuring a stylized tree was attached to the doorframe.

After a minute with no response, Rios knocked louder.

"Maybe she's not in," said Johnson.

"Or maybe our friend Doug gave her a call after all." She pounded with her fist. "Sarah Cohen, it's the Cortes County Sheriff's Office. Please open the door."

From inside came the sound of bare feet padding on hard floors. "What do you want?" croaked a tired voice.

"It's about your roommate. Please open the door."

The door creaked open. A young woman with a head of short, dark hair stood in the doorway, wearing gray sweatpants and a paint-spattered sweatshirt. A set of white earbuds hung from her neck down to a phone clipped to her waistband.

"Sarah Cohen?" asked Rios.

"Yeah." The young woman eyed them suspiciously. "Who are you? What's this about Genette?"

Rios held up her shield. "Detective Rios. This is my partner, Detective Johnson. You mind if we talk inside?"

Without a word, Sarah opened the door further to let them in and led them into a two-story loft that left Rios breathless. Vaulted ceilings, hardwood floors, and a black spiral staircase rising to the second-floor bedrooms and balcony. Floor-to-ceiling windows afforded stunning views of the distant mountains. Numerous framed modern abstract paintings decorated the interiors walls. In the center of the room, an aluminum easel held a painting in progress on top of an old drop cloth.

Sarah led the detectives to a beige leather settee and matching loveseat, arranged around a glass and stainless-steel coffee table. Sarah collapsed onto the loveseat. Rios and Johnson sat nearby on the adjacent settee.

"When was the last time you saw Genette?" asked Rios.

"About nine last night. Genette and some of her Alpha Nu sorority sisters went out clubbing."

"On a Monday night?"

Sarah shrugged.

"You didn't go with them?"

"The sorority Susies aren't really my crowd." Sarah picked at a speck of dried blue paint on her hand. "Why are you asking about Genette? She's not in jail, is she?"

"Why would you think she'd been arrested?" asked Rios.

"She didn't come home last night. This morning you come banging on my door asking questions about her. Figured maybe she got busted for something."

"Do you know which clubs they went to?"

"They usually go to HausMusik, Rush, or the Trip Hop. I'm not sure where they went last night."

"And you didn't hear from her after she left?" asked Johnson.

"No—wait, yeah, she drunk dialed me around midnight."

Shortly before she died, thought Rios. "What did she say?"

"She didn't say anything, just made a bunch of weird

noises. 'Muh-muh-muh.' Like baby talk or something." Sarah paused. "There was someone else in the background yelling at her."

"One of her sorority sisters?" Rios made a note in her notebook.

"Maybe." A cloud of concern crossed Sarah's face. "Why all these questions? She's okay, isn't she?"

"Do you know the names of the people she was with last night?" asked Johnson.

"I don't know. She was meeting them at the Alpha Nu house. What's this about? Has something happened?"

Rios reached out a put a hand on the young woman's trembling hand. "Sarah, I'm sorry to tell you this, but Genette was found dead this morning in downtown Ironwood."

"What? No! You're wrong." Sarah knocked over a ceramic vase full of lilies and roses on the coffee table. She righted it, but left the puddle of water. "She . . . she's with her sorority sisters. She's gotta be."

"I'm afraid it's true," said Johnson.

"But why? How?"

"That's what we're trying to figure out," Rios answered. "Did she ever use drugs?"

"Drugs? No, never. Why would you ask such a thing?"

Johnson smiled sympathetically. "Because she died after taking a mixture of ecstasy, heroin, and strychnine."

"Strychnine? You mean like rat poison?" Sarah's breathing quickened.

Rios studied her reaction. There was grief, but also something else. Fear? Guilt? "Did Genette ever take hex when she went clubbing with the girls?"

Sarah didn't answer right away. Rios let the silence thicken between them, and hoped Johnson would, too. Sarah glanced back and forth between them, then stared at her mug. "She told me she'd sometimes have a little bump of hex. Just to let loose, you know? A lot of people do it."

"Who sold it to her?"

"I don't know. ." Sarah stared at the floor. "She never said."

"You ever take any yourself?"

"No, never."

"Sarah, we're not looking to arrest anyone for using hex. But we have to stop whoever's selling it so no one else dies."

"I don't know anything about it. Never touched the stuff."

Rios waited again, hoping Sarah would leak a name or mention a particular club. Grief and guilt had a way of eating at someone, compelling them to leak out bits of the truth. But the young woman just sat silently, pulling up her legs and resting her head on her knees.

"Anything else we should know about who may have poisoned Genette?"

"I don't know anything. Really."

Time to switch gears. Rios handed Sarah the search warrant. "I'm going to have to ask you to step outside the condo while we conduct a search."

Sarah examined the warrant. Her expression changed; sorrow gave way to anger. "No way, this is my place, too. You have no right."

Johnson pointed to the warrant. "Actually, this says we do."

"I realize it's an inconvenience," said Rios. "But we're looking for who sold Genette the tainted hex."

"I'm in the middle of a painting. It's a commissioned piece. I'm on deadline."

Rios nodded. "I promise it won't take more than a couple of hours."

"Fine, I'll just stay in my room until you're done."

Johnson shook her head. "No, I'm sorry you'll have to—"

"That will be fine," interrupted Rios, holding up a hand to Johnson. "We're not interested in your room."

Sarah picked up her mug, glaring at the two detectives, and stormed up the staircase to one of the bedrooms.

"Why did you let her stay here? Procedure dictates that—"

"Relax. I think Ms. Cohen knows more than she's telling, but I don't think she's our dealer. I'm willing to give her a little slack."

"Where do we start?"

Rios pulled on a pair of latex gloves and handed a pair to Johnson. "Upstairs in the victim's bedroom."

After a two-hour search, Rios and Johnson had turned up very little, other than some photos of the victim with her sorority sisters and a flyer for Ladies' Night specials at the Trip Hop Lounge. No drugs other than over-the-counter medications.

Rios knocked on Sarah's bedroom door. The young woman opened it, looking more disheveled than when they had first arrived. Her eyes were red, her face wet with tears.

"We're done with our search," said Rios. "I'm really sorry for your loss, ma'am."

"Who's going to call her folks? Someone's gotta tell them what happened."

"We have her parents' number," said Johnson. "We'll be contacting them later today."

Rios handed the woman her business card. "Please contact us if you think of anything that can help us find who poisoned Genette."

9

SHEA SAT ALONE in the Iron Goddess office staring into space. Terrance had left for a doctor's appointment shortly after finishing Chlöe Stansbury's paperwork.

She felt pulled in all directions. She was busy enough back when it was just her and Jessica. Now she had Annie to take care of. And Rios pushing her to hang around the Athena Sisterhood. Even her work here at Iron Goddess was getting complicated with employee conflicts and rushed projects.

A knock on the door pulled her from her pity party. Lakota stood in the office doorway. "I talked to Switch about the music and we came up with a solution."

"Oh yeah? What's that?"

"I got an old iPod that I can load up with all the Frank Sinatra, Michael Bublé, and Perry Como music she can stand. She can crank it up as loud as she wants without disturbing the whole crew."

Shea nodded. "Thanks for that. There's another situation I need you to discuss with her."

"Now what?"

"Switch's been calling Kyle names: midget, shorty, and so on. He's complained to me about it. Think you can get her to stop?"

Lakota sighed. "I can talk to her. Whether she'll stop is another matter."

"I understand she's got issues. Hell, we all got issues. I can't be tippytoeing around her when she's making things difficult for everyone else. I gotta set boundaries. If she can't handle it, then I gotta let her go."

"Do you know what that would do to her? Working here is the one thing in her life she loves. It's her anchor. If she loses this job, she'll end up on the streets."

"Then convince her to stop calling Kyle names. Otherwise, she's out the door."

"You're right. I just wish it wasn't me that always has to talk to her."

"She trusts you more than she does anyone else. But if you want me to talk with her instead, I will. You're our engineer, not Switch's baby-sitter."

"No, I'll talk to her."

"I appreciate it." Shea glanced at her watch. "It's after five. Let's get outta here."

Shea spent the next ten minutes closing up the shop. When everyone had left, Shea set the alarm and walked out the back door of the garage.

The setting sun was partially obscured by a blanket of heavy clouds moving in from the west. The temperature had dropped fifteen degrees from when she was outside earlier. The smell and promise of a November drizzle was in the air. Fortunately, she didn't have far to go and could relax with Jessica and Annie for the evening.

Sweet Betsy roared to life and Shea was soon navigating the twisting switchbacks down Sycamore Mountain. As she dropped in elevation, the temperature warmed to a more comfortable level and Shea picked up the pace, leaning harder into curves, and occasionally scraping her footpegs on the asphalt.

At the bottom of the mountain, the terrain leveled out, stretching across scrub desert dotted with saguaro cactus. A half mile farther, she turned into her neighborhood, which butted up against a low ridgeline topped with boulders that always reminded her of the spiny back of a dragon. Cotton-woods and sycamore trees dominated the rugged yards, along with wild grasses and other native plants. No mani-cured lawns or decorative rock. The homes themselves were a few decades old and some in urgent need of main-tenance.

Jessica's car was parked next to their garage because there was no room inside, a source of increasing complaints. Shea pressed the remote in the left pocket of her hoodie. Her garage opened to reveal her stable of motorcycles.

Once inside, Shea pressed the button again. The garage door groaned and clanked as it rolled back down. She pulled off her helmet and stepped into the house. The smell of take-out hamburgers and french fries put a smile on her face. *I deserve a break today,* she hummed to herself.

In the kitchen, a wrinkled McDonald's bag rested on the counter, next to a brightly colored kid's meal box. Shea grabbed a plate, pulled the remaining hamburger out of the bag, along with a half-empty box of fries, and sauntered to the living room.

Jessica sat on the love seat, staring blankly across the room. A half-eaten hamburger and fries lay on a plate on the coffee table. The place was unnervingly quiet.

"Hey, hon. Where's Annie?"

Jessica stared up at Shea, her arms crossed. "In her room," she said through gritted teeth.

"Uh . . . did she eat?"

"Nope!"

Shea sat next to her and put an arm around her shoulder. "What's going on, babe?"

Jessica took a deep breath and let it out slowly. "I'm losing my mind."

"I lost mine years ago. Don't really miss it."

"I'm not in the mood for jokes."

"Seriously, what happened?" Shea took a bite of her burger.

"Annie came home with a note from her teacher for calling another student the N-word."

"Oh."

"Don't you dare excuse it by saying she grew up hearing that word."

"Wouldn't think of it. There's no excuse for her using that word. Have you talked with her?"

"I thought you should have the honors."

"Fair enough." Shea set her own plate on the coffee table. "If it's any consolation, I really appreciate all that you do for her. You've really gone above and beyond since Wendy got killed."

"I can't be the only one around to deal with Annie. I have a job, too, you know."

"You're right. I need to do more."

"I feel like the black nanny raising the kids."

"You're not." Shea took Jessica's hand. Their eyes met. "You are my family. I love you more than anything else in this world."

"I love you, too, but it doesn't change how I feel." A tear spilled down her cheek. "You work sixty hours a week. It was bad enough when it was just the two of us, but now . . ."

"I know. I hate that the shop keeps me so busy."

"Annie's got some issues. This problem at school may

be linked to the trauma she's endured. She needs help. Professional help."

"Maybe she does, but right now I don't have the money to pay for it. Those shrinks don't come cheap."

"Maybe if you sold some of the bikes in the garage, Annie could get the help she needs and I'd finally have a place to park my car."

Shea sighed and pressed her forehead against Jessica's. "I'll see what I can do, okay? You're important to me. So is Annie. I'll figure something out." She gave her a kiss on the lips. "In the meantime, I'm gonna have a talk with our girl."

Shea hung her hoodie in the hall closet and opened the door to Annie's bedroom. Annie sat knees to chest on her bed with her back against the headboard. Her face was red and puffy from crying. Her pigtail braids were loose and ragged.

"Hey, Doodlebug. I . . . uh . . ." Shea struggled for words. Having kids was never in her life plan. "I hear you had an . . . *interesting* day."

Annie shrugged.

Shea straddled the royal blue, child-size chair next to the smallish wooden desk. "Wanna tell me what's going on?"

Another shrug.

"How 'bout we start with why you used the N-word at school today."

"Naomi Harris was mean to me."

"How was she being mean to you?"

"She wouldn't let me jump rope with her and the other girls. She said dumb rednecks don't know how to jump rope. So, I called her a nig—"

"Don't say it! Don't you *ever* use that word again."

"Why? Naomi says it all the time."

Shea rubbed her face, wondering how to explain racial

politics to an eight-year-old. "She shouldn't be using that word either. It's a very hateful word."

"I don't hate her. I just wanted to jump rope. Besides, she called me a dumb redneck."

"Which she shouldn'ta done."

"So why did I get in trouble and she didn't? It ain't fair."

"No, it ain't. But here's the thing. You can't control what other people do. All you can do is keep your side of the street clean."

"What street?"

"It's just a saying, kiddo. It means don't do nothing bad, no matter what other folks is doing. When you got kidnapped, I did some pretty stupid things. Things I regret. Things that made the situation worse. And I had to pay the consequences."

"What is consequences?"

"Consequences is what happens when you do stuff you shouldn't. When you used the N-word, you got sent home with a note. Then Jessica sent you to your room without any dinner. That's consequences."

"I don't like consequences."

"Nobody does. But what you said was wrong. It hurt Jessica's feelings."

"I didn't mean to. I didn't say it to her."

"Whether you meant to or not, it still upset her."

"I'm sorry."

"I ain't the one you need to be telling sorry. How about this: You tell Jessica how sorry you are for hurting her feelings. Then I'll give you your dinner. Deal?"

Annie nodded.

"Good. Now go apologize to Jessica."

10

THE NEXT MORNING, Shea parked Sweet Betsy in a space between a candy-apple-red BMW convertible with a CAU window decal and a green Subaru sporting a VEGANS TASTE BETTER bumper sticker. Despite her friendship with the owner, LezBeans Coffee and Books wasn't Shea's kind of place.

Inside the café, the cacophony of multiple conversations and espresso machines enveloped her like a clingy lover. The pungent aromas of pumpkin spice and coffee assaulted her.

What was it about fall that made every coffee shop want to flavor everything like pumpkin pie? She hated that shit.

Her last memory of this place fueled her foul mood—the night she had ended her relationship with Debbie. Shea had told her she was too busy working on a custom bike to attend one of Debbie's campus protests.

"What the hell's wrong with you, Shea?" Debbie had demanded. "Too busy making a buck to stand up for women's equality?"

Shea rolled her eyes. "That's not it and you know it. I have other responsibilities."

"You have a responsibility to your sisters to stand up against the good ol' boy network running this university and let your voice be heard. It isn't just about you. Maybe if you showed some solidarity, women could make more than seventy-four cents for every dollar a man makes. But no, you'd rather let the fucking patriarchy continue to oppress women."

Shea had risen to her feet, knocking over her cup of coffee. "You want me to stand up for myself and let my voice be heard? Then hear this. I'm tired of your shit. You're too busy organizing protests and lobbying politicians to show up for a fucking date once in a while. I can't remember the last time we had sex."

"Shea, lower your voice." Debbie's face colored. She straightened her posture, glancing around the room.

"Which is it, Deb? Lower my voice or let it be heard? You know what, don't answer that. I don't need your feminist theory answers. I grew up with the patriarchy, too."

"Yes, poor Shea and her troubled childhood. Turned you into a car thief."

"Fuck you!" Shea leaned into Deb's face. "I don't need your pity or your condescension. Go find yourself a new plaything. This relationship's over."

Shea had stormed out, revving her engine in the parking lot before roaring off into the night.

And now here she was years later, back in this bastion of Sapphic sisterhood, filled with androgynous lesbian hipsters chatting inanely about sports teams, the latest fashion trends and who's dating whom while sipping chai lattes and green tea.

"Holy shit, if it isn't the world-famous Shea Stevens, bike builder to the stars," said the woman behind the counter. Despite having a bit more silver in her seventies-style afro than Shea remembered, the woman offered a gleaming smile that was as warm as ever.

"Morning, Nita." Shea stretched over the counter and gave her a hug.

"I saw them bikes you built for the Pink Trinkets. Damn fine work."

Shea managed a smile. "Thanks."

"So, what'll you have? Pumpkin spice lattes are on special."

Shea's upper lip curled in disgust. "No, thanks. Small cup of regular coffee'll be fine."

"Iced or hot?"

"Hot."

"Room for cream?"

"Nope. Just hot, dark, and bitter." Shea laid a fiver on the counter. "You seen Debbie in here yet?"

"Ha! Speaking of hot, dark, and bitter." Nita poured the coffee and popped a lid on the cup. "Don't tell me you're seeing her again?"

"No. Not romantically anyway."

"Thank Goddess for that. Something to do with that feminist biker club she got going?"

"Yeah, the Athena Sisterhood." Shea gathered up her change. A woman behind her in line frowned, looking impatient. Shea stepped aside to let the woman up the counter. "She here?"

"Front room overlooking the street. Watch your back, sister."

Shea raised her cup in acknowledgment, then shuffled through the labyrinth of tables and bookshelves to the front room. Bright morning light poured through the plate glass window. Shea squinted to make out faces.

Debbie sat in the corner reading a hardback book with

a blue and yellow cover. Her makeup and wedge-cut chestnut hair was immaculate as always. A silver earring in the shape of a labrys—a double-sided battle-ax—dangled from each ear. She wore a black leather vest, called a cut, over a pale pink button-down shirt, like a mashup of Martha Stewart and Joan Jett.

Two small rectangular patches, one above the other, had been sewn to the right pocket on the front of the vest. The top read LABRYS, the bottom PRESIDENT, in Pepto-Bismol pink lettering on a white background. A similar patch with the word IRONWOOD was on the left pocket.

A wave of memories crashed over Shea. Debbie throwing her a birthday party composed mostly of people Shea didn't know. The two of them making love in Deb's office at the university. Marching in the Ironwood Gay Pride Parade. Shea teaching Debbie how to ride a motorcycle. The two of them arguing over Shea's failing to live up to Deb's ideal of what a true feminist should be and feel and think and do.

"Hey." Shea approached the table, forcing a smile.

Debbie's face went from serious to joyful in an instant. "Oh, sweetie, I have missed you." She stood, arms opened wide for a hug.

Shea held up her hand and backed up a step. "Not quite ready for hugs yet. Still healing from a broken collarbone."

"Yeah, you mentioned something about an accident." Debbie put a hand on the side of Shea's face and pulled her in for a quick peck on the lips before sitting back down.

Shea grabbed the other chair and took a deep breath, ignoring the writhing ball of emotions in her gut. "What're you reading?"

Debbie held up the book. "*By Any Means: Feminist Strategies to Winning the War Against Women.* Sort of a militant feminist's manifesto."

"Huh." Shea took a sip of coffee and gazed absently out the window. *Typical Deb and her obsession with politics.*

"Rachel Maddow's raving about it." Debbie paused. "I'm boring you, aren't I?"

"Maybe a little."

"Never were much of a reader, were you?" Debbie pushed the book aside and folded her hands. "What kind of bike are you riding these days?"

"Iron Goddess 750 Custom. You?"

"Indian Roadmaster. I'm a bit conflicted about supporting a company that appropriates Native American culture for the sake of a buck, but I have to say, it's a comfy ride. Of course, I still commute in the Green Machine. Remember that?" Debbie asked with a devious grin.

"I remember it being very cramped," said Shea, recalling the times the two of them had made out in the convertible Audi roadster. The memory sent a wave of warmth into her groin.

Debbie's face flushed. "I hear you have a new girlfriend. What's her name?"

Shea shot her a wary glance. "Jessica."

"She hot?"

"*I* think so."

"Any kids? Other than that moody cat of yours, I mean."

"My niece, Annie, lives with us. She's rather fond of Ninja."

"Since when do you have a niece?"

"My sister's daughter. I became her guardian after Wendy got killed." The image of Wendy with half her face blown off had burned into Shea's memory.

"Oh yeah. I heard about that on the news. Tragic." Debbie paused for a moment. One corner of her mouth curled into a half smile. "Funny, I never pictured you as the mommy type. How old is she?"

"Eight."

"And how long have you and Jessica been an item? "

Shea's nose crinkled in disgust. "Geez! What's with the interrogation?"

"No interrogation." Debbie shrugged. "Just making conversation."

"'Bout six months, if you must know." *Just get through this, girl. The sooner you start hanging out with the Athenas, the sooner you can give Rios the information she wants.*

"Six months? That's like a record for you, isn't it?"

"Not really."

"Wow, serious relationship *and* a kid. Never thought I'd see the day when the wild mustang Shea Stevens would be domesticated." Debbie's voice dripped with condescension. "One big happy fucking family."

Shea glanced out the window at the people walking past, resisting the urge to storm out like last time. "Talk to me about the Athena Sisterhood."

"Ooh, what do you think of our cuts?" Deb stood up and twirled to show off the three-part patch on the back of the cut.

A rounded rocker patch, emblazoned with the words ATHENA SISTERHOOD in pink letters, curved across the top of the cut. The word ARIZONA curved upward in the bottom rocker. Between the two rockers was the club's emblem—a stylized silver owl with pink accents on the outstretched wings. A rectangular patch with the letters MC had been sewn on to the right of the emblem.

"Pretty snazzy, huh?" Deb said as she sat down, beaming.

"It's nice." Shea tapped one of the patches on the front "What's LABRYS mean?"

"It's the double-headed ax, a lesbian symbol. Damn, don't you know anything about lesbian culture?"

"I know what a labrys is. Why you got it on a patch?"

"It's my road name."

"Subtle."

"I think it fits. I am, after all, fighting for the rights of women."

"You get permission from the Confederate Thunder to start a motorcycle club in Cortes County?"

Debbie's glee faded into a glower. "I don't need a man's permission. I am a woman. I have the right to do what I want, associate with whom I want, wear what I want, and identify how I want."

"Normally I'd agree with you. But the Thunder's the dominant biker club around here. Starting an MC in their territory and wearing outlaw-style cuts is considered disrespectful."

"You think I give a shit what those sexist rednecks think? They don't deserve respect."

Shea leaned in. "Deb, the Thundermen ain't like the corporate or academic types you're used to going up against. You go riding around on your bikes in your pretty new cuts emblazoned with a pink MC patch, there's gonna be trouble. People are gonna get hurt."

"They lay a hand on me, I'll sue them for every nickel they got."

Shea wiped her face with her hand and sighed. "They're not just gonna call you dirty names. They'll fucking tear you apart. These guys are animals."

"All the more reason for us to stand our ground. We have a right to the same freedoms they have. That includes starting our own motorcycle clubs. And if that means we have to fight, so be it."

"No matter who gets hurt or killed in the process?"

"You'd have us cower in fear from these criminals? Act like we're their property?"

"That's not what I'm saying. But you gotta understand the consequences."

"Does that mean you don't want to join us?"

Yeah, I really don't, Shea thought. "I'd like to hang around the club and get to know you guys first."

"*Women,* not guys," Debbie corrected sharply.

"Sorry! I'd like to get to know you *women.* Iron Goddess has a bike night event coming up. Gonna be a lot of female bikers there. Be a great way for the Athena Sisterhood to attract new members. Maybe y'all could sponsor a booth."

"I'd rather sponsor you as a prospect."

"A prospect? And be your whipping girl for a year?"

"Hey, I'm the president. I'll go easy on you. I might even be persuaded to fast-track you and get you patched after only a few months."

"Let me get to know the other women first. See how it goes." Shea stood up. "Right now, I gotta go open the shop."

"Join us for drinks tonight at Gertie's."

"Gertie's? Why are y'all meeting in a dyke bar? Is the Sisterhood a lesbian club?"

"No, but Fuego, the owner of Gertie's, is the club's VP. She lets us use their back room for meetings."

"That's convenient."

"It is." A coy grin creased Debbie's face. "So, you'll join us for drinks?"

Jessica's gonna be pissed when she finds out I'm spending time around Debbie instead of taking care of Annie. But what choice've I got? Let Rios send me back to prison? Not a chance.

"When should I be there?"

"Nine."

"On a school night?"

"Oh my, aren't you the little soccer mom now." Debbie giggled. "What's wrong? Got a PTA meeting to go to? Or does Jessica have you wrapped around her finger?"

"I was working until almost midnight last night. I gotta sleep sometime."

"The Shea Stevens I knew didn't need much sleep. Join us! I'll make it worth your while."

Yeah, I'll bet. Shea chugged the last of her coffee and pitched the cup into a nearby trash can. "Fine, I'll see you at nine."

"Oh, and you're going to need to introduce yourself by your road name."

"What road name?"

"Whatever it was you used to go by way back when."

"I'd rather just go by Shea, if it's all the same to you."

Debbie's face hardened. "It's not all the same to me. We use road names in the Sisterhood. It's for your protection and for everyone else's. So no one can track us down."

"I'm not worried."

"It's not a request. You want to hang with us, you use a road name."

Shea's jaw tightened. The more time she spent with this woman, the more she wanted to kick her ass. "I went by Pantera when I was a teenager boosting cars."

Labrys scrunched her eyes. "Pantera seems too ethnic for you." Her gaze wandered around the room and stopped at an abstract painting with the word HAVOC in bold white letters against a grungy background. "Havoc. That's your road name."

"Havoc? Seriously?"

"See you at nine, Havoc."

11

———————

After spending eight hours working with Lakota on the engineering specs of Chlöe Stansbury's cafe racer, Shea arrived home to a smorgasbord of savory aromas.

A pair of tapered candles flickered on the coffee table. Jessica stood in front of the stove stirring a pot of soup while keeping an eye on two other boiling pots.

"Hey, babe, what smells so good?" Shea kissed her temple.

Jessica wiped away dots of perspiration from her forehead. "Lentil soup and a Mediterranean salad for starters, followed by homemade gnocchi with marinara sauce. And for dessert, poached pears in a pomegranate wine reduction."

"I got no idea what most of that is, but if you made it, I know it'll be delicious. What's the occasion?"

"You don't remember?"

Shea got a sinking feeling in her stomach. *What'd I miss?* "My birthday's not till February. Yours was last month."

"Think back to May."

"Last May? Oh, that's when we started dating, right?"

A look of frustrated bemusement played across Jessica's face. "Yes, and that makes tonight . . ."

"Wednesday?"

"Our six-month anniversary."

"Oh." *Is this a big deal? Should I have brought flowers?* Shea wondered. "Well, happy six-month anniversary." She grinned nervously and pulled Jessica close for a more intimate kiss.

The warmth and tenderness of Jessica's lips reminded Shea how much she needed her. And how pissed she would be when Shea told her she was going out later.

"Where's Annie?" Shea asked when she came up for air.

"Terrance and his new boyfriend are baby-sitting her, so you and I can have a night alone." Jessica's eyes twinkled with promise and seduction.

Guilt pressed on Shea's conscience and she pulled away from the embrace. "Hon, there's something I gotta tell you."

Jessica frowned. "What?"

"I met with Detective Rios the other day. She's pressuring me to spend time with the Athena Sisterhood."

"The Athena Sisterhood? Why?"

"A few women have died recently from hex laced with rat poison. Rios thinks someone in the club's selling it."

"Why get you involved?"

"They think that with my background I can find out who's dealing." She deliberately didn't mention her meeting with Debbie. *No need to make Jessica more upset.* "It's bullshit, but I ain't got no choice. I signed that goddamn confidential informant agreement. She's got me by the short hairs."

"What about Annie? I can't be the only one taking care of her. You're her guardian."

"I know. You and Annie are the most important people in my life." She reached out to Jess and pulled her close. "But if I don't do this, Rios is gonna send my ass back to prison."

Jessica sighed and stirred a pot of sauce with a wooden spoon. "So, when does this undercover assignment begin?"

"Tonight."

"Tonight? Damnit!" Jessica threw the spoon into the sink, splattering tomato sauce against the wall. "I spent the past two hours making a special dinner for us. It's the first night we've had alone in forever."

Shea embraced her from behind. "I'm sorry, honey. I really am. You did all this for me, for us. It's wonderful."

"And it's all going in the garbage."

"No, it's not. I don't have to be show up until nine. Let's just enjoy the amazing dinner you made, and then we should still have time for a little sumthin'-sumthin'."

Jessica turned around, cradled Shea's face in her hands, and sighed. "I wanted tonight to be special."

"It is. You made it special. I shoulda done something too. I've just been so busy with work, I barely got a brain cell to spare. But you mean the world to me."

Shea leaned in and kissed Jessica. Lips and tongues intertwined. Shea allowed the walls of her heart to come down. Anger, frustration, and fear faded.

After a few minutes, a timer went off, pulling the two of them back into reality. Shea smiled, not caring that it made the childhood scars on her face seem deeper. She stepped back as Jessica finished preparing dinner.

Jessica switched off the burners on the stove. "Help me dish up."

"I'd invite you to come with me, but I know how nervous you get riding on the back of my bike at night."

Shea filled two bowls of lentil soup while Jess plated their salads. The two of them sat down on the love seat in the den and Shea put a hand on Jessica's thigh. "I won't stay long. Probably have one drink, shake a few hands, and head out."

"You swear?"

"Cross my heart and hope to die."

"No dying! Please! Just come home safe." Jessica pecked Shea on the cheek. "I don't know why I put up with you."

Shea pulled Jessica closer, her body coming alive with need. "Because you have an unhealthy attraction to bad girls." She kissed Jess hard.

Jessica moaned and stretched out on the love seat. "So my therapist tells me."

Shea's hand slipped under her girlfriend's shirt, grazing her back ever so slightly, causing Jess to gasp. "And I'm really good with my hands."

Jessica pushed Shea back with a sigh. "Promise me something first."

"What?" asked Shea, feeling more than a little frustrated.

"You won't sign up to be a pledge, okay?"

"A what? You mean a prospect?"

"Whatever they call it in biker clubs."

Shea scoffed. "Trust me, I got no intention of spending the next year as a prospect. I don't even want to be a hangaround."

"Just promise me."

"Yeah, yeah, I promise." She kissed Jessica's throat. "Now can we get back to celebrating our semi-anniversary?"

"The soup's going to get cold."

"Soup can wait. I'm hungry for dessert."

AFTER POURING her fourth beer from the pitcher on the table, Shea felt her cellphone vibrate in her pocket. In the crowded bar, she couldn't hear it ring above the noise. She opened her phone. Jessica was calling. It was nearly midnight. A flick of her thumb sent the call to voicemail.

"Sorry," said Shea to the stocky woman with a square jaw and a blond buzz cut sitting across from her. "You were about to tell me how you got the name Savage."

"It's stupid, really." The patches on the front of her cut identified her as the club's sergeant at arms.

A woman who was sitting next to Savage, with the nickname Indigo, nudged her playfully. "I think it's a funny story." She swept her mahogany braids behind her shoulders.

Savage rolled her eyes. "Fine. Before I became an EMT, I was a navy corpsman assigned to a marine outfit in Iraq. A guy in my unit was really into 1950s pulp fiction. One night after he'd had a few too many, he started calling me Doc Savage. The name stuck."

"But wasn't Doc Savage a guy?" asked Shea.

Savage shrugged. "What did I care? How 'bout you? What'd you do to earn the name Havoc?"

"You'd have to ask Labrys." Shea paused, feeling her head swim from the alcohol. "So, how long've y'all been a part of the Athena Sisterhood?"

"A year and a half," said Indigo. "Started out as just a women's riding group, but then the Athena Sisterhood approached us about starting a local chapter. I was apprehensive at first, but I really love being part of this family."

"It's a great group of women," said Savage.

"Y'all ain't worried the Confederate Thunder's gonna push back?" asked Shea.

"Crazy white boys with guns? Been dealing with that shit my whole life," said Indigo with a half-serious grin.

Savage nudged Indigo. "Labrys says they talk real big, but they ain't nothing to worry about."

Shea shook her head. "Labrys doesn't know them like I do."

"How do you know them?" asked Savage.

"I grew up with them. My father was their president when I was a kid."

Indigo glanced at Savage, then at Shea, an embarrassed look on her face. "Sorry, didn't mean no offense by that crazy white boy's comment."

"Relax," said Shea. "They are crazy. And dangerous. My old man murdered my mama just for trying to leave him."

"Damn!" Savage took a drink of her beer and shook her head. "That must've been awful."

"Ancient history." Shea swirled the beer in her bottle and shrugged. "But that's what I mean when I say they're dangerous."

"Your father give you them scars on your face, too?" asked Savage.

"Naw. Got attacked by a dog when I was a kid. My old man of all people saved me."

"Shit. You had a helluva childhood." Indigo grimaced. "I guess what don't kill ya makes ya stronger."

"So they say," said Shea.

A woman wearing an Athena Sisterhood cut over a purple flannel shirt walked over, carrying a tall bottle of San Pellegrino sparkling water. "Hey! Y'all seen Orphan?"

"You just missed her, Pipes," said Savage. "Left about five minutes ago."

Pipes shook her head. "Dammit, I needed to talk to her."

"I heard her roommate just died," added Indigo. "Over-dose or something. So sad."

"Pipes, you met Havoc?" asked Savage.

Pipes shook Shea's hand. "You gonna be joining us?"

"We'll see."

"Pleasure to meet ya." She finished the bottle of sparkling water and slammed it down on the table. "Okay, y'all have a good night. I'm outta here."

Indigo pretended to pout. "So soon?"

"Yeah, got a meeting with one of my Narcotics Anony-mous sponsees in the morning."

"See ya, Pipes." Savage waved.

Shea looked Indigo in the eye, then at Savage. "Mind if I ask y'all a question?"

Indigo nodded. "Uh, sure."

"I heard somebody in the club is dealing hex. You know anything about that?"

Indigo shifted and looked away. "Never heard that."

"Hex?" asked Savage. "Who told you that?"

Shea shrugged. "Just people talking."

"Despite what you *might have* heard, we don't allow no drugs in the club," insisted Savage. "No dealing. No using. As the club's sergeant at arms, I make sure of that."

"No one?"

"What are you?" asked Indigo. "A cop?"

"No," answered Shea, feeling a rush of indignation.

Indigo looked askance at Shea. "Sure about that? You seem awfully curious about this whole drug thing."

Shea pulled out a business card and slid it over to Indigo. "I build custom motorcycles for a living."

Indigo examined the card. "You work at Iron Goddess? You know Terrance?"

"He's my business partner."

"Interesting. He and I go way back." Indigo tucked the

card into her purse. "I may have to stop by next time my bike needs servicing."

A couple of men in Confederate Thunder cuts walked into the bar. Shea recognized them right away. One-Shot, the club's president, stood six-foot-something with a military-style crew cut. His VP, Mackey, a stout guy with the face of a weasel, scanned the room.

Shea reached over and tapped Labrys' shoulder. "Hey! We got trouble."

Labrys set down her beer, mouth agape. "Um . . . maybe they're just here for a drink."

"At Gertie's? I don't think so."

Mackey nudged One-Shot and pointed to the tables where the Sisterhood was sitting.

"Crap." Shea felt her body tense. "They spotted us."

"What do we do?" asked Indigo.

"Y'all sit tight. I got history with these guys. Lemme see if I can diffuse the situation." Shea grabbed her glass beer mug and walked around their table to intercept the two Thundermen.

"Hey, One-Shot," said Mackey. "Look who it is—the dog-faced diesel dyke."

Shea hoped the beers hadn't slowed her reflexes too much. "What do y'all want?"

"You with the Barbie bikers, lesbo?" asked Mackey.

"What business is it of yours?" The bar grew quiet as patrons noticed the confrontation.

"Cortes County's our territory," said One-Shot in a monotone bass voice. "They wanna start a club, they need to talk to us first. You know this."

"Aw, come on, One-Shot. They're just women who like to ride," said Shea. "They ain't honing in on your little crystal meth empire, if that's what's eating you."

"They wanna ride? They can ride. But not while

wearing outlaw-style patches." One-Shot folded his arms. "No one starts an MC here without our permission. It's disrespectful."

"Fuck you, Lurch!" Labrys appeared next to Shea. "I don't need a man's permission to tell me what I can and can't wear."

One-Shot took a step toward Labrys.

Shea recognized the look on his face. If she didn't do something fast, the situation would turn bloody. She stepped between them. "One-Shot, wait!"

He paused and turned to Shea, but remained silent.

"You and I both grew up with the Thunder. I respect that you're president of the club now. So, don't screw it up and make the same mistake your predecessor did."

"And what mistake's that?"

"Stirring up trouble where there ain't none. Hunter's dead because he stole dope from the Jaguars."

Mackey shoved Shea's shoulder. "That's a goddamn lie. He's dead because you lured him up to the Jaguar's warehouse by claiming they had his kid. Never woulda gone back there otherwise. His death is on you."

More than you know, Shea thought as she remembered the bullet she'd put in Hunter's head. "Be smart, One-Shot. Leave the Athenas alone. They ain't hurting no one."

She could see the wheels turning in One-Shot's head as he considered the situation. Her grip tightened on her beer mug. *Come on, man. Just walk away.*

He shook his head. "No one but the Thunder wears the MC patch in this county. If they don't take off those cuts—"

"Not gonna happen, asshole," yelled Labrys.

Mackey swung at Labrys, but Shea caught his arm with her free hand. Mackey drove his other fist into Shea's jaw, splitting her lip. She spat blood in his face and clocked him with her mug, knocking him off his feet. Blood trickled from a cut above his eye.

Shea pointed the beer mug at Thunder's president. "Leave us alone, One-Shot." Members of the Sisterhood circled around her.

One-Shot helped Mackey to his feet. "Final warning. Next Barbie biker I see riding with an MC cut is gonna get hurt."

Mackey wiped the blood on his face and pointed to Shea. "You just earned yourself a death sentence. I don't care who your old man was."

He turned and the two Thundermen marched out the front door.

For a few minutes, the place was deadly quiet. Half the patrons had left. The rest sat wide-eyed staring at the Sisterhood.

"Well done, Havoc." Labrys clapped Shea on the back as they returned to their seats. "I named you well."

"You sure can throw down," said Indigo. "We could use your street smarts."

Savage appeared with a bar towel wrapped in ice. "Here, put this on your lip. Should reduce the swelling."

"Thanks. I should really get home." Shea wiped the blood from her chin and pressed the cool, damp cloth to her face. Her jaw was still in one piece, but her lip and cheek felt fat and numb. "Y'all may think being in a motorcycle club is cool . . ." Her mouth hurt to talk. "But a fucking MC patch ain't worth dying for."

"That's why we need you," said Labrys. "You know the Thunder better than anyone."

Shea's phone vibrated again. A text message from Jessica asking if she was okay. "I gotta head out. It's late."

"Aw, come on, Havoc" said Indigo. "One more round at least. My treat."

"Another time." She took a step toward the door, then stopped and turned. "And in case you're interested, Iron Goddess Custom Motorcycles is hosting a women's bike night event tomorrow. Would love to see y'all there."

Indigo gave her a mock salute. "We'll be there."

12

——————

WHEN SHE ARRIVED HOME, Shea immediately pulled a bag of frozen peas from the freezer and placed it against her aching jaw. She shuddered from the sudden jolt of cold and pain before the numbing effects of the frozen peas took the edge off. With her free hand, she grabbed a bottle of vodka, closed the freezer with her elbow, and ambled toward the love seat where Jessica sat, her face a mask of resentment.

"What happened to your face?" Jessica's harsh tone felt like nails in Shea's aching skull.

She considered telling Jessica the truth but didn't want her to worry. "Tripped and banged my chin on a table. Hurts," Shea mumbled. She plopped down next to Jessica and took a long drag of vodka.

"Maybe if you'd stayed home in the first place, this wouldn't have happened." Jessica peeked under the bag of peas. "Goodness, this is really swollen. And you smell like a still." Her nose crinkled as she sat back.

"Just trying to get that bitch Rios off my back. She's so mean."

"I called you a dozen times. Why didn't you answer?"

Guilt intensified the pain in Shea's head. "It was just so loud in there. So loud. Must not have heard the phone ring."

"Is this what I have to look forward to from now on? Taking care of Annie by myself while you go out drinking and come home looking like you've been in a fight?"

"Jess, can we not do this now? My head is killing me." Shea took another pull on the vodka, enjoying the bite at the back of her throat. Jessica grabbed the bottle and slammed it onto the coffee table.

"Hey, I was drinking that," Shea slurred, reaching for the bottle.

Jessica moved it out of reach. "You've had enough for one night, I think."

Shea pouted. "Don't be mad at me, Jess. I'm sorry I was out so late. But I don't wanna go back to prison. Rios is just mean. So mean."

"You spent more time with her tonight than you did with me."

"Rios? She wasn't there."

"No. Your ex-girlfriend. Debbie." Jess practically spat the name.

"I invited you along but you didn't want to come."

"'Cause it's our anniversary."

"Well, six-month anniversary." Shea made a goofy face. "Is that really a thing? I don't think it's a thing. I mean, do they even sell Hallmark cards for that?"

Jessica's eyes watered. "I wanted some alone time with my girlfriend for once. Is that a crime? The past few months have revolved almost entirely around Annie. You and I need some couple time."

Shea struggled to focus on what Jessica was saying, but random thoughts chased each other through her inebriated mind like rabid squirrels. Her jaw throbbed relentlessly. Her stomach was turning somersaults. "I need to go to bathroom." She struggled to her feet and the room swayed.

Jessica magically appeared in front of her. "We need to discuss this."

"Jesus Christ on a cracker, Jess. I'm tired. I'm drunk. My jaw's killing me. And if you don't move outta my way, I'm gonna hurl all over you. Now piss off!"

"Fine." Jess stepped out of the way.

Shea went to take a step and stopped short when her niece appeared in the hallway between the bedrooms. "Annie?"

"Why are y'all fighting?"

"Oh shit. Sorry, Annie." Shea stumbled toward her. Annie backed up, eyes wary.

"What's wrong with you, Aunt Shea?"

"Rough night, kiddo."

Jessica stepped between them. "Go back to bed, sweetie. We're sorry we woke you." The two of them disappeared into Annie's room.

Shea leaned against the wall to steady herself against the swirling sensation. "Shit, Wendy." She tried to remember her sister's face before she was killed. But the only images that came up were the ones with half her face blown off by a cop's bullet.

Shea's stomach lurched and she threw herself into the hallway bathroom, splattering the floor and toilet lid with the liquefied remnants of dinner. The reek of tomato sauce and bile only made the memories of Wendy's shattered face more vivid. Shea heaved again as she struggled to lift the toilet lid.

So sorry. So, so sorry, she thought, struggling to stop the dry heaves several minutes later.

"Oh, Shea, what'd you do?" asked Jessica, entering the bathroom.

"I messed up."

"I'd say you threw up."

Shea wiped her mouth with her arm. Something cool and wet was wiping across her face and body. "Jess." She reached out to cup her girlfriend's face, but Jessica pulled away in time to avoid getting smeared with vomit.

"Why do I put up with you, you dopey girl?" Jessica's voice was kind once again, mothering.

Shea pointed to deep scars crisscrossing her face. "Cause chicks dig butches with scars."

Jessica chuckled. "Oh, is that it? Well, let's get you cleaned up."

"Kiss me, baby."

"Ugh, I don't think so." Jessica scrunched her nose and turned away as she pulled off Shea's soiled shirt.

Shea pouted as she sat in just her bra and jeans on the floor. "But it's our six-month-iversary. We should have sex."

"Shoulda thought about that before you went drinking with your biker buddies. Come on, get up." Jessica lifted Shea off the floor and steered her out of the bathroom and into their bedroom.

"We gonna have sex?"

"Darling, that ship has sailed. You need sleep and I gotta clean up the mess you just made in Annie's bathroom."

13

AT SEVEN THIRTY the next morning, Shea was using an angle grinder to cut a stock motorcycle frame to fit the specs for the Stansbury bike, when Terrance walked into the shop. Her jaw still ached from getting punched the night before, and the vibrations from the grinder weren't helping her hangover any.

"Geez, Shea, you look like hell," said Terrance as Shea finished a cut and set down the grinder.

She pulled off her gloves and rubbed her temples. "Rough night hanging out with the Athena Sisterhood."

"Athena Sisterhood? You and Jessica were supposed to be celebrating your anniversary."

"'Supposed to be' being the operative words."

"I don't understand. What happened?"

"Well for one, no one told me Jessica was planning a special evening. I didn't even know six-month anniversaries were a thing."

"So, you made other plans."

"Detective Rios has been pressing me to spend time

with the Sisterhood. She thinks one of them's selling hex. So last night I hung out with them and had a few drinks."

"I bet that went over like a lead balloon. What'd she say when you told her your ex is their president?"

"She already knew. Sorry you and your boyfriend got roped into watching Annie for nothing."

"Damn, girl," said Terrance with a chuckle. "You are seriously deep in the shit."

"To make matters worse, One-Shot and Mackey showed up demanding the Sisterhood stop calling themselves an MC or wearing outlaw cuts."

"And you got in the middle of it?"

"What was I supposed to do, T? Those gals are nice, but they ain't hardcore bikers like the Thunder. They're college kids and office workers who think it's cool to wear outlaw-style cuts. If I didn't step in, Mackey and his crew woulda mopped the floor with them."

"Don't go looking for trouble with them, Shea."

"I don't go looking for it. It finds me all on its own." Shea leaned against the bike.

"Just make sure the Thundermen don't show up here looking to settle scores. We have enough to deal with without a bunch of redneck bikers shooting up the place."

"Trust me, if I had my druthers, I'd have nothing to do with either club. I just want to build bikes, make love to my girlfriend, and help Annie get over her issues."

"She still having problems?"

Shea nodded. "Bad dreams at night. Trouble at school. And she keeps begging to see Monster and his old lady."

"Tough being a parent, isn't it?"

"I'm not sure I'm cut out for it, honestly."

Terrance clapped her on the back. "We all feel that way. You'll figure it out."

AT TEN O'CLOCK, Rios arrived at a small tan stucco house in Ironwood's historic Winslow district, after Dispatch called her about another suspected poisoning. Three patrol cars sat parked along the street, all with lights flashing. People from neighboring houses stood in their yards looking for clues into the drama inside. Rios pulled on a pair of latex gloves, gathered her leather-bound notebook, and approached the house.

Deputies Graham and Cruz were talking with a petite Asian woman just outside the carport where a black and chrome Honda Shadow Phantom motorcycle sat next to a faded blue eighties model Toyota Corolla hatchback. Aguilar stood guard just outside the crime scene tape, which stretched between the front porch's wooden supports.

Rios walked up the lantana-lined driveway to steps leading up to the porch, bracing herself against another hostile confrontation.

Aguilar shook his head like a disapproving father. "Still haven't figured out who's dealing this bad dope, eh, Detective? The bodies are piling up. Goodman's gonna have your ass if you don't wrap this thing up soon."

"Shut up, Aguilar, and stick to what you're good at: standing around doing nothing." Rios glared at him. It took all of her willpower not to punch that smirk off his face.

"Maybe if you weren't a rat you'd 'ave gotten more cooperation from your squad."

"Maybe if you weren't such an asshole, you would have made detective by now."

Rios pushed past him and stepped through the open front door to find herself in the house's living room. The midcentury modern furniture surrounding a thirty-six-inch television screen felt straight out of *Leave It to Beaver*. The place wasn't terribly worn, but definitely lived in. A few dozen books, ceramic pots, and other knickknacks filled a floor-to-ceiling bookshelf that separated the living room from the kitchen, where the center of activity seemed to be.

A round maple table with matching chairs and cabinets dominated the kitchen. The back door leading outside was ajar with a shattered windowpane nearest the lock.

Johnson, Winslow, and Tobias, the crime scene photographer, had gathered around a woman's body on the floor. She was wearing an Athena Sisterhood vest over a purple check flannel shirt and lay on her side next to a chair in an all-too-familiar arched posture. Elbows sharply bent, fists held against her chest. Froth and vomit covered her face. No doubt another hex-related death.

A thick paperback book lay open near the center of the kitchen table. Orange juice surrounded a knocked-over cup and had dribbled off the table's edge to form a secondary puddle on the scuffed linoleum.

"Morning, everyone. What do we know?" asked Rios.

"The victim is Piper Anderson," said Johnson consulting her notes. "Ms. Mikiko Sakamoto, the victim's neighbor, called 911 after she broke through the back door and found the deceased unresponsive."

"According to the patches on the front of her vest," chimed in Winslow, "she went by the nickname Pipes and was the Athena Sisterhood's road captain, whatever that is."

Rios carefully lifted the front of the book by the edge and leaned over to glance at the cover. "Looks like the Narcotics Anonymous big book."

Johnson crinkled her nose. "Kinda strange."

"What do you mean?" Rios looked up at her.

"Hex is a party drug, not something you'd take alone sitting at the kitchen table."

"You're thinking she was intentionally poisoned?"

"I have no idea. You're lead detective on this, so I defer to you."

"Definitely something to consider." Rios bent down to examine the body. The eerie grin caused by the strychnine threatened to unsettle her stomach. She shifted her focus to the clothing, reaching into pockets, half expecting to find a bag of hex or other drugs. But the only things that turned up were a canvas wallet, a black pocketknife, and a set of keys. The wallet had a driver's license, a debit card, thirty dollars in cash, and discount cards to Safeway, Walgreens, and Target.

Rios stood back up, considering Johnson's observation about the book and hex being an odd combination. *Why would someone use hex to kill someone? Unless they wanted to cover it up as another overdose. If that was the case, were the other cases also intentional?*

"I'm going outside and talk to the neighbor. Winslow, work the scene around the house, particularly the carport, driveway, and the entryways. Look for anything indicating recent visitors. Johnson, work the scene in here. Let's get fingerprints and DNA from all doorknobs, kitchen surfaces, any cups or silverware in the sink or dishwasher. Get a sample of the liquid from the drinking glass and bag anything that might explain how she died. Tobias, I want photos of the deceased, the book, the door, and anything else Johnson or Winslow find."

Rios walked out the back door, ducking under the crime scene tape and around the house where she found the neighbor still standing with Graham and Cruz. "Gentleman, can you give Detective Winslow a hand canvassing the yard for evidence? I think he's around back."

"Sure thing," said Graham as the two of them hustled toward the backyard.

"Mrs. Sakamoto?"

The woman looked up with a sad smile. "Yes?" she asked. Her silver hair was tied in a bun. Her pale skin had the texture of wrinkled tissue paper.

"Ma'am, I'm Detective Rios. Could you tell me what happened this morning?"

Mrs. Sakamoto nodded. "As I was telling the deputies here, I called Piper to see if she was ready to go for coffee. We often grab a cup over at LezBeans Coffee and Books. Have you ever been there?"

Rios face grew warm as she noticed Graham and Cruz looking at her for an answer. She didn't like discussing her sexuality at work and this was getting uncomfortably close to admitting she was a lesbian. "I've heard of it."

"LezBeans is a such a lovely café, so much nicer than Starbucks. Piper and I kind of have a standing coffee date there."

Rios arched an eyebrow. "You two were dating?"

"Oh heavens no. I'm happily married to my husband, Joe. Piper and I have sort of a mother-daughter bond. We like to get together and 'shoot the shit,' as she likes to say."

"When did you call her?"

"Eight o'clock. When she didn't answer, I walked over because I could see her motorcycle and car were still in the driveway. I went around to the back door and that's when I saw her . . . lying on the floor. I . . . I . . ." Her voice choked with emotion, she bowed her head, covered her mouth, and took a deep breath. "I could tell something was wrong, so I broke in hoping I could save her. They taught a first-aid course at our church a month ago. I was best in my class, if you can believe it."

Rios offered a sympathetic smile. "So, you broke in . . ."

"Oh . . ." Ms. Sakamoto shook her head. "She didn't

have a pulse and her skin was cool. I knew she was gone. So, I called the police."

"Did Piper ever take drugs?"

"Well, I think she did take something regularly, what was it? One of those medicines that sounds like a creature from a Gojira movie. Lipitor maybe? It was for cholesterol, I think."

"I'm more interested in whether she was taking any illegal drugs. Heroin, marijuana, ecstasy?"

"No, well, not recently. She was addicted to meth before I met her. But she's been clean for—what?—five years I think it was on her last sobriety birthday."

"Could she have relapsed?"

"I suppose it's possible. But if she had, I never saw it."

"Did she go out to the clubs much?"

"No, not really. I'm a part of a local canasta club myself. Every Wednesday. They say it's good for the mind, especially at my age."

"I meant does she ever go to bars?"

"Only one that I know of: Gertie's. She said that's where her motorcycle gang met."

"How often did she go there?"

"Oh, I really don't know, maybe once a week. They're not like those bikers you see on TV or hear about on the news getting into trouble. They put on rallies to support women's causes."

"When you get together for coffee, what do you discuss?"

"Oh, everything. Movies, politics, art, just whatever."

"Have you seen anyone hanging around lately?"

"No, not really. There's one gal who comes around every so often. Real tall, like one of them women basketball players. I think she was Piper's NA sponsor."

"Did she ever have any of her fellow members of the

Athena Sisterhood stop by? Did you hear any motorcycles recently?"

"No, not recently. And believe me, when they're in the neighborhood, you hear them. Those bikes are so loud they shake my windows. But I haven't heard them in the past few weeks."

"Was anyone upset with her that you know of?"

"Why? You think someone killed her?" Ms. Sakamoto put a hand to her chest. "Why would someone hurt such a sweet soul like Piper?"

"We're looking into all possibilities. So, she didn't have a disagreement with anyone?"

"Honestly, no. Everybody in the neighborhood liked her."

Rios finished up her interview notes. "Well, thank you for speaking with me. If you remember anything else you think will help us, please let us know."

"Of course." Ms. Sakamoto wandered slowly into the adjacent yard and disappeared into her house.

Rios returned to the deceased's kitchen. "How's it going, Johnson?"

"Found a piece of paper tucked inside the book with a list of names and phone numbers." Johnson handed Rios the paper sealed inside an evidence bag. Only first names and occasionally a last initial were written in multiple hands.

Rios had seen a similar list before. "Looks like a contact list of people from the victim's twelve-step groups. My sister used to keep one when she went to NA. You find her cellphone?"

"Right here." Johnson handed her an iPhone in a pink protective case. "I haven't bagged it yet."

Rios pressed the power button and was grateful to see

that it wasn't locked. "Looks like her last phone call was 11:07 last night to an Elizabeth S."

"We have an Elizabeth S. at the top of the phone list," said Johnson. "Maybe that's her sponsor."

"Let's find out." Rios hit the callback button, then the speaker button.

"Pipes? Is that you?" asked an alto voice with a thick New York accent.

"This is Detective Rios with the Cortes County Sheriff's Office. Is this Elizabeth?"

"Uh . . . yeah. How'd you get this number?"

"It'd be best if I explain in person. Why don't you meet me at the sheriff's substation in Ironwood? I can fill you in. Say around three o'clock this afternoon."

"Where's Pipes? And what're you doing with her phone?"

"I can answer all your questions at the station. Can I expect you at three?"

There was a long pause. "I can't come out there. I'm at work."

"I understand. It's just that Pipes could really use your help right now. She's your friend, right?"

"Yeah, she's my friend. But I can't just walk outta work, ya know?"

"Or if you prefer, I can send a patrol car to pick you up. I'd be happy to explain it to your boss. Where do you work?"

"Naw, no need to send a patrol car. I'll be there at three."

14

———

Wʜᴇɴ Rɪᴏs ʀᴇᴛᴜʀɴᴇᴅ to her desk around two in the afternoon, she had a message from the medical examiner's office stating Piper Anderson had died between six and eight o'clock that morning.

She began running reverse lookups on the phone numbers from the victim's NA contact sheet. A few people on the list had criminal records, usually for possession, DUI, and one with an aggravated assault charge: Elizabeth Schwartz. The case was a few years old and the charges had eventually been dropped.

Her phone interrupted her train of thought. "Rios here."

"Detective, an Elizabeth Schwartz is here to see you."

"Thanks, Sergeant. I'll be right down." She hung up, grabbed a legal pad and the folders for the related cases, and hustled down to the station lobby.

Rios immediately recognized Elizabeth Schwartz from her mugshot. She stood six nine with an athletic build, angular cheekbones, and coffee-brown hair tied in a pony-tail. Although her physique made her look like she could play for the Phoenix Mercury, her blue Oxford shirt and navy slacks suggested an office job.

"Elizabeth Schwartz?"

"Yeah." The woman crossed the room in a couple of strides and towered over Rios.

"I'm Detective Rios." She shook the tall woman's hand. "Let's take a seat in one of our interview rooms.

Rios led her down the hall to interview three, a small room with a metal table and four chairs. A stainless-steel ring was secured to the center of the table and another to the floor. A video camera hung from the corner ceiling.

"I appreciate your coming down here." said Rios. "Would you care for some water?"

"Nah, I just wanna get this over with." Even with Schwartz sitting in the chair, her knees bumped the table. "How'd you get Pipes' phone?"

"When was the last time you saw Pipes?"

"Last night around midnight. She was upset about something and asked me to come over."

"Why was she upset?"

Schwartz shifted in her seat and glanced around the room. "Look, no offense but I can't really talk about that."

"Oh? Why is that?"

"We're in a recovery group together. It's anonymous and confidential."

"Narcotics Anonymous, right?" Rios pulled a photo of the book out of the case file. "We found the book on her kitchen table."

"You were in her house? Did something happen to her?"

"Why was she so upset she needed her sponsor to come so late?"

"I shouldn't be discussing this. I mean, it's anonymous, ya know? That's how the program works."

"I used to go to Nar-Anon and Al-Anon because of my sister. I understand the need for anonymity. But you and me are both trying to help out Pipes, right?"

"Is she in trouble?"

"Yes, I'm afraid she is. That's why I need you to tell me why she was upset." Rios watched a series of emotions play across the woman's face. Getting a recovering addict to break confidentiality wasn't going to win Rios any friends, but it might lead her to a suspect.

"Well, it's just life, you know? She broke up with her girlfriend awhile back. Her bike needed work. Just regular shit. She was worried she might start using again. So, she called me."

"What time did you leave?"

"I don't know. About one, I guess."

"How was she when you left?"

"Better. Still a little stressed, but okay. Why? What happened to her?"

"Well, I'm afraid I've got some bad news."

"She's dead, isn't she?" Schwartz sat there grim faced.

"I'm afraid so." Rios looked for any sign of surprise, but didn't see one. Maybe she figured it out after being called into the station. Or maybe she knew all along. The woman was hard to read. "Did Pipes ever use hex?"

"Not that I heard."

"She ever go to nightclubs or bars?"

"Definitely not. Hanging around bars is a great way to slip and start using again."

"You think that's what happened?"

"If she took hex, something happened."

"Where would she have bought the hex?"

"I got no idea. I never used it."

"You ever hear people discussing it in the meetings?"

"Yeah, but they never say where they got it."

Rios sighed. This was turning into another dead end. "Okay, anything else you can think of that might help us find out who sold Pipes the hex?"

Schwartz shook her head. "That's all I know."

"Well, Ms. Schwartz, I appreciate you coming in today. And I'm real sorry for your loss."

Rios escorted the woman back to the lobby. She was going to have to start calling names on Piper Anderson's contact list. Hopefully someone might know who was dealing hex.

Shea was welding the shortened frame for the Stansbury bike when Terrance called over the PA system, "Shea, please report to the office."

She pulled off her welding mask and dropped the welder. "Now what?"

Shea walked into the office to find Detectives Rios and Johnson sitting in front of her desk. "Shit."

Terrance glanced first at the detectives, then at Shea. "I'll give you ladies some privacy." He patted Shea on the shoulder as he passed through the door. "Keep your cool, girl."

"Morning, Ms. Stevens," said Johnson.

"What the hell do y'all want?" Shea glowered at the detectives as she settled behind her desk. "I got work to do."

"What have you learned from the Athena Sisterhood?" asked Rios.

"That drug use is strictly forbidden among the club. Biker Express charges more than we do for oil changes. Oh, and one of the patched members is allergic to strawberries."

"That's it?" Rios took a seat and leaned over the desk. "You think this is some kind of joke? People are dying."

"Gimme a fucking break, will ya? I'm doing the best I can." Shea pulled a glass and a bottle of Bushmills from the bottom drawer, and downed a shot. The ibuprofen she'd taken earlier wasn't doing anything for her headache or her jaw. "Last night me and my girlfriend were s'posed to celebrating our six-month anniversary . . ."

"Miss Stevens, you need to listen—" said Johnson.

Shea ignored her and poured herself another shot. "But instead of a romantic evening with my girlfriend, I was out drinking at a bar with my ex and her buddies in the Athena Sisterhood." She tossed the whiskey down her throat, savoring the burn.

Rios looked indignant. "Shea—"

"But you know what the best part was? The fucking Confederate Thunder showed up and damn near broke my jaw." A warm sensation spread from Shea's belly to the rest of her body.

"I'm sorry to hear that, but—" pressed Rios.

"You're ruining my life, Detectives. You know that?"

Rios leaned toward her and met her gaze. "Shea, listen to me. A member of the Sisterhood is dead."

Shea narrowed her gaze. "What? Who?"

"Piper Anderson. I believe she went by the nickname Pipes."

"Pipes?" The whiskey turned sour in her stomach. "I was just talking to her last night. How can she be dead?"

"Strychnine-laced hex. That makes four deaths in two weeks. If you don't find out who's behind this, there'll be more."

Shea's head throbbed worse than before. "I'm spending time with the Sisterhood like you asked."

Rios pulled out a notebook. "Why don't we begin with the members you've met."

Shea grew increasingly uncomfortable. This was it. She was becoming a snitch. "All I know are road names."

"It's a starting point. Maybe a brief description of each."

Shea looked from Rios to Johnson and back again. She was cornered. Then again, maybe giving them a list of road names would be enough to get them off her back. "Let's see, there's Labrys."

"That's your ex-girlfriend Deborah Raymond, right?" asked Johnson.

"Yeah. I talked with a woman named Savage—kinda butch, has short spiky hair. Said she was an EMT. Also a tall, attractive African American woman who goes by Indigo. Ugh, who else? Orphan—a few inches shorter than me, dark hair. And Pipes, but then . . ." Shea's voice trailed off.

"Any of them seem like they would be selling drugs?" asked Johnson.

Shea scoffed. "These women? Doubt it."

Rios continued writing notes. "What else can you tell us?"

"That's it. I'm a hangaround. They ain't gonna tell me shit about any club business. I told you that."

Rios nodded. "I think you're right."

"Thank you! Finally, you're starting to listen."

"That's why we want you to become a prospect, Miss Stevens," said Johnson.

"Look, lady, do you have any idea what being a prospect involves?"

Johnson sat a little taller in the chair. "It's Detective, actually."

Shea rolled her eyes. "Fine. Let me explain something to you. Prospects are at every patched member's beck and call, twenty-four-seven. I'm already in the doghouse with my girlfriend because of this. I don't have time to be a prospect. You wanna throw me in jail? Then do what you gotta do, *De-tec-tive*."

Rios shook her head and folded her arms. "I'm disappointed in you, Shea. Pipes is dead and you don't give a rat's ass about anyone but yourself. How many women have to die before you care?"

"That's bullshit and you know it. I care a lot. But the gals in the Athena Sisterhood ain't outlaw bikers. More like feminists college-types who drink lattes and eat kale. They sure as shit ain't drug dealers."

"We have a witness that says otherwise," said Johnson.

"Then your witness is fulla shit. I know the Thunder's dealing hex 'cause I was with them when they stole it from the Jaguars. Probably why they showed up at Gertie's last night. They're worried another motorcycle club might interfere with their drug business." Shea rubbed her jaw. "But the Sisterhood has a strict no-drugs policy. All they care about is women's rights."

Rios looked closer at Shea. "Is that how you got that bruise on your face?"

"Yeah, their VP, Mackey, got in a lucky punch."

Rios met Shea's eyes, "Regardless, our evidence points to the Athena Sisterhood as the source of these recent hex deals. So, you need to do your part and become a prospect and let us know who all is involved."

"I don't have time for this. My niece is having PTSD problems. My girlfriend hates me. And we're extremely busy at the shop. Snitching on the Sisterhood'll have to wait."

"So, you're refusing to honor your CI agreement?" Rios stood and pulled out a pair of handcuffs.

She's bluffing, Shea thought. She stood with her arms crossed. "I guess I am."

In a flash, Rios slammed Shea against the wall, snapping the cuffs on her wrist. "Shea Stevens, you are under arrest."

"This is bullshit." Shea struggled to back away but she was literally cornered.

Rios and Johnson each grabbed an arm and pulled her out of the office and through the showroom in front of a handful of gawking customers. Johnson droned through a Miranda warning, but Shea didn't pay attention. *Just a fucking scare tactic,* she told herself.

When they stepped through the front door, Rios pulled out her phone. "Dispatch, this is Detective Rios. I need a patrol car to Iron Goddess Custom—"

"Wait!" Shea's shoulder throbbed as visions of Annie living with Monster played in her head.

"Hold on, Dispatch." Rios turned to Shea. "You got something to say?"

"I'll do it."

"Do what?" Rios leaned into Shea's face. "I want to hear you say it."

Shea took a deep breath and let it out. "I'll be your snitch. I'll ask about becoming a prospect."

"Cancel that, Dispatch." Rios hung up and removed the handcuffs.

"But there's no guarantee they'll approve me."

"You're a smart woman, Shea. I'm sure you can convince them."

Shea rolled her sore shoulder and winced. Jessica was going to have a shit fit.

15

———

THE POUNDING beats of the Pink Trinkets' latest album, *Singing Mammogram,* blared from speakers set up on the Iron Goddess back lot. Around the perimeter, vendors were selling riding gear, embroidered patches, and motorcycle insurance.

Rows of Iron Goddess motorcycles gleamed under the overhead lights. Dozens more bikes belonging to attendees filled the rest of the lot and choked the surrounding side streets.

Shea nursed a bottle of Sam Adams from the comfort of a lounge chair, watching the growing mass of people circulate through the assortment of chrome and steel. Jessica sat beside her sipping a bottle of water, while Annie sat on the ground playing a handheld video game.

Terrance breezed by carrying a case of bottled water.

"Not a bad turnout, eh, T?" asked Shea.

Terrance set down the case of water and surveyed the crowd. "Yeah, I was afraid it'd be too cold. Maybe we'll sell some bikes tonight."

Jessica pointed to a cluster of women wearing Athena

Sisterhood cuts. "Don't you have a rule against people wearing club colors?"

"Since they're not an outlaw club," said Shea, "I decided to make an exception."

Terrance frowned. "You make an exception for them, others will want one, too. Next thing you know someone's been stabbed or shot in the showroom. We don't need that kind of publicity."

"Ah, you worry too much, Terrance. Most Thundermen wouldn't be caught dead shopping at Iron Goddess. The only other MC bikers we get in the shop belong to law enforcement clubs. It's a nonissue."

"You say that now." Terrance hefted the case of water again. "Why don't you make yourself useful and mingle with the crowd, sell some bikes."

"Hey, I set up the tents. You mingle with the crowd. I'd rather sit here and people watch."

He left, shaking his head. "Suit yourself."

A member of the Sisterhood with short dark hair approached holding hands with a guy sporting a bushy beard, deep-set eyes, and unruly hair. "Hey," said Shea. "It's Orphan, right?"

"Hey, Havoc. Good to see you. This is my boyfriend, Richard."

Jessica looked at Shea with a quizzical look. "Havoc?"

"My road name." Shea muttered.

Jessica chuckled. "Oddly appropriate."

Shea shook Orphan's hand and then Richard's. "Glad, y'all could make it. This is my girlfriend, Jessica."

"Nice to meet the two of you." Jessica said.

Orphan kneeled down near Annie. "And who is this cutie?"

Annie made a face when Shea ruffled her niece's hair. "This is Annie."

"Aunt Jessica, I'm hungry," Annie got to her feet and brushed dirt off the back of her pants.

Jess gave Shea a knowing look that seemed to say, *You need to take care of your niece.* She was right, Shea knew. And yet she also needed to get closer to the members of the Sisterhood. "Jess, you mind?"

"I got it," said Jessica with a passive-aggressive tinge to her voice. She stood and took Annie's hand. "Come on, kiddo. Let's you and me grab a bite while Shea talks with her biker friends." The two of them disappeared into the crowd.

"Is that your daughter?" asked Orphan.

"My niece. She came to live with Jess and me after my sister died."

"It's tough losing family. I lost mine when I was eleven."

"You may have lost your folks, Orphan," said Savage walking up, arm-in-arm, with Indigo. "But now you have the Athena Sisterhood."

Orphan's face brightened. "Hey, sisters!" she said as she gave each of the women a hug.

Shea felt a twinge of jealousy at the women's sisterly affection for one another. She missed being a part of the extended family of a motorcycle club.

"You got some kickass bikes, Havoc," said Savage, gesturing to some of the Iron Goddess motorcycles on display.

"Thanks." Shea keyed into Indigo's somber mood. "You okay, Indigo?"

Indigo shook her head and wiped a tear from her face. "You hear what happened to Pipes?"

Shea sighed and raked her hand through her hair. "Yeah. It's terrible."

"What happened?" asked Orphan, a worried expression playing across her face.

Savage looked away. "Dead from a drug overdose. After five years of being clean, no less."

"Police picked me up this afternoon and questioned me for more than an hour." Indigo's eyes glistened with anger and hurt. "Treated me like I'm some kind of criminal. How'd they even get my number?"

"Beats me." Shea stared out at the crowd, feeling like the worst person to walk the earth. "They questioned me, too."

"You?" Indigo gave Shea a quizzical look. "You only met Pipes the other night."

"That's what I told them."

Orphan's lower lip trembled. "You sure it was Pipes? I mean, maybe the cops got the ID wrong. It happens sometimes, ya know?"

"Naw, it was her," said Indigo. "The cops showed me a photo."

Bile burned Shea's throat as she recalled the horrific picture. She took another pull on her beer, but it was empty. When she grabbed another out of a nearby cooler, she caught Savage's eyeing her and let it sink back into the icy water. "Cops said Pipes overdosed on hex cut with rat poison. Any idea where she got it?"

Savage gazed out at the crowd. "Not from any of us."

"Really? 'Cause the cops thought someone in the club was dealing." Shea realized too late that she was pressing too hard.

Savage narrowed her gaze at Shea. "And why would they think that?"

Shit. Don't blow your cover, girl. "Hell if I know."

"I wanna go home," Orphan pulled herself closer into her boyfriend's embrace.

"Don't go, Orphan," said Shea. "The night is young."

Indigo kissed Orphan on the top of her head. "And you got us here for support."

"Thanks, but I just don't feel like being around people right now. C'mon, babe."

Savage patted her on the back. "Get home safe, Orphan. Take care of her, Richard."

"I will. Y'all have a good night," said Richard as the two of them wandered off.

Shea raised an eyebrow. "What's with the sudden vanishing act?" Could Orphan be the one dealing hex? She didn't seem the type, but Shea knew some people were good about hiding their dark side. Her father for one.

"Pipes sponsored Orphan as a prospect in the club. They've known each other for a while. Orphan really looked up to her as a big sister." Indigo let out a long breath. "First her parents, then her roommate, and now Pipes. It's a lot for anyone to deal with."

"You don't think Pipes got the hex from Orphan?"

"Why are you so hung up on this idea that one of us is dealing?" Savage put her hands on her hips and glowered at Shea. "You a narc or something?"

"No, of course not." Shea looked from Savage to Indigo. *Why did Rios push me into this situation? I'm no snitch.* "My old man ran the Confederate Thunder when I was growing up. They were into a lotta bad shit. Drugs, guns, dogfighting. I didn't want to hang around another club like them."

"The Athena Sisterhood is nothing like that bunch of misogynistic assholes you used to call a family, Havoc." Labrys appeared next to Shea and put an arm around her waist. "We don't deal drugs or any of that nonsense. We have one mission—to fight the patriarchy and make this world safer for women."

Shea felt a wave of heat through her body. The familiar

scent of Labrys' perfume aroused her, but brought with it the anxiety of their contentious past. "Glad to hear it."

"If you were one of us, you'd know this." Labrys planted a kiss on Shea's cheek that would have landed on her lips if Shea hadn't turned her head at the last second. "I really missed you, you know?"

"What the hell's going on here?"

Shea pushed away from Labrys' grasp as Jessica marched toward them with Annie in tow. "Nothing, sweetie! We were just discussing motorcycles."

"Oh, is that what we were discussing?" An evil grin played across Labrys' face. "I thought we were discussing you and I spending more time together."

"What?"

"She's kidding, honey." She reached for Jessica's hand. "But I am considering becoming a prospect."

"A prospect?" Jessica stepped away from Shea. "Since when?"

"Jess, this isn't just about me."

"Damn right, it's not just about you. This affects me and Annie."

"Lighten up, Jess," said Labrys. "The Athena Sisterhood looks after its own."

"You need to mind your own business, lady." Jessica got into Labrys' face. "Shea and Annie are *my* family. Not yours."

"Really? I don't see a ring on your finger."

Shea's feelings of discomfort turned to anger. "Back off, Labrys."

"Aw crap," said Indigo, looking out across the parking lot. "They're here."

"Who?" Shea scanned the crowd and spotted several Thundermen on the far edge of the parking lot. "Motherfucker! I'll deal with this."

16

SHEA PUSHED her way through the crush of bodies and spotted Mackey straddling and punching Dragon, a member of the Sisterhood, in an attempt to steal her cut.

"Leave her the fuck alone, Mackey!" Shea rushed toward them, but One-Shot blocked her path.

"We warned you 'bout them outlaw patches," he grumbled. "Now we're taking your cuts."

"Like hell you are." She tried to shove him out of the way. He grabbed her hoodie with one hand and drove his sledgehammer fist into her face with the other.

Shea stumbled as everything went hazy and gray. A kick to her stomach knocked the wind out of her. She spit out blood and bile as she forced her mind to focus. *Can't let these fuckers win.*

As she struggled to her feet, One-Shot grabbed her by the back of her collar. She elbowed him in the solar plexus. He fell, grabbing his chest and gasping for air. She drove the heel of her palm into his chin, whipping his head back and sending him spiraling to the ground.

Shea found Dragon laying on the ground, alone and missing her cut. She wiped blood from her face.

"You okay?" asked Shea.

When she nodded, Shea turned back to Mackey, who was now using Labrys' face for a punching bag while holding her up by her hair. Shea kicked his legs out from under him, knocking him on his ass and away from Labrys.

Shea pulled Labrys to her feet, blood dripping from her nose. "You all right?"

"Look out!" Labrys pointed.

Shea turned in time to see Mackey charging her like a bull. Shea hit the pavement hard, but managed to roll before he could pin her. She scooped up a helmet from a nearby motorcycle and brought down on his head. He crumpled facedown on the blacktop.

A muscular arm locked around Shea's neck and lifted her off the ground, jolting her so hard she dropped the helmet. She tried desperately to scratch her attacker's face, but couldn't make contact. She kicked at his kneecaps with the heel of her boot, but the beefy arm only tightened around her neck, cutting off air and her blood supply.

Using her attacker's arm for leverage, Shea swung her knees over her head, nailing him in the head. They tumbled backward. Shea landed on One-Shot's chest. He wasn't moving, his eyes closed. She didn't know whether he was dead or merely unconscious. She didn't care.

"Get off me!" said Indigo as Monster was pulling at her cut.

Shea looked for the helmet she dropped but it had rolled out of sight. She ran up behind Monster and kicked the inside of his knee. His leg buckled, forcing him to release his grip on Indigo's cut. A haymaker to his temple drove him to the ground. Shea planted a knee on his chest and grabbed him by the collar.

"This is why I refuse to let you see Annie."

"You know the rules, Shea-Shea." He looked up at her, eyes struggling to focus. "No new clubs without the Thunder's permission."

"Your rule. Not mine. Not the Sisterhood's."

Multiple police sirens pierced the noise of the melee. Thundermen scrambled for their bikes. The air shook with the roar of multiple Harleys starting at once and disappearing into the night.

Shea's grip on Monster's shirt tightened. "Stay away from my family, my shop, and the Athena Sisterhood. Or I will burn your club down like Sherman torching Atlanta. You got me?"

"I know you killed Hunter." Monster's face twisted into a smirk. "I kept it to myself. Till now. Whaddya think the boys will do when they learn you murdered their president."

Shea's heart pounded. "What makes you think I did it?"

"Security camera on the back of the Jaguars' warehouse. Recorded the whole damn thing. I grabbed the computer with the recordings before we left that day."

"Then you know I only shot Hunter in self-defense."

"You think Mackey and One-Shot will see it that way? What will Annie think?"

"You best destroy that video if you ever hope to see Annie again, asshole. Wendy shared a lot of the club's dirty laundry with me before she died. I could send every member of the Thunder to prison for years." It was a bluff, but she didn't have any other cards to play.

"You a snitch now, Shea-Shea? Working for Buzzkill?"

Shea winced at the accusation. Monster blindsided her with a right cross and scrambled to his feet.

"This is Thunder territory. We will not be disrespected.

We'll plant the Barbie Sisterhood in the ground if we have to." He brushed himself off and vanished into the crowd of attendees fleeing the party.

"Keep on yapping, old man," Shea muttered to herself as she dabbed the blood from her split lip. "We'll see who gets buried."

Shea found several members of the Sisterhood gathered under an abandoned vendor tent, nursing wounds and commiserating. "Y'all all right?" she asked.

Labrys looked up at her ruefully, holding an ice pack to the side of her face. "They got Dragon's cut. Raven's and Fuego's, too."

"I'm real sorry that happened."

Terrance offered Shea a damp shop towel. "Here. Clean yourself up."

"Thanks."

"I told you letting the Athenas wear their cuts was a bad idea."

"T, now is not the fucking time for *I told you sos.*"

"Everybody freeze!" Deputy Aguilar and several of Sheriff Buzzkill's goons had their weapons drawn and were waving back and forth at the Athena Sisterhood.

"Well, if it isn't Deputy Commando. Put away your dick, Aguilar," said Shea. "You missed the party again."

"We got a call that a biker club was causing a disturbance," said Aguilar, refusing to lower his weapon as his fellow deputies reholstered theirs. "I'm guessing by the looks of things it was the Athena Sisterhood."

"It was the Confederate Thunder, you idiot. Not the Sisterhood."

Jessica ran up to Shea, a worried expression on her face. "I can't find Annie."

Shea's heart thudded. "I thought she was with you."

"She slipped out of my hand," said Jess, shaking her head. "I lost track of her in the chaos."

"What a minute. Who are you? And who's Annie?" Aguilar slipped his service weapon back into his holster.

"Annie's my niece." Shea stepped away from Aguilar.

"Hold on a minute, Stevens. I still have some questions for you."

"Fuck you. I got an eight-year-old to find. You wanna stop me, you're gonna have to shoot me." Shea searched through the parking, looking around the remaining motorcycles and anywhere else she might hide. "Annie! Where are you?"

Shea's heart pounded in her chest, echoing in her ears. *Did Monster grab her on his way out?* "Annie!"

Others joined in the search, filling the air with the girl's name. Shea reached the edge of the parking lot where the pavement ended at the base of a steep hill covered with brittlebush, cholla, and prickly pear. In the sandy ground, she found a series of small shoeprints.

"Annie? You up there?" The echo of her own voice was the only response.

The dark was too deep and the hill too treacherous to try without a light source. She tried to use her phone as a flashlight, but it wasn't bright enough. "Annie, if you're up there, say something."

There was no reply.

Shea raced back across the parking lot, calling for Annie the whole way. "Any sign of her?" she asked Jessica as she passed her.

Jessica shook her head, tears in her eyes. "No."

"I'm gonna grab a flashlight from the workshop. I think she ran up the hill." Shea opened the back door and stopped short. "Annie?"

Annie sat on a creeper stool next to Switch, who was repairing a motorcycle on one of the lifts. "Hi, Aunt Shea. What was all the noise outside?"

Shea swallowed the urge to yell, not wanting to trigger Switch's freak-out mode. Shea took a deep breath and let it out. "We been looking for you, Doodlebug. 'Fraid something mighta happened to ya."

"I'm just in here, talking to Switch."

"Hey, Switch. Whatcha working on so late?"

Switch looked up with her usual emotionless face. "Turn signal's not working."

"Oh." Shea nodded. "How long you planning on staying?"

"I'll lock up when I'm done," said Switch, her attention almost entirely on her work.

Deputy Aguilar burst through the back door, followed by Jessica.

"Oh, thank God," said Jessica.

"She was here the whole time." Shea put an arm around Annie.

"Annie, you scared the hell out of us!" Jessica's voice reverberated off the walls.

"Shhhh." Shea put a finger to her lips.

"Don't shush me! This is important!"

Switch turned, a hint of panic in her expression.

Shea held her hand up to Jessica and looked at Switch. "It's okay, Switch. Jessica was just worried about Annie. No one's in trouble."

Switch's eyes moved from Shea to Annie. "Annie is a good girl. She helps me." The wire cutters in her hand trembled.

Annie reached out and took Switch's free hand. "Switch is good, too." Annie smiled.

The wire cutters stopped shaking. Switch's eyes relaxed, her expression softening. "Annie is a good friend."

"Sorry," said Jessica. "Forgot about Switch's . . . issues." There was still tension in her voice, which Shea knew she would have to deal with once they were out of earshot of Switch.

Shea nodded. "Tell you what, Annie. You hang out and help Switch while the rest of us clean up outside. Okay?"

Annie nodded.

"And don't go nowhere else. Promise?"

"I promise."

Aguilar stepped up to Shea, a notebook and pen in hand. "Now that you found your kid, I need to know what the hell happened."

Shea gestured toward the door. "Let's take this outside."

The three of them walked back out to the parking lot. Terrance was giving an ice pack to Labrys, who winced as she put it to her face. The other deputies were interviewing the few remaining Athenas.

The instant the door closed, Aguilar stepped in front of Shea, a scowl on his face. "So, what happened here tonight, Stevens?"

"Iron Goddess was hosting a bike night for women when the Confederate Thunder showed up and started attacking my guests."

"Why would they do that?"

"Because they're assholes."

Aguilar glanced over at Labrys and a few other Athenas, then turned back to Shea. "So, this isn't a gang war between the Athena Sisterhood and the Thunder?"

Shea balled her fists. "If it is, we didn't start it."

"We? So, you're a part of the Athena Sisterhood, too?"

Shea caught a terse look from Jessica. "I'm just a woman who likes to ride, same as the Athenas."

Aguilar scoffed. "You know, word on the street is that the Sisterhood is trafficking hex."

"That's bullshit!" Labrys appeared next to her, holding the ice pack to her face. "Just rumors spread by the patriarchy to shut us down. We don't allow drug use in our club."

"And you are?"

"Labrys, president of the Athena Sisterhood. You cops should be out chasing down the Thunder instead of harassing us. They're the ones that attacked us."

"You want to make a statement? Fine, let's start with your legal name. None of this biker nickname nonsense."

"You want my statement? Here it is. We were here having a good time. The Thundermen showed up, attacked me and several other Athenas, and only left when they heard your sirens. End of statement. No one else has anything else to say." Labrys gave a stern look to Shea and to the other Athenas who had gathered around. "Now go arrest those sexist fuckers."

Labrys walked away, followed by the rest of the sisters.

"Now, hold on," said Aguilar, following after them. "If I don't get names and contact information, I'm going to haul you girls down to the station."

Dragon turned and pulled a card out of her cut. "You want my name? I'm Rebecca Li, attorney-at-law. Here is my contact information. The Athenas are my clients. So unless you plan to arrest any of us, I suggest you contact me in the morning with any further questions. Are we clear?"

Aguilar examined the card and frowned. "We're clear." He put away his notebook and signaled for the other deputies to follow him back to their patrol cars.

"Thanks, Dragon." Shea felt some of the tension release as she let go of a breath she hadn't realized she was holding.

"No problem. But we're going to have to figure out what

to do about the Thunder. This is the second time. And from what I've seen, the sheriff's office doesn't seem as gung ho as they once were to prosecute them."

Shea watched the sheriff's cruisers disappear up the road. "I've noticed that, too."

17

"You wanted me to join a women's group," Shea explained to Jessica after they put Annie to bed. "The Sisterhood *is* a women's group."

Jessica sat beside her on the love seat. "I didn't mean one where you get beaten up all the time by the Confederate Thunder. Especially with Annie around. What's to stop that guy Monster from just taking her?"

"Me!" Shea slapped her chest. "I would stop him."

"You can't be with her all the time. He could grab her from school or when she's with me." Jessica stared at the floor, arms folded across her chest. Fear crept into her voice. "Those guys fucking scare me, Shea. And they have a real hard-on for the Sisterhood."

"I know." Shea put a hand on Jess' back. "They scare me, too."

"I don't want to be watching over my shoulder all the time, afraid some redneck biker is going to come after me to get to you. I can't live that way. I will move out before I let that happen."

"You don't mean that."

"Like hell I don't. It's bad enough being black in this goddamn redneck county. But I will not have the Confederate Thunder breathing down my neck just so you can ride with your friends."

"That's not why I'm doing it and you know it."

"I don't care. I *really* don't. My mama didn't raise no fool. I love you and I love Annie, but I will leave if you put me in that situation. And if you love me, if you *truly* love me like you say you do, you won't force me to make that choice."

Shea let out a hard breath. "I get that. I do. It's just that I feel something when I'm with these women. Something I ain't felt in a while."

"What?"

"A sense of family."

"Shea, *we're* your family." Jess faced her, cradling Shea's face in her long, delicate fingers. "Me and Annie."

Shea felt herself drawn into the warmth of Jess's chestnut eyes. "You are, I know. It's just . . . I don't how to explain it. I ain't good with words."

She closed her eyes, struggling for a way to explain. "Growing up around the Thundermen and their families, it was like its own community. Anytime somebody needed something, it was taken care of, you know? When a Thunderman went to jail or got killed, his old lady and kids never worried about paying bills or having enough to eat. The club provided. Always."

"Shea, are you listening to yourself? They're criminals. Drug dealers. Gunrunners. Racist, sexist, homophobic thugs. How can you miss that?"

"But that's my point, Jess." Shea met her girlfriend's gaze. "The Sisterhood isn't like that. They're a motorcycle club without all the bigotry and violence. They could help baby-sit for us. We could go out, just the two of us, more than once in a blue moon."

"But they're dealing drugs."

"So far, I haven't seen it. Except for Pipes, the girl who OD'd the other day. But she was an addict. I think Rios is wrong. The Sisterhood isn't dealing drugs."

"Why does Rios think they are?"

"She's one of Buzzkill's drones. They get some bogus tip that claims the Sisterhood's dealing and they treat it like gospel. Honestly, my money's on the Thunder. They stole the hex from the Jaguars. Then they recut it with rat poison to increase their profits. They don't care if people die because of it. They're only interested in the Benjamins."

"Which brings us back to my main objection. Every time you get together with them, those damn Thundermen show up. Have you looked in the mirror lately? You look like you lost a boxing match to Muhammad Ali."

"Aw, baby, that's just my look," said Shea, hoping to lighten the mood. She tried to smile but it made her face hurt worse.

Jess smirked. "I'm sorry, but black eyes are not a good look for you. I prefer you with a little less color."

Shea sat for a moment, just holding her hand, letting ideas bubble up in her tired mind. "What if . . . what if the Thunder wasn't a problem?"

"What do you mean? They are a problem."

"I know, but what if there were a way I could make them not be a problem anymore. Then would you be okay with me being a prospect for the Athena Sisterhood?"

"You're not planning on gunning them all down, are you?"

"Shea chuckled in spite of the pain. "Tempting, but no."

Jessica took in a deep breath and let it out slowly. "You really think we could go out more often, just the two of us?"

"Yes."

"But you said prospects are at their beck and call twenty-four-seven."

"Orphan told me it isn't that bad with the Sisterhood. Not like what the Thunder puts their guys through."

"Well . . . in that case, I guess I could live with it. But how will you keep the Thunder from being a problem? They're adamant about breaking up the Sisterhood. And Monster seems determined to see Annie."

"I know where the Thunder keeps their stash of drugs and guns that they sell. Or at least where they used to. I just need to verify they still keep it there. Then it's just a matter of calling Rios and having them bust the Thunder."

"Why haven't you given Rios this information before?"

Shea shrugged. "It's kind of a nuclear option. There's a chance, however slim, they might've moved their stash. And even if they haven't, once I turn over the info, they will probably suspect I'm the one that snitched. Unless they stay locked up, there could be consequences. But right now, I don't see any other choice."

"What if they catch you?"

"I'll be careful. Maybe I can get some of the Athenas to help me."

Jessica sat silent for a moment, clearly processing the situation. "If they put the Confederate Thunder behind bars, then I'm on board with you joining the Sisterhood. Otherwise, you either stay away from Athenas or stay away from me. That's all there is to it."

Shea embraced Jessica as a tide of gratitude and want washed over her. "I'll find a way to make it happen. I promise."

～

THE NEXT MORNING, after a quick stop at Iron Goddess, Shea walked into the Cortes County Sheriff's Office Ironwood substation. Her face was still swollen and deeply bruised, but the pain was subsiding. In the light of day, the potential blowback from using the nuclear option seemed too risky. She hoped that by talking with Rios, she could get Confederate Thunder Motorcycle Club thrown in jail for the previous night's brawl.

The desk sergeant, a woman with a weathered face and a name tag that read DVORAK took one look at Shea and said, "What the hell happened to you?"

"I need to talk to Detective Rios," said Shea, minimizing her jaw movement. Speaking, as it turned out, was still painful.

"Yeah, what about?" Caution tempered the sergeant's tone.

"She'll know."

"Listen, lady, no one gets past me unless I know who you are and why you're here."

Shea struggled to keep her cool. "Fine. I have some information about a case she's working."

"Now we're getting somewhere." Dvorak picked up the phone, her hand hovering over the keypad. "Your name?"

"Shea Stevens."

Dvorak punched in the extension. "Detective, I got a Shane Stevens wants to see you."

"It's Shea. Like the stadium." Frustration made the throbbing in her jaw worse.

Dvorak rolled her eyes. "I gotta a *Shea* Stevens to see you. Says she has some information on one of your cases." She nodded and hung up. "Take a seat. Rios'll be up in a bit."

Shea plopped down on one of the molded plastic chairs and absently watched a handful of people come and go through the lobby. Shea caught a towheaded six-year-old boy staring at her like she was a circus freak. Shea flipped him off. He returned the gesture and turned away.

It occurred to her this was one of the few times she had been here and not been handcuffed. She hoped to keep it that way. Being beaten up, however, was still par for the course.

Twenty minutes later, Rios opened the door leading to the rest of the station. "Shea? What the hell happened to you?"

Shea shuffled up to within a few inches. "We need to talk," she mumbled.

Rios studied her for a moment. "Okay, let's go into one of the interview rooms."

Shea followed her down a brightly lit hallway papered with an assortment of notices, historic photos, and memorials to fallen officers.

Rios paused when they reached the interview rooms. "Crap. They're all three occupied at the moment. You want to talk at my desk?"

"I want the Confederate Thunder arrested. Every last one of 'em. Else I'm done being your snitch."

Rios sighed. "Well, let's see if we can't work this out." Rios led her farther down the hall and through a door marked VIOLENT CRIMES DIVISION. They skirted past several large cubicles and stopped at the last one. Inside were two adjacent desks. One looked like it had been pared down to the essentials—a phone and a computer. The other had a few knick-knacks, a couple of photos tacked to the wall, and a small sky-blue-and-white flag crammed into a stuffed pencil cup.

She sat down at the empty desk, feeling like she was walking on somebody's grave. "This where Edelman sat?"

A shadow of regret passed over Rios' face. She took a

deep breath and let it out slowly before meeting Shea's gaze. "Why don't you tell me what's going on."

"You hear about what happened last night?"

"Why don't you tell me."

Shea gave her a quick rundown of the previous night's events. "I want them all arrested. Not just a few of them, but every fucking one of them. And no bail. Otherwise they're gonna keep coming after the Sisterhood and putting every-one, including my family, in danger."

"Shea, I can't just arrest them even if I wanted to. I have to have proof they committed a crime."

Shea set a thumb drive on the desk. "Here's the security video of the parking lot from last night. I woulda thought Aguilar would've asked about it, but he didn't seem too interested in going after the Thunder."

"Well, let's take a look." Rios inserted the thumb drive into her computer and pulled up the video. "It's really grainy. Between the bad lighting and the camera angle it's hard to make out any faces."

"But you can see the Confederate Thunder is attacking us. That's Mackey," said Shea, pointing to a blurred figure on the screen. "There's One-Shot. And the big guy there is Monster."

"Detectives Morris and Bello are working that case. I can give this to them, but I can't guarantee the DA will press charges, much less be able to have them held without bail."

"Tell me, Rios. How many of you are on the Thunder's payroll?"

"Shea, it's not like that."

"Like hell it ain't. It all makes sense. The Thunder wants the Sisterhood disbanded, so they send you to do it for us, using me as your snitch, no less. And if I get killed in the process, or my niece or my girlfriend, you couldn't care less."

"Shea, I do care about you." Rios put her hand on Shea's. "And your family."

Shea was tempted to pull away, but too many conflicting thoughts and emotions were crowding her tired brain. "If you want me to infiltrate the Sisterhood, I need you to put the Thunder in jail and keep 'em there."

"I'd love to. It's just that we need more than a low-quality video to do it. Especially on assault charges. If you had something more solid on more serious charges . . ."

The nuclear option was looking more and more like her best option. It was dangerous, possibly suicidal. But if it worked, Thunder would be behind bars and Rios would know they were the ones dealing hex.

"You want your something solid? I'll get you something solid." Her legs protested as she stood. "And when I do, I expect you to lock their asses up."

18

WHEN SHE REACHED her bike in the parking lot, Shea pulled out her phone and called Deb.

"Professor Raymond. How can I help you?"

"Hey, Deb. I mean, Labrys. It's Havoc."

"Hey, sweetie! How's your face?"

Shea cringed at the word *sweetie*. "Swollen, but it'll heal. How's everyone else?"

"Okay, from what I've heard. Mostly bumps and bruises. You showed some real grit out there, girl. You sure I can't talk you into becoming a prospect?"

"Well, that's part of why I'm calling. But first I need a favor."

"Sure, anything for you, baby."

It took all of Shea's willpower not to let herself get distracted by Labrys' game playing. "I think the Confederate Thunder is behind these hex poisonings. Including Pipes."

"Really?"

"They're the ones that stole a ton of hex from the

Jaguars last summer. And I know where they used to stash their drugs and illegal guns. If I'm right, maybe I can get them busted and out of our hair for good."

"That would be awesome, Havoc. So what help do you need from me?"

"Well, not you specifically. I was wanting someone from the club to go with me. Watch my back. That kinda thing. Someone with combat or fighting experience."

"I'll come with you. Orphan, too. She's here with me in my office."

"No offense, Labrys, but I was thinking someone more like Savage."

"Hey, just because I'm a college professor doesn't mean I can't fight. I've taken a self-defense class or two in my time. Besides, there's nothing I'd like better than to shut those dumb rednecks down."

Shea thought about it. If everything went as planned, it could solve all of her problems. But if things went sideways, Orphan or Labrys could get hurt or killed. "I don't want to see you get hurt. Orphan either, for that matter."

"Hey! You want to be a prospect? You gotta learn we stand with each other. So, it's either Orphan and me or you can forget joining the Sisterhood."

"What does Orphan have to say?"

"Orphan's a prospect. I'm the president. She does what I tell her. Don't worry, she can hold her own."

Shea sighed. "All right. I gotta pick up a few things from home before I head up to their stash house. You want meet somewhere in Ironwood in about an hour?"

"Sure. How about LezBeans?"

"A good a place as any." Shea sighed. "See you in an hour."

Shea hung up and pulled on her helmet and gloves,

imagining what life would be like as a prospect with Labrys as a sponsor.

On her way to LezBeans, Shea stopped at home to put on her bulletproof vest and slip her .40-caliber Glock in a holster at the small of her back. Shea felt pumped. Once they confirmed the drugs were still in the old stash house, she'd take some photos, send them to Rios, and hopefully be done with this mess forever. That was the plan, at least.

As she climbed back onto Sweet Betsy, her cellphone rang. Shea hoped it was Labrys calling back to say she had changed her mind. A quick glance at the screen revealed it not to be the case. The caller ID read CORTES UNIFIED SCHOOL DISTRICT. "What now?"

She was tempted to ignore it, but feared something might have happened to Annie at school. Something like Monster showing up and taking off with her. Annie would probably be too happy to see him not to go.

She pulled off her helmet and hit the answer button on the third ring. "Yeah, this is Shea."

"Miss Stevens, this is Principal Everett Howell at Pineview Elementary School. We've had a situation involving your niece, Annie."

"Is she okay?"

"She's fine. But we do need you to come pick her up right away."

"Why? What's happened?"

"It's best if we explain in person."

"Yeah, okay." Shea ended the call and immediately dialed Jessica at work.

"Shea? I can't really talk now. I'm at work." Jessica sounded a bit frustrated.

"It's Annie. Something's happened at school."

"She all right?"

"I think so. Her principal says we need to go down and pick her up."

"And by we, you mean me. Yeah, I can't do that. I'm tied up with a client right now. She's your niece. You need to biker up, as you say, and handle the situation yourself."

"Come on, Jess. Just this once. I got something important to do."

"Oh really? And what might that be?"

Shea did not want to tell her about her plans to visit the Thunder's stash house. "Never mind. I'll deal with it."

"I love you, Shea."

"Love you, too," Shea grumbled before ending the call. "Fuck."

Shea called Labrys back. When she answered, Shea said, "Hey, change of plans. I can't do this now."

"Shea, don't even think about doing this without Orphan and me."

"No, it's not that. My niece's school just called. I gotta go pick her up."

"So, pick her up and meet us at LezBeans. Orphan can watch her while you and I take care of business."

Shea stood there speechless for a moment. Leaving Annie with someone Shea had only met a few times while she and Deb rode off to a remote shed in the woods? What would Jessica say? But then, something had to be done about the Thundermen. "Okay, I'll meet you two at LezBeans. Probably be closer to two hours."

"I'm looking forward to it, darling."

"Labrys . . ." These endearments were really getting on Shea's nerves.

"Yes?"

"Never mind."

～

WALKING down the hallway toward the Pineview Elementary main office brought back a flood of memories—the smell of Elmer's glue, the sound of safety scissors cutting brightly colored construction paper, and her father's booming voice arguing with school administrators over the school's prohibition against little girls playing kickball.

She strolled past an exhibition of third-grade artwork, a bulletin board festooned with pumpkin and skeleton cutouts, and a poster announcing the upcoming county fair. Beyond that stood the glass-enclosed principal's office. The door squeaked as she pulled it open.

With her arms wrapped tightly around her skull-and-crossbones book bag, Annie sat slumped on the same wooden bench outside the principal's door that Shea had warmed more times than she could count. As Shea approached, Annie looked up, her mouth a thin line, eyes defiant. Shea offered her a knowing smile.

"May I help you?" asked the receptionist. The nameplate identified her as Esther Cavanaugh. She was a stocky woman wearing oversized, red-rimmed glasses and a white turtleneck underneath a maroon corduroy jumper that looked homemade.

"I'm Shea Stevens, Annie Wittmann's aunt. Y'all called me to come in." Shea unzipped her leather jacket.

"I'll let Principal Howell know you're here." She picked up the phone, delivered the message, and hung it up. "The two of you can go right in."

"Come on, Doodlebug. Let's see what kinda trouble you're in."

Shea opened the heavy wooden door. A man with a gaunt face stared up at her from behind a mahogany desk. "Please come in and have a seat." He gestured to the smallish chairs in front of the desk.

Annie climbed up onto one of the chairs, her feet dangling several inches above the floor. Shea closed the door and took a seat beside her.

Principal Howell adjusted his glasses and narrowed his gaze at Shea. "Ms. Stevens, what happened to your face?"

"I got mugged last night." Close enough to the truth.

"So, there's not an abusive situation at home that I need to be aware of?"

"Thanks for your concern, but no. Now, ya mind telling why I'm here?"

Principal Howell sat up tall with his elbows on the desk, his fingers forming a tent. "Miss Stevens, earlier today during recess, Annie's teacher informed me that your niece struck another student."

"He was calling me names again," said Annie defiantly.

Principal Howell narrowed his gaze. "Young lady, you will speak when you are being spoken to and not before."

Shea felt a twinge of fire at his scolding of her niece. She turned to Annie. "Who called you names?"

"Jeremy Pierce. He called me Little Orphan Annie and said I was white trash."

Shea raised an eyebrow and turned to the man. "Is this the kid she's accused of hitting?"

"It is. Her teacher, Ms. Hargrove, witnessed it."

"Well shit, if someone called me that, I'd deck 'im, too."

"Miss Stevens, we do not tolerate profanity in this school. Neither do we tolerate physical violence."

"Oh, but you tolerate name calling and bullying?"

"Ms. Hargrove made no mention of such statements from the boy Annie assaulted. And even if she had, it does not excuse hitting another student."

"My niece has survived a horrible trauma, a helluva lot worse than anything she could have doled out to some snot-nosed brat who thinks it's okay to bully girls."

"Which is why we're not filing criminal charges against Annie. But we are suspending her for three days."

"You're kicking her out of school for defending herself?"

"She's not expelled, just suspended. For now. I can have Ms. Hargrove email you her assignments so that she doesn't get behind in her studies."

"And the kid who was bullying her? He getting a suspension, too?"

"As I said, I have no corroboration of Annie's claims of verbal harassment."

"So, he gets off scot-free. Well aren't you just the paragon of justice." Shea wasn't entirely sure what a paragon was, but she had heard the expression used one or twice.

"Miss Stevens, we have a zero-tolerance policy toward violence. I suggest if your niece has trauma-related issues and is unable to keep herself from lashing out at others, you look into getting her counseling."

"And I'd suggest you have a talk with that kid and his parents. Because if I hear he's bullying my niece once more, him getting walloped by Annie is gonna be the least of his worries."

"Miss Stevens, are you threatening one of our students?"

"I'm just saying karma can be a real bitch." Shea stood up. "Come on, kiddo. Let's blow this joint."

Annie stuck her tongue out at Howell and followed Shea out, dragging her book bag behind her.

"I saw that, young lady!" Howell bellowed.

When they reached the parking lot, Shea handed Annie a small leather jacket and helmet, taking her book bag and securing it in her motorcycle's saddlebags.

"Are you mad?" Annie asked as Shea fastened the strap on the girl's helmet.

Shea frowned. "No, I'm not mad. A little frustrated, maybe."

"Frustrated with me?"

"Not you, kiddo. Just the situation." With her own helmet in place, Shea threw a leg over the bike then helped Annie onto the passenger seat. "Don't worry. I got sent to the principal's office a bunch of times for punching some smart-mouthed kid."

"So, what I did wasn't bad?"

Shea sighed. "Thing is, I understand why you did it. Unfortunately, doing it can get you in a lot of trouble. When I was a kid, you get caught fighting, they make you clean erasers for a week. But these days, it gets you kicked out or worse. Best thing to do when they start calling you names is walk away."

"But it's not fair. Why should he be allowed to call me names? It hurts my feelings." Annie's voice cracked with sorrow.

"I know, Doodlebug. It ain't fair. But sometimes it ain't about fair. It's about surviving. Understand?"

Annie nodded, the helmet exaggerating the movement like an oversized bobblehead doll.

"Now that we got that settled, I'm gonna need ya to stay with a friend of mine for a bit while I go take care of some business."

"Do I know 'em?"

"You mighta met her at the Bike Night party. Her name is Orphan."

"That's her name?"

"Just a nickname. She's part of the Athena Sisterhood MC."

"She really an orphan like me?"

"Yeah, she is. Lost her folks a few years back."

"Okay."

"All right, now hold on!" She started the motorcycle and revved the engine as loudly as she could, setting off a few car alarms in the process. Annie squeezed her tight and they raced out of the parking lot.

19

———

SHEA HELD the door for Annie as they entered LezBeans. The place was still busy with their midafternoon crowd. Nita waved and stepped out from behind the front counter. "Oh my goddess, Shea, what happened to your face? D'you get in an accident?"

"A fight actually. Some guys caused a bit of trouble at yesterday's bike night event."

"Damn! Well, knowing you, I'm sure you gave as good as you got."

Shea shrugged.

"And who is this little cutie pie?" Nita kneeled down to Annie's height.

"This is my niece, Annie."

"Pleasure to meet you, Annie. How's your day going so far?"

"I got kicked out of school." Annie's lower lip poked out in a pout.

"Uh-oh." Nita looked up at Shea.

"Some kid at school was harassing her and she stood up

for herself. So naturally, they suspended her for three days."

"Ain't it always the way. Blame the victim." Nita smirked. "Well, chin up, Annie. I'm sure you'll be back in school before you know it."

"Listen, Nita, you seen Deb in here?"

"Yeah, she and another member of her motorcycle gang grabbed a table twenty minutes ago. Looked almost as beaten up as you. Must've been one helluva fight."

"It was." Shea ruffled Annie's hair. "Come on, Doodlebug."

Shea found Labrys and Orphan at a table tucked in the far corner of the café. Labrys' face was swollen, but most of the bruising was expertly covered up by makeup.

Labrys jumped up and wrapped Shea in a hug that lasted a moment too long for Shea's comfort. She stepped back and Labrys gave her a wink. "They really beat the hell out of you, too, huh? Thank goodness you don't get by on your looks."

Shea ignored the remark. "Labrys, Orphan, I think you met my niece, Annie, last night."

"Good to see you again, Annie." Orphan reached out and shook Annie's hand.

"Good to see you," echoed Annie shyly.

"I 'preciate you looking after her." said Shea. "With a little luck, maybe Labrys and me can get you-know-who off our backs and in jail for good."

Orphan handed Shea a piece of paper. "Here's my address where you can pick her up afterward."

Shea folded it and put it in her pocket. "Annie, I'll pick you up in an hour or two, okay?"

Annie nodded.

Labrys zipped up her jacket. "Enough chatting. Let's ride."

Shea rode north along the Ironwood bypass with Labrys on her five-o'clock riding a red and ivory Indian Roadmaster. The air was cool as they flew past ranches with names like the Rolling J and the Lazy 8.

The stash house was off Jefferson Highway, a few miles on the other side of the Church, a former church that now served as the Confederate Thunder's clubhouse. Shea didn't like the idea of driving past the Thunder's base of operations, but coming from the south it was unavoidable.

Assuming they weren't spotted, they would drive down the unmarked road where the stash house sat on land belonging to the club. Shea hadn't been there in nearly two decades, but shortly before her death, Wendy had confirmed the club still used it.

It was almost never guarded and rarely visited unless the club needed to drop off or pick up contraband—guns, drugs, and the like. Shea was hoping the large plastic bins filled with hex that the Thunder stole from the Jaguars would be there, possibly recut with rat poison.

As the private drive to the Church came in view, four bikers riding side by side—outlaw style—crested a distant hill. *Oh shit.* Shea ducked down onto her tank, flipped down the tinted visor inside of her helmet, and twisted the throttle, hoping the extra speed would make them less easy to recognize. In her rearview mirror, Shea saw Deb tuck in close behind her.

Thundermen blasted by in a flash, the rumble of the Harleys drowning out the roar of the wind. Shea spotted One-Shot and Monster, but wasn't sure about the other two. Had they recognized her?

Shea's heart pounded in her ears. She watched her side mirrors to see if Thundermen turned around. They didn't.

A honk from Labrys caught Shea's attention. She glanced up to see she was drifting off the road. She straightened out, narrowly avoiding a large rock. Shaken and embarrassed, she revved her engine and raced down the two-lane highway.

Her body was charged with adrenaline. They needed to get to the stash house, take photos of whatever contraband they found, and get the heck out of there before anyone showed up.

A half mile farther, Shea turned down an unmarked dirt road and Labrys followed. The road was riddled with ruts and pockets of loose sand, making the ride treacherous. Periodically, trees and bushes on the side of the road smacked against Shea's legs, no doubt adding to her collection of bruises.

The road ended in a clearing in front of a small wooden cabin. Shea killed her engine and Labrys followed suit. The smell of autumn was in the air. Among the overwhelming green of ponderosa pines and juniper, a few deciduous trees were showing off the last of their fall colors.

"Was that them we passed on the road?"

"Yeah."

"Maybe we shouldn't do this." Labrys' usual confidence was fading.

"If they were going to come after us, they would have done it already. We should be okay," Shea said, trying to convince herself as much as Labrys.

"If you say so."

"Besides," said Shea drawing her Glock. "I brought along some insurance. We'll be fine."

The wood of the cabin was gray and worn. A large rusted padlock secured the door, covered in peeling green paint.

Labrys lifted the padlock and let it whack against the wood. "Now what?"

Shea pulled a narrow leather case from her jacket and opened it. "Not a problem." She fished out two thin pieces of steel, an L-shaped tensioner and a pick with two triangular tabs on the end. "One of the few useful skills Ralph taught me," Shea said tersely referring to her father.

Labrys looked around with a grim expression on her face. "Just hurry. This place gives me the creeps."

"Relax. We'll be in and out in no time." Shea set the short end of the L-shaped tensioner in the padlock's keyhole, her thumb resting lightly on the long end. Then she inserted the pick above it and worked the tumblers. Shea visualized the inside of the lock, feeling as she went which tumblers were set and which ones still needed to be. A few moments later, the cylinder turned and the padlock popped open.

"Damn, girl. Color me impressed."

"It's all in the touch."

"Shit, you can touch me like that anytime."

"You had your chance," Shea said in a humorless tone.

"Maybe I'll have a chance again."

Shea glared at her. "Is that why you want me in the club? So you can seduce me?"

"No, I want you in the club because you're a badass feminist."

"Uh-huh, right." Shea removed the padlock and opened the door to reveal a pitch-black room. She tried the pull string of the bare bulb near the inside entrance. Nothing happened. "Either the bulb's blown or they got no power. Run back to my bike and grab the flashlight outta my tank bag."

"Excuse me? You giving me orders? You're the one who wants to be a prospect."

Shea rolled her eyes. "Forget it. I'll get the goddamn flashlight."

She walked back to her bike and pulled a flashlight out of her tail bag. As she closed the bag, she thought she heard a rumble like thunder in the distance. She froze for a moment and listened. Nothing but the breeze blowing through the trees. "Geez, girl, getting all jumpy."

She hustled back to the cabin, stepped inside, and flicked on the flashlight. The odors of mildew, gasoline, and animal feces hung heavy in the air. "Smells like some rats have been making their home here." To her right, several assault rifles leaned against the wall: AR-15s, AK-47s, Steyr AUGs, and a few others she didn't recognize.

"Damn," said Labrys, mouth agape. "What's with the fucking arsenal?"

"Some they use, others they sell." Beyond the rifles sat a can of gasoline, a case of tequila, and a few boxes of rat poison. At the far end she found boxes of ammunition stacked on top of two large red plastic bins.

"Hot damn, they're still here," said Shea, giving one of the red bins a kick.

"What's in there?"

"The dope they stole from the Mexicans. Probably worth a few mill on the street. Help me with these boxes."

"What's that sound?" asked Labrys.

Shea stood still and heard a rustling in the corner. "Just a rat, most likely. Maybe a skunk."

"No, that rumbling."

Shea listened again and heard it, too. She hoped it was thunder or maybe a passing jet. But as it grew louder, she knew it wasn't. "Shit, we gotta get out of here. Run!"

With no time to relock the door, the two of them rushed back to their bikes. Shea pulled on her helmet without bothering with the chin strap. She turned the key, hit the starter, and Sweet Betsy roared to life. Deb started her bike but bobbled the clutch. The motorcycle jerked and tumbled on its side. Deb frantically struggled to right it.

"Leave it!" shouted Shea. "Get on the back of mine."

"I'm not leaving my bike."

Shea's survival instinct screamed at her to save herself and drive off. But she couldn't bring herself to abandon Labrys to the Thundermen's brutality. She kicked down her side stand and ran to help Labrys lift her bike. At nearly half a ton, there was no way Labrys could lift the heavy touring bike on her own.

"Grab the rear seat. I'll get the handlebars," Shea instructed. "Now lift!"

Shea put all of her strength into her legs and pushed the bike upward. Pain erupted in her shoulder and back. The bike rose a foot off the ground before the seat slipped from Labrys' hand, forcing Shea to lay it back down. Before they could try again, four Confederate Thunder motorcycles roared into the clearing.

20

AFTER MEETING WITH SHEA STEVENS, Rios had uncovered numerous complaints filed against the Confederate Thunder over the past year. But despite the mounting evidence, no charges had been filed against the club. This included the bloody clash last August between the Thunder and the Jaguars street gang that had left several of the Mexican gang members dead. District Attorney Lloyd Russell's office had cited a lack of evidence implicating the motorcycle club. Ever since District Attorney Lloyd Russell was elected the previous November, his office hadn't prosecuted a single case against the club or its members. The question was why.

It was no secret that the D.A. had limited courtroom experience, and had until recently worked as a second-year associate for a personal injury firm. Many believed he got the job because his father was a major contributor to the Cortes County Republican Party. Was the inexperienced Russell afraid of losing in court? Or did his reluctance to prosecute run deeper than that?

And what of Sheriff Keeler? For years, he had promised

to drive the Confederate Thunder out of the county. But now even he seemed less concerned about their criminal enterprises.

It was worrying. But Rios was hesitant to look deeper. She'd already crossed the blue line once. Doing so again could have serious repercussions.

What did concern her about the Confederate Thunder was their growing conflict with the Athena Sisterhood and its potential impact on breaking the strychnine poisoning cases. She couldn't risk losing Shea Stevens as an asset. The body count was rising and she had few clues. More deaths were sure to follow unless Stevens infiltrated the Sisterhood and located the supplier of the deadly hex. She didn't need the Thunder interfering with that.

Rios stopped by the cubicle belonging to Detective Elyssa Morris and her partner, Johnny Bello. Morris was at her desk looking up someone's profile on the system. Bello was elsewhere.

"Elyssa, you and Bello were assigned last night's assault cases at Iron Goddess Custom Cycles, right?"

"There's no case. We got a few statements from the alleged victims claiming the Thunder ambushed them. But no other witnesses placing anyone from the Confederate Thunder at the scene. No security video."

Rios handed her the thumb drive that Stevens had given her. "We got video."

Morris plugged in the thumb drive and played the video. "Hard to make out anything it's so dark."

"Did you interview any of the Thundermen?"

"A few. They claim the Athena Sisterhood attempted to kick them out of a public event because they were men. It's all 'he said, she said.' Why the interest?"

"I have an informant helping me locate the source of the strychnine-laced hex that's been killing club patrons.

We have a witness saying the supplier's in the Athena Sisterhood. These brawls with the Confederate Thunder are complicating my investigation. Charging some of the Thundermen on this assault would help a lot."

Bello walked up holding a coffee mug that read #1 DETECTIVE. "Don't tell us how to work our case, Rios. Last I heard, your clearance rate isn't looking so good."

"What's wrong, Bello? The wife not putting out anymore? She find out you've been sticking it where you shouldn't?" asked Rios.

"Ho! You should talk. At least I ain't sleeping with one my witnesses."

"That's bullshit!" Rios gripped the wall of the cubicle to keep from punching him.

Bello scoffed. "Not what I heard."

"Okay, guys, cut it out!" said Morris.

"Who's spreading rumors I'm sleeping with a witness."

Bello smirked and turned his back to Rios as he sat at his desk. "I ain't saying. But a picture's worth a thousand words."

"What the hell you talking about?"

Morris stood and held up a cautious hand to Rios. "Just drop it," she whispered. "And don't give guys like him any more ammunition. Just back off and let us work our cases. All right?"

Rios wanted to press the issue, but she had enough on her plate. Dealing with the rumor mill could wait. She turned around and headed back to her desk, passing Detective Johnson along the way.

"Hey, Toni, I got a bunch of security videos from several Ironwood dance clubs. They're on a thumb drive on your desk."

"Thanks."

Rios arrived at her desk. Next to the thumb drive was a

printout of a photo. Rios picked it up and saw it was an image of her with her hand on Shea Stevens' from earlier that day. The words DYKES IN LOVE had been written on the photo with a permanent marker.

Rios glanced around the room and spotted Aguilar walking out of the door. "Goddamn him!"

~

SHEA DREW her Glock as she recognized the approaching Thundermen. Mackey, One-Shot, Monster, and Gator, a lanky guy with a long jaw, scraggly teeth, and greasy, shoulder-length hair. There was no way this confrontation was going to end without bloodshed.

The men shut off their bikes. In the startling silence, Shea's pulse pounded in her ears. She nudged Labrys behind her, shielding her with her body. "Just let us out of here, One-Shot and no one gets hurt."

"What the hell are you doing here, you fucking skank?" demanded Mackey. His little rat face was bright red. He drew a large Smith & Wesson revolver. One-Shot pulled a side-by-side, double-barrel shotgun out of a long holster mounted on his bike. Gator and Monster both held 9mm handguns, one a Walther P99, the other a Beretta 92FS.

"We didn't steal nothing if that's what you're thinking."

"Shea," said Monster. "You got no reason to be here."

"Let us leave and you won't see us again."

Mackey glared at her. "It ain't enough you bitches set up your own club in our territory. Now you think you can trespass on our property?"

"Drop the gun, Shea-Shea," said Monster.

"Don't do it." Labrys' voice trembled. "Shoot them. Shoot them now!"

Shea weighed her options. They were outnumbered

and outgunned. At best she could take out one, maybe two of them. But it was going to take more than firepower to get out of this alive.

"Toss the gun and we'll let you two go." One-Shot raised his shotgun, gazing down at her through the sights. "But we keep your girlfriend's cut and her bike."

"Over my dead body!" said Labrys.

"Happy to oblige." Gator pulled back the hammer on his revolver.

"Wait! Stop!" Shea took her finger off the trigger and tilted up the gun in surrender. "Just let us go. No harm, no foul."

"Put it on the ground." One-Shot lowered the shotgun. "Her cut, too."

"You can have her cut and my gun, just let her keep her bike." Shea laid the Glock on the ground.

"What are you doing, Shea?" Labrys' voice squeaked like a mouse. "They'll kill us."

"No they won't. Just take off your cut."

Labrys glared as she pulled off her cut and dropped it next to Shea's gun. "You and I are going to have a serious talk when we get out of this," Labrys whispered.

"There," said Shea. "Now let us go."

Gator approached her. "Sorry. Can't do that." He punched her in the gut.

Shea doubled over in pain. She opened her eyes in time to dodge the next blow aimed at her head and dove for her Glock.

Gator kicked the gun away before she could reach it. She drove her fist into his crotch, dropping him to his knees. "Take that you asshole."

One-Shot pointed the shotgun. Shea pulled Gator to his feet, using him as a shield. The shotgun blast to Gator's chest sent the two of them tumbling backward. Shea scooped up Gator's Walther and nailed One-Shot in the shoulder. He fell to one knee, yelling and gripping his bloody shoulder, dropping the shotgun in the process. Gator was making gurgling sounds, his chest a gaping hole of gore.

Shea grabbed the shotgun. Monster and Mackey were kicking Labrys in the back as she lay on the ground.

"Fucking skank!" Mackey gave Labrys another kick.

"Stop or I'll blow your fucking heads off!" Shea aimed the Walther at Mackey's head, with the shotgun tucked against her other shoulder, pointing at Monster's abundant belly. "And drop your guns."

Behind her One-Shot was moaning. Gator was dead silent.

"What the hell'd you do?" Mackey hunched down, looking like he would charge her.

"I'll do the same to *you* if y'all don't fucking do what I say."

The two men glared at Shea, but let their weapons fall to the ground.

"Shea-Shea," said Monster, breathing heavily. "You ain't gonna shoot me. We're family."

"You wanna bet your life on that, old man?" Her finger slipped onto the shotgun's second trigger.

"I'm gonna skin you alive, ya goddamn dyke." Mackey spit on the ground.

"That's right, Mackey. Gimme another reason to put one through your thick skull. Now help my friend up."

Monster grabbed Labrys by her arm and lifted her to her feet. She was a mess. Face swollen and covered in blood and dirt. Her body drooped like a rag doll.

"You all right, Deb?" Shea asked.

Deb coughed. "It's Labrys, goddammit."

A grim smile forced itself across Shea's face. "Can you walk?"

Labrys pulled away from Monster, stood a little straighter, and wiped her face. "I think so." She took a few uneasy steps.

"Can you ride?"

With a few grunts, she pulled on her cut and picked up Shea's Glock, her hand shaking as she pointed it at Monster. "I can ride. If someone picks up my bike."

"Monster," said Shea, "you and Mackey pick up her bike."

Mackey scoffed. "Like hell I will."

Shea fired a shot that just missed Mackey's ear. He ducked, eyes wide open. "Fuck me!"

Without another word, the two men heaved the bike onto its side stand. Meanwhile, Labrys gathered up their guns.

With the bike upright, Monster started walking toward Shea. "Whoa! Where you think you're going?"

"Our guys are bleeding to death, Shea."

"What do we do, Havoc?" Labrys stood beside her bike with an armful of the Thunders' guns.

Shea put pressure on the Walther's trigger. "Put their guns in your saddlebag and get outta here."

"What about you?"

"I'll catch up."

Labrys dumped the guns in one of her saddlebags, started the engine and disappeared up the dirt road.

Shea considered what to do with Monster and Mackey. She had killed people in the past, but always in self-defense. But if she let them go, they would come after her.

Shea aimed the shotgun at Mackey's bike, a Harley Fat Boy Lo. The tank sported the club's emblem known as the

Johnny Reb, a skull painted against a Confederate battle flag with lightning bolts at each corner.

"Don't you dare shoot my bike! No, no, no!" Mackey took a couple of steps toward her.

Shea pulled the trigger, ripping open a grapefruit-size hole where the painted skull had been. Gasoline trickled into a puddle on the ground.

Mackey looked terrified and more than a little grief stricken. "You fucking bitch. Ya coulda blowed us all to hell."

Shea pointed the Walther at him again. "Hell is where you belong, asshole."

"Don't do it, Shea-Shea." Monster held up his hands, pleading with her. "You a lotta things, but you ain't no murderer."

She stared at Mackey, willing herself to pull the trigger. He glared at her, as if daring her to do it. But something in her held her finger. Maybe Monster was right.

She pushed the barrel of the shotgun into the ground, plugging up the end with clay and gravel, then hurled it into the woods. It would take a good cleaning before it would be safe to fire.

"Go help your friends." She tucked the Walther into her waistband, hopped onto her bike, and raced out of the clearing. A bullet whizzed past her helmet. Another shattered her right side mirror. "Shit!" Someone must have had another gun tucked away somewhere.

She ducked down and twisted the throttle, charging up the trail before they could pull off another shot.

21
———

A MILE DOWN THE HIGHWAY, Shea caught up to Labrys, who was chugging along just under the speed limit. Shea waved her to go faster, but Labrys didn't speed up.

Come on, let's go! Shea thought, feeling like she had a target on her back. Maybe something was wrong with Labrys' bike. Or maybe she was just spooked. She was a college professor, after all. Not a street thug.

When they reached the tiny town of Granite, Labrys pulled into a two-pump gas station with an office the size of a single wide. Shea stopped next to her.

"You all right?" Shea asked.

Labrys lifted her tinted visor. Her chest shook sobbing. Her right eye was dark purple and swollen shut. Her nose was crooked and still bleeding.

"It's all right, Deb. We're safe."

Labrys glanced in a side mirror. "Oh shit, I look horrible." Her voice had a shaky nasal quality.

Shea chuckled ins spite of her concern. "That's what you're worried about? How you look? You just faced down four Thundermen. And survived."

Labrys cried harder. Shea's heart sank.

"I'm sorry. You might oughta go the hospital. I'll ride with you."

"I don't want anyone seeing me like this." Labrys took a deep breath and let it out. "You kill them?"

Shame warmed Shea's face. "I wanted to. But I couldn't do it."

"It's okay. If it hadn't been for you, who knows what they would have done to me."

"Yeah, well, don't get all sentimental on me. I been meaning to kick their asses for a while now."

Labrys started to laugh, but it turned into a choking fit. "Fuck, that hurts."

"How's your back?"

"My helmet and the armor in my jacket protected me from the worst of their kicks."

Shea nodded. *She's tougher than I thought.* "You still should get checked out. Make sure you ain't got a concussion or internal bleeding."

"I just want to go home, take a Percocet, and climb into bed." Labrys began to sob again. "I never thought it would be like this . . . never this violent."

"I tried to warn you. These guys don't play. They're outlaw."

"So I noticed." Labrys gingerly touched her bloodied nose and winced. "Ugh, I think they broke my nose." Labrys' good eye narrowed. "What happened to your mirror?"

"Bastards shot it. One of 'em must've had a backup gun."

"You think the guys who got shot are dead?"

"One-Shot probably survived. I only winged him. Not so sure about Gator. One-Shot nailed him with a chest full of buckshot."

"They're going to come after us, aren't they?"

Shea glanced back the way they came, half expecting the entire club to come roaring over the hill, guns blazing. "We should keep a low profile for a while. Might wanna put those Sisterhood cuts away till things cool down."

"And the guns in my saddlebag?"

"There's a cattle guard five miles outside of Ironwood. We'll stop there and get rid of our unwanted cargo."

"I'm sorry for dropping my bike. I feel like an idiot."

Shea avoided Labrys' gaze as old feelings threatened to surface. "Coulda happened to anyone. I was an idiot to get you involved. I'm sorry."

Labrys reached out and lifted Shea's chin to face her. Their eyes met. Shea's body trembled. She told herself it was the adrenaline burning out of her system.

"You saved my life, Shea," Labrys whispered. "Thank you."

Shea turned away and ran a hand through her hair. "Don't get all girly on me. Fuck." Shea felt a tightness behind her eyes. "Let's get moving. I gotta pick up Annie."

"Of course."

Labrys slowly rolled back onto the highway. Shea followed her, checking her remaining mirror every minute or so for signs of the Thunder.

Now that the adrenaline had worn off, her belly hurt from the punch she took. Lifting Labrys' bike didn't do her back or shoulders any good either. None of that mattered if she could get Rios to raid the stash house and lock up the Thundermen for good.

She'd been tempted to call Rios when they stopped back in Granite, but Shea didn't want to linger too long until they had some miles between themselves and the Thunder. Unfortunately, the longer she waited, the more likely it became that the club would remove the drugs and guns from the stash house. She prayed that Monster and Mackey were too busy saving their fallen comrades to worry about the cops raiding their drug stash.

When they stopped at the cattle guard on the outskirts of Ironwood, Shea opened Labrys' saddlebag and replaced the stolen Walther in her holster with her Glock. Then she gathered up the Thundermen's guns, wiped each one with her T-shirt, and slipped them between the bars of the cattle guard.

"Won't someone find them here?" asked Labrys.

"Probably not for a while. And even if they do, they'll likely get traced back to the Thunder, not us. Speaking of which, I gotta make a call." Shea pulled out her phone and dialed a number on her speed dial list.

"Detective Rios speaking."

"It's Shea Stevens. I found your hex dealer."

"Who?"

"The Confederate Thunder. Just like I told you."

"I'll need some proof."

"And you'll find it. There's a dirt road off Jefferson Highway three miles northeast of the Confederate Thunder clubhouse. Leads to a one-room cabin where they keep shit they don't want the cops to find. They still got the hex they stole from the Jaguars."

"You're sure?"

"I was there thirty minutes ago. Big, red plastic bins underneath a cases of ammo. They also got an arsenal of weapons that probably ain't legal. If you raid the place, you can shut this whole thing down and look like a fucking hero."

"I'm hoping you didn't just break in there. Otherwise, anything we find there could get tossed."

Aw shit. Time to cover my ass. "Break in? Don't be ridiculous. I was there with a few members of the Thunder."

Technically true. "But it should be unguarded now." Assuming Monster and Mackey took their comrades to get treated for their wounds.

"Uh-huh," replied Rios, clearly unconvinced. "I'll see if I can get a judge to sign off on a warrant."

"You do that. And then put their asses in jail. I'm tired of dealing with their bullshit."

Shea hung up and looked over at Labrys. "Follow me over to Orphan's. After what you've been through, you shouldn't be alone. And Orphan could use the company."

Labrys sat for a moment. Then said, "Yeah, all right."

IT WAS dark by the time Rios, Johnson, and Winslow bounced along in Rios' car down the dirt road leading to the Confederate Thunder's stash house. The scraping of branches along the side of her car left Rios worried she was going to need a new paint job. A K9 unit squad car followed behind them.

"You sure we shouldn't have called SWAT in on this?" asked Winslow from the backseat.

"My informant said the place wasn't guarded," Rios replied, hoping Shea was right.

"Then how come we're wearing vests?"

"In case my informant was wrong."

The road widened into a clearing. Rios pulled straight in, illuminating the small wooden structure with her high beams. A heavyset man with a long white beard wearing a Confederate Thunder cut sat on a lawn chair in front of the cabin, a Remington hunting rifle on his lap. She recognized him from his mug shot.

"Get the fuck out of here," shouted Monster as he

shielded his eyes from the headlights. "This is private property."

Rios stepped out of her car with her service weapon drawn. "Cortes County Sheriff! Search warrant! Get on the ground!"

"Motherfuckin' commies. You can't do this. This is America." He stood up, holding the rifle waist high.

"Toss the gun and get on the ground, or we *will* shoot you," said Johnson as she held up the warrant in one hand, her service weapon in the other.

Monster spat, then tossed the rifle. "There."

"Lay your ass on the ground, hands behind your head, fingers laced, ankles crossed." Rios picked up the rifle and handed it to Winslow. The man grunted as he complied with the commands.

"What's your name?" asked Winslow.

"Monster."

"Otherwise known as Vernon Mueller," said Rios. "A couple of assault charges back in the day. You still on probation, Monster?"

"I invoke my Fourth Amendment right to silence."

Rios chuckled. "I think you mean the Fifth Amendment, but feel free to keep your mouth shut." She cuffed him. "I'll take these off once we're done here. Unless we find something illegal."

"Y'all smell that?" asked Johnson.

Rios sniffed the air and caught a whiff of fumes. "Gasoline?"

Johnson followed the scent and stopped over a damp spot on the ground. "Someone must've spilled some gasoline."

"You getting sloppy gassing up your bikes, Monster?"

While Johnson cuffed Monster, Rios stepped up to the cabin door and found it padlocked. Deputy Peterson, a stocky K9 officer with a crew cut, approached with a Malinois named Misty. Misty stopped and pawed at the front door. Drugs were inside.

Gotcha, thought Rios. "Where's the key to that lock?"

"I'm just guarding the place. Got no key."

"Of course, you don't." She holstered her pistol, walked to the back of her car, and pulled a battering ram out of her trunk. "Not a problem."

"Hey you can't do that," moaned Monster. "That's destruction of private property."

"You got another way in?" asked Johnson.

"No."

Johnson kicked his boots. "Then shut the hell up."

Peterson and Misty moved aside as Rios returned to the door. "Knock, knock." She swung the battering ram. The door cracked but didn't open. A second blow smashed the door inward, ripping the lock out of the wood. Rios dropped the ram and pulled the flashlight off her belt to look around. "It's clear. Peterson, do your thing."

"Okay, Misty." Peterson led the canine into the cabin.

Rios guided them with her flashlight. Misty started on the left, sniffing boxes, musty furniture, and motorcycle parts. When she reached a pair of red plastic bins, Misty sat and pawed at the bins.

"We got a hit," said Peterson. "Good girl, Misty." He and the dog exited as Winslow entered.

Rios turned to him. "Help me move these ammo cases. Let's see what's in these bins."

When the ammo cases were moved off to the side, Rios inspected the top bin, looking for possible booby traps. A year earlier, a detective had lost an arm and his vision after opening a container of coke rigged with explosives. Rios didn't see anything to suggest a threat.

"These bins match the ones we found at the Jaguars' warehouse a few months ago," said Winslow.

"Yeah, I thought they looked familiar." Rios released the locks on the ends of the bin and grabbed a pry bar she found in the corner of the cabin to lift off the cover. No explosion.

Rios took a deep breath, looked inside, and found a jumble of tools, a stereo receiver, and a twisted nest of electrical cords. She pried the lid off the receiver hoping to find drugs hidden inside, but found nothing but electronics. "No drugs. Let's check the second bin."

They moved the first bin to the side and popped the lid off the second one. Again, no contraband, just an assortment of biker-themed Christmas decorations and a blanket with a Johnny Reb sewed on it. Rios felt like the grinning skull was mocking her. "Shit."

She scanned the rest of the cabin. "My informant also said there was an arsenal of weapons, but I'm not seeing them. Just cases of ammo."

"How'd the dog get a hit when there's no drugs?" asked Winslow.

"If drugs were stored there at one time," said Peterson, "there could still be enough residue for Misty to get a hit."

Outside the cabin, Monster chuckled. "Need help finding something?"

Johnson kicked his boot again. "Quiet."

"So now what?" asked Winslow.

"Let's tear this place apart. There's got to be something we can arrest these guys on."

Rios and her team pulled everything out of the cabin, digging into boxes, tearing apart furniture, and disassembling motorcycle parts. But after two hours, they had found nothing illegal. And Misty didn't get a hit off of anything but the empty red bins.

"All right, folks. Let's pack it up." Rios' temper was simmering. Whatever had been here was gone now. She couldn't be sure the bins had even contained the hex she was looking for.

"What about our door?" grumbled Monster as Johnson uncuffed him.

"Be glad we don't arrest you for threatening a deputy with a deadly weapon." Johnson cycled the bolt several times, letting five finger-length rounds clink onto the ground, and handed the unloaded rifle back to Monster. "Have a nice day, sir."

"Goddamn pigs."

Rios, Johnson, and Winslow piled back into her car and drove off, followed by Peterson in the K9 vehicle. Shea had some serious explaining to do.

22

———————

SHEA PULLED into her garage and helped Annie off the back of the bike.

As the two of them pulled off their helmets, Shea said, "Listen, Doodlebug, I'd appreciate it if you didn't tell Jessica about seeing Labrys, all right?"

"Why not?"

Shea fussed with her jacket zipper that refused to release. "Well, I don't want her to worry." She jerked the edge of the jacket and the zipper let loose.

"Why was she all beat up? Did you hit her?"

Shea felt like she'd been sucker punched for the second time in as many hours. "No, I would never do that." Though there had been times in the past she had wanted to. "Some guys roughed her up a little, but I made them stop. It's no big deal." *Close enough to the truth.*

"Looked like someone hit her."

Shea hung their helmets from hooks mounted on the wall. "Why don't we go inside and see what Jessica has for dinner. I think I smell pizza."

"Real pizza or one of Jessica's weird pizzas with weird ingredients like artichokes?" Annie made a face.

"I dunno. Let's go find out."

She took a final glance outside, still haunted by visions of the Thunder showing up en masse to seek revenge. Her fist pounded the switch on the wall that set the garage door clanking closed.

Inside the house, a large pizza box lay on the kitchen counter. Shea lifted the lid. "You're in luck, kiddo. It's pepperoni and sausage. Now go wash up."

"Yay, real pizza!" Annie hustled off to the hallway bathroom.

"So, what happened at school?" asked Jessica from the living room love seat.

Shea pulled out a dispenser of pumice hand soap, determined to remove any gunshot reside from her arms and hands. "She got suspended for defending herself against that bully."

"They suspended her?" Jessica asked between bites.

"Three days. That same punk was harassing her, so she decked him. I'da done the same thing." Shea put some pizza slices on a couple of plates and sat down next to Jessica.

"What are we going to do?"

"I have someone who can watch her for a few days next week while we're at work."

Jessica's eyes narrowed. "Who?"

"Orphan. She's an artist and doesn't have a day job. She'd be perfect."

"From the Sisterhood? Do you even know her real name?"

"Sarah something."

"Sarah something? You want to let someone whose last

name you don't know watch your niece for eight to ten hours a day?"

Annie walked in and sat on the sofa with her plate. "She watched me this afternoon."

Shea choked on a piece of pepperoni. *What's she gonna blurt out next?* "Jess, don't freak out. I had some errands to run. Orphan agreed to watch her. It was no big deal."

Jessica set aside her plate and leaned toward Annie. "You like hanging out with Orphan?"

"Yeah, it's kinda fun. She showed me how to paint. I just didn't like the scary woman that was there."

Sucker punch number three. *Could the Thunder have gotten to her that fast?* "What scary woman?" Shea asked.

"I dunno. She was hanging out at her door when we got there. Orphan told her to go away."

"What did this scary woman look like?" asked Jessica.

"Big. She said mean things to Orphan that made her scared."

Jessica locked eyes with Shea. "You seriously want Annie staying with Orphan when there are big scary women showing up at her door?"

Shea wasn't sure whether to be worried about this scary stranger or to be relieved it wasn't the Thunder. "I'm sure it's nothing serious. If Orphan thought she was in trouble, she would have said something to me or to—" *Aw shit.*

Jess cocked her head. "Or to whom? Who else was there?"

"I didn't want to say anything 'cause I knew you'd overreact."

"Oh you did, did you? And would this other person's name happened to be Deb?"

"Uh-huh," said Annie.

Shea smirked. "Thanks a lot, kid."

"And what errands were you and your ex-girlfriend doing all afternoon?"

"It's not what you think."

"Then please. Enlighten me."

"We went to a place where the *other motorcycle club* keeps their stash of . . . *contraband*." Shea tilted her head in Annie's direction, not wanting to mention the Thunder in front of her. "I figured if I can get them arrested for selling this contraband, I won't have to be Rios' snitch no more."

"Really?" Jessica crossed her arms, her face a mask of anger and disbelief. "And did you and your old girlfriend find any *contraband* at this *other club's* place?"

"See, that's the good part." Shea forced a placating smile. "We found the . . . uh, *contraband* they stole from the Jaguars. They're as good as busted."

"And Deb got beaten up," added Annie, followed by a throaty belch. "Can I have some more pizza?"

"Beaten up?" Jess' crinkled in concern. "By whom?"

"We ran into a little trouble."

"What kind of trouble?"

"Some of the guys in the other club. Trust me, they got the worst of it." A memory of Gator's bloody chest surfaced in Shea's mind. She pushed it back down with a bite of pizza. "The important thing is when Rios busts them and sends them all to prison, you and me can live happily ever after."

"Let's hope so." Jessica lay back and stared at the ceiling. "You still planning to join the Sisterhood?"

"Yeah. With the Thunder no longer a problem, there's nothing to worry about."

"Except for your psycho ex-girlfriend."

Shea set aside her plate and cradled Jessica's face. "Deb is ancient history, Jess. I love you. I'm committed to you. My heart overflows with love whenever I'm with you."

"I love you, too." Jess kissed her.

"Ewww!" Annie carried her plate into the kitchen. "I'm gonna eat in my room."

Shea chuckled. "Just don't spill anything on the carpet."

Jessica climbed onto Shea and planted a series of kisses on her face and neck. Shea sighed as the troubles of the day evaporated.

"Can we go out tomorrow night? Just the two of us?" whispered Jess.

"You want me to ask Orphan to watch Annie?"

"I asked Mrs. Collins next door to watch her, hoping you'd say yes."

"In that case, yes." Shea kissed her deeply.

RIOS COLLAPSED into her chair and laid her head on the desk after returning from the fruitless search on the Thunder's so-called stash house. It was well after nine o'clock. She was tired and hungry, but more than anything she was angry. She had given Shea Stevens the benefit of the doubt, only to end up looking like a fool.

It was bad enough being known as the department's IA snitch. The photo someone had taken of her holding Shea's hand didn't help. After the search turned up nothing, it would be a miracle if she didn't get transferred out of the department.

She sat up and thumbed through the case files. What little evidence she had pointed to someone in the Athena Sisterhood being the source of the hex. She needed Shea working the Sisterhood from the inside.

Rios was about to call Shea when her cellphone rang. "Detective Rios."

"Hey, it's Morris." There were conversations and music in the background.

"What's up, Detective?"

"You were concerned the rivalry between the Confederate Thunder and the Athena Sisterhood was going to get bloody?"

"Yeah?"

"It just did. We got a dead Thunderman. Looks like a shotgun wound to the chest. Thought maybe you could offer some insights."

Rios sighed. The last thing she wanted was to spend the next several hours at another crime scene. "Where are you?"

"Bootlegger Bob's."

"Someone killed a Thunderman at their favorite watering hole?"

"We're thinking it's a body dump. Victim was most likely killed somewhere else. My gut says the Athena Sisterhood's responsible."

Rios found it hard to believe, but clearly her instincts had been off lately. "Your victim got a name?"

"Patch on his cut reads GATOR. Driver's license IDs him as Edward Applewhite. You know him?"

"I've heard the name. Skinny, kind of a Jay Leno chin."

"That's him."

"Served time for a couple of B&Es, as I recall. You want me to come down there?" *Please say no.*

"If you wouldn't mind."

"Bello won't think I'm trying to steal your case?"

"We both want this solved before more bodies start piling up. Any help you can give is appreciated."

"All right. I'll be there in thirty minutes."

"Thanks, Detective. See ya then."

Rios grabbed her purse and her leather-bound notebook and headed out. As she drove, her mind sorted through the evidence she had so far. None of the members of the Sisterhood she'd identified had a criminal record, outside of a few protest-related trespassing charges. No assaults. Murder seemed like a big step.

Then again, she had a witness claiming one or more of them was dealing drugs. Murder and narcotics often went hand-in-hand. And there were the rumors that the Sisterhood was linked to the firebombings. The recent clashes with the Thunder certainly gave them motive.

For all she knew, Shea Stevens could have killed Gator. She had mentioned she was at the stash house with members of the Thunder. Odd considering her concerns for her family's safety. Maybe Shea wasn't giving her the whole story.

The bright lights of Bootlegger Bob's parking lot appeared in the darkness. The entrance was blocked off with two CCSO barricades. Rios showed her detective's shield to the deputy standing guard, who moved one of the barricades and let her through.

She parked next to a marked patrol car. Most of the vehicles in the lot were motorcycles, many with the words CONFEDERATE THUNDER or the Johnny Reb painted on the tanks.

As she gathered her notebook and purse, a stain on her passenger floor mat caught her eye. Upon closer examination, she saw it was dark reddish partial shoe print. "What the hell?"

Rios pulled out her phone and dialed.

"Detective Johnson speaking."

"Where are you?"

"At home. Eating dinner. Why?"

"Check the bottom of your shoes."

"My shoes? Why?"

"I think you stepped in something tonight."

"Ugh. Please tell me it wasn't manure. Hold on. Let me check."

As she waited, one of the field techs assigned to the scene walked past. "Hey, Hank!"

He turned around. "Evening, Detective."

"You have a presumptive blood test kit handy?"

"Sure, I'll be right back with one."

He returned a moment later with a small kit. "You found something here in the lot?"

Rios grimaced. "Sort of." She pulled out the floor mat. "My team executed a search warrant on one of the Thunder's properties earlier. I think one of the detectives may have stepped in blood and transferred it to my floor mat."

"Well, let's take a look." With a cotton swab wet with ethyl alcohol, he swiped the dark stain on the mat. A drop each of reagent and hydrogen peroxide confirmed her suspicion as the cotton swab turned hot pink. Blood. "Positive. We'd have to take it to the lab to confirm. You want me to bag it?"

"No, that's all right. I'll do it. Thanks for your help."

"Anytime." Hank walked away to return to his duties.

Johnson came back on the line. "Tell me this isn't what I think it is."

"It's blood. I just ran a test on a stain your shoe left on my floor mat."

"But how?"

"Must have stepped in it around the Thunder's stash house. Bag the shoes and meet me at Bootlegger Bob's."

"Now?"

"We have a dead body. Your shoes are evidence."

Rios hung up, folded the floor mat, and stuffed it into an oversized evidence bag. This wouldn't help her reputation, but it might solve this homicide.

She carried the bag toward the long wooden building. The words BOOTLEGGER BOB'S glowed in ten-foot neon above the front entrance. Signs advertising brands of beers flashed in the windows.

Detectives Morris and Bello were standing over Gator's body ten feet laid out on the ground from the front door. Flies buzzed around the large bloody hole in his chest.

"Evening, Detectives."

"Thanks for coming, Toni. What's in the bag?" asked Morris.

"You said you thought the deceased may have been killed elsewhere?"

"Yeah. Not much blood here. We did find a shotgun nearby. The whole thing looks staged."

"I may have found your primary crime scene."

23

———

The next morning, Shea was lacing up her boots when Jessica walked into the bedroom. The scent of maple syrup drifted in with her.

"You joining us for breakfast? I made pancakes."

"Sorry, don't really have time. Me and the team are working on this custom bike. It's a rush job."

Jessica put a hand on her hip. "But it's Saturday. I thought you were going to be spending more time with Annie."

"I plan to, but just not this minute." Shea stood up and gave Jess a peck on the lips while slipping on her armored hoodie. "Some suit wants a custom café racer before it gets too cold for her to ride."

"What time will you be home?"

"In plenty of time for dinner. I promise."

Jess sighed. "You better."

Someone pounded on the front door. No polite knock, but an insistent hammering that only came from unwanted guests.

"You expecting someone?" Shea asked.

"No," replied Jessica.

Shea hustled into the living room, with Jessica trailing behind her. Annie was sitting on a stool at the breakfast bar with a plate of pancakes, a worried expression on her face.

"Take Annie into the back." Shea picked up the baseball bat she kept near the front door and peeked through the peephole. A uniformed deputy she didn't recognize stood on the front step. "Shit."

Shea opened the door, holding the bat behind her back. Just in case. "Yeah?"

"I'm looking for Shea Stevens."

"You got her."

"I'm instructed to bring you to the Ironwood station for questioning."

"Questioning? I don't have time for this. If Rios wants me to make a statement about the drugs she seized last night, have her call me." Shea started to close the door, but the deputy pushed it back open, stepping into the room.

"Shea, what's going on?" Jessica called from behind.

The deputy drew his pistol. Jessica shrieked.

Shea held up her hands, making sure her body was between the deputy and Jessica. "Whoa, whoa, whoa! No need for guns. Rios wants me to answer some questions, I'll answer some goddamn questions."

The stern-faced deputy looked from Jessica to Shea, then reholstered his weapon.

Shea turned to Jessica. "It's okay. Just a misunder—Hey!" She felt the bite of cuffs zipping closed on her wrists. "What the hell?"

"Let's go!" The deputy grabbed her arm and dragged her down the sidewalk to his waiting patrol car.

∽

AFTER BEING DUMPED UNCEREMONIOUSLY in a CCSO interrogation room, Shea waited for an hour before two detectives, a man and a woman, walked in.

"Shea Stevens," said the male detective, "my name is Detective Bello. This is Detective Morris."

Shea looked at one then the other. Something wasn't right. "Why am I handcuffed? And where the hell's Rios?"

"Detective Rios is not currently assigned to this case," answered Morris.

"What the hell you talking about? I'm her CI." Blank stares. "The one that told her where the Thunder were storing the hex they been dealing."

"You're referring to the cabin off Jefferson Highway?" asked Bello.

"Yes," said Shea with considerable relief.

"No drugs were found there."

"What? That can't be. They were there." If no drugs were found, that meant the Thundermen hadn't been arrested.

Bello opened a case file and pulled out an eight-by-ten of Gator's body, showing the bloody mess that had been his chest. "We are investigating the death of this man. Do you recognize him?"

I am so fucked, thought Shea. "I ain't saying nothing else without my lawyer."

WHEN DRAGON ARRIVED two hours later, Shea gave her a brief rundown of the previous day's events. When they were ready, Dragon called the detectives back into the interrogation room.

"So," said Detective Bello, once again holding up Gator's photo. "Do you know this man?"

Before Shea could answer, Dragon spoke up. "My client

did not kill this man, although she was a witness to his death. She will tell you what she knows in exchange for full immunity for all past offenses."

Bello's eye's narrowed almost imperceptibly. "We'll listen to what she has to say. If it has sufficient value, we'll talk to the DA about immunity."

Dragon gave Shea a nod.

"He's a member of the Confederate Thunder," said Shea. "Goes by the name Gator."

"Well, he did," said Morris. "He was found shot to death last night outside Bootlegger Bob's, a biker bar in Bradshaw City."

"I've never been there." It was the truth. By the time Shea was of drinking age, she had ended any affiliation with her father's club.

"We believe he was shot here." Bello pulled out another photo, this time of the stash house. "You have been here, am I right? This is the cabin where you told Detective Rios they would find a considerable quantity of hex."

Shea looked at Dragon, who nodded.

"The Thunder'd stolen two red bins full of hex from the Jaguars last summer. I figured that's where they'd've stashed it, so I went there to confirm it was still there. But before I could, four Thundermen showed up."

Morris took notes on a legal pad. "What are the names of these Thundermen?"

"Gator, One-Shot, Monster, and Mackey."

"Who shot Gator?" asked Bello.

"One-Shot, the club's president."

Morris raised an eyebrow. "Why would he shoot his own guy?"

"He was shooting at me. I ducked behind Gator. One-Shot hit him instead."

"Clearly, the one you want is One-Shot," said Dragon. "My client is completely innocent."

"Except," said Bello, "that doesn't explain how your fingerprints were on the shotgun we recovered."

Shea's chest tightened. She had forgotten about picking up the shotgun and shooting Mackey's tank. She felt like an idiot.

Dragon leaned over to Shea. "You picked up the gun?" she whispered.

"Just to keep them from coming after me again. I didn't shoot anyone with it. I just jammed mud in the barrels and tossed it."

Dragon looked up at the detectives. "You found mud in the barrel of the gun, did you not?"

"We're still waiting for the final report to come from the lab. But what if there was? We have your client's fingerprints on the outside of the barrel and the trigger."

"After One-Shot murdered Gator, and acting strictly in self-defense, my client grabbed the shotgun and held it to ward off further attacks. Prior to leaving the scene, she packed the end of the barrels to prevent it from being used against her."

Morris continued making notes. "What is One-Shot's full name?"

"Gerald Dewey," said Shea, remembering him from when both of their fathers were in the club.

"Unless you have any further questions, I believe we are done here."

Morris and Bello looked at each other. Morris shook her head, then turned to Shea. "You're free to go for now. But be available should we have any further questions."

Shea followed Dragon out of the building. "Thanks for your help. You mind giving me a ride back to my shop?"

"Perhaps." Dragon stopped and locked eyes with Shea.

"But first, explain something to me. Why are you working as a confidential informant for the sheriff's office?"

Shea held her gaze, trying to look sincere. "Look, I'm not looking to rat anyone out in the Sisterhood, if that's what concerns you. I can keep club secrets."

"So why are you a CI?"

"A few months back, the cops caught me at a crime scene with a gun that was linked to a series of murders. It wasn't even my gun. I'd taken it away from a member of the Confederate Thunder after he and my sister's old man, who was the club's president at the time, tried to drag her outta my shop. Detective Rios threatened to send me back to prison unless I agreed to be a snitch."

Dragon studied Shea a moment before saying, "I understand."

"The Sisterhood ain't doing nothing illegal, are they?"

"Sometimes the club engages in acts of . . . civil disobedience. To raise awareness of how women are marginalized and mistreated. I trust we can count on your discretion."

"Fine with me. I've engaged in civil disobedience plenty of times. To say nothing of some not-so-civil disobedience."

"That's good to know."

"Now about that ride."

24

SHEA STOOD at her front door, key in hand, for what felt like an eternity after Dragon dropped her off. She had left a message on Monster's voicemail on the way from the sheriff's station. He was the last person she wanted to talk to, but the Thunder would soon be looking to avenge Gator's death. Her only hope for survival was to somehow get Monster to convince the Thunder to call a cease-fire. It seemed impossible. But she had no other option.

The door opened. "Shea? What happened?"

Jessica looked concerned. But not as concerned as Shea felt. It was all starting again. Her efforts to get out of a troublesome situation were making things worse, putting those she cared about in danger. The Thunder wouldn't think twice about hurting Jessica.

Shea hugged her. "We need to talk."

Jessica pulled back. "Shea, what's going on? Did they arrest the Thunder for the drugs?"

A truck rumbled past the house. Shea watched it warily. "Maybe we should discuss this inside."

They walked in and sat on the love seat. "Where's Annie?" asked Shea.

"Down the street at her friend Hailey's house. Tell me what's going on."

Shea stared across the room as the fight at the cabin replayed in her mind. "Turns out the drugs at the Thunder's stash house were gone by the time Rios showed up. Maybe they moved them after Deb and I were there. But for all I know, they coulda sold 'em a long time ago and just used the bins they were in for something else."

"Then why'd that cop pick you up?"

Shea ran a hand through her hair. "A Thunderman got killed last night. The cops thought I did it."

"You didn't, did you?"

Shea filled in the details about what had happened. "I called Monster and left a message on his voicemail. Maybe he can get the club to back off somehow if I agree to let him see Annie. I don't know. I'm just winging it at this point."

"And if he doesn't? They could come after us."

Shea looked deeply into Jessica's eyes, brimming with tears of fright. "I won't let them hurt you. I will turn myself over to them before I let that happen."

Jessica shook her head, hand covering her mouth. "No, no, no, you can't do that. That's suicide. Can't you call Rios?"

"Rios can't do shit. They didn't bust them for their attack on the Jaguars last summer. They haven't arrested anyone for harassing us at Gertie's or Bike Night. We're on our own."

"And what about the Sisterhood? Aren't they supposed to protect you?"

"I'm not even a prospect, so they aren't obligated to do shit. But I can call Labrys and see—"

"No, don't." Jessica sat up straight and wiped her face.

"We don't need her. You and me, we'll figure this out ourselves."

Shea cupped Jessica's cheek, impressed by this new show of resolve. "Yes. Yes, we will."

SHEA HAD TRIED Monster's number twice more by the time she and Jessica were getting ready for their date. Still no call back. The lack of response worried her.

Shea suggested they stay home, but Jessica remained adamant. She wasn't going to let the Thunder rob her of a long-awaited night out.

Shea walked out of her walk-in closet in a T-shirt featuring an abstract printed design that incorporated the Iron Goddess Custom Cycles logo.

"You're not really going to wear that are you?" asked Jessica, wearing only pantyhose and a bra.

"What? It's a perfectly fine shirt. It's clean, at least. No holes." Shea inspected the T-shirt to double-check she hadn't missed any tears.

"It's an Iron Goddess T-shirt. Don't you have anything nicer?"

"We're just going to Emperor Dragon. People wear jeans and T-shirts there all the time."

"I know, but this is our first date night in weeks. I want it to be nice." Jessica dug out a dress shirt from the back of Shea's closet and handed it to her. "Try this."

Shea pressed her forehead against Jessica's as she took the shirt. "For you, I'd go naked. It'd kinda go with what you're wearing."

"Tempting, but I think the health department might object. And I plan on wearing a dress over this." Jessica chuckled as she disappeared into their bathroom.

She brushed a layer of dust off the shoulders of the shirt. *How long's it been since I wore it?* Her phone rang as she was buttoning it.

"Don't answer that," Jess said. "This is our night out. Whoever it is can wait."

Shea glanced at the caller ID. It was Labrys. *Has the Thunder retaliated already? Had a member of the Sisterhood been attacked?*

Shea hurried into the living room and answered the call. "What's up, Labrys?" she asked in a hushed tone.

"Be at Gertie's at six o'clock. When you arrive, tell the bartender who you are. She'll instruct you from there."

"Why? What's wrong?"

"The Sisterhood is having our weekly meeting."

"That's it? A club meeting? Now's not really a good time. Jess and I have dinner reservations."

"Havoc," said Labrys is a stern voice. "You want to be a prospect?"

"Of course, but—."

"Then do what I say, when I say it. Period."

Shea's chest tightened as she caught a glimpse of Jess's reflection in the bathroom mirror. "What am I supposed to tell Jessica?"

"She's *your* girlfriend. You figure it out. Just be at Gertie's at six."

"Is this what being a prospect for the Sisterhood's gonna be like?"

"What do you mean?"

"Ordering me around, even if it screws up plans with my family."

"*We* are your family. We need to know you're committed to the cause, sister. So, are you in or are you out?"

Jess was going to have a shit fit. But Shea didn't have a lot of choice. She needed all the allies she could get at this point. Even if the Athenas weren't as street smart as Shea wished they were.

"I'll be there. Just gimme a heads-up next time, all right?"

"See you there. Give my love to the missus."

Shea felt like putting her fist through a wall. Or better yet, Labrys' head. The bitch was enjoying this way too much.

Jess walked out of the bathroom. Her flowing scarlet dress was accented with a double-stranded gold and red coral necklace. She stood with arms crossed, the vision of a spurned goddess. "You answered it, didn't you?"

Shea squirmed under her disapproving eye. "I gotta go take care of something. I'm sorry."

"We've got a date. You bailed on our six-month anniversary. You are not skipping out now."

"It's Athena Sisterhood stuff. Labrys insists I be there."

"Oh, Labrys insists?" said Jess with dripping sarcasm. "You're ditching me to hang out with your ex? Again?"

"I think they're voting me in as a prospect. I gotta be there."

"You don't have to be there for them to vote, do you? Let's just go to dinner. They can call you and tell you whether you're in or not."

"Jess, it doesn't work that way. I need to be there."

"You need to be with me."

"I know, I know. But I can't be in two places at once."

"Then you have to decide which is more important—me or your ex."

"Stop making it about her. We need the help of the club to deal with the Thunder. Trust me, it will be like having an extended family, everyone having your back."

Jessica stood silent for a moment. "No."

"No? Jess, this ain't up for debate. I have to do this. My

freedom, maybe even our lives, depends on it." Shea grabbed her motorcycle hoodie from the coat closet and slipped it on. As she turned to go, she saw Jessica's face wet with tears.

"I really thought I mattered to you."

Shea's insides twisted. "You do." She reached out to her, but Jessica pulled away.

"Just go." Jessica turned and disappeared into their bedroom, slamming the door behind her.

Shea wanted to follow and make everything all right. But so much depended on her joining the Sisterhood.

25

THE SQUARE in downtown Ironwood was lively with CAU students out for a good time. Not unusual for a Friday night. Shouting, laughter, the thumping beat of multiple music sources, and tempting aromas from the numerous restaurants filled the cold night air. Shea's stomach rumbled, reinforcing her anger at Labrys for spoiling her dinner date.

She strolled into Gertie's. It was early evening and the place was only a quarter full.

"I'm Shea Stevens," she said to the bartender, a gal with a tattooed flowering vine wrapping around her left arm. "Labrys told me you'd give me instructions."

The bartender poured shots for a couple of customers at the end of the bar, then looked up at Shea. "Don't have any instructions for a Shea Stevens."

Shea sighed. "How about for Havoc?"

The bartender nodded with a knowing smile. "Your instructions are to wait."

Shea grimaced. More of Labrys' power games, no

doubt. She ordered a beer and drank it, wishing she were at home with Jessica.

She didn't blame Jess for being upset. So far, Shea hadn't lived up to her promise to spend more time with her and Annie.

Not that Rios had left her much choice about getting closer to the club. Going back to prison wouldn't help Jess or Annie. But it was more than that. Shea liked spending time with these women and being part of the MC world again. And if she had to suck it up and endure Labrys's bullshit for a year as a prospect, maybe it would be worth it in the end.

Just as Shea was finishing her beer and about to order another, Savage emerged from the hallway that led to the back of the restaurant, a grim expression on her face. "You! Come with me. Now!"

Shea slapped a fiver on the bar and followed Savage into a large meeting room filled with two dozen members of the Sisterhood. A table had been set at one end, behind which Labrys, Fuego, the club's VP, and Savage sat. They glared at her as if mad about something she had done.

What the hell's going on? Shea wondered.

Labrys banged the gavel three times. "Havoc, please stand before the officers' table."

Shea complied. *What if they didn't vote me in? What am I gonna tell Rios?*

"Havoc, you have requested to join our ranks despite being a hangaround for only one week. We have discussed your qualifications to be a member of the esteemed Athena Sisterhood Motorcycle Club." Labrys's voice was stern and filled with drama. "We know you are a former convict that has engaged in violence on numerous occasions. We are a passionate, but peaceful group that does not take kindly to violent criminals. And yet you have the nerve to ask to join our club. What say you for yourself?" Havoc appeared to be enjoying herself. Maybe too much.

"You really want me to answer that? Fine." Shea turned her back on the officers' table, folded her arms across her chest. "I was born into the MC culture. My asshole father used to be the Thunder's president. I've tangled with them on occasion over the years. And since y'all saw fit to declare yourselves a motorcycle club in their territory, you might want someone who knows what you're up against."

"And how do we know you'll be loyal to our club?"

Shea turned and locked eyes with Labrys. "I saved your ass last night, didn't I? How's that for loyalty?"

No one spoke for a few minutes. The smirk on Labrys's face faded as she nodded to Savage, who picked up a leather cut from under the table. It bore a top rocker patch that read ATHENA SISTERHOOD and a bottom rocker with the word PROSPECT. No club emblem. No MC patch

"Havoc," said Savage, "you are hereby designated a prospect of the central Arizona chapter of the Athena Sisterhood for a period of no less than one year from today."

Shea pulled on the cut. It was a little big, but the lacing on the side could be tightened. It felt good even if it was just a prospect's cut. The Athenas applauded at Labrys' announcement. Several stood up and hugged her.

Shea took an empty seat between Indigo and Orphan.

Indigo gave her a peck on the cheek. "Glad to have you, sister."

"Thanks."

"Hey, Indigo," whispered Orphan, "where's Raven, Pixie, and Goth?"

Indigo shrugged. "I don't know. They should've been here."

Labrys pounded her gavel on the table to get the other

women's attention. The conversations in the room went quiet.

"Sisters, now that we have that out of the way, a lot of you have asked what happened to my face. I'm here to tell you. We are at war. Not with the enforcers of the corporate glass ceiling or the good ol' boy network down in our state legislature. We are at war with the Confederate Thunder."

A murmuring rose in the room.

"They have attacked us in this very bar. They ambushed us at Bike Night. I suspect they murdered Pipes. And yesterday they tried to kill me. Thankfully, Havoc, our new prospect, was there to stop them."

Labrys stood up, a pained expression on her face. Shea suspected she was still hurting from the day before. "Why is the Thunder so hell-bent on shutting us down? We represent a threat to their drug dealing, gun running, and womanizing. Our refusal to submit to their authority is a slap in their sexist faces. They call us disrespectful. They claim we don't know what we're doing."

Shouts of anger and profanity erupted from the group.

"So far, the cops have done little to help us, claiming they don't have enough proof. They've all but written off Pipes' death as a simple overdose. Meanwhile, the Thunder is free to deal drugs and assault us without consequences. Well, I for one will not stand for it. They can break my nose and bruise my ribs, but I will not back down."

"Hell yeah!" shouted Savage.

"Fuck the cops!" added another member of the club. "Fuck the Thunder!"

"The Thunder has declared war on us. They are vicious. They are experienced. And they are armed. But we are women. We've been fighting for our right to exist since the beginning of time. They may be vicious, but we are tough. They may be experienced, but we are smart. And they aren't the only ones who know how to fire a gun. Together, we will stand up to these bullies and show them that the Athena Sisterhood isn't afraid of anyone."

Cheers and applause shook the room.

"Havoc!" Labrys pointed to Shea. The room went silent.

"Yeah?"

"Your first duty as a prospect is to find us some tables out in the bar. Now move your ass. I'm thirsty."

26

———

Shea walked out of Gertie's into the cold to clear her mind from the effects of the four beers and three shots of tequila she'd had.

During a conversation with some of the Athenas, Indigo admitted she didn't currently have a job and yet somehow often could afford to go out dancing a few times a week. Plus, there was a peculiar guardedness about her that set off red flags in Shea's mind. Indigo was hiding something. *Is she the one dealing drugs at local clubs?*

Nearby laughter down the street caught Shea attention. A group of hefty leather-clad men stood outside the Bear's Den, a men's bar. A familiar figure caused Shea's jaw to drop. She rubbed her eyes to make sure she wasn't imagining this. Under the bright overhead lights illuminating the front of the bar, Monster stood making out with a Hispanic man.

"Holy shit." The Thunder would kill him if they knew. His wife wouldn't be too thrilled either.

She pulled up the hood of her armored hoodie and slipped out her phone, opening the camera app with the flash turned off. With her heart hammering in her chest, she strode past the men and discretely snapped a couple of photos of Monster and the other man. They paid her no attention, too wrapped up in each other's embrace.

A few doors down, Shea stopped to examine the photos. The first was a little blurry, but the second clearly showed Monster locking lips with his lover. The sign for the Bear's Den glowed in the background.

Under normal conditions, Shea would never out someone, not even the deeply closeted right-wing hypocrites who spouted homophobic rhetoric by day while cruising clubs at night.

But these weren't normal conditions. The Thunder would be coming after her. So, if she had to blackmail Monster into getting the club to back off, so be it.

She texted the photo to Monster with the message: *Naughty little Monster. Call me.*

She followed that with a copy to Labrys saying they now had some leverage against Thunder retaliation.

Shea stumbled through the dark house, the booze in her system causing her to slam against the wall and into the breakfast bar. *Probably shouldn't have driven home like this,* she thought.

Chlöe Stansbury's patronizing voice echoed in her mind: *Alcoholism can destroy your life.*

Fuck Chlöe Stansbury and her fucking pink café racer. I made it home in one piece. And I caught a photo of Monster making out with another man.

She stumbled and face-planted on the carpet. "Shhh!" she said to no one.

Glad that Jessica wasn't waiting up for her, she pulled

herself to her feet and debated whether she should crash on the couch or risk sneaking into bed.

Jessica's gotta understand I'm doing what I have to do. Surely, she can't still be mad. And even if she is, so what? This is my fucking house. I'm sleeping in my goddamn bed.

In the bedroom, Jessica snored quietly. Shea tossed her hoodie and prospect cut onto the floor and fell against the dresser as she pulled off her boots. Twice mis-entering the combination of the small gun safe on the upper shelf of her closet. Once opened, she locked her pistol inside.

"Shea? You home?" Jessica's voice was muffled by her pillow.

Shea shimmied out of her clothes and slipped into bed. "Yeah. It's me."

"What time is it?"

"Late." The bed was starting to spin. "Hoo boy!"

"I really missed you tonight."

"I'm sorry, baby."

Jessica turned toward her. "So, you are a prospect now, huh?"

"Yeppers."

"This mean you'll be out drinking till all hours every night?"

"Nah, baby. I didn't mean to stay so long, but . . . ugh." She paused, trying to control the bed spins. "But I think I know who's selling hex at the clubs."

"Who?"

"Wait, uh, what's her name? Indigo. Yeah, that's it. Indigo, that fiend."

"The sister I met at Bike Night with the butch girl-friend? Why her?"

The vertigo began to fade. "No job, but all the time she's going out, partying, drinking. I mean, who does that with no job, right? Also, she drives this new fancy schmancy

BMW K1600GT. Fucking six-cylinder behemoth. All farkled up. Akrapovič exhaust, custom saddle, and all these electronic gizmos. Shit."

"She could have bought the bike before she lost her job. Or maybe her girlfriend paid for it."

"Maybe. But all night long, she kept excusing herself to take private calls. When I asked her what's up, she got all squirrelly. Like she's hiding something. I just know it's her."

"You really think the Confederate Thunder would have sold hex to a black member of a rival club?"

"When it comes to drugs, the only color the Thunder cares about is green. I'm telling you something hinkey is going on with that girl."

"So, what do you plan to do?"

"I need to get proof! Proof she's dealing."

"The last time you tried to prove someone was selling drugs, you and your ex got beat up and a Thunderman got killed. How long before the Thunder comes after you?"

"Ahhh . . . I have a solution to that. I saw Monster tonight." A satisfied smile crept across Shea's face.

"What'd he say?"

"Didn't say nothing." Shea giggled. "I just took his picture."

"His picture? I don't understand."

Shea reached down to the floor. The bed spins started up again. She steadied herself, pulled her phone out of her jeans pocket, and showed the photo to Jessica. "How's that for some proof?"

Jessica squinted as her eyes adjusted to the brightness of the phone's screen. "Is that Monster? Kissing a guy? I thought he was married. And straight."

"He is. But here he is outside the Bear's Den next to Gertie's. That dirty, dirty boy!"

"Oh my! What are you going to do with the photo?"

"I am gonna tell him that the Thunder better leave me and the Sisterhood alone. Otherwise, I'm gonna let the Thunder in on his secret."

"What'll the Thunder do if they learn he's gay?"

"Kick him out of the club. Kill him. Who knows?"

"Shea, I don't like this. Outing a man knowing they'll kill him for it? That's not right."

"Better him than us."

"And the guy he's kissing? Would they kill him, too?"

Shea laid the phone on the nightstand. Her eyelids felt heavy. "I don't know, Jessica. Right now, I'm too tired and too drunk . . ."

Jessica said something about coming up with an answer soon, but Shea was already drifting off.

27

"WHAT THE HELL IS THAT?" asked Terrance the following morning as Shea walked in and hung her hoodie and prospect cut on the coatrack in the Iron Goddess office.

"What?" Her head ached from the previous night's drinking. She poured herself a cup of coffee from the pot Terrance had made.

"You know damn well what. That vest. We agreed: no club colors. That includes you."

"I'm not wearing it. I hung it up."

Despite her suggestion that the Athenas lay low, Labrys had insisted the sisters—patched and prospect alike—wear their cuts whenever they rode. As if this show of solidarity would intimidate the Thunder.

So for now, she was wearing her prospect cut. Under her hoodie. It might get her booted from the club, but it might also save her life.

Terrance harrumphed as he sipped his coffee. "Since when are you a member of the Sisterhood anyway?"

"Since last night. I got voted in as a prospect."

Lakota appeared in the open doorway. "Shea, someone pulled up to the garage asking for you."

Shea grinned. *Monster.*

"Who is it?" asked Terrance warily.

"One of her Athena Sisterhood buddies from the looks of it."

Shea's smile faded. "Oh. Okay, I'll be right down."

"Shea, don't get messed up in something you can't get out of."

"Hey, that's what I'm best at." Shea took a long drag on her coffee before shuffling through the service bay.

Outside the garage doors, Indigo sat tall on her black and electric-blue BMW K1600GT. She wore a matching modular helmet with the front tipped up. "Morning, Havoc."

"Morning, Indigo." Shea had to admit it was a beautiful bike. *Amazing what a little drug money can buy you.* "What can I do for you?"

"The custom saddle I had made was supposed include the heater that came with the original seat. But so far, it doesn't seem to put out any heat. I was wondering if you could take a look."

"Where'd ya have the custom seat made?"

"Ojai, California. And I don't feel like driving out there. When I lived down in Phoenix, I went to MotoGhost for service. But since I moved to Bradshaw City, I can't find anyone that'll work on a Beemer. Can you help me out? I can pay cash."

"I'll have my crew take a look at it. Follow me to the sales counter. We'll get your work order written up."

Indigo dismounted her bike and followed Shea through the service bay, past the office, and into the showroom. "Wow, there really are some nice bikes here."

"Thanks. We try," said Shea as they arrived at the sales counter. "Lemme get your info, so I can put your real name and address in the computer."

Indigo set her driver's license on the counter, then pulled out a packet of tissues and blew her nose. She wasn't looking too good. Face ashen. Eyes watery. Is it a cold? The flu? Withdrawal?

Shea glanced at the ID as she typed the information into the system. "Zia Pearson. Cool name."

"Thanks," said Indigo. "I prefer Indigo though."

"How'd you get that road name?"

"My mother had a dress when I was a kid. The deepest blue I'd ever seen. I loved it. Just something magical about the hue. I asked her what color it was and she said indigo. Been my favorite ever since. Every time I see that color, I think of her."

"She still alive?" From her tone, Shea had a feeling Indigo's mother was dead.

"Naw, she died when I was thirteen."

Shea frowned. "Sorry to hear that."

"Yeah, it was rough. My daddy did all right, though we don't speak much anymore."

"Oh? How come?" *He not approve of your involvement in the drug trade?*

"Different journeys, different values," Indigo said with a dismissive shrug. She sneezed.

Shea winced as she felt the spray hit her in the face.

"Oh God, I'm so sorry. I think I'm coming down with something. I hope you don't get sick."

Shea wiped her face with a nearby shop rag and forced a smile. "Hey, it happens. No big deal. I'll have my electronics specialist take a look at your saddle, see what's up with the heater. You got a ride or d'you wanna wait for it?"

"I'll wait for it. I got nowhere to be this morning."

Shea pointed to the corner in the back of the store. "Waiting room's over there. Coffee's fresh. TV works most of the time."

"I appreciate it, Shea. I'm so glad you're a part of the Sisterhood."

"Me, too," said Shea. *But maybe not for the reasons you think,* she thought.

Shea returned to the service bay and handed the work order to Switch. "See if you can figure out why the heater's not working on this custom saddle."

"I can do that."

"Good. Everything kosher between you and Kyle?"

"I'm not Jewish. I'm Latina," said Switch with a straight face.

"Of course. My mistake. You two getting along?"

"Why wouldn't we?"

Shea opted not to answer. "Let me know when you've fixed the heated seat. Client's waiting on it."

Time to do a little research on Ms. Zia Pearson, Shea thought as she returned to the office.

"Was that Indigo I saw come in?" asked Terrance.

"You know her?"

His smiled faded, replaced by a look of embarrassment. "Yeah, I, uh, saw her at Bike Night."

Shea narrowed her gaze at him, smelling a lie. He was usually a straightforward guy, so when he wasn't, Shea knew it. "Why you got a weird look on your face, T?"

"What do you mean?" He stared at his computer.

"There's something you're not telling me."

"I don't know what you're talking about."

"You're a goddamn liar, Terrance Douglas. What the fuck's going on? You two used to date or something?"

"No, nothing like that."

"Well, there's something not right about that girl."

"What do you mean?" Terrance looked up from the computer.

"I think she's the one dealing the tainted hex and getting all these people killed."

"That's ridiculous. She'd never do anything like that."

"Okay, then what aren't you telling me?"

"I can't tell you. It's confidential."

"Since when do you keep secrets?"

"Shea, trust me. She's not the one you're looking for. She's a good person."

Shea grimaced, unconvinced. "Fine. If you say so."

Shea typed in Indigo's real name, Zia Pearson, into her browser. The first few hits were some Facebook pages and LinkedIn accounts. She clicked on each of the links, but found that the accounts didn't belong to Indigo. "Seems our girl is keeping a low profile online."

She did a news search for the name and came across a headline that read PHOENIX BILL COLLECTOR ARRESTED. She clicked on the link, but the news site only provided a teaser that revealed nothing other than the suggestion that Indigo had been arrested several months back. To read the article, she would have to become a paid subscriber. "Shit. Damn paywall."

"Are you Googling Indigo?" Terrance glared at her. "Leave the poor woman alone."

"Fine." Shea shoved her keyboard aside. "I'm gonna go work on the Stansbury bike."

"How's it coming along?"

Shea rolled her eyes. "We've got the frame done. I'm working on the tank. Kyle's working on the fenders. Still gotta do the front end, handlebars and oil pan, and then send the whole thing to paint."

"We need to move faster if we're going to meet our rush

deadline. Maybe if you spent more time here working on the bike and less time screwing around with the Athena Sisterhood."

"Oh please, the Sisterhood is our target market. If you were hanging out with them, you'd call it marketing or public relations or some such nonsense."

"Nevertheless, you miss our deadline, it's going to cost us money."

"All right, T! Geez! I get your point." Shea stood. "Everybody fucking wants something from me."

"Life's tough sometimes."

"Yeah, well there's only so much Shea awesomeness to go around."

She left the office, walked through the service bay without so much as a look at the Stansbury bike, and stepped out the back door to make a phone call.

"Detective Rios. How can I help you?"

"Hey, it's Shea. I wanted to let you know that I got voted in as a prospect with the Athena Sisterhood. And I think I may know who's dealing the tainted hex."

"I don't want a repeat of our raid on the Confederate Thunder's cabin. I need solid proof if I'm going to get a warrant."

"I know. I'm working on that." Her call waiting beeped in her ear. "I gotta go. I'll call you when I got something."

Shea clicked over to the other call. "Yeah?"

"Shea-Shea, we gotta talk."

A big grin broke out across her face. "Hello, Monster. Screw any cute boys lately?"

"Where the hell'd you get that photo?"

"Snapped it last night when you and that guy were making out."

"It wasn't me."

"Bullshit. I saw you clear as day. Walked right past ya. Woulda stopped and said 'Hey,' but you seemed a little busy giving your boyfriend a tonsillectomy."

Monster was silent for a moment. "All right, look. It was a onetime thing. I ain't no faggot."

"Whatever you say. I'm a dyke, so it ain't like I care either way. But your buddies in the Thunder might. And we both know this wasn't no onetime thing."

"Look, I can't talk right now, but you and me, we need to come to some terms."

"Yeah, I'll say. Nice job, by the way, framing me for killing Gator."

"Come by the house tomorrow night. Julia can cook dinner. And bring Annie and that colored girl of yours."

"Her name is Jessica."

"Fine, bring Jessica."

"How do I know this ain't just a setup to kill me and Jess, so you can take Annie for yourself?"

"Shea-Shea, how could you think such a thing? You're family."

"Don't bullshit me, Monster. Gator's dead because One-Shot tried to kill me while you and Mackey were kicking the shit out of my club president. You wanna meet? We do it public."

"Fine, where?"

"The county fair. Me and Jess are taking Annie there tomorrow evening. You meet me by the Ferris wheel around seven, we'll talk."

"Julia and me can spend some time with Annie while I'm there?"

"Depends how things go. They go well, sure. They don't go so well, everybody finds out about your tastes in men. And FYI, something happens to me or my family, my lawyer has instructions to post that photo and a few others I took all over social media."

"Fine. Tomorrow night at seven by the Ferris wheel."

28

WHEN INDIGO HAD SETTLED up her bill, Shea escorted her to her bike and handed her the keys. Indigo's eyes were dull and watering, her voice hoarse. "No offense, Indigo, but you look like shit."

"I feel like shit. I just want to go to bed and zone out." Indigo blew her nose and rubbed her head. "Unfortunately, I still have one more errand to run."

Errand, huh? Like scoring some dope? "Is it something I can do for you?" Shea forced a smile.

"Oh no. It's kinda personal." Indigo pulled on her helmet. "But thanks for offering. And thanks for fixing my seat heater. As achy as I feel, I'm going to need it on my way home."

"Ride safe out there."

Indigo started the bike, then gave Shea the thumbs-up. Shea waved and ran to the office, slipping on her hoodie.

"What's up?" asked Terrance.

"Be back in a while." She grabbed the keys to one of the production sports bikes. "Gonna take one of the bikes for a test ride."

"A test ride?"

She raced out of the office, into the garage, hopped on the bike she'd grabbed the keys for and headed around to the main road. *Which way did you go, Indigo?* she wondered. *North or south?*

To the left the road descended Sycamore Mountain and south toward Shea's neighborhood. There wasn't much else in that direction for miles. She turned right and raced north through town hoping she didn't get stopped by one of Sheriff Buzzkill's deputies.

Five minutes later and still no sign of Indigo. *Did I turn the right way?* Had she gone south instead?

Shea twisted the throttle further. The speedometer creep past eighty, ninety, and into the triple digits. The motorcycle blazed past cattle ranches and roared through sweeping turns that wound among the high desert hills.

She spotted a single motorcycle chugging along a couple of miles ahead of her. Was it Indigo? There was a lot of motorcycle traffic this time of the year. Riders came up from Phoenix and Tucson to see some fall colors.

Shea narrowed the gap to half a mile and could make out a tall rider sitting upright on the distinctive six-cylinder engine of BMW K1600GT. *Indigo!*

Tailing someone wasn't really in Shea's wheelhouse. Most of the time, she was the one being pursued, either by cops or by gangsters. So, she wasn't sure how close was too close. She didn't want to lose her, but also didn't want to spook her quarry.

What's Terrance not telling me about Indigo? she wondered. Twenty years earlier he'd served time for possession. Maybe they went to the same NA meetings. That would explain his keeping Indigo's secrets. It wouldn't be the first time a drug dealer hung out at NA meetings, trolling for business.

The first traffic light near Ironwood turned yellow as Indigo approached it. Shea feared Indigo would zip through the light, leaving Shea stuck until it turned green again. But Indigo stopped. As Shea drew closer, she feared Indigo would recognize her.

A single car crossed through the intersection. The light remained red. Indigo glanced at Shea through her mirrors.

Don't look at me. Don't look at me. Goddamn it, why doesn't the light turn green? Why can't ADOT program these damn lights better?

The light turned green. The K1600GT's six cylinders rumbled and Indigo flew down the road. Shea kept her distance and was able to put a few cars between them, alleviating her fear of being recognized.

As they got into town, Indigo turned north onto Shadow Rock Road and pulled into the Bradshaw Park parking lot. A decade earlier, families came to Bradshaw Park for picnics, to feed the geese, and to ride two-person pedal boats across the pond.

But over the years, the park changed. Dope fiends and hustlers had replaced the pedal boats and geese. Every sign and picnic table was tagged with graffiti. Dirty needles and used condoms littered the weed-choked lawn.

Shea parked on the opposite side of the lot, took cover behind a large Ford pickup, and pulled out her phone hoping to record Indigo making a buy.

Indigo approach a tall person in a hoodie holding a paper grocery bag with the top rolled closed. They hugged and appeared to exchange pleasantries. Indigo unrolled the paper sack and pulled out a gallon-size plastic bag of what looked like syringes, though it was hard to tell from where Shea's stood.

Indigo returned the plastic bag to the paper sack and pulled out a small cardboard box, from which she withdrew a small vial. The supplier gestured with his hands like he was explaining something important Shea couldn't hear.

What the hell's in the bottle? Morphine? Fentanyl? Keta-mine? Whatever it is, it sure ain't legal if she's buying it here.

Indigo glanced around, shifting her weight from one foot to the other.

You goddamn junkie, Shea thought. *I'm gonna nail your ass to the wall for killing Pipes and them other women.*

Indigo handed the bag person a thick envelope. Shea guessed it contained cash. The two shook hands and Indigo hustled back to her bike, where she locked the paper sack in the top case on her bike.

Shea rushed back to her own motorcycle. The video she took with her phone would help, but she needed a closer look at whatever was in the sack. She couldn't afford to let Indigo get out of this.

Indigo cruised out of the lot.

SHEA KEPT at least two cars between her and Indigo as they traveled to the east side of Ironwood, not far from the Central Arizona University campus. Ten minutes later, Indigo pulled into a CVS Pharmacy parking lot. Shea hoped Indigo would be in there long enough for her to get a peek at the drugs.

When Indigo walked inside, Shea raced over to Indigo's bike and pulled out her lock-picking kit. She'd never picked a BMW top case before. The lock was quite different from normal door locks. But Shea was determined to see what was inside.

She slipped in the tension wrench and then used a pick the explore the interior of the lock. The tumblers moved out from the center rather than from one side and there were eight of them rather than the usual five or six. She applied the slightest pressure on the tension wrench and managed to set two of the pins right away.

She glanced at the front door of the pharmacy, but there was no sign of Indigo. *Good.* She hunkered down and focused on the remaining six pins. The third one gave her some trouble but finally set. Then the fourth. She glanced up once again. Still no sign of Indigo. *Maybe things are finally going my way.*

She set the final pins in a matter of seconds, turned the cylinder, and the top case latch released, giving her the same thrill she got from boosting cars when she was fifteen.

Shea lifted the lid of the top case and dug into the paper sack. Sure enough, the plastic bag was filled with syringes. Roughly a hundred of them. Shea pulled out her phone and took a quick snapshot. She was about to fish deeper into the bag when someone grabbed her from behind and threw her to the ground.

"What the fuck're you doing with my bike?"

Shea glared up at Indigo. "Catching a murderer."

"Havoc? What the hell?"

"Don't give me that shit. You're the one dealing drugs."

"Dealing drugs? Have you lost your damn mind?"

"Oh yeah?" Shea scrambled to her feet and held up the bag of syringes. "Then what are these for?"

"Maybe I'm diabetic."

"Since when do they sell insulin at Bradshaw Park? Don't bullshit me, Indigo. You're the one dealing the hex that's killing those women."

Indigo's eyes brimmed with tears. "You don't know a goddamn thing."

"If I'm wrong, prove it."

"You wanna know what I bought, Miss Busybody?" Indigo held up the bag, her arm shaking with rage. "Fine!"

She reached into the sack and pulled out a box and tossed it at Shea. "Read for yourself."

Shea examined the label. "Estradiol valerate? Why would . . . oh shit! I'm so sorry. That's why Terrance knew you."

"Terrance told you I was trans?" shrieked Indigo, tears streaming down her face.

"No, he just said he knew you. Wouldn't say how. I had no idea you were transgender."

"Well, now you do." Indigo snatched the box from Shea's hand and jammed it back into the bag. "Satisfied?"

"But I read online you got arrested."

"What? You been checking up on me? Damn you, Havoc!"

"So, you weren't arrested?"

"Some punk cop named Aguilar clocked me as trans and arrested me for soliciting."

"Soliciting?"

"Yeah, he figures I'm black and I'm trans, so I must be a ho. Because who could possibly believe that a black trans woman could actually have a job?"

"I thought you said you're currently unemployed."

"After that asshole Aguilar arrested me, my boss fucking fired me because I was in jail for a weekend when I shoulda been at work."

Shea felt like shit. This was not what she wanted to be doing. "I'm so sorry. Really. I've run into Aguilar before. You're right. He is an asshole."

"He's not the only asshole." Indigo glared at her. "Stalking me. Breaking into my top case. I should have you arrested, you know that?"

Shea sighed. "Please don't. I was wrong, I know that. And I won't tell a soul you're trans." She put her hand on

Indigo's arm and was grateful she didn't pull away. "I was upset about Pipes dying."

"You realize I had to fight just to be allowed *in* the Sisterhood. Labrys was against it. Didn't feel I was a *real* woman. Treated me like I was some tired old drag queen invading women's spaces."

"I don't think that way. You're a woman, same as me. End of story. Anything else is none of my business."

"Damn right it's not." Indigo pulled out her pack of tissues, blew her nose, and wiped her eyes. "Like I need this shit. I'm coming down with the flu or a cold, and now I catch you poking around in my shit."

Shea held out her arms. "How about a hug?"

Indigo continued to glare at her for a moment. Then her face softened and she embraced Shea. "I hope you catch whatever I got."

"If I do, I deserve it."

29

———

AROUND SIX THE NEXT EVENING, Shea and Jessica led Annie past the Cortes County Fair entrance. The brisk air smelled of cotton candy, cooking grease, and livestock. Laughter, screams of delight, and tinny carnival music created a familiar mixture that summoned one of Shea's few happy childhood memories. Annie's eyes went wide with wonder at spectacle.

"Wow! Can I go on one of those rides?" Annie pointed to a towering machine swinging cockpits full of people side to side, spinning end over end.

"Ugh, makes me sick just seeing it," said Jessica with a horrified look.

"You sure you can handle it, Doodlebug?" asked Shea. She had to admit it did look like fun. And better to ride it now than when Annie had a belly full of snacks. "Looks pretty intense."

"I ride on the back of your motorcycle, Aunt Shea. I think I can handle *that*."

"Well, let's go see how long the line is."

Annie grabbed Shea's hand and dragged her through

the crowd as fast as she could go with Jessica trailing behind. A couple of dozen people stood in the line.

"How long's the wait?" Shea asked the machine's operator, a fiftyish man with a scruffy goatee, a round belly, and a dull expression.

"Hell if I know. I just run the machine."

Shea compared the number of people on the ride with those still in line. "Looks like it might be fifteen, twenty minutes. You wanna wait that long?"

"Yes, yes, yes! I want to ride it," replied Annie, jumping up and down.

Shea shrugged. "Okay, well, you're the boss."

"Really?"

"Well, not of everything. Just what we do this evening. Within reason."

"I'm getting kind of hungry myself," said Jessica. "You mind if I check out the food vendors?"

Shea gave her a kiss and grinned when she caught a passerby gawking. "Take a picture! It'll last longer."

The gawker flipped her off and stomped away.

"Shea, stop teasing the straights."

"As you wish. Maybe you could get us some weird deep-fried things."

"Weird deep-fried things?"

"You know, deep-fried Snickers bars. Deep-fried birthday cake. Deep-fried coffee."

"Deep-fried coffee? How does that even work?"

"Got no idea. But they're always frying up something crazy."

"I'll see what I can find. Y'all be careful on that contraption."

Shea and Annie took their place at the end of the line. Above them, people screamed and cheered as the ride whirled them in all directions. Despite the bustle of people, Shea found herself relaxing for the first time in weeks. No worrying about drug dealers or motorcycle clubs. Just a time to be a normal family, whatever the hell normal was.

"Well, look who's here?"

Shea turned to see Labrys walking up to her wearing her Sisterhood cut over a navy quilted coat. *Please, not now.* All the joy escaped from her like air out of a balloon. "Uh, hi, Labrys."

"Taking the little one for a ride, prospect?"

"Something like that." Shea looked around to see if Jessica was in view. The last thing she wanted was for the two of them to get into a shouting match. Or worse.

"You're not wearing your cut, I see."

Shea shrugged. "No, just a night out with the family. It's not a club function."

"You should be wearing it. Even with your, uh, leverage photo, we need to demonstrate Sisterhood solidarity. To show those assholes from the Thunder we will not be intimidated. I saw one of them walking around earlier with his old lady."

"Tell me, Labrys. Did you ride your bike here?"

"No, I took the Audi. Why?"

"Most MCs prohibit wearing club colors unless you're on a bike."

Labrys tilted her head and folded her arms across her chest. "Did I just hear a *prospect* try to tell her *president* the rules of our club?"

"Hello, Deb." Jessica returned carrying a large drink and something wrapped in red-checkered waxed paper. Her expression hardened into a mask of contempt. "Why are you here?"

"Excuse me? I don't recall needing your permission to be here."

"Why are you here talking to Shea? Is this some club meeting I'm not aware of?"

"Havoc, you need to muzzle your old lady."

Jessica's jaw dropped. "Shea, you need to tell this bitch to step off before I show her how tough she's not."

Shea stepped between the two women and held up her hands. "Hey, can we take things down a notch in front of my niece?"

"Fine," said Jessica, "but she needs to go. This is our family time. You promised."

Labrys scoffed. "Havoc, you—"

"Labrys, shut it!" Shea's eyes locked on Labrys, whose face flushed pink.

"What did you say to me?"

"I know I'm just a prospect, but we're here for some family time. Club business and solidarity and whatever will have to wait for another night."

"Oh really? Dictating terms are we, prospect?"

"If that means I'm outta the club, so be it. But I been neglecting my family for the past week or so and I intend to make up for that."

Labrys glowered at Shea and Jessica.

"Aunt Shea, the line's moving!"

Labrys' expression softened into a fake half smile as she glanced down at Annie. "Family is important. So, I'll leave y'all to it."

"Thanks, Labrys."

"But from here on out, I expect you to follow orders. Are we clear?"

"Crystal."

"Y'all have a good night." Labrys walked off whistling Melissa Etheridge's "Come to My Window."

"Jessica, before you say anything, know that I hate her as much as you do."

"I doubt that's even possible. You have no idea how much I despise that woman."

"Yeah, well, get to know her as long as I have, you'll learn to hate her even more. Trust me."

"Aunt Shea, come on! It's our turn." Annie grabbed Shea's hand and dragged her off.

"Y'all have fun!" Jessica waved as they passed through the gate and took their seats aboard the ride.

AT FIRST, the ride was like racing up a twisty mountain road at high speed, spinning the car they were in around and at various angles. Annie giggled and screamed with delight, bringing a smile to Shea's face.

Then the flipping and rolling began.

Shea was feeling a little green when their car finally came to a stop. The operator unlocked their restraints. Annie jumped off and bounced up and down, "Can we go again? Can we?"

Shea stumbled a bit as her equilibrium readjusted. "Maybe in a bit, Doodlebug. Your auntie needs a moment to regain her land legs."

They followed the crowd and found Jessica by the ride's exit. "Wanna try one of these deep-fried Sriracha balls?" She held out a white plastic fork, on the end of which was what looked like a reddish hush puppy.

Shea's stomach did a cartwheel at the thought of spicy food. "I'll pass for now."

"I wanna try one!" insisted Annie.

"I dunno, Annie. They're spicy."

"I like spicy."

"What do you think?" Jessica looked to Shea.

"I'm the boss, Aunt Shea. You said so."

Shea shrugged. "Let her try a bite."

Jessica held out a Sriracha ball to Annie. "I'm telling you, it's hot."

"I can handle it." Annie bit into it. For a second, she appeared to enjoy it. Then her cheeks flushed. Her eyes and mouth opened wide with pain, her hand fanning the bite of Sriracha ball on the edge of her tongue, hopping around. "Hot, hot, hot!"

"Here ya go, little princess." Monster emerged from the crowd along with his wife, Julia. He handed her a large Styrofoam cup.

Annie grabbed it and took a long drag on the straw. After a moment the pink faded from Annie's face and she took a deep breath.

"So good to see you again, Shea-Shea," said Julia, reaching out to her. She had put on weight since Shea last saw her. Her skin was tan as always, but more weathered and sagging beneath the eyes. The thick braid that had always been her trademark had turned from mahogany to silver. She still wore a cut that read PROPERTY OF MONSTER on the back.

"Good to see you, Aunt Julia." Shea embraced her, catching a whiff of weed from her hair.

Julia had always been like a fun aunt to her. At thirteen, Shea had confided to Julia about her attraction to girls. Julia hadn't batted an eye and never told a soul as far as Shea knew, not even Shea's mother, with whom Julia was close.

And now Shea held proof of a secret that would devastate her marriage to Monster. It saddened Shea for what it would do to Julia. She hoped she wouldn't have to play that card. But if Monster wouldn't or couldn't keep the Thunder from retaliating, she would do what was necessary.

"Julia, Monster, this is my girlfriend, Jessica."

"Nice to finally meet you," said Julia, shaking Jess' hand.

"Likewise," said Jessica.

"You're early," said Shea to Monster. Never in the years she'd known him had he set off her gaydar. *Some people just hide it better than others,* she thought.

"Just enjoying the fair with my old lady." He gave Julia a squeeze, then bent down to meet eyes with Annie. "Whatcha been eating that set your mouth on fire, little princess?"

"Aunt Jessica gave me Sriracha fire balls." She continued to fan her mouth with her free hand, the drink firmly gripped in the other.

Julia raised an eyebrow. "You giving this child spicy foods?"

"First of all, she insisted on trying it," said Shea. "Second of all, she's fine. Mexican kids eat spicy food all the time." Shea glared at Monster.

Annie hugged Julia. "I missed you, Gramma Julia."

"Missed you, too, sweetheart."

Monster's expression grew serious. "Shea, you and I need to talk."

"Jess, I'll be back in a minute." Shea led Monster over to a place next to one of the tents, out of the flow of traffic."

"So," said Shea, unable to keep from smirking. "Now you switch-hit for the all-boys' team, huh?"

Monster wouldn't meet her gaze. "I don't have to explain myself to you."

"No, but you might have to explain yourself to Julia. Or even One-Shot and the boys."

Monster looked up at her, fear and anger in his eyes. "Shea-Shea, please. You tell Julia, it'll kill her. You tell the club, well . . ."

"They'll kill you. I know that. But right now, they want to kill me and the gals in the Sisterhood. So, if you want this to remain our little secret, you best convince them to live and let live."

"How'm I supposed to do that? Gator's dead. One-Shot's still recovering from the bullet you put in him. All 'cause you tried to break into the cabin. What the hell were you looking for, anyways?"

"The hex you stole from the Jags. Somebody recut it with rat poison and people are dying."

"We sold that shit a while ago."

"To who?"

"I never met 'em."

"But you know who it is."

"Shea, if they found out I told you anything—"

"And if you don't tell me, I post that photo to the club's Facebook page."

Monster rubbed his face and beard. "Why you gotta be like this?"

"Because women are dying, Monster. Innocent women."

"Fine. We sold the hex to someone named Bonefish."

"Bonefish? Never heard of him."

"Me neither. I wasn't involved in the exchange, so I never saw the dude. Just heard the name."

"How do I find this Bonefish?"

"I hear he owns a bar."

"What bar?"

"Sports bar called the Tenth Inning."

"In downtown Ironwood?"

"Yeah." He took a deep breath and let it out. "Jesus Christ on a cracker, I'm a dead man."

"Long as the Thunder backs off, you ain't got nothing to worry about."

"Yeah, easier said than done. Now can Julia and me start spending time with Annie?"

Shea studied him. She'd never seen him so humbled

and broken like this. In his prime, he'd been a ruthless enforcer for the club. How long had he been living this double life? Years? Decades? And now the threat of exposure had completely unraveled him.

"A few hours once a month."

"Bless you, Shea-Shea."

"Supervised."

"Supervised? What do ya think we're gonna do? Molest our own grandbaby? I may be, uh . . ."

"Gay? Come on, you can say the word."

"Fine. I'm gay. But I ain't no pedophile."

"You prove you can handle this *and* you're not involved in any violence, then I'll consider unsupervised visits. I can't risk exposing Annie to more of the club's shit."

Monster crossed his arms and kicked the dirt. "I guess it's a start."

"But I'm serious. I hear the Thunder's hurt someone and you're involved in any way, that'll be the last you see of Annie. And I post the photo of you and your little bear cub. Oh and one more thing, that video of me shooting Hunter. I want it gone and not a word to anyone."

"Hand to God, I swear." He held out his hand and Shea shook it. "Now let's get back with them. I need to spend some time with my old lady and my grandbaby."

30

———

Indigo rode her K1600GT north on the dark road to Bradshaw City after she and Savage had spent the evening at Orphan's apartment. Savage was riding at her five o'clock on her Honda Shadow 750.

The worst of her cold symptoms were gone thanks to the home-remedy concoction Savage had given her, some pungent combination of kale, spinach, ginger, garlic, and horseradish. Maybe the cold germs found the remedy as distasteful as she did and skedaddled.

The full moon glowed orange over the eastern horizon, burnishing the distant hilltops. This was the bliss she had longed for in the lonely days before her transition. Being acknowledged and accepted for who she was by friends who didn't feel the need to put her in a box.

Savage's romantic interest in her had taken her by surprise. Indigo had all but given up on ever being in a relationship again. Too many lesbians wanted nothing to do with trans women. But Savage didn't seem to have a problem with it. Indigo was almost afraid to hope this could turn into something long term.

The ribbon of highway climbed through a series of sweeping curves. Mountains rose up to their right, blocking their view of the moon. To the left, the land fell away into a deep valley.

A cluster of headlights appeared in her left-side mirror. At first, she figured they were a couple of cars, but the throaty rumble of their engines told a different story. A group of Harleys. Four, maybe five of them.

The Athena Sisterhood cuts she and Savage were wearing suddenly felt like giant targets on their backs. Indigo tried to ignore the tremor of fear creeping up her spine. *Plenty of motorcycles around. Chances of them being Thundermen are slim.*

The other bikers caught up with Indigo and Savage and pulled alongside them in the oncoming lane.

Nothing to see here. Just go on past.

Indigo looked over. The biker next to her pulled ahead just far enough for her to see his Confederate Thunder patches gleaming in the moonlight. Her heart pounded.

"Leave us alone!" shouted Indigo, her voice all but drowned out by the roar of the wind.

The Thunderman kicked at her front tire. Indigo's BMW bobbled for a second but recovered. She twisted the throttle. Her bike rocketed away from her pursuers.

In her left-side mirror, she watched in horror as the other bikers converged on Savage, who's 750cc Harley Street had no chance of outrunning the Thundermen's larger bikes. Savage's headlight wobbled to the right and disappeared off the side of the road.

Indigo tried not to think about what they would do to her as a trans woman of color if they caught her. But she couldn't abandon her girlfriend to those animals. She had to turn around.

The Thundermen caught up to her as she slowed, surrounding her in front, on her left, and from behind.

She swerved onto the shoulder and locked up her brakes. The Thunderman zipped past, one nearly clipping her. They disappeared around a curve.

Indigo took a moment to catch her breath, then turned her bike around to look for Savage. The shoulder of the northbound lane, where Savage had disappeared, had a small gulley, unlike the steep downhill on the southbound side.

Indigo putted back down the road in first gear with her high beams, struggling to hear or see anything that would indicate Savage's presence. A glow of a headlight caught her eye. *I see ya, girl. I'm coming.*

As she approached, the Thundermen came charging up behind her like a pack of lions. A heavyset Thunderman on a beefy Electra Glide kicked the side of her bike. Indigo struggled to maintain control but at the lower speed, she didn't have enough inertia to resist the blow. The bike swerved off the road and plummeted down the hill. For an instant, Indigo felt the crushing weight of her motorcycle roll over her before she slid into unconsciousness.

SHEA LAY in bed next to Jessica, gazing into her eyes, after the two of them had made love for the first time in weeks. "God, I've missed this."

Jessica grazed her nails along the back of Shea's neck. "Maybe if you spent more time at home . . ."

"I know, baby. I know." Shea closed her eyes, riding the high of her last orgasm, amplified by Jess's electric touch. "If Monster can get the Thunder to back off, and if this lead on the hex pans out, maybe the three of us can take a vacation somewhere. Once I get this one custom bike finished, that is."

"That's a whole lot of ifs," said Jessica.

"Trust me, it'll happen." Shea's phone rang. "Good Lord! Who the hell's calling this time o' night?"

"Just send it to voicemail."

"I intend to." Shea rolled over picked up the phone from the nightstand. "Shit. I gotta take this."

"Why?"

"Labrys, it's eleven thirty at night. What the fuck?"

"Got a call from Savage. A group of Thundermen ran her and Indigo off the road four miles north of Ironwood on Highway 89."

"They okay?"

"Savage is fine. Indigo's a little banged up, but she'll live. You've got a bike trailer, right, prospect?"

"Yeah . . ." Shea didn't like where this conversation was going.

"Does it have a winch on it?"

"Yeah, it's got a winch."

Jessica scrunched her face in annoyance and shook her head. Shea held up her free hand and shrugged her shoulders.

"Go pick them up."

Shea took a deep breath and let it out. "Yeah, all right. This is why we should be laying low right now. Not wearing our cuts everywhere."

"Don't tell me how to run my club, prospect. I will deal with the Thunder."

"How?"

"Never you mind. Just get out there and rescue Indigo and Savage."

"Labrys, don't do nothing stupid. You'll get yourself killed."

"I know what I'm doing. You just do what you're told, prospect."

"Shit. All right. I'll go pick them up." Shea slammed the phone on the nightstand. "Dammit!"

"What's going on?" asked Jessica.

"Indigo and Savage got run off the road by the Thundermen."

Jessica buried her face in her hands. "I thought Monster was gonna get them to lay off."

"Maybe he hasn't had a chance to talk to them. Or maybe he did and they blew him off. I don't know. But I can't let Savage and Indigo freeze to death out there."

"So why do you have to go? Can't someone else pick them up."

"For starters, I have a motorcycle trailer. And as a prospect, I'm at the bottom of the pecking order."

"How long will you be gone?"

Shea rubbed her face and sighed. "Not more than a few hours."

"Well, hurry home. This bed gets awfully lonely without you."

Savage was sitting with her arm around Indigo on the side of the road when Shea pulled up in the shop truck pulling the enclosed bike trailer. The full moon was almost directly overhead, giving everything a silvery glow.

"Y'all all right?" asked Shea as she climbed out of the cab of the truck. She shined her flashlight at them.

Savage shielded her eyes from the light. "I'm fine. Not so sure about Indigo. Her bike landed on her when she went tumbling down that hill over yonder."

Shea kneeled down in front of Indigo. "How ya feeling, girl?"

"Cold," Indigo grumbled, her hands on her temples.

"She was seeing double earlier and having a hard time walking straight," added Savage.

"I'll be all right once I get warm," said Indigo rather tersely. "Don't need to go to no hospital."

"Indigo, you should have a doc look at you. You could have a concussion, internal bleeding, broken ribs." Shea put a hand on Indigo's arm.

Indigo pulled her arm away. "Don't tell me what to do, Havoc. I'm still mad at you for the other day."

"Look, I'm real sorry about that. Truly I am. But concussions ain't no joke. Seriously, I had a cousin die from one."

Indigo scoffed. "Last time I went to Cortes Regional, they refused to treat me 'cause I'm trans. I was running 104-degree fever and they were all, *'We don't know how to treat your kind.'* Such bullshit. I ain't going back there."

Shea sighed. "I'm sorry that happened to you. I know a good doctor in the ER. I can make a call if you want."

"I'll see how I feel in the morning." Indigo started shivering.

"Well, let's get you warm at least." Shea helped her up and into the cab of the truck, then started the engine. "Sit tight while we get your bikes."

Shea closed the door and turned to Savage. "You guys call the cops?"

"Naw, we called Labrys first. She said not to."

Shea grimaced. "You get a look at the guys who did this?"

"Four or five Thundermen. There was a medium-sized guy with long dark hair and scrunched-up face."

"Probably Mackey."

"A really tall guy with a big revolver on his belt."

"Sounds like One-Shot."

"I didn't get a good look at anyone else."

Shea scanned the area with her flashlight and spotted Savage's motorcycle lying on its right side in a gulley. She climbed down the embankment, hefted the bike onto its side stand, and inspected it. "Tires look okay. No damage to the wheels. Gotta mean scratch the length of the tank. Your front fender is bent, but I may be able to make it drivable. You try to start it?"

"Not yet. How we gonna get it up out of the gully? It's all rocky and I can't hardly see shit," said Savage.

"Lemme deal with this fender first. Don't need it tearing up your tire. Then we'll see about getting it outta the gully."

Shea climbed back up to the truck, opened the trailer, and pulled out a long pry bar, which she used to bend the bike's front fender away from the wheel.

Satisfied, she tossed the pry bar up onto the shoulder of the road. "Let's see if it still runs." She swung a leg over the seat, turned the key, and pressed the starter. It revved a little but didn't quite catch.

"You think the engine's busted?" asked Savage.

"Probably just needs a little coaxing. Bikes ain't meant to be on their side." Shea pressed the starter again, and after a little encouragement with the throttle it sputtered to life.

"Whew," said Savage. "That's a relief. How you gonna get it back onto the road?"

"You'll see. Better scoot back. It'll probably kick up some rocks."

Savage stepped back toward the truck. When she was clear, Shea gunned the motor, sending up a rooster tail of debris, then floored it up the steep embankment onto the road.

"Fuck yeah! That's what I'm talking about," said Shea, her heart pounding with excitement. "That shit'll make your butt pucker. Whew!"

"You think it's okay to ride home?"

"I reckon so. I didn't see any disconnected lines and don't smell any fuel, so should make it home at least. If it gives you any problems, gimme another call. Now, where's Indigo's bike?"

Savage pointed down the hill on the other side of the road. "Down there somewhere."

Shea's joy evaporated. "Crap." She shined the flashlight down the grassy hillside until the light glinted off of something metallic. "There it is! About forty feet down the hill."

"How we gonna get it up here?"

"Truck's got a winch on it. I think we can pull it up here. Probably ain't ridable." Shea walked to the front of the truck and pulled out the hook and cable to its full length, then shimmied her way down to where Indigo's bike lay.

All fairings had ripped off and the tank was naked. The front tire was torn around a twisted wheel and hanging on to a bent telelever front end. Shea hooked the cable around the forks just above the "A" arm.

"Savage," called Shea, "you know how to operate the winch?"

"Yeah, I think so."

"Take up the slack. Slowly. I'll let you know when to stop."

The winch motor hummed and the cable grew taut. "Okay, stop!"

Shea readjusted the cable to make sure the hook wasn't going to slip off. "Okay, ease her on up."

The cable groaned and strained. With a grind and crunch, the bike dragged up the hillside, cutting a groove in the prairie grass and mowing down the occasional prickly pear cactus. Shea followed along beside it.

The groaning grew more pronounced. With a loud crack, "A" snapped free and the front end broke off the frame. The rest of the motorcycle slid back down the hill about ten feet.

"Hold it!" Shea shouted. "Put the winch in neutral."

Shea pulled the hook and cable back down and ran the cable through the front wheel, then down the hill again to hook it to the main bike frame. "Okay, pull her up again."

The winch dragged both sections of the motorcycle up to the street.

Savage came over as Shea inspected the broken front end.

"Damn, that bike is toast," said Savage.

Shea sighed. "That'd be my guess. Let's get it onto the bed of the truck."

The two of them heaved the pieces of motorcycle up the ramp and into the back of the trailer, then strapped them in place with tie-downs. Once Shea was sure they were secure, she stepped over to the cab of the truck.

Indigo rolled down the window. "How bad is it?"

"Well, I'll tell it to ya straight. You, my dear, are the proud owner of seven hundred pounds of scrap metal."

"Fuck. Just what I needed." Indigo held her temples in her hands.

"I can haul what's left of it back to Iron Goddess so your insurance adjuster can take a look at it. You need me to drop y'all off somewhere?"

"We were going up to Indigo's place for the night," said Savage. "I guess we can ride two-up on my bike."

Shea looked at Savage's Street. "Not much of a passenger seat and no sissy bar. You think you can hold on?" she asked Indigo.

Indigo opened the door and gingerly stepped out of the truck. "I should be okay. Thanks for helping us, Havoc." She gave Shea a fist bump.

"Anything for my sisters." Shea turned to Savage. "You ever hear back from those three members that were missing a few nights ago?"

Savage's face darkened. "Raven, Goth, and Pixie? No. I'm really worried. I hope the Thundermen haven't gotten to them, too."

Shea nodded. "Let's hope. Take it slow going home. I can follow y'all as far as Bradshaw City."

"I appreciate it," said Savage as she tightened the chin-strap on her helmet.

Shea leaned into Savage, as if to give her a hug. "Drive her over to the new hospital up there in Bradshaw City," Shea whispered. "Maybe she'll have better luck with the staff. S'pposed to be state of the art."

"Will do, Havoc. Thanks again." Savage patted her on the back and mounted her bike.

Indigo winced as she pulled her helmet back on and climbed onto the back of Savage's bike, wrapping her arms around Savage's husky middle. They eased down the road, keeping to the speed limit.

Shea followed them until they hit the limits of Bradshaw City. After a quick stop for a bag of spicy pork rinds at a convenience store, she turned around and headed south to Sycamore Springs.

On the way back, she nibbled on the pork rinds, letting the burn keep her awake on the dark road.

Something from earlier still worried her. Was Labrys planning to retaliate against the Thunder? The last thing they needed was for the violence to escalate.

She flipped on the radio to pull her out of her thoughts. "You're listening to today's country, KORT-FM, Ironwood," said the radio announcer. "A heads-up for folks on the road near Bradshaw City—we just got word from the Cortes County Sheriff's Office that Pine Road is closed in both directions due to a massive fire at Bootlegger Bob's, a popular biker bar just east of town. No word yet of any injuries, but we will—"

Shea switched it off. Bootlegger Bob's was a Thunder bar. Shea's gut told her Labrys was somehow responsible.

Rios arrived at her desk to find a yellow Post-it note attached to her monitor.

See me when you get in this morning. —LT

She took a deep breath and let it out. She hadn't heard anything back from Shea about her supposed lead on the tainted hex. While security footage from Trip-Hop and other clubs showed members of the Sisterhood dancing, it failed to confirm the one witness' story that the Sisterhood was dealing hex in the restrooms. Interviews and background investigations on the victims had also led to dead ends.

No doubt Goodman was calling her into his office to chew her out for not closing these cases.

The glass door to his office was open. Goodman had a half-eaten breakfast burrito in one hand and was wiping something off his tie with the other.

"You wanted to see me?"

"Yeah, come in." He set the burrito down, wiped his hands on the napkin before handing her a note from a phone message pad. "Got a call from the fire marshal. Someone burned down Bootlegger Bob's last night."

"The Confederate Thunder's bar?" Rios' jaw went slack from disbelief as she stared at the note. "Holy crap! Any casualties?"

"Five dead. Four more admitted with serious burns. Several others treated at the scene for smoke inhalation."

"Who'd be insane enough to set fire to Bootlegger Bob's?"

"Interesting you should ask that question." He picked up three case files and set them in front of her. "These are those other three arson cases I mentioned to you before. They were originally assigned to Property Crimes. All have similar burn patterns and multiple ignition points, suggesting a coordinated attack. The fire inspector's saying this latest one at Bootlegger Bob's has the same MO."

Rios thumbed through the files. A strip club. State senator's office. A church. The Athena Sisterhood had staged protests at all three locations. And now Bootlegger Bob's, not long after a couple dustups between the two biker gangs. "You think the Athena Sisterhood burned down the bar?"

"I do. Combine that with the Thunderman who was recently murdered and the four deaths from strychnine poisoning and you have ten homicides, all linked to the Athena Sisterhood."

"Do we have any physical evidence tying the Sisterhood to any of the fires?" She flipped through the case files.

"We just got forensics back on the first two. Still waiting on the third. Property Crimes hasn't had a chance to go through it. But now they're our cases. District Commander Bedford is requesting a task force to investigate and shut down the Athena Sisterhood. Since you're already looking into them for the strychnine poisoning cases, I want you to head it up."

"Yes, sir."

"How are those poisoning cases coming, by the way?"

"Detective Johnson and I have been going through security footage and have spotted several people wearing Sisterhood vests on the night in question. Still putting names to faces. I got a CI working them from the inside. She called the other day saying she thinks she knows who the dealer is."

"Do we have a name?"

"Not yet. I told her we need solid proof."

"I want a name. Sooner rather than later. And have your CI look into these arson cases, too. I'm assigning Detectives Morris and Bello to work with you and Johnson. And check with Escobar and Chen in Property Crimes. These first three arson cases were theirs to begin with."

"Yes, sir."

"I want to make this clear, Detective. This is our top priority. Bedford wants members of the Athena Sisterhood taken down and in bracelets before they kill anyone else. Any questions?"

"No, sir."

"I expect to see a progress report on my desk by end of day. Dismissed."

Rios gathered up the case folders and walked down to the cubicle shared by Morris and Bello. "You two are assigned to my new task force."

"Bullshit!" said Bello, looking up from his computer. "We already got a full caseload."

"So do I. Talk to Goodman if you have a problem with it. I need y'all to work these cases." Rios handed Morris the three older arson case folders.

Morris glanced over the folders. "These are Property's cases. Why are you giving these to us?"

"Same firebug killed five people last night at Bootlegger Bob's, most likely someone connected to the Athena Sisterhood. I'm on my way over there now to talk to the fire inspector. So far ten deaths are linked to the Sisterhood. We're tasked with building a case against them."

A big smile spread across Bello's face. "Well, why didn't you say so before? 'Bout time we shut them bitches down."

Morris opened one of the files. "Where should we start?"

"Go through all the forensics reports we just got back. Reinterview witnesses. See what you can find that points to the Sisterhood. Goodman wants a report by the end of the day, so let me know what you come up with by this afternoon."

"This afternoon?" Bello asked. "What about my other cases?"

"This takes priority. Bedford wants them shut down before anyone else gets killed." Rios walked farther down the aisle to Johnson's desk. "Grab your coat. You and I are taking a ride up to Bradshaw City."

TWO DOZEN MOTORCYCLES lined the street surrounding the entrance at Bootlegger Bob's. Normally, at nine o'clock in the morning the place would be all but deserted. But now a crowd of Thundermen, old ladies, and hangarounds stood vigil, pressing against the police barricades under low clouds that threatened rain.

"You really think the Sisterhood burned down the Thunder's bar?" asked Johnson, gazing out the window. "They'd have to be suicidal."

"So far, that's what it's looking like."

Rios inched her car into the driveway past faces filled with anger and violence. Deputy Graham was standing guard at the crime scene, as he had at the Genette Abrams crime scene. Dressed in rain gear, he stood with a wary eye scanning the leather-clad crowd, his hand resting on his service weapon.

Rios rolled down her window and was hit with the acrid stench of burned rubber and scorched wood. She flashed her detective's shield. "Keeping the crowd under control, Deputy?"

"Trying to."

"Fire marshal still here?" Drizzle dotted her windshield.

"Under the white tent." He pointed to where a group of people stood under a canopy.

"Thanks. Stay dry."

He waved her through. Rios parked next to a dark blue CCSO patrol car. "You want an umbrella?" she asked Johnson as she grabbed her notebook.

Johnson squinted up into the ash-white sky. "No, thanks. A little drizzle never hurt anyone."

They found Fire Marshal Wayne Denetclaw talking with one of the evidence techs underneath the white canopy. Water droplets dotted the high cheekbones of his weatherworn face. Silver hair peeked from under a Cortes County Fire Department baseball cap.

"Morning, Wayne," said Rios. She had first met him when she was a uniformed officer. His demeanor always reminded her of her father.

"Antonia!" He said, using her given name. When he hugged her, his eyes vanished into slits with his smile. "So good to see you. Who's your friend?"

"Fire Marshal Wayne Denetclaw, meet Detective Ebony Johnson."

He shook Johnson's hand. "Pleasure to meet you, Ebony. You Toni's new partner?"

"No, just working with her on this case."

"Ah yes." He turned to the smoking ruins and put his hands on his hips, his smile fading. "Five fatalities I know of so far. A few others with second- and third-degree burns. Very sad."

"We know the fire was deliberately set?" asked Rios.

"Without a doubt. Multiple ignition points. One in back. Two in front. One on the east side. All within minutes of each other. Follow me, I'll show you." He trudged around the building and gestured for Rios and Johnson to follow. They stopped at the rear, where there was little left but the scorched foundation. He pointed to a particularly dark scorch mark. "Fire started here around midnight last night. Burn pattern and glass fragments suggest some sort of improvised incendiary device."

"A Molotov cocktail?" asked Rios.

"Yup. To make matters worse, the bar stored cases of liquor back here, so once it lit . . ." Denetclaw shook his head.

"You say the arsonist also hit the front and sides of the building?" asked Johnson.

"They did." He walked back around the east side of the building, which had also burned to the foundation with similar scorch marks. "Another ignition point here at the east exit. We found three of the bodies here."

Denetclaw continued on and stopped near the smoking remnants of three motorcycles that had been parked near the front entrance. "Two more devices on the front. One at the front door, another hit these motorbikes. And like I said, all within a few minutes according to witnesses."

The rain was coming down harder and forming

puddles. "That's a lot of ground to cover in just a few minutes," said Rios. "You thinking multiple suspects?"

Denetclaw shrugged. "Maybe. But based on the burn patterns, these Molotov cocktails all hit from roughly the same angle and with considerable speed, which spread the glass fragments over a greater area than if thrown from just a few feet."

Rios studied the hill that overlooked the bar. "So, you're thinking they threw all four fire bombs from the same location?"

"That would be my guess."

"Thanks, Wayne. Johnson and I will check the hill for evidence."

"Good hunting, Antonia!"

By now the rain was coming down steadily. Although Rios' jacket provided some protection against the weather, her hair, pants, and shoes were soaked. Detective Johnson's lips were shivering from the cold.

"Can't we wait until it stops raining?" Johnson asked as the two of them trudged up the slippery hill. A carpet of pine needles covered mud and hidden rocks, which threatened to twist an ankle.

"I thought you said a little rain won't hurt," said Rios, wiping water from her face.

Johnson grimaced, pulling her jacket over her head. "This is more than a little rain. This is a deluge."

"The longer we wait, the more evidence will get washed away." Rios grabbed a tree just in time to keep from losing her balance.

Johnson sighed and pointed ahead where the land leveled out a bit. Something yellow had been tied around a tree trunk. "What's that there?"

Rios hustled over to it and examined it. "It's like a thick band of rubber. There's another one on this other tree."

"Property markers, maybe?"

"No, property markers are usually thin red plastic ribbon. I've never seen anything like this being used. And why on two trees just a few feet apart?" Rios sniffed the air as she caught a hint of something. "You smell that?"

Johnson took a whiff. "Yeah, gasoline. Or maybe kerosene. Stronger closer to the ground," she said as she bent down.

"We could have lost that if we'd waited much longer. Arsonist must have been up here." Rios took out her phone and took a photo of something on the ground.

"What'd ya find?"

Rios slipped on a pair of latex gloves and picked up a pink disposable lighter, holding it by the top and bottom to avoid smudging any prints. Rios recognized the Gertie's logo printed on the side. "Arsonist must have dropped this in the dark." She slipped the lighter into an evidence bag she pulled out of her coat pocket.

Rios looked down the hill at the burned-out building. "Man, whoever did this must've had a hell of an arm. Got to be at least forty, fifty feet from here to the edge of the bar. Even farther to hit the back and front entrances with any accuracy."

"Wait a minute, I think I know what this is," said Johnson, staring at one of the yellow bands tied around a tree. "My oldest, Jeremy, has one."

"What is it?"

"One of them giant slingshots. My son uses it for throwing water balloons back and forth with his friends."

"Could use one to launch a Molotov cocktail?"

"I don't see why not. Long as it doesn't catch fire."

Rios looked back and forth between the yellow band and the burned-out building. "I think you're right. With a little practice one of those would be the perfect launcher.

Let's get the evidence techs up here, see what else they can find. Meanwhile, you and I will be getting some witness statements."

Shea made three calls before heading to work the next morning, but all had rung through to their respective voicemails.

The first was to Monster. He had certainly seemed motivated by Shea's threats of outing him. Had he tried to get the Thunder to back off? Or did the attack on Indigo and Savage happen before he had a chance? It was impossible to know without talking to him.

She just left a curt message. "Call me today or I start posting photos on social media."

Shea's second call was to Savage. When the call went to voicemail, she said, "Just checking to see how Indigo's doing. Call me when you can."

Maybe they were just sleeping in. Or maybe Savage had convinced Indigo to go to the hospital. Either way, Shea was confident that Indigo was in good hands.

Her final call was to Labrys. The fire at Bootlegger Bob's worried her. The most recent reports on the news had said that half a dozen people had been killed and that a dark green convertible was seen leaving the area shortly after the fire began.

Is this what Labrys meant when she promised to "deal with the Thunder"? It seemed like a stretch, even for Labrys. The girl was a control freak and a manipulator, but Shea had never known her to be violent.

But even if Labrys wasn't responsible, the Thunder might assume someone in the Sisterhood was. The war between the clubs had escalated, even if Labrys hadn't done anything. They had to find a way to call a cease-fire before someone else got hurt. Otherwise, the Thunder might very well kill everyone wearing Sisterhood colors.

The one bright spot in all of this shit was that at least she had a lead on the person the Thunder had sold the hex to. Bonefish, whoever he was, owned the Tenth Inning. If she could track him down and maybe record herself buying a few hits of hex off him, Rios could arrest him and hopefully release Shea from further obligations as a CI.

At Iron Goddess, Shea spent the morning fabricating the clip-on handlebars for Stansbury's café racer. Once completed, she attached them to the front forks, followed by the triple clamp and gauges. It would have to be taken apart again before sending the various parts to be painted, but the project was finally starting to look like a motorcycle.

A few hours later, she stepped into the office after getting most of the grime off her hands and arms. "Yo, T, I'm heading out for lunch."

Terrance glanced at his watch. "It's only eleven. Why so early?"

She pulled her Glock out of her desk drawer and tucked it into the holster at the small of her back. "Got an errand to run in Ironwood."

"You're packing heat for an *errand*? You planning on robbing a bank?"

"Ran into Monster last night at the fair. He told me who the Thunder sold all that hex to."

"The stuff they stole from the Jaguars?"

"Yup. Sold it to a guy who goes by the name Bonefish."

"How'd you get him to tell you that?"

A wicked smile crept across her face. "Some good old-fashioned blackmail. With a photo I shot of him kissing a guy in front of the Bear's Den."

"You caught him kissing a guy and you're threatening to out him?" Terrance crossed his arms and gave her a disapproving look.

"I know. I'm a horrible person for threatening to out a gay person. But if it stops more people from being poisoned to death, not to mention keeping the Thunder away from me and the Athena Sisterhood, I count that as a win."

"And what do you plan to do with this Bonefish fellow?"

"Record him selling me some of the tainted hex."

"So why do you need the gun?"

"Just being cautious."

"Uh-huh. When will you be back?"

"An hour. Two at the most."

"Unless you end up in the hospital or the morgue."

"You're such a pessimist."

"No, I'm a realist with a long memory of you getting yourself into trouble."

"I've also gotten folks *outta* trouble. You see that hunk of twisted metal in the garage?"

"I did. What is it?"

"What's left of Indigo's bike after a bunch of Thundermen ran her and Savage off the road last night."

Terrance sat up, a worried expression on his face. "She's all right, isn't she?"

"She was pretty banged up, but I think she'll recover. Savage took her home on the back of her bike."

"You see? This is what I'm talking about. How long before someone shoots up this place? Again."

"I'll make sure that doesn't happen, okay?"

Terrance held her gaze for a moment. "You hear someone burned down Bootlegger Bob's?"

Shea looked away as she zipped up her jacket. "Probably an electrical fire. That place was always a death trap."

"Cops are saying it's arson. Six dead so far."

"Huh," said Shea as nonchalantly as she could manage. "Tragic."

"You know anything about it?"

"Me? Seriously, T?" Shea turned around and frowned at him. "You really think I would do something like that?"

"When push comes to shove? Maybe. Just seems awful strange that the Thunder's bar burns down the same night they run a couple of Athenas off the road."

"I may be a lotta things, but a firebug ain't one of them." She pulled on her helmet and stepped to the door. "I'll be back soon."

THE TENTH INNING was on the east side of Ironwood's Downtown Square, set in one of the area's historic buildings that dated back to the state's nineteenth-century mining boom. The walls, floor, and bar were aging hardwood, the ceiling covered with decorative tin tiles. On the more modern side, four TVs mounted near the ceiling played an array of sports channels—women's basketball, downhill slalom skiing, a Formula One race, and a football highlights program.

A handful of patrons drank silently at a table, nursing their liquid lunches. The barstools stood empty while the bartender, a rangy guy with bulging eyes and a shock of dark hair, cleaned beer mugs while periodically cursing at the basketball game.

"Come on, you bitches! Throw the damn ball!"

Shea slid onto a stool at the bar, wondering if the bartender was Bonefish. She was tempted to ask straight out, but decided on a more subtle approach. "Bushmills, please. Neat."

"Yeah." The bartender kept his eyes glued to the set as

the team in the white jerseys grabbed the ball and drove it down the court for a three-pointer. "Goddamn bitches ain't worth shit this year." He turned to Shea. "Sorry, you said Bushmills neat?"

"Yeah." Shea glanced up at the basketball game. "Didn't realize the WNBA was playing this time of year."

The bartender poured the whiskey into a glass and slid it over to Shea. "It's EuroLeague. Got a cousin who plays for the Wisla Can-Pack Krakow, but the team can't seem to get their act together this season."

Shea laid a ten next to the glass, then took a sip. The smoky liquor fired up her courage. "Excuse me, I'm wondering if you could help me."

"Yeah?"

"I'm looking for someone."

"Ain't we all."

Shea forced a smile. "A guy named Bonefish."

The bartender's demeanor changed from frustrated to suspicious. "Who the hell are you?"

"Someone looking to make a buy."

"Buy?" He narrowed his gaze. "Buy what exactly?"

"Party favors. Hex, specifically." She laid ten twenties on the bar next to the ten. She normally didn't carry much cash, but she'd stopped by the ATM and pulled out as much as she could afford. Jessica would have a fit.

"Who sent you?"

"Does it matter?"

"Don't know nothing about hex or anyone named Bonefish. I suggest you finish your drink and go."

"Look, I ain't no cop. I'm a motorcycle builder. I'm friends with the Thunder. Honest. I just need to score some hex. Got a rave coming up."

The bartender leaned over the bar and growled. "In case you hadn't noticed, this is a sports bar, not some hip-hop disco. You looking for hex, try one of the clubs around the corner." He shoved the stack of bills back at her. "Now get the hell outta here before Werner over there rips you a new one."

A burly man from one of the corner tables stood up. Bald, handlebar mustache, and wearing a wifebeater that revealed two sleeves full of neo-Nazi ink. He cracked his knuckles as he lumbered over.

Shea got to her feet and held up her hands in compliance. "All right, my mistake. I can take a hint." She backed out the door. The mountain of a bouncer followed her, stopping at the threshold to watch Shea shuffle down the sidewalk.

Had Monster just fed her a line of bullshit so she would let him and Julia spend time with Annie? Anything was possible. But if it was bullshit, why would this string bean get so angry all of a sudden?

She walked back to Sweet Betsy parked a few doors down from the bar. She unlocked her helmet and was pulling it on when she heard the rumble of an approaching motorcycle. Shea ducked down, concerned it might be a Thunderman.

A rider wearing an Athena Sisterhood cut drove past on a familiar brick-red Indian Roadmaster. *Labrys*.

Labrys pulled into a space on the other side of the Tenth Inning. Shea wasn't sure why, but her gut was telling her not to say hello. Maybe she didn't want to listen to Labrys scold her again for not wearing her prospect cut. Maybe she was starting to believe that her ex-girlfriend really was an arsonist and a murderer.

Labrys left her helmet dangling from handlebars and pulled a fat white envelope from her jacket's inner pocket before strolling into the Tenth Inning.

Shea watched the bar's front door, frustrated at once

again being pulled into Labrys' shit. So much for being a part of a motorcycle club that wasn't dealing drugs.

Shea considered rushing in and confronting her, but she didn't want to risk becoming Werner's punching bag. A glance at her phone told her it was past noon. She needed to get back to the shop.

The back of Shea's neck prickled as if someone was watching her. She scanned the street and noticed an unusually tall woman with an MMA fighter's physique smoking a cigarette outside a nearby vacant storefront that was an art gallery until a few months ago. Despite the chilly weather, the woman wore only a tight black T-shirt, jeans, and Doc Martens.

Shea realized how suspicious she must look squatting behind her motorcycle, watching the Tenth Inning's front door. Shea smiled and waved. The smoking woman disappeared into the vacant storefront.

As Shea's legs were starting to cramp from squatting, Labrys walked out of the bar carrying a brown paper sack.

More dope to sell, no doubt. Debbie Raymond, you are the worst feminist on the planet.

Shea'd had enough. If Labrys was willing to kill people to make a buck, someone had to stop her. Shea hustled down the street and reached Labrys just as she was locking the paper bag in her top case.

"What the fuck's in the bag, Labrys?"

Labrys jumped and turned, eyes wide with fear. "Good Goddess, you scared the shit out of me!"

"Answer the question."

"It's my lunch. Why?" Labrys' expression grew more stern. "And why aren't you wearing your cut, prospect?"

"Don't give me any of that prospect shit. You're dealing drugs."

"Like hell I am! And how dare you speak to your president that way."

"Don't lie to me, Debbie. I saw you walk into the Tenth Inning with a fat envelope. You gonna tell me it wasn't fulla cash?"

"Lower your damn voice." Labrys looked around, then faced Shea. "Yeah, it was full of cash. I . . .uh . . . I placed a bet on last Saturday's CAU football game. The barkeeper has a sports book going. I thought it would be an easy way to make some quick cash. Just a one-time thing, you know? Unfortunately, the Sentinels got their asses kicked last Saturday. So, I had to pay up. A lot."

Shea studied Labrys' face. She'd always been a fabulous liar. "Since when are you a college football fan? I remember you calling it another example of men getting preferential treatment over women."

"I could care less about the game. I just figured since the school is making millions off the game, why shouldn't I get a piece of that action? How was I supposed to know Ahmed Jackson was going to tear his ACL the day before the game?"

The story seemed a little too convenient. Shea wasn't buying it. "How much exactly did you lose?"

"Not that it's any of your business, but a little over two grand."

"This is the first time you've bet on a game and you risked two grand?"

"Okay, maybe it's not the first time I bet on a game. But yeah, I lost two grand. Don't believe me, go in there and ask Tony."

"Who the hell's Tony?"

"The bartender. He runs the sports book."

"That's interesting. Because I heard the Confederate Thunder sold the hex they stole from the Mexicans to the bar's owner. A guy named Bonefish. And the next day, you walk in there with a wad of cash and walk out with a bag of something."

"You think I bought drugs?"

Shea studied Labrys' expression. "Show me what's in the bag and prove me a liar."

Labrys held her gaze for a long moment, then turned away and pulled on her helmet. "I don't have time for this nonsense. I have a class to teach in half an hour."

"And what about the fire?" Shea pressed.

"What fire?" Labrys threw a leg over the bike and pulled on her gloves.

"Bootlegger Bob's burned down after you told me *you'd* deal with the Thunder for running Indigo and Savage off the road. News report says a green convertible was spotted leaving the scene. Sounds like your Audi."

"You think *I* had something to do with it? Really, Havoc, you need to have your head examined. You're delusional."

"Six people are dead, Debbie."

"Oh well. Shit happens."

"What's the rest of the club gonna think when they learn their president is a drug dealer and a murderer?"

Labrys glared at Shea. "You better check yourself, prospect. I'm beginning to wonder where your loyalties lie. We'll discuss this later." Labrys started the bike, pulled out of the parking space, and cruised down the road.

Shea returned to Sweet Betsy, revved the engine, and jetted down the road, narrowly missing a pedestrian in a crosswalk.

So far, she had a few pieces of the puzzle. But it wasn't enough to present to Rios. She still couldn't confirm who Bonefish was. And despite what her gut was telling her, she couldn't prove Deb was dealing drugs. Not yet anyway.

35

———

SHEA SPENT the rest of the day showing Kyle how to use the pipe bender to fabricate the exhaust pipes. So far Kyle's attempts resulted in bends marred with ripples, flat spots, and collapses. The lesson would have gone a lot smoother if Shea hadn't been so distracted thinking about her run-ins with Labrys and the bartender at the Tenth Inning.

"Dude," said Kyle. "I don't know what I'm doing wrong."

Before Shea could answer, her phone rang. The caller ID told her it was Savage. "Hold on a minute. I need to grab this."

She walked away to a quieter corner of the garage. "Hey, Savage. How's Indigo?"

"Better. I talked her into going to the ER. Slight concussion and some bruised ribs. Nothing broken, thank God."

"Glad to hear it. You hear about the fire?"

"Bootlegger Bob's? Yeah. Part of the reason I'm calling. Labrys asked me to put out the word that we're having an emergency meeting tomorrow night. Don't know who started that fire, but no doubt the Thunder's going to be blaming us."

"I have a feeling I know who started it," mumbled Shea. As soon as the words slipped from her mouth, she regretted it. It was just speculation. And if she was wrong, she would be causing division in the club when they needed to be standing together.

"Really? Who?"

"Never mind. Rather not say till I know for sure."

"Regardless, we need you at Gertie's tomorrow night at eight."

"Yeah, I'll be there."

"Good. Until then, keep your head down."

Shea hung up as Lakota walked past, waving. "See you tomorrow, Shea."

"Yeah." Shea glanced at the time. It was five.

Kyle was still working on a bend when Shea returned.

"Dude, I think I got it." Kyle pulled the piece of metal from the pipe bender and handed it to Shea. The bend was clean with the center exactly as marked.

"Good job. We'll see if we can finish it up tomorrow. Now get on outta here. It's quitting time."

When the rest of the crew was gone and the shop locked up, Shea walked out to the parking lot. The sun had dipped below the horizon and the light was dim and hazy. As she unlocked her helmet, something fell out of it.

"What the hell?" She picked it up and discovered it was a piece of paper. She walked under the glow of one of the outdoor security lights. The words *Mind your own damn business or you'll get hurt* were written in what looked like a woman's handwriting.

Shea looked around the empty lot. *Labrys. It's gotta be. Fucking bitch thinks she can push me around, she's got another think coming.*

Shea took a photo of the note with her phone, attached it to a text she sent, then dialed a number.

"Detective Rios speaking."

"Hey, it's Shea Stevens. I found your hex dealer. It's Deborah Raymond, aka Labrys. She's the president of the Athena Sisterhood."

"You're sure? I can't afford another false lead like last time."

Shea explained about her experience at the Tenth Inning, including her confrontation with Labrys and the note she'd found in her helmet.

"I'll look into it," said Rios.

"I think she also started the fire at Bootlegger Bob's."

"What makes you think that?"

"Just something she said. After the Thundermen ran a couple of our members off the road, Deb told me she was gonna deal with the Thunder, but never explained how. Next thing I know, Bootlegger Bob's gets firebombed. Also, she drives a dark green Audi Quattro roadster."

"Convertible?"

"Yeah."

"Okay, thanks for the lead. Anything else?"

"Yeah, police protection for my family. I can handle myself, but I can't always be there to protect Annie and my girlfriend. Now I'm worried about retaliation from both the Thunder and Deb."

"I'm sorry, Shea, we don't have the resources."

"You put me in this situation. It's your responsibility to protect my family."

"I wish I could, Shea. We're understaffed as it is. We're not the U.S. Marshals Service."

"Goddamn it, Rios. You got no problem putting civilians in danger, but ya won't do shit to protect them once they are. Shoulda known better than to trust you."

"Hey, I'll look into Ms. Raymond. If we can get something to hold her on, we will, okay?"

"And the Thunder? On second thought, forget it. I'll take care of my own damn situation."

"Shea, don't try—"

Shea hung up, hopped on Sweet Betsy, and raced north into the darkness. She should have turned south and headed home, but she wasn't just going to let this threat go unanswered.

When she arrived at Deb's place, the house was dark. Shea marched up the porch steps, pounded on the door, and waited for a minute or so, but there were no sounds from within.

"Where the hell are you, bitch?" Shea yelled at the door.

Her phone rang. The caller ID told her it was Jessica. "Hello?"

"Shea, I need help." Her voice sounded frantic. "I—" The call dropped.

Shea's pulse raced as redialed Jessica's number. It went straight to voicemail.

A chill ran up her spine. *Jessica!*

Shea pulled on her helmet without bothering with the chin strap. Her motorcycle tore down the street like a rocket while visions of Deb attacking Jessica—or God forbid, Annie—played through Shea's mind.

When she hit the highway, her speedometer pushed well into the triple digits. The bike blurred past any cars she encountered. She didn't even care about cops or wildlife. All that mattered was making sure Jess and Annie were okay.

She blazed through Olde Towne Sycamore Springs and down the twisties on the south side of Sycamore Mountain. Cascades of sparks erupted from the pavement as she scraped her footpegs in the corners.

When she finally pulled into her garage, there was no sign of Jessica's car. Like Deb's house, all the inside lights were out. Shea tripped over Ninja, the cat, in the dark living room. Her chest tightened. Her pulse pounded in her ears. "Where the fuck are you?"

Again, she called Jessica's smartphone, but it went straight to voicemail. "Goddammit!" Her mind raced. She considered calling Rios or even Savage, but there wasn't much they could do.

Her mind was too stressed to come up with a rational solution. She needed to calm down and think. Instinctively, she reached for the bottle of Bushmills on the top shelf of the pantry. There was only a quarter bottle left, a lot less than she remembered. Jessica hated the stuff. Was Annie sneaking drinks now?

"Shit, girl, now you're getting paranoid." She filled a tall glass with whiskey and took a long drink. Her body relaxed the instant it hit her throat.

"Okay, now think." She plopped onto the love seat and tried to think of ways to track down where Jessica might be. She had emptied the glass and was pouring the last of the bottle in when the front door opened.

"Hey! Sorry we're late. Got a flat tire after I stopped at the market." Jessica walked inside carrying several plastic grocery bags with Annie trailing behind, all bundled up in her winter coat. "Fortunately, this really tall woman stopped and helped me change it. I swear she looked like an WNBA player."

Shea pounced on Jessica like a tiger, wrapping her in an embrace. "Thank God, you're home."

Relief washed away her most immediate fears, but Deb remained a threat.

Jessica pulled away. "Shea, what's wrong? You're scaring me."

Shea held Jessica's gaze for a moment, struggling for the words to say.

"Aunt Jess, I'm hungry."

Without breaking eye contact with Shea, Jessica said, "Dinner'll be ready shortly. Go play in your room for a bit. Shea and I have to talk."

As Annie ambled off, shedding her coat, Jess led Shea to the couch. "What's going on, babe?"

"I need you to take Annie and stay in a motel room."

"A motel room? Why?"

Shea handed Jessica the note. "It's just too dangerous."

"What the hell, Shea? Who wrote this?"

A pained expression plastered itself across her face. "Deb, I think. It looks like her handwriting."

"Why would she threaten you?"

"She's the one dealing hex and she knows I'm on to her. She burned down that biker bar and killed several people. Now she's after me. I need you two out of harm's way till I can resolve the situation."

"How long will that take? Annie's just now back in school after her suspension. This kind of disruption isn't good for her."

"Just until Rios has enough evidence to arrest Deb. Shouldn't be more than a day or so."

"What about you?"

"I can protect myself. I can't always be there to protect you and Annie. You need to get someplace safe right now. Stay at a friend's or at a motel, anywhere but here."

"We're about to have dinner."

"Dinner can wait. Your safety can't. I can call Terrance if you want."

"I got his number. I can call him." Jessica cupped Shea's cheek with her delicate hand. "I'm worried about you, you crazy biker chick."

"I'll be all right." Shea laid her hand on Jessica's. "Just

lay low at Terrance's. Things will be back to normal soon enough."

"Feels like this *is* the new normal."

"Let's hope not." Shea stood up. "Give Terrance a call. I'll help Annie pack a bag."

36

DETECTIVES Rios and Johnson slipped into a lecture auditorium in Mofford Hall and took seats at the back of the room. The lights were dark while a popular sword-and-sorcery television show was being projected onto a screen. In the scene, a male character forced himself on a female character, while she struggled to resist his advances.

"Geez, this is supposed to be educational?" whispered Johnson with a look of disgust on her face.

Rios nodded. "Makes you wonder, doesn't it?"

At the conclusion of the scene, the video stopped and the lights went up. Professor Deborah Raymond stood at a lectern at the front of the room.

"Once again, a popular show depicts rape as just another everyday occurrence with no repercussions. The hero of the show is free to treat women as objects to be used, abused, and thrown away. It is this normalization—"

"But Professor Raymond," interrupted a male student, "If she didn't want to have sex, she should have spoken up and said no."

Professor Raymond appeared to consider his response. "Interesting observation, Mr. Dobson. Anyone else?"

A female student raised her hand. "She did say no. Twice."

"Ah, the plot thickens." Raymond's eyes widened in mock surprise as she turned to the young woman. "Ms. Cox, did you actually hear Lady Madeleine verbally object to having sex?"

"Yes, I did."

"Show of hands—who heard Lady Madeleine say no?" Two-thirds of the students, all women, raised their hands. "And how many did not hear her say no?" The remaining third of the class, mostly guys, raised theirs.

"There seems to be some disagreement on this. Shall I replay the scene?"

"No!" came the overwhelming response from the student audience.

A wry smile crept across Raymond's face. "I agree, once was enough. However, I have watched this scene more times than I like. Not only does Lady Madeleine say no, she does so not once, not twice, but four times. And yet for some reason the men in this room didn't hear her say it even once."

The room grew uncomfortably quiet.

"But Professor, get real. It's just a TV show," said Dobson.

"Do you think rape only occurs on TV?"

"No, but seeing it on TV isn't going to make guys want to rape someone. I watched the scene when it first aired a few months ago and I haven't raped anyone."

"How do you know you haven't if you can't hear when a woman objects to having sex, Mr. Dobson?"

The two locked eyes for a moment. Rios felt the room crackle with tension.

"My goal is not to shame Mr. Dobson or anyone in this room, but to encourage you to question your assumptions about what rape is, how it happens, and what role it should play, if any, in the entertainment we consume." She glanced at her watch. "Okay, that's all for today. I'll see you tomorrow."

The room erupted with the sounds of notebooks snapping shut, book bags being shuffled, and students talking as they left the auditorium. Raymond gathered her belongings from the lectern.

"Professor Raymond! Might I have a word?" asked Rios as she Johnson meandered through the last of the stragglers.

"May I help you?" asked Raymond.

Rios held up her badge. "Detectives Rios and Johnson, Cortes County Sheriff's Office. Interesting presentation."

"Thank you, I wasn't aware the sheriff's office was so interested in my course on the depiction of women in media."

"We're not. We actually have some questions for you."

"About?"

"Perhaps we should do this in your office."

Raymond regarded Rios and her partner. "Very well. Come with me."

PROFESSOR RAYMOND LED Rios and Johnson up a set of stairs and along a corridor past a bulletin board littered with pamphlets advertising opportunities to study abroad, postcards offering tutoring services, and flyers asking for study partners. The linoleum floor inclined sharply for a few feet as they entered an older section of the building. Doors to professors' offices were festooned with a listing of office hours, postings of recent test scores, and printed versions of *Bloom County* and *Far Side* cartoons.

Raymond unlocked her office door and escorted them inside, where framed certifications and overstuffed bookshelves lined the walls surrounding a small, cluttered desk, a minifridge, and a few chairs. "Have a seat," said Raymond.

"Thanks." Rios studied the cramped surroundings. No photos of family or pets anywhere.

"So what does the sheriff's office want to know?" Raymond sat behind her desk, fingers steepled.

"Ms. Raymond, in add—"

"It's Professor Raymond."

Rios forced an apologetic smile. "Of course. *Professor* Raymond, in addition to your work here at the university, you are the president of the Athena Sisterhood Motorcycle Club. Is that correct?"

Raymond eyed them with suspicion. "Yes, that is correct. Why?"

"I understand you gals have been having some trouble with the Confederate Thunder?"

"We *women* have been repeatedly harassed and assaulted by those racist, sexist criminals, who feel it's their privilege to decide who calls themselves a motorcycle club. Can I assume you've made some arrests?"

"We are looking into it. However—"

"In other words, no, you haven't."

"Not as of yet. We're here on a separate matter." Rios laid out photos of the five overdose victims. "Do you recognize any of these women?"

Raymond briefly glanced at each one then shook her head. "No, I don't. Should I?"

Rios raised an eyebrow. "None of them look familiar? Check again."

The professor sighed and looked closer at the photos.

She pointed to one of them. "That's Pipes. She was a member of the Sisterhood. Unfortunately, she was a drug addict. Guess her disease finally caught up to her."

"All five of these women died from ingesting hex laced with strychnine. Are you familiar with the drug hex?"

"It's heroin cut with ecstasy, right?"

Rios smiled. "Trust a professor to know the right answer, especially one as in tune with popular culture as yourself."

"What's any of this have to do with me?"

"We have a witness that claims she saw a member of the Sisterhood dealing hex in the ladies' room at the Trip Hop Lounge."

Raymond's face turned to stone. "You've been misinformed. We have a strict prohibition against illegal substances in our bylaws. If Pipes hadn't overdosed, she probably would have been kicked out for using."

"I understand that motorcycle clubs are very territorial," said Johnson. "Why is that?"

Rios wasn't sure where Johnson was going with this new line of questioning, but decided to let the young detective run with it.

"Any number of reasons. Ego and control, mostly."

"That would include control of income streams, right?" asked Johnson.

"In some cases, yes."

"So hypothetically, an existing club that's dealing, say, methamphetamine wouldn't appreciate a new club in their territory that's dealing hex, for instance."

Rios smiled as she saw Johnson's angle and watched Raymond squirm.

"Hypothetically speaking, yes."

"Is that why the Confederate Thunder doesn't want you gals—excuse me, you women, around?"

"I told you, the Athena Sisterhood does *not* deal drugs." Raymond's hand gripped the side of the desk, her knuckles turning white. "The question you should be asking is why the county sheriff gives the Thundermen a pass, while you harass the very people who are fighting for your equality."

"Well, I'm not—" Johnson tried to interject.

"Don't interrupt! We filed a complaint when they harassed us at Gertie's. Anyone arrested then? No. Any arrests after they attacked us at an Iron Goddess event? Of course not. How about when they killed a dozen Mexicans with a bomb a few months ago?"

"Professor Raymond!" said Rios firmly. The professor's eyes burned holes into her. "While I certainly appreciate your concerns, the DA felt there wasn't sufficient evidence to charge anyone in the Jaguars case. That said, I am interested in further discussing the conflicts you and your organization have had with the Thunder."

"Well it's about goddamn time."

Rios opened her notebook to an incident report. "I understand that two of your members were run off the road on Tuesday night. Is that correct?"

Raymond's jaw went slack. "How did . . . who told you that?"

"So, it did happen?"

"I'm not sure. I may have heard about something like that."

"You're not sure? I have a report that a Zia Pearson, who I believe goes by the nickname Indigo, was treated at a medical center in Bradshaw City the next morning for injuries sustained in that incident. I would think as president of the Athena Sisterhood, you would be aware of that."

"I may have heard something about that."

"Where were you that night?" asked Johnson.

"I was in bed. I had a class to teach the next morning."

Johnson pulled a copy of the arson investigator's report on the Bootlegger Bob's fire from Rios' notebook and laid it in front of Professor Raymond. "Are you familiar with Bootlegger Bob's?"

"Should I be?"

"It's a biker bar popular with members of the Confederate Thunder. A witness saw a dark green convertible leaving the Bootlegger Bob's parking lot shortly after it was firebombed on the same night your club members were run off the road. What kind of car do you drive?"

Raymond looked from Johnson to Rios. "Do I need to call my lawyer?"

Rios shook her head. "Not at all. We were just hoping you might have some information about who might have started a fire at Bootlegger Bob's that killed six people."

"I drive a green Audi. But I don't know anything about the fire. Like I said, I was in bed."

"You sure?" asked Johnson. "We're running fingerprints and DNA on evidence found at the scene, so if there's anything you want to tell us, now would be the time to do it."

Raymond fidgeted ever so slightly. "I wasn't there so how would I know anything?"

Rios shrugged. "Maybe someone in your club knows something. You won't mind providing me with a list of names of all of your members, would you? Including prospects?"

"Why should I?"

Rios leaned over the desk and glowered at Raymond, all niceties cast aside. "Because there is a growing pile of bodies connected to your club. Four dead from taking hex laced with strychnine, which someone in the Athena Sisterhood is selling. One Thunderman named Gator dead from a shotgun blast to the belly. Witnesses put you there as well. And now six people affiliated with the Thunder burned to death immediately after two of yours got run off the road. And coincidentally enough, you drive a car matching one spotted leaving the scene."

Professor Raymond's gaze flicked down for a second before once again meeting Rios'. "If you had any solid evidence that I committed any crimes, you would have arrested me by now instead of badgering me in my office."

Rios stared at her, unflinching, for what seemed like hours, letting the tension build once again. It didn't bother Rios. This might be the professor's office, but interrogating suspects was Rios' game.

Raymond smiled. "You know? I recognize you. You hang out at LezBeans Coffee and Books every Sunday, don't you?"

Rios' face warmed. She preferred to keep her personal and professional lives separate. "You don't want to provide me a list of names, fine. We'll get them another way. But we will find who in the Athena Sisterhood is dealing hex. We will find the arsonist who burned down Bootlegger Bob's. And everyone involved, directly or indirectly, will be charged with murder. Enjoy your freedom while you can, Professor." Rios stormed out.

Johnson caught up with her halfway down the hall. "You really go to that gay bar every week?"

"LezBeans isn't a bar," said Rios as she hustled down the stairs. "It's a coffeehouse and bookstore."

"Are you gay?"

Rios wheeled around and glowered at Johnson. "Would you have a problem with it if I was, Detective?"

"Um, no. I guess not. Just caught me by surprise is all."

Rios fixed her eyes on Johnson. "Let me make one thing

clear. My personal life has nothing to do with this job. You got me?"

Johnson stared at the floor. "Yes, ma'am."

"People are dying out there. It's up to us to prevent more from dying. We've got eleven homicides to close. And I intend to close them."

37

THE FIRST BULLET made a nickel-size hole in the Kokopelli Cafe's exterior wall a few feet in front of Shea. A fraction of a second later, the second bullet ripped through the paper bag she held containing two coffees exploded. Time slowed to a crawl as she turned to face the shooter, catching a fleeting glimpse of a dark green convertible with top up. *Labrys!*

Shea was drawing her Glock from her waistband when the third bullet slammed into her chest. Searing pain radiated throughout her body, driving her to the ground. Her jaw tensed.

She willed herself up again, ignoring the screams of onlookers. Her free hand went to her chest as she winced. *No blood. Kevlar. I'm okay.*

Down the street, the convertible ducked behind a semi and disappeared over the next rise heading north toward Ironwood. "Fuck me! You ain't getting away that easy." Her voice was hoarse and gravelly.

She hopped on Sweet Betsy, reholstering her pistol in

the process, and blazed out of the parking lot, sending pedestrians scrambling for safety.

Her eyes teared up as the icy wind blasted her unprotected face. Every heartbeat amplified the pain in her chest. Shea didn't care. The only thing that mattered at this point was giving Labrys what she deserved.

After a few moments, Shea spotted the semi. The convertible had to be on the other side, but oncoming traffic prevented her from passing the truck.

When the lane finally cleared, Shea pulled into the left lane, but Labrys' car was nowhere to be seen. *Where the hell is she? Did she pull off?*

Shea glanced all around, checked her mirrors. The adrenaline shooting through her system made it hard to focus. Her mind jumped around like a rabbit. *What roads could she have pulled off on? There aren't any. Did I really see her? Did she go after Jessica? No, Jess is at work. What about Iron Goddess? God, I need a drink. Annie's stealing my whiskey. Wait, where am I?*

She realized she was parked on the side of the road, shivering. Her face numb. Hands stiff. Stomach churning. A wave of nausea hit and she puked on the ground next to her, droplets of vomit sizzling as they hit the hot engine.

Slow down, girl. You're alive. She took a deep, painful breath, and let it out slowly. She kicked down her side stand, unlocked her helmet, shoved it on her head, then pulled back onto the highway.

"I know where you work, bitch."

SHEA PAID for parking in one of the guest lots on the Central Arizona University campus, then ran to Mofford Hall, where Labrys' office was located. Though it had been years since Shea had been there, her feet still knew the way even if her head was still a bit muddled. Inside, she took the steps two at a time to the second floor, charged through a knot of students milling about the hallway, and pounded on Labrys' office door.

"Office hours aren't until two," said a muffled voice. "Come back then."

Shea pounded again. "Open the fucking door, Labrys, or I swear I'll kick it in."

Shea could hear two distinct voices inside, followed by the sound of the door being unlocked. Shea raised her fist ready to strike. The door opened to reveal a twenty-something with short red hair. Her blouse was half tucked in and her hair mussed.

The young redhead jumped back in fear. "What the hell?"

Shea lowered her arm. "Where's Deb Raymond?"

Labrys appeared in the doorway, looking equally unkempt. "Go on, Parker. We can finish this later."

"What's your damage, bitch?" The redhead walked out with a quick glare at Shea.

Shea pushed her way into the room and locked the door behind her.

"What the hell is wrong with you, prospect?"

Shea drew her Glock and pointed it at Labrys. "You think you can kill me?"

Labrys took a step back, a mixture of fear and resolve in her eyes. "Put that gun away, Havoc, before someone gets hurt. What in hell's going on?"

"This is what's going on, you fucking psycho!" From her jacket pocket, Shea pulled out the threatening note she'd received and shoved it in Labrys' face. "You think I wouldn't recognize your handwriting?"

Labrys snatched it from Shea's hand and examined it. "What is this?"

"Like you don't know. "

"You think I'd threaten you? Have you lost your mind?"

"Oh, so you didn't just try to shoot me down in Sycamore Springs? Bullshit! I saw your green convertible as you drove by."

"That's impossible. I was just with . . ." Labrys gestured to the door. "Well, you saw her. How could I be here and in Sycamore Springs at the same time?"

Shea mind spun in twisted circles. Nothing was making sense. Was Labrys telling the truth? If it wasn't her, then who? She holstered the pistol.

"Here. Sit." Labrys led Shea to a chair. "You want something to drink?"

"Whiskey. Bushmills, if you got it."

"Well, you'll have to settle for bottled water." Labrys pulled a Dasani from the minifridge. The blue plastic top crackled as she opened it and handed it to Shea. "Now talk to me. Did someone really try to kill you?"

"Little bit ago. In front of Kokopelli's." Shea stuck her finger in the hole in her jacket.

"Holy shit, Havoc." Labrys unzipped Shea's jacket and touched the dimple in the Kevlar vest underneath. "Are you all right?"

"Sore, but I'll live." *Is she lying to me? Fucking with my head the way she always did?*

"It wasn't me, I assure you. Nor did I write this note."

"Looks like your handwriting."

"It's not. Sure, I was miffed at you for accusing me of dealing drugs. But you're a prospect of the Sisterhood. Hell, we have a history together. I would never do anything to violate that."

Shea sipped the water. The pain in her chest had dulled. "The Thunder sold hex to someone named Bonefish at the Tenth Inning. I show up looking for Bonefish and find you walking in with a big envelope full of cash and walking out with a big bag. What was I supposed to think?"

"Why are you so obsessed with this hex business? We're not cops. Yes, it sucks that Pipes died, but she was an addict. She relapsed. It happens."

"It's not just Pipes. Four other women are dead from taking the drug. Ain't we supposed to be protecting women?"

The two locked eyes for a moment. Shea could see the wheels turning in Labrys' mind.

"Havoc, are you working for the cops?"

Shea caught her breath. "Why would you ask that?"

"Two detectives were here earlier today, asking me about hex *and* about Bootlegger Bob's burning down. Somehow they knew the Thunder ran Indigo and Savage off the road. Now how would they know that? Are you a snitch?"

Shea folded her arms across her chest and stared at the floor. The jig was up. "I got jammed up last summer and got caught with a gun I'd taken off Mackey, a Thunderman. Turns out it was linked to a murder. This Detective Rios threatened to send me back to prison if I didn't become a CI."

"Damn, never thought I'd see the day that Shea Stevens would be one of Buzzkill's snitches. Gotta say I'm a little disappointed."

"I didn't have no choice. Besides, I fucking hate drug dealers. I don't want anyone else to die from taking drugs laced with rat poison. It's gotta stop." Shea sighed. "This mean I'm outta the club?"

"Disloyalty is a big deal. I should kick you out."

"I did what I had to do. You do what you gotta do. But someone in the club's dealing this shit. Who better than me to help you find her?"

An awkward silence settled in the room. Shea replayed the shooting in her mind. A figure in a dark green convertible. Face just a blur, obscured by the fog of the bullet's impact. *Who the hell was it?*

"Someone really shot you?" Labrys' finger hooked the bullet hole in Shea's jacket.

Shea wrapped her hand around Labrys' and felt a surge of emotions she had once buried. Passion. Excitement. Need. "Yeah."

"You don't go down easy, do you?"

"No." Shea met Labrys' gaze.

"You're still a prospect. For now. But no more snitching. If someone in our club is dealing, we'll handle it ourselves."

"Thanks." Shea's hand pulled away and rubbed the spot where the bullet had hit the vest. "Tell me the truth. You burn down Bootlegger Bob's?"

Labrys looked Shea straight in the eye. "No, I did not."

"Good to know." Shea still wasn't sure whether to believe Labrys or not. She drank the last of the water and tossed the bottle into a wastebasket.

"You know about tonight's emergency meeting?" asked Labrys.

"I'll be there."

"Good. Now get out of here. I've got a class to teach."

Steel-gray clouds threatened rain as Shea walked out of the building and across campus to the guest parking lot. She rubbed the aching impact point on her chest.

If it wasn't Labrys, then who the hell shot me? Was it the same green convertible seen leaving Bootlegger Bob's?

She closed her eyes and tried again to see the face of the shooter as he or she sped past in that dark green convertible.

She nearly jumped when her phone rang. It was Terrance. "Yo, T? What's up?"

"What's up? There was a drive-by next door at the café. Ms. Brooks said she saw you get shot."

"Drive-by, huh?" Shea forced a chuckle. It hurt to laugh. "Wasn't me. I had an errand to run in Ironwood. I'll be down at the shop soon."

"Ms. Brooks seemed awfully convinced it was you. Cops even stopped by asking for you."

"Which cops?"

"I don't know. A couple deputies I didn't recognize. Why? What's going on?"

"Nothing, T."

"Nothing? Then how come your girlfriend and your niece are crashing at my place? Who's after you, sister girl?"

Shea sighed. "Honestly, I'm not sure. Probably has to do with the people who are dealing that jacked-up hex at clubs. I must've pissed off someone while looking for the dealer."

"Should I close the shop till this blows over?"

"Shop should be fine. It's me they're after."

"Be honest with me, Shea. That shooting next door? Were you there?"

"Let's just say I'm thankful for Kevlar."

"Dammit, girl, why didn't you just say that to start with?"

"Didn't want you to worry is all. Look, I'm okay. Whoever's after me probably thinks they got me, so the shop's in no danger. Besides, we can't afford to stop work on the Stansbury bike, right?"

Terrance grumbled into the phone. "You best be right. Now get your ass back here."

"Will do."

"Oh, and one more thing. Call Jessica. She's worried about you."

"I'm on it, T."

38

———

RIOS PRINTED OUT THREE MONTHS' worth of Professor Raymond's bank statements, handed one month to Johnson, and kept the other two for herself.

"What am I looking for?" asked Johnson.

"Anything other than groceries, paying the light bill, the usual."

"All right."

Rios went line by line through the first statement. In addition to Raymond's twice-monthly paycheck from the university, there were several cash deposits. The size of the deposits varied from a couple of hundred dollars to a few thousand. But nothing that would have triggered the bank to report the deposit to the government. There were also numerous large cash withdrawals, as well as payments to organizations like the Women's Equality Fund and the Athena Sisterhood National Chapter. She highlighted the suspicious transactions.

"Find anything interesting?" Rios glanced over at Johnson's statement, several lines of which were highlighted in pink.

"She moves around a lot of cash, both in and out. Also, there's a purchase at Roy's Toy and Hobby. She doesn't have any kids," said Johnson. "Could be where she bought a giant slingshot for launching Molotov cocktails."

Rios considered it. "You could be right. How long ago was the purchase at Roy's Toy and Hobby?"

"Two months."

"We can check to see if the shop has a record of what was purchased. I think we can get a search warrant of Raymond's home based on bank statements, the matching car, the lighter." She picked up her phone and called the DA.

Dressed in body armor and with a search warrant in hand, Rios and Johnson led the Special Tactics Unit up to Professor Raymond's front door as the day's shadows were getting long.

The house was a well-kept if smallish bungalow in a historic Ironwood neighborhood. White flowers bordered a lawn of winter rye. A rainbow flag hung from a pole mounted on the side of the front porch.

Rios pounded on the rustic mahogany door. "Open up. Police! Search warrant!" When there was no response after a minute, Rios tried again.

"I didn't see her Audi in the carport. Just a motorcycle," said Johnson. "She's probably not home."

Rios turned to the STU officer with the battering ram. "Okay, break it down."

With one swing, the doorjamb shattered, knocking the wooden door wide open. The members of the Special Tactics Unit rushed in armed with assault rifles. Rios wasn't expecting any serious resistance, but she didn't want any surprises. She and Johnson followed the STU through the door, sidearms at the ready.

Inside, the house was filled with expensive hardwood furniture and antiques. Abstract paintings and shelves filled with hardcover books lined the wall. A sculpture of two entwined stylized women stood as the centerpiece of a coffee table. In the small kitchen, high-end cooking pans hung from a rack mounted to the ceiling.

Lieutenant Pasco, who ran STU, approached Rios and Johnson. "The house is clear, Detectives."

"Okay, thanks. Have your men stand down, but keep an eye out for the owner showing up. Oh, and bring in Peterson with the dog."

"Roger that." He signaled to the rest of the team and they filed out of the house.

A moment later, Deputy Peterson walked in with Misty, the Malinois. He led her systematically through each room, opening cabinets, closets, and any other space that might hide drugs. Rios and Johnson followed at a distance, looking for potential contraband or any evidence that might connect the good professor to dealing hex or involvement in the Bootlegger Bob's fire.

"What the hell is this?" shouted a familiar voice from outside. "Who the hell are you people?"

"And we have company." Rios closed the kitchen cabinet she'd been checking and strode out to the front porch. "Professor Raymond, welcome home."

Raymond's face was flushed and full of anger. Lieutenant Pasco blocked her from the porch. "What the hell are you people doing?"

Rios handed her a copy of the search warrant. "Ma'am, we are conducting a legal search of the house. I'll need you to stay outside while we do so."

"On what grounds are you searching my house? You

have no probable cause." Raymond tried to push past the lieutenant, but he held on to her.

"Tell me, Professor," asked Rios, "what's with all of the large cash transactions in and out of your bank account?"

"They're none of your damn business, that's what they are." She glared at Rios. "You and your storm troopers best leave my home at once."

"You best sit tight or you'll be arrested. You understand me?"

"I'm calling my lawyer and putting a stop to this bull-shit." Raymond pulled out her phone.

Peterson and Misty walked out. When his eyes met Rios', he shook his head. "No joy. Sorry."

Rios got a sinking feeling. She couldn't afford another failure. "Are you sure? Maybe she missed something."

Peterson shrugged. "It's possible. There are limits, but I'm reasonably sure that if there were illegal drugs in there we would have found them."

"That damn dog better not have pissed in my house," yelled Raymond.

"What now?" asked Johnson as Peterson and Misty returned to his vehicle.

"We keep looking. Maybe she keeps the drugs else-where, but maybe she has some of that cash here. Or rat poison that we can have the lab match to the strychnine in the hex. I'm not giving up so easily."

Rios walked back into the house. But after a few hours of searching, the most incriminating thing they could find was an out-of-date prescription bottle of hydrocodone, an empty gas can, and a rattrap that used poison, but not strychnine. The search was another bust. "Come on, John-son. Let's go home."

When they walked outside, Raymond was standing with Rebecca Li, the Athena Sisterhood's attorney.

"Professor Raymond, we're all done. You can go inside now." She turned to Pasco. "Thanks, guys! We're out of here."

"Wait a minute!" said Li, following the two detectives to Rios' car. "Who's going to pay for my client's door?"

Rios pulled out a pamphlet from her notebook. "She's free to submit a claim for damage to the County Manager's Office. Have a nice day, Counselor." She and Johnson climbed into her car and rode off.

39

———————

THE BACK ROOM at Gertie's buzzed with multiple conversations.

"I thought this meeting was supposed to start at eight," Shea said to Savage and Indigo. "It's almost eight thirty."

Her phone rang with Jessica's ringtone. Shea silenced it and sent the call to voicemail.

"The wife gotcha on a short leash?" joked Indigo, who had been acting goofy since she arrived.

Shea shook her head. "Just anxious is all."

"Don't pay no attention to her," said Savage. "It's the pain meds talking."

"And they're damn good, too!" Indigo chuckled then winced, grabbing her right side. " 'Cept when I laugh."

"Just take it easy on those." Shea winked at her. "Don't want to see you get addicted."

"Oh, don't even start with that drug talk." Indigo crossed her arms.

Shea glanced around the room. "Where's Orphan? I thought all meetings were mandatory for prospects."

Savage shrugged. "Dunno. I called her several times and left messages."

"I hope she's okay."

"I'm sure she's fine," said Indigo, giggling. "She's got that fine boyfriend of hers looking out for her. If I had a boy like that, I wouldn't be here either. I'd be home rocking his world."

Savage rolled her eyes. "Still no word from Raven, Pixie, or Goth, either. It's been more than a week. Something's going on. Something bad. I can feel it."

Labrys and Dragon stormed into the room and the conversations quieted down. The women settled into their seats. Savage joined the other officers behind the table at the head of the room. Labrys alone remained standing.

"As I have said previously, we are at war. Over the past couple of weeks, there have been several confrontations between ourselves and the Confederate Thunder. Most recently, they drove two of our Athenas off the road, totaling one of our bikes. We have tried to pursue legal remedies. But Sheriff Buzzkill and his good ol' boys don't care about us. On the contrary, they think *we're* the problem. Just a few hours ago, Buzzkill's goons broke down the door to my home and turned the place upside down, claiming to be looking for drugs." Labrys gave a steely glare at Shea.

Oh shit, thought Shea. *She's definitely going to kick me out now.*

"After sending their drug dog all over my house, guess what? They didn't find anything. Because the Athena Sisterhood does not do drugs. Unlike the Confederate Thunder. Bottom line: the patriarchy takes care of its own. Always has, always will."

"What about the fire at Bootlegger Bob's?" asked Savage.

"Not surprisingly, the cops are saying it was arson," replied Labrys. "But who are you going to believe? According to the county's own record's, that bar has been cited for numerous electrical violations over the years. But now they're looking to pin the fire on one of us."

"Have you talked to the national chapter about this?" asked Indigo. "Maybe they've dealt with a similar situation before."

"We don't need national to rescue us," said Labrys with a smug look on her face. "We're smart, strong women. We can weather the storm."

"Perhaps we can sit down with the Thunder and work it out," suggested Dragon.

Labrys shook her head. "Those animals can't be reasoned with. They started this. They want war, we'll give them a war."

Shea struggled to keep her mouth shut, but her history growing up with her dad as the head of the Thunder wouldn't let her leave it alone. She stood up. "Labrys, you can't win like this."

"Sit down, Havoc. You're out of order," snapped Labrys. "Prospects are not allowed to speak during meetings."

"Fuck order! Y'all are gonna get yourselves killed."

Savage frowned. "Havoc, please sit down."

"Look, all due respect to the rules of order, but I grew up watching the Thunder do their thing. And I saw what they did to the Jaguars. They did the same thing to an MC with ties to the Bloody Brotherhood. Before that it was a Korean street gang."

All eyes were on Shea, but no one said anything. Labrys looked like she would shit bricks.

"Six Thundermen are dead. Their favorite bar is burnt to the ground. Don't matter whether we did it or not.

They're gonna blame us. Savage, how many times you try to call Orphan and the others that are missing?"

"All damn day," said Savage grimly.

"They ever miss a meeting before?"

"No."

Shea let the word hang in the air. "Labrys is right about one thing. This is war. And the Thunder don't take prisoners. How many of y'all been in the military?"

A few hands were raised.

"Any y'all seen combat?"

One hand remained. Savage's.

"Any of y'all cops?"

No one raised their hand.

"The Thunder won't cut us any slack just 'cause we're women. All we are to them is bitches with the gall to call ourselves bikers. And to declare ourselves an MC? Might as well have insulted their mamas, far as they're concerned. They will brutalize us and rape us and murder us and not think twice." Shea took a deep breath and let it out. "If we hope to survive, we're gotta work out a peace agreement with them."

"Oh yeah? And who's gonna do that, prospect? You?" asked Labrys. "You're not even a patched member."

"No, but I have contacts there. They may not like me much, but they respect me."

An uncomfortable silence settled on the group until Indigo said, "I move that Havoc reach out to the Confederate Thunder to set up a meet to negotiate a peace agreement."

"I second it," added Dragon.

Labrys seethed. "All in favor?" she grumbled.

"Aye," said a majority of the women, hands raised.

"Opposed?" Labrys raised her hand, as did a few others. She banged her gavel. "The ayes have it. Motion passes.

Havoc will reach out to one of her contacts at the Thunder and arrange a meeting to discuss a peace agreement."

After the meeting, Shea stepped out of the room and switched her phone off vibrate. She was about to call Monster when Labrys slammed her against the wall. "What the hell did you think you were doing in there?"

Shea glowered at her. "Saving your ass. This isn't some protest you're planning. This is gang warfare and you don't know the rules."

"Hell I don't." Labrys gave Shea a knowing look. "You think I don't know how to play rough? Trust me, I do."

Shea's jaw dropped. "Jesus Christ, you did burn down the Thunder's bar."

"Me? Never! Even if those people had it coming."

The bitch was lying. Shea could tell. Her hand curled into a fist. It took all her restraint to keep from decking Labrys. "You're gonna get more of us killed if you keep this up."

"Don't tell me how to run my club, prospect. You're lucky they asked you to reach out to the Thunder. I was ready to boot your ass for good. And once this is over, I just might."

"When all this is over, you won't need to. I don't want to be in your goddamn club. You got no clue what you're doing. Only reason I'm reaching out to the Thunder is to protect the other women of this club from your fucking stupidity."

Shea pushed away from her, marched down the hall, and stepped out Gertie's back door. "Jesus fucking Christ!" She kicked a loose rock across the alley that ran behind the row of shops, then pulled out her phone. It rang twice before Monster answered.

"Shea-Shea, you got some balls calling me after what

your club done. Killed four patched members and two old ladies."

"Don't start with me, Monster. You were gonna get the Thunder to leave us alone."

"Look, I tried. But I can't help what a few of our guys do after they've had a few."

"Oh, is that your excuse? Boys will be boys? Cut the bullshit. We gotta stop this nonsense before anyone else gets killed on either side."

Shea heard Monster sigh into the phone. "Yeah, I s'ppose you're right. Let's talk, but not over the phone."

"Where then?"

"Can I convince you to come over to my place?"

"So you can ambush me? I don't think so."

"No ambush. Word of honor. You're family. I wouldn't do that to you."

Shea thought about it. He had raised Wendy, her sister. "I'll be there in forty-five minutes. But if anything happens to me, that photo of you and your Latin lover goes viral."

40

———

A FLOOD of childhood memories filled Shea's mind as she pulled up to the home shared by Monster and Julia Mueller. The night she stayed there when her sister, Wendy, was born. Countless summer parties eating watermelon and homemade ice cream while her father and the rest of the club drank, argued, and had midnight lawn tractor races down the street.

But the most vivid memories were the long nights she cried herself to sleep wrapped in Julia's arms after Ralph, her father, murdered her mama.

Shea parked Sweet Betsy on the street, let herself through the gate in the white picket fence, and strolled up the weed-riddled walk to the house. Ratty beige lawn chairs sat on either side of the door.

Shea knocked. A moment later Monster opened the door, his Beretta in a holster on his hip. His face was puffy and wet with tears. He reeked of smoke and BO. Shea'd seen him drunk several times, but not like this.

He let her inside without a word and led her to the kitchen table where a half-empty bottle of Jack Daniel's stood beside a tall glass decorated with flowers. His cell-phone lay next to it.

The interior of the house was like a time capsule, circa 1950. The kitchen appliances had rounded corners and matched the peach-colored cabinets and the faded linoleum. Monster grabbed a tumbler from the drying rack next to the sink, set it in front of Shea, and filled it half full of Jack.

"Whole world's gone to shit," mumbled Monster.

Shea took a sip of her whiskey, reminding herself not to drink the whole thing. Too much on the line to get shit-faced. "Where's Julia?"

"At her sister's in Lake Havasu." His lids were heavy. Sweat glistened off his forehead, despite the coolness of the room.

A question formed on Shea's lips, but she hesitated to ask. With another long swallow of Jack, she found her courage. "You tell her about the Bear's Den?"

"Hell no! Think I'm stupid? She went with some of the other old ladies for an extended girls' getaway weekend in Vegas."

"How come you ain't been returning my calls?"

"Been busy."

"Busy? You're fucking retired, old man. People in our clubs are getting hurt. What the hell's keeping you so busy you can't return a call?"

"Doctors' appointments." He looked her straight in the eye. "I'm dying, Shea-Shea."

"Aw shit!" Shea felt like she'd been sucker punched. "Not AIDS, is it?" She knew it was a stupid stereotype, but couldn't keep the words from coming out.

"Fuck no! Doc says I got ass cancer. Stage 4."

"That's bad I take it." Shea poured herself another drink.

"Well there ain't no Stage 5."

"Sorry, man."

"Sorry don't do shit for me. We're all sorry—sorry sacks o' shit. Don't mean nothing when karma comes and bites you in the ass. Literally."

"They can cure that now, can't they? Radiation, chemo?"

"Even with all that crap, doc says I got two chances: slim and none. Told me to start putting my affairs in order. *Affairs!*" Monster laughed bitterly. "What affairs I gotta put in order?"

Shea took a deep pull on the Jack. She was here for a reason and it wasn't to play nursemaid to Monster, even if he was dying. "Look, man, I'm sorry you got cancer. That's fucked up, but like you said, ain't shit anybody can do about it. But there is something *we* can do. We need a truce between our clubs."

"Who the fuck cares about the goddamn clubs?"

Monster finished his glass and started pouring himself another. Shea grabbed the bottle from his hand and slammed it on the table.

"Listen, you selfish son of a bitch. This keeps up I will see to it that Buzzkill locks up every Thunderman in Cortes County."

Monster burst out laughing. "Not fucking likely, Shea-Shea."

"Oh yeah? Why's that? He's always hated the club."

"Who you think bankrolled his reelection campaign?"

Shea bit her bottom lip in anger. No wonder the sheriff's office hadn't locked up any Thundermen. "Maybe you don't care about the clubs, but what about Annie? Care about her? 'Cause sooner or later, she's gonna get hurt, unless you and I stop this senseless gang war."

He gazed dully at her for a moment. "Fine. You wanna peace agreement? Here are the terms: *either* the Athena

Sisterhood takes off their cuts and stops calling themselves an MC *or* they declare themselves to be a Confederate Thunder support club subject to our supervision."

"Bullshit! Ain't no way either one of those're ever gonna happen."

"Also, you turn over whoever's responsible for burning down Bootlegger Bob's."

"Do you even hear yourself?" Shea looked away, frustrated at the impossibility of forging a peace. As much as she hated Labrys for burning down the bar, giving her up only put the club at more risk. "For the record, I don't know who burned down your bar, but it wasn't us."

"And one more thing, Julia gets to see Annie whenever she wants. Unsupervised."

"Oh, that's part of the Thunder's demands?"

"No, that's my demand. Or a dying wish, whatever you wanna call it."

Shea emptied her glass and resisted the urge to pour herself some more. "Look, I can see about you and Julia spending some time with Annie. She's been begging to see y'all, too. But there is no way in hell the Sisterhood is going to give up being an MC, nor are they going to be a support club to a sexist, racist outlaw club like the Thunder."

"Those dykes on bikes got no business calling themselves an MC. They got no understanding of MC culture or history."

"No, but I do."

"Just 'cause your father was president don't mean you know what goes on inside the club. And dressing up in outlaw-style patches don't make you an outlaw."

"I know enough. Besides, the Sisterhood may not be outlaw, but they are bikers and hardcore feminists to boot. You push us, we push back harder. And don't forget, I still have that picture of you and your boy toy. Don't risk what precious time you have left."

"I'm already a dead man. Only thing outing me'll do is hurt Julia. After all she did for you after your Mama died, I'da thought you'd be a bit more charitable."

"You're the one who's been cheating on her, you piece of shit."

Monster lunged at her over the table, but the booze had slowed his reflexes. He landed with a thud on the tabletop.

"You're a real fuck-up, Monster," Shea said as Monster fell back into his chair. "Tell the Thunder to leave the Athena Sisterhood alone or we will put more Thundermen in the ground."

"You do what you gotta do," grumbled Monster. "I just don't care anymore."

Shea glowered at him. Until he sobered up there was no more use talking to him. She took a final pull directly from the bottle of JD. "If you care about Julia and want her to see Annie when you're gone, you best find a way to make this truce happen." She stormed out.

As she pulled on her helmet, a gunshot shattered the quiet night. "What the fuck?"

It sounded like it had come from inside the house. Shea rushed back in and found Monster slumped in his chair, a gaping hole in the side of his head. Blood spatter covered the wall. His Beretta lay on the floor below his still hand.

"Jesus fucking Christ, Monster! What did you do?" A tidal wave of sadness hit her, making it hard to focus. "Goddamn, why would you do that?"

Her mind raced. *I should call Julia. Or maybe someone else in the Thunder. No, not them. Savage. No, don't get her involved. Rios? Hell no, definitely not Rios. Aw, fuck, I don't know. I don't know.*

The ding of a cellphone pulled her out of her head. A

text message from Julia appeared on Monster's phone, saying what a great time she and her friends were having in Vegas. A photo of her grinning and holding a bottle of champagne followed.

Somewhere in the night, a police siren wailed and grew closer. "Shit, shit, shit!"

In a surge of adrenaline, she wiped down the glass she drank out of and put it upside down on the drying rack and grabbed Monster's phone, before dashing back out to her motorcycle and driving away.

She resisted the urge to drive like a bat out of hell. *Just be cool,* she told herself as two police cars whizzed past toward Monster's house. But the whiskey was kicking in strong, muddling her mind and messing with her sense of balance.

Skidding brakes and an angry car horn sent a jolt through her as she blew through a red light. She flipped off the driver, who was stopped in the middle of the intersection behind her. *Fucking asshole!*

Just gotta get home. Just get home. Everything'll be all right. But she couldn't get the image of Monster out of her head, which morphed into the face of her sister with half her face shot off, and then into her mother, dark blood pouring out of her neck through Shea's slender fingers.

As she sped through a tight left turn, she felt the bike drift off the road and slip sideways out from under her. The ground slammed her left side.

The next thing she remembered was looking up at the Milky Way cutting a swath of stardust across the night sky. Her left shoulder throbbed to the rhythm of her chattering teeth. Despair and sorrow wrapped around her like a boa constrictor and squeezed.

She sobbed uncontrollably for what seemed like hours, her consciousness dissolving into the emotion. Self-loathing spread throughout her body and settled in her stomach. She barely managed to lift her helmet visor before she puked repeatedly on the ground beside her. When the dry heaves subsided, she was left feeling empty, a dry husk of what she could have been if she hadn't been such a fuck-up.

Her back ached and she realized she'd been lying on her Glock. She peeled off her gloves and pulled the gun from its holster. It felt icy in her hand, and yet comforting. How easy would it be to put it to her head and pull the trigger? *Everyone would finally be rid of me. Annie could grow up with someone that didn't ignore her. Jess could find someone that treated her with the respect she deserved. Terrance could close the shop and get a job making a lot more money somewhere else.*

She pulled off her helmet with her free hand and rested the gun against the side of her face. It felt so solid, the weight reassuring. Her index finger slipped inside the Glock's trigger guard. *I can do this. I deserve this. Sweet fucking oblivion.*

The muffled sounds of Melissa Etheridge's "I Want You" interrupted her train of thought. Jessica's special ringtone. "Oh, Jess. I'm so sorry for being such a disappointment."

Is this how you want Jess to find you? said a voice in her head. *Are you really such a chickenshit loser that you would hurt her like this?*

"Fuck!" She dropped the gun and unzipped her jacket, fishing out her phone. "Hello?" she choked out.

"Shea, are you okay? I called and left several messages. I got worried."

"Sorry." Shea wiped her face. "Sisterhood meeting ran long. Heading home now."

"Why does your voice sound so funny?"

Shea sniffled. "Cold air making my nose run. I miss you."

"I miss you, too. When can Annie and I come home?"

"Soon, babe. I promise."

"Okay, well, I love you."

"Love you, too."

Shea put the phone away and struggled to her feet. Her body trembled, as if she'd been rung like a bell. Her head slowly cleared. She stuffed the Glock back in its holster and wandered over to Sweet Betsy.

Grabbing hold of the handlebar and rear of the bike she heaved it up onto two wheels. Aside from some scratches and a loosened mirror, it seemed to be in one piece. Moments later, she was back on the road.

41

Rios yawned and rubbed her eyes as she took a seat in Goodman's office.

"What's the word on this dead biker, Detective?"

"Name's Vernon Mueller, goes by Monster. Member of the Confederate Thunder. Single gunshot to the head. Appears to be a suicide. But..."

"But what?" Goodman cocked his head.

"Neighbors say they heard a motorcycle drive away shortly after the gunshot. It may be nothing though."

"Or it could be the Athena Sisterhood."

"Maybe. No sign of forced entry. Haven't been able to reach the wife, Julia Mueller, but have left a couple messages. Could be a domestic dispute turned deadly."

"Keep me updated. Where are we with the strychnine cases?"

"We're up to six confirmed deaths, so far. My CI gave me a name: Bonefish. Supposedly bought a large amount of hex from the Confederate Thunder last August and is one of the owners of the Tenth Inning sports bar. I checked the database. No one using that alias."

"What about the Tenth Inning?"

"Neither of the owners have a criminal record. No liquor license violations. No felons on the payroll. Not even a bad rating from the health depart—"

"I need some arrests, Detective," interjected Goodman. "Redouble your efforts on the Athena Sisterhood. You've got a witness who says she saw one of them dealing at a club."

"There you are!" Morris popped her head in the door with a case file in her hand.

"You need something, Detective?" asked Goodman.

Morris pointed to Rios. "Sorry, Lieutenant. Just a quick question for Toni. Weren't you at the Desert Vistas condominiums complex the other week doing a notification?"

Rios nodded. "One of the strychnine victims lived there. Why?"

"We got a homicide victim in the same complex."

"What's the unit number?"

Morris opened the case file in her hand. "Victim, Richard Hayden, lived in building D, unit 210. Found his body just outside unit 209."

"That's where my strychnine victim lived." Rios picked up the Abrams file that was sitting on Goodman's desk and thumbed through it. "Yeah, unit 209. Vic's name was Genette Abrams; roommate is a Sarah Cohen. We interviewed her, but didn't come up with anything. Art student with no priors."

"Cohen's down in interview room one if you want to take another crack at her. I got a feeling she's hiding something."

Rios turned to Goodman. "We done here?"

He shooed her away with his hand. "Go! See if you can't close these damn cases. There's too much red on that board out there," he said referring to the unsolved cases.

She followed Morris down to the interview rooms and stepped inside the monitoring room. Sarah Cohen appeared on the screen marked INTERVIEW 1, her head buried in her arms, obscuring her face.

"Just to bring you up to speed, the victim's throat was slashed in his own apartment, then the body dumped on Ms. Cohen's doorstep. He still had his wallet with fifty-seven dollars in cash, so robbery doesn't appear to be a motive."

"Sounds personal, like someone sending a message," said Rios.

"I agree. Perhaps one of her ex-boyfriends with a grudge," explained Morris. "We've asked her about any exes. She claims she broke up with her previous boyfriend more than a year ago and it was amicable."

"Who called 911?"

"She did. This morning. Six hours after time of death."

"Interesting. Let's go see what we can find out."

Rios and Morris walked down the hall and entered the interview room.

"Sarah Cohen?" said Rios as they took their seats. "You remember me? I'm Detective Rios."

Sarah sat up. Her left eye was blackened, and her lower lip split. Her swollen face and shirt were speckled with blood. A hand-shaped bruise marked her right arm. "I remember."

Rios studied the woman. Somehow this was all connected—the poisoned roommate, the murdered neighbor, and what appeared to be an assault on Sarah herself. But Rios wasn't sure yet how it all fit together. "Been a rough couple of weeks, huh?"

Sarah shrugged and stared absently at the table.

"Tell me what happened."

Emotion spread across Sarah's face. Tears rimmed her

eyes. "I opened my front door to . . . to take out some trash and . . . I found him." She gasped for air between heaving sobs. "Blood . . . blood everywhere. I . . . I called 911, but . . ." Her eyes shut tight as if warding off the memories. "He was dead."

Rios pulled a pack of tissues from her pocket and handed it to Sarah. "Tell me, Sarah, did Richard beat you up?"

Sarah shook her head vigorously.

"Then who?"

"No one," she said through gritted teeth. "I . . . I fell off my motorcycle."

Rios raised an eyebrow. "You ride a motorcycle?"

Sarah nodded.

"How'd you fall off?"

"Not paying attention."

Rios had seen her share of motorcycle accident victims. These injuries didn't fit the pattern. Particularly the red handprint on Sarah's arm. "You a member of the Athena Sisterhood, by chance?"

"Why?" Sarah met Rios' gaze, fear evident in her eyes. "What's that got to do with Richard getting killed?"

"That's a really good question. What does it have to do with who killed Richard?"

"Nothing."

"So, who killed Richard?"

"Beats me." Sarah covered her mouth with her hand.

"You want to help us catch who did, right?"

"Yeah."

"You two dating?"

Sarah looked away and blew her nose. "I didn't really know him. Just saw him around the complex, you know?"

"Was Richard dating your roommate Genette?"

"Maybe. I don't know."

"You don't know who your roommate was dating?"

"We traveled in different circles."

"Makes sense. She was a sorority girl. You're an artist and a biker. What's your road name, by the way?"

"Why? It doesn't have anything to do with anything."

"You never know. Devil's in the details, they say."

This brought a glare from Sarah. "It's Orphan, if you must know."

Rios saw an in. "Interesting name. I'm an orphan, too."

"Yeah right." Sarah scoffed.

"It's true. My parents were killed in Guatemala when I was sixteen. How about you?"

"Plane crash. I was eleven."

"You grow up in the system?"

Sarah shook her head. "My aunt and uncle took me in."

"Good to have family," said Rios. "So, why would someone kill Richard and dump his body on your doorstep?"

"I got no idea." Sarah wrapped her arms around her, staring intently at the table.

"Sarah, I know you want to help us find who killed Richard, so I need you to be honest with me. Were you two intimate?"

Sarah blushed. "Yeah." She buried her face in her hands and sobbed. "Why is all this happening to me?"

"What is happening to you? What aren't you telling us, Sarah?" asked Morris in a stern voice.

"Nothing, I swear."

"Did Richard hurt you?" asked Rios.

"No, he'd never *do* that." Sarah sat up and wiped her face. "He was always sweet to me."

Rios met her eyes. "So, who beat you up?"

Sarah gasped and covered the bruise on her arm. "No one. I told you, I dropped my bike."

"That handprint on your arm didn't come from a motorcycle accident."

"I don't know what you're talking about."

Someone outside knocked on the door, then opened it. Rebecca Li stood there in a tan business suit. "Morning, detectives. Is my client under arrest?"

Rios grimaced. "No."

"Excellent. Then this interview is over."

"Counselor," said Morris, standing, "we are investigating the murder of your client's boyfriend. I would think that you and your client would want to help us find the killer."

"Maybe if you spent less time harassing members of the Athena Sisterhood and more time investigating the Confederate Thunder for their numerous criminal activities, you'd find the suspects you're looking for."

"Are you suggesting the Thunder is responsible for this murder?" Rios looked at Sarah. "Is that what happened, Orphan?"

Sarah shrugged. "The Thunder's been going after us any chance they get. They attacked us at Gertie's and then again at Iron Goddess. Ran a couple of us off the road a few nights ago. But y'all don't do anything. So, what's it matter what I say? Y'all never arrest them."

Rios felt a pang of guilt over the lack of response by the sheriff's office. "I'm sorry if we've dropped the ball." Rios shot a glance at Morris. She and Bello were responsible for a lot of these cases. "But I will personally look into these matters."

"I think we're done here," said Li. "Come on, Sarah. Let's go."

42

———

"Why aren't you working on the Stansbury bike?" Terrance walked into the office. "We're behind schedule as it is."

Shea lifted her aching head from her arms nested on the desk. "Geez, T, you gotta yell like that?"

"I'm not yelling. But if we miss our deadline . . ."

"Relax! We're almost done with fabrication. Should be ready to send it out for paint in another day or so."

"So, why's Kyle the only one working on the bike?"

"I'll be out there soon as the ibuprofen kicks in. Kyle knows what he's doing." Shea rubbed her temples and emptied her coffee cup. "We're only a few days behind schedule. I'll make it up when the parts come back."

Terrance sat across from her, gave her coffee cup a sniff, and glowered. "We should discuss your drinking problem."

"I ain't got no drinking problem."

"Really?" Terrance yanked open her desk drawer and pulled out the bottle of Bushmills. "Then why's your coffee cup smell like an Irish pub?"

Shea gave him a bleary-eyed stare, but said nothing.

"Shea, I'm a recovering addict. I'm not judging you. I've been where you are."

Shea shook her head and was rewarded with a fresh wave of pain. "You ain't never been where I am. I'm dealing with a lotta shit right now."

"Like what?"

"Like Monster."

"He still pressuring you to—"

"He's dead, T. Killed himself last night." She could still smell the metallic tang of Monster's blood in the air and it made her want to hurl.

Terrance knitted his brow. "Suicide? Why? Because of that photo you took?"

"No. At least, I don't think so. I don't know." Tendrils of guilt tightened around her battered psyche. "He was dying. Ass cancer, he said. Terminal."

"Were you there? Did you try to stop him?"

Shea bore holes into Terrance. "I didn't know he was going to do it. He was just drunk and depressed. I walked outta his house and was about to drive away when I heard the shot."

"You call the cops?"

Shea chuckled darkly. "Yeah, right."

"No, I suppose not." Terrance put a hand on Shea's arm. "I'm sorry, sister girl. I know he was family, sort of."

"Annie's gonna be devastated."

"All the more reason for you to get your shit together. She's going to need you to lean on. Maybe you should look into AA."

"Maybe you should mind your own fucking business." Shea stood up and brushed past him. "Don't need another of your lectures." In the hallway, she almost stumbled over Kyle.

"Dude," said Kyle, trying to keep her upright. "One of your biker club friends is out back asking for you."

"We'll continue this discussion later," called Terrance.

"Let's not," she mumbled, and shuffled into the garage.

Just outside the open garage door, Orphan stood next to her Harley Sportster 883.

"Damn, Orphan. What happened to your face?" Shea hugged her gingerly.

"I, uh, dropped my bike. Hoping you could knock out some dents. I think the back fender may be scraping. I can pay cash."

Shea walked around the bike, inspecting the damage. Softball-size dents covered the tank, fenders, and exhaust. The headlight was cracked. Gauges dangled from their mountings. Both side mirrors were gone. "How'd this happen?"

"Laid it down to avoid a coyote. Must have hit some rocks or something."

"Or something." Shea's finger traced the outline of a dent on the side of the tank. No scraped paint or chrome. Just dents, even in places there shouldn't be if it had been dropped at speed.

Orphan had the jittery eyes of a frightened rabbit. Shea grew up seeing the same look in her abused mother's eyes. "Cut the shit, Orphan. We both know you didn't drop your bike. Is Richard abusing you?"

"Richard? No!" Orphan shook her head, wiping tears from her face.

"Look at me." Shea held her gaze. "If it's him, just tell me. I'll personally beat the ever-loving shit outta him so he never does it again."

"It's not him." Orphan collapsed onto the seat of motorcycle, buried her face in her hands, and sobbed. "Richard's dead."

Shea stood there stunned. Seeing Orphan overcome with emotion evoked Shea's own conflicted feelings about Monster's suicide. "Shit! How'd it happen?"

"Oh God, I'm such a horrible person."

"Why? What'd you do?"

"If I tell you, you'll hate me."

"I won't. Trust me, no matter what it is, I've done worse."

Orphan took a deep breath. "I've been living off the trust fund my parents left me when they died. Paid for my condo. My bike. Past three years of college." She wiped her face. "Then my accountant tells me the balance is running low. Tuition's been going up. Property taxes, health insurance, all the other shit. I tried finding a job, but no one willing to hire an art student is wants to pay what I need to make. So, a friend of mine told me she was making a mint dealing party favors at clubs."

"And by party favors, you're not talking glow sticks and beads."

"Poppers, weed, and ecstasy, mostly. A little acid and Special K now and then. But nothing serious, you know? No meth or dope or coke. She hooked me up with her supplier. Good money, so why not, ya know?"

Shea glowered at her. "Other than getting yourself or someone else killed."

"Everything was fine until my supplier wanted me to sell this new kind of ecstasy, something called hex. Didn't know what was in it at first. Just that it was like ex, but with a bigger kick. Customers loved it."

"Until . . ."

"Until my roommate tried some and . . . and she died. Turns out my supplier had recut it with rat poison. Cops said a few other folks died, too." Orphan broke down in sobs. "Oh God, I never meant to hurt anybody. Just trying to make a little bank, ya know?"

Shea felt sick. She'd been so sure Deb was the one dealing the hex. After all the shit Deb had put her through, Shea had been only too happy to turn the manipulative woman over to the cops. But now that it was Orphan, she didn't know what to do. Shea saw a lot of herself in Orphan. She wasn't ready to give her up to Rios. "Jesus, girl."

"I know. I'm a horrible person."

"You gotta quit. Now. Before anyone else gets hurt."

"I tried. My supplier won't let me. Says I'm too good an earner. When I tried, they killed Pipes and made it look like an OD, to let me know they're serious. Then . . . they showed up at my condo. Insisted I start earning again. Brought ten grand's worth of product for me to sell. When I refused . . ." Orphan stared out across the back parking lot. Her face hardened with anger. "This morning, I found Richard's body on my doorstep. Throat cut."

Shea started putting the pieces together. "Your supplier go by the name Bonefish?"

Orphan gasped. "How'd you know that?"

"Bonefish bought the hex the Confederate Thunder stole from the Jaguars. Where do I find him?"

"Him who?"

"Bonefish."

"Bonefish isn't a he; she's a she."

"So how do I find her?"

"I have a phone number. I call it and Lizzie Black, one of her enforcers, drops off the drugs and picks up the cash."

"What's Bonefish's real name?"

"I don't know. Everybody just calls her Bonefish."

"They do this to your face and bike?"

"Yeah."

"Just so you know, your days of dealing drugs are over," said Shea matter-of-factly.

"I can't. They'll keep hurting people I know. Maybe even you."

"Then we'll get the club involved and make sure they don't."

"No, I don't want anyone else to get hurt. It's my problem. I'll deal with it."

"When they killed Pipes, they made it the club's problem." Shea pulled out her phone and called Labrys.

"What do you want, Havoc?" asked Labrys in a nasty voice. "I'm busy."

"Look, I'm sorry I accused you of dealing hex."

"Well, that's a first! Shea Stevens apologizing. I should—"

"But I found out who is."

There was a pause. "Who?"

"She's right here." Shea handed the phone to Orphan.

"Hello?" Orphan looked like a dog about to be whipped. "Yeah, it's me." Her face crumpled in humiliation.

Shea couldn't make out Labrys' words, but could tell she was yelling. Orphan related the same story about her dealings with Bonefish.

"Labrys wants to talk to you." Orphan returned the phone to Shea, looking utterly defeated.

"What's the word?" asked Shea.

"I honestly don't know what to do. Bad enough we have the Thunder breathing down our necks. And now this Bonefish bitch is killing our members? I'm out of my depth here. What do we do?"

"Wow! Debbie Raymond asking my advice? That's a first! I should—"

"Yeah, yeah, you made your point. You've dealt with people like this before. I haven't."

A plan formed in Shea's head. "I got a few ideas."

"Like what?"

"Hold on for a sec." Shea covered the mic on the phone. "Orphan, you got that stash of Bonefish's drugs, right?"

"At my condo. Why?"

Shea turned back to the phone. "Call Savage and the rest of the club. Have them meet me at Orphan's place in an hour, armed if possible. Everyone but Dragon."

"Why not Dragon?" asked Labrys.

"She's the club's lawyer. What I'm proposing ain't exactly legal."

Labrys huffed. "I have a class to teach in twenty minutes."

"This is for the safety of your club, Lady President. What are your priorities?"

"Shit! Fine, I'll call my department head. Tell him I've got menstrual cramps. He won't ask any questions. See you in an hour."

Shea hung up. "Follow me." Shea led Orphan to the shop's office. "Yo, T! Gotta run an errand. I'll be back . . . well, it might be awhile." She slipped on her Kevlar vest.

"What are you doing? The Stansbury bike's our number-one priority"

"Kyle can handle it. I got other priorities." Shea tossed him the keys to Orphan's bike. "Also, write up an estimate to repair the damage on the Sportster out back."

"Shea!" Terrance grumbled as Shea pulled on her jacket and helmet. "This is not the way to run a business."

"No, but if I'm real lucky, I might save a few lives." She pulled her Glock out of her top drawer and tucked it into her waistband holster. "Time to pay the piper, Orphan!"

"What am I driving?"

"You're riding bitch. Grab your helmet."

43

AS SHEA REACHED the top of the stairs outside Orphan's condo, her eyes were drawn to the rust-colored stain on the concrete. Shea could still smell the scent of blood. A trail of drops led to the other end of the breezeway. Orphan whimpered and covered her mouth, a tear streaming down her left cheek.

"Come on, girl." Shea put a hand on Orphan's shoulder. "Let's get inside."

Orphan unlocked the door. Shea found herself gazing wide-eyed around at the condo. "So, this is the kinda crib dealing drugs gets ya, huh?"

Orphan didn't respond.

"Sorry, guess that was uncalled for. So, where's the stash?"

Orphan led Shea to her kitchen area, pulled a large Stouffer's lasagna box from the freezer and set it on the table. She opened the cardboard flap and took out the foil container. "In here."

Shea removed the aluminum foil cover to reveal a

plastic bag filled with smaller bags, each containing black pills.

"Weren't you afraid your roommate would cook it, thinking it was lasagna?"

"Genette's allergic . . . *was* allergic to gluten."

A loud pounding at the door set Shea into high alert. She wrapped a hand around the grip of her Glock.

"Who is it?" asked Orphan in a timid voice.

"It's Savage. Labrys, Fuego, Brillo, and Indigo are with me, too."

Orphan opened the door and let them in. "You have any problem getting through the gate? I told the guard to let in anyone on a motorcycle asking for me."

"No problem at all," said Savage as she hugged Orphan.

"Nice place." Brillo, a lanky woman with freckle-dusted ivory skin and tight curls of coppery hair, stopped at the bag of drugs on the kitchen table. "Holy shit! What the hell's this?"

Orphan lowered her head and sunk into a brass-framed chair.

"I know what it is." Fuego glared at Orphan. "It's ecstasy mixed with *chiva*. They call it hex, and for good reason. That shit killed Pipes. You a drug dealer, *mija*?"

Shea folded her arms and met the gazes of the other women. "Orphan's been dealing at the clubs, not realizing her supplier recut it with rat poison."

"Geez, prospect!" Labrys picked up the bag of hex and tossed it at Orphan. "You been doing this under our noses the whole time?"

"Didn't mean for no one to get hurt. Just trying to keep my condo."

"Aw, *pinche pobrecita*." *Poor fucking girl.* Fuego kicked the leg of Orphan's chair. "Don't care who she kill, long as she keeps her fancy crib, eh, *pendeja*?"

"Havoc, you gonna report her to that cop you're working for?" asked Indigo.

Shea's face warmed as all eyes turned to her. "No."

"You a snitch, prospect?" Fuego shoved Shea's shoulder.

"Not by choice. Some detective jammed me up on bogus charges a while back." Shea straightened her jacket. "If we turn Orphan over to the cops, her supplier will likely come after us."

"Why?" asked Brillo. "We're not involved."

"To keep Orphan from talking."

"Did you sell this shit to Pipes?" asked Savage. The other women pressed in around Orphan.

She looked up at them like a wounded puppy. "No. My supplier, Bonefish, had Pipes killed when I threatened to quit."

Labrys cuffed Orphan's ear. "This is why we don't allow drugs in the club, you idiot. Shit likes this happens."

"Point is," said Shea, "we're all in danger here. We need to work together."

Labrys pressed her palms against her temples. "You said you have a plan?"

"Yeah. Are the rest of the gals coming?" asked Shea. "We need all the muscle we can get."

"This is it. Most couldn't get out of work." Labrys' face darkened as she exchanged a glance with Savage.

"So, what's the plan?" asked Brillo.

Shea held up the hex. "This bag's worth ten grand or more—money Bonefish probably doesn't want to lose. I'll call the number Orphan has for her, tell her to meet us somewhere. When Bonefish and her enforcer, Lizzie Black, show up, we take them out."

"How you going to convince her to show up, *mija*?" asked Fuego.

"I'll tell her we have her drugs and want to negotiate a truce."

"What if she doesn't want a truce?" asked Brillo.

"I'm sure she won't. And even if she did, she wouldn't keep it. Not after all the shit she's done. But she'll want her drugs back. I just need her in my gun sights."

"Havoc, you're talking murder," said Indigo. "Since when are we an outlaw club? Can't we just scare them?"

"We're not outlaw," insisted Labrys. "But we have a right to protect ourselves. Against the Thunder. Against these drug dealers."

"I've dealt with people like this several times. They don't scare easy. Putting a beat down on them ain't enough. They'll come right back atcha when you ain't looking. Either they die or we do." Shea looked from one face to another. "So, are we ready to do this?"

"Hold on, prospect," said Labrys. "We're a club. We vote on these things."

Shea shrugged. "You're the one who said you were outta your depth."

Labrys smirked. "All in favor of Havoc's plan?"

All but Indigo and Brillo raised their hands and said, "Aye."

Indigo shook her head. "I can't risk going to prison. Not in my situation. They would fucking kill me in there. Or worse."

Savage put an arm around Indigo. "You wanna sit this one out, babe, I won't blame you."

"Brillo?" asked Labrys.

Brillo knitted her brow and sighed. "Sorry, I can't risk losing custody of my kids again."

"That's fine. The rest of us are in," said Fuego.

Savage nodded. "Damn straight."

"Absolutely," said Shea.

Orphan shook her head. "Y'all don't know who you're dealing with. Lizzie Black—she's huge. And fast. I heard she served in the Israeli military. She could probably take out all y'all with one arm tied behind her back. She fights dirty."

"So do I." Shea pulled out her Glock and chambered a round, then reholstered it. "And the fact that she's big just makes her a larger target."

Tears ran down Orphan's face. "I'm sorry I got y'all into this. I'll do whatever you want. They killed Richard. They killed Pipes. I'm in it to the end." She pulled out her phone, tapped through a few screens, then held it up to Shea. "Here's the number."

Shea dialed the number on her own phone. It rang five times before a recorded female voice said, "Leave a message."

"Hello, Bonefish. My name's Shea." She silently cursed herself for not using her road name. "I have the hex you gave Orphan. Reckon it's worth ten grand or more. You want it back, call me. If I don't hear back from you by midnight, I'll flush it down the toilet."

"What do we do when she does call back?" asked Brillo. "Where we going to meet her?"

Shea thought about it. "Black Rock Mine. There's a lot of equipment there we can use for cover."

"Mine's closed," said Savage.

"Yup," Shea said with a nod. "But I can pick the lock on the gate easy enough."

"Let's show this bitch we mean business." From a shoulder holster under her jacket, Labrys pulled a Glock, identical to Shea's, holding it cocked sideways at arm's length and swinging it around.

"Jesus Christ!" Shea pushed Labrys' arm down until the

pistol was pointing at the floor. "You even know how to use that thing?"

"Yeah. Sort of."

"Sort of will get you killed, Lady President."

"Fine." Labrys holstered the pistol. "You teach me."

Shea rolled her eyes. "Take a fucking class."

"I need to learn now. You want me to show up unable to defend myself?"

Fuego nudged Shea. "She's got a point, *mija*. We don't know how many Bonefish got working for her. We need all the firepower we can get. If she don't know how to shoot, she's no good to us."

"As your president," said Labrys with a smirk, "I order you to accompany me to the gun range and teach me how to shoot."

"Oh good lord!" Shea hated to admit it, but Fuego was right. "Fine. Let's go. Anyone else wanna come on this field trip?"

"Nah," said Savage. "We'll stay here and keep an eye on Orphan. Just in case Lizzie Black shows up again."

Shea picked up the bag of hex. "I'll take this with me. If Bonefish or one of her crew shows up, tell her she needs to call me."

44

———

SHEA STOOD behind Labrys in the stall at the Avid Marksman Indoor Gun Range. Each wore a pair of rented ear muffs. "Keep the index finger of your shooting hand parallel to the slide, with the rest of your fingers wrapped around the grip. Put your thumb down on the other side or it could break it when you fire."

Labrys pressed her body against Shea's. "Like this?" Her voice had a hint of breathiness in it that brought heat to Shea's groin.

Shea tried to ignore it. "Lay the thumb of your other hand on top of the first one and wrap the fingers of your left on top of your right fingers."

"Like a golfer's grip."

"I suppose. Never played golf."

"Really? You'd love it. We'll have to go sometime. I can teach you. Only fair since you're showing me how to shoot."

"Deb . . ."

"It's Labrys!"

"Whatever! Let's stick with the subject at hand. We ain't got a lotta time."

"Sorry, sweetie."

"And don't call me sweetie. I ain't been your sweetie in a long time."

"Geez, Shea, what crawled up your derrière and died?"

"Can we just focus on shooting?"

"Fine. Now what?"

"Okay, is the safety off?"

Labrys lowered her pistol, pointing it toward Shea as she examined it. "Umm..."

"Hey, careful!" Shea pushed the barrel away. "Ya gotta pay attention to where your gun's pointed."

"Sorry! How do I tell if the safety is off?"

"It's a trick question, actually. Glock's don't have a safety except on the trigger itself. That's why you keep your finger out of the trigger guard until you're on target and ready to shoot. Now look down the barrel and line up your sights."

"Okay, got it."

"Slip your finger onto the trigger and slowly squeeze. Don't pull!"

"What's the difference?"

"Squeezing means smoothly tightening your whole hand. Pulling is jerking your finger."

Labrys squinted her eyes shut and began squeezing.

"Stop! What are you doing?"

"I'm squeezing."

"Why you got your eyes closed?"

"It's going to be loud."

"We've got ear protection on. Just relax. Forget the bang. Take a breath. Now let it out slowly as you squeeze, keeping your sights lined up on the target."

Labrys once again squinted and pulled the trigger. The gunshot visibly shook her. "Holy shit, that was loud. Where'd I hit the target? I don't see a hole."

"You missed it completely. Set your gun on the shelf

and step aside. Lemme show you how it's done." Shea moved in to where Labrys had stood, raised her pistol, and squeezed off three shots, all three a bull's-eye.

"Whoa! How'd you do that?"

"Years of practice. You didn't hit the target because you closed your eyes. You gotta stop anticipating the gunshot."

"Okay, let me try again." Labrys stepped up and fired off two more rounds. Both hit several inches away from the bull's-eye. "I did it!"

Labrys laid down her gun, threw her arms around Shea, and kissed her on the lips.

Before Shea realized what was happening, she found herself kissing Labrys back, slipping into the well-worn groove of their former relationship until Jessica's face appeared in her mind

Shea pulled away. "Fuck!"

"Shea, it's okay. We still love each other."

Shea flinched. "No, you had your chance. I love Jessica now."

"Shea, how can you love her? She's not a biker. She doesn't understand the feel of the wind in your hair, the thrill of whipping through twisties, the roar of a 1200 cc engine throbbing between your legs." Labrys put a hand on the inside of Shea's thigh.

Shea batted it away. "I don't care. She treats me with respect. And I . . . I just betrayed her."

"Oh please! It was just an innocent kiss."

"I think I should go home."

"Shea," Labrys took Shea's hand. "Don't leave me. I need to learn how to do this. My survival depends on it."

Shea pulled away. "You just need to practice. I can't be your teacher. There's too much history."

"Prospect, as your president, I am ordering you to stay here and help me. We are in this together. We are sisters."

Shea glowered at her. "This is why I left you, you know? You and your fucking control issues."

"You would abandon your sisters when we need you the most? That's so typical of you and your commitment issues."

Shea balled her fist, but resisted the urge to pop Labrys in the mouth. "Fine. I'll see you through this. But I am fucking sick of you ordering me around like I'm a child. Maybe I ain't all college educated like you, but I got a brain. I know shit you have no clue about."

"Then use that brain of yours to teach me how to protect myself."

Shea fumed and found herself staring into Labrys' deep chestnut eyes. Old feelings rumbled beneath the surface. Anger, longing, frustration. "Get up to the line and try again. And keep your fucking eyes open."

AN HOUR LATER, they stood alongside their bikes parked on the street as they geared up to ride. Labrys was droning on about some politician caught fooling around on his wife.

The low rumble of Harleys shook the air. Shea immediately recognized the two bikers wearing Confederate Thunder cuts cruising toward them. Mackey and One-Shot. For an instant, she and Mackey locked eyes.

"Get down!"

"What'd you say?" Labrys asked.

Mackey raised a pistol and let loose several shots. Shea drew hers, but held her fire to avoid hitting passing cars. In an instant, Mackey and One-Shot had vanished into traffic.

Shea turned to Labrys. "You okay?"

Labrys lay on her back with a bullet hole in the front of her helmet, just above the open visor. Her eyes were wide, unfocused and dilated, her face pale and expressionless.

"Fuck! Deb, hold on." Shea lifted Labrys' head and found a larger exit hole near the back of the helmet. "Shit! Shit! Shit!"

Shea gently pulled the helmet off Labrys' head. To Shea's surprise there was very little blood. The bullet had gone through the helmet's padding, but only grazed Labrys' scalp.

"Ughn..."

"You're okay, sweetie. You're just in shock."

"They...they shot."

"They got your helmet. You hit anywhere else?" Shea searched Labrys' chest for signs of wounds, but didn't find anything. "You're gonna be okay."

Labrys took a deep breath. "I'm...I'm alive?"

"Yeah, you're alive. Can you ride?"

"I...I think so."

"Okay, let's head back to Orphan's place."

"No, no. Just...wanna go home."

Shea grimaced. They needed to get back to the safety of the group. But she didn't feel like arguing. She put her own helmet on Labrys' bleeding head. "Okay, Lady President. You're the boss. We'll go to your place."

RIOS WAS MULLING over her notes from her interview with Sarah Cohen, trying to fit it in with the rest of the evidence, when a stack of case files dropped on her desk, pulling her out of the zone. "What the hell?"

Morris wore an expression of concern tinged with shame. "I found these. They were 'misfiled' with some cold cases," she said using air quotes. "I found them by chance."

Johnson stopped what she was doing as Rios rifled through them. "Somebody killed three members of the Athena Sisterhood?"

"And sexually assaulted them. Maintenance worker found the bodies behind a building at a rest area off I-17."

"This happened a week ago. Why am I just seeing them now?"

"Not only were the cases misfiled, they were marked CLOSED—UNSOLVED on the system."

"I remember that call out," said Johnson. "Why would someone close it unsolved right away?"

Rios' blood boiled. "Who changed the status on the system?"

"According to the computer, Detective Needham in Property Crimes."

"Needham?" asked Rios. "He retired last month."

Morris nodded. "He did. But get this: the cases were never assigned to him."

"Who were they assigned to?" Rios closed the files and crossed her arms.

Morris' face warmed. "You."

"Me? I've never seen these before in my life." Rios scanned the room. *Who would hide these cases? Aguilar, maybe. But he's just a deputy, and not too smart. Someone higher up must be involved.* "You tell anyone about these?"

"Just you two."

"Keep it that way for now. Someone's sabotaging my investigation. I aim to find out who it is."

Morris nodded. "You got it."

Rios held up the files. "Thanks for this."

"No problem." Morris started to walk away.

"Hey wait! Where are you with those assault cases—the one at that lesbian bar and the one at Iron Goddess?"

"Nowhere. We had some recent random shooting cases that took priority. Why?"

"You mind if I take a crack at them?"

"I'll bring them over. Anything else you want to take off my hands?"

"That'll do for now. But keep your ears open for anything else suspicious."

"What are you thinking?" asked Johnson.

"I have a CI claiming someone here's running interference for the Thunder. She may be right." Rios pulled out her phone and dialed, but the call went to voicemail. "Shea, we need to talk. Call me ASAP."

"Can we just take these cases like this?"

"Goodman wanted me to put an end to the violence between these two clubs. That's what I intend to do." Rios searched her phone directory, pulled up a familiar name, and called it.

"Federal Bureau of Investigation, Special Agent Marc Obregón speaking."

"Marc, it's Toni."

"Hey *chica!* Long time, no see. You still slumming with Sheriff Keeler?"

Rios grimaced. "'Fraid so. Listen, you ever hear of someone going by the name Bonefish?"

Obregón chuckled darkly. "Bonefish, huh? Yeah, why?"

"I'm investigating six deaths involving hex laced with strychnine. One of my CIs claims this Bonefish guy bought it from the Confederate Thunder, recut it, and is selling it in local clubs."

"Well, Bonefish isn't a guy. Bonefish is a woman, and she's a ghost."

"A ghost?"

"Her name pops up every now and then, but we haven't

been able to get anyone to tell us much," explained Obregón. "Apparently she's got some serious muscle behind her. One rumor is that she's a local businesswoman, but that's all we got. You say the Thunder's connected to this?"

"Only that they stole the hex from the Jaguars, then sold it to Bonefish. That said, I also have a stack of assault and homicide cases that I suspect are linked to the Thunder."

"Really? We've been investigating the Thunder's meth operation for a while now. So far without much help from your beloved sheriff. Want to compare notes? Maybe we can nail both the Thunder and your Bonefish."

Rios glanced at Johnson, who was listening eagerly. "Yeah, I'll stop by your office in a bit."

"I look forward to seeing you."

Rios hung up. "Come on, Johnson. We're taking a trip to the FBI."

45

LABRYS WHIMPERED as Shea helped her off with the helmet and laid it on the all-too-familiar handmade quilt on Labrys' bed. The bedroom was cozy, organized, and very pink, just as Shea remembered it.

"How's it look?" Labrys asked through gritted teeth.

"Bleeding stopped. It's all kinda dried and caked in your hair. How you feel?"

"Ugh. Hurts like hell." Labrys touched her scalp gingerly and winced. "But I don't feel as jittery as I did."

"We should clean out the wound. Make sure there's no gunshot residue or anything in there that could get infected."

"Sounds painful, but you're probably right." Labrys wriggled out of her jacket and tossed it next to the helmet. "Been awhile since you've been here, huh?"

"Looks the same." The place was filled with ghosts of better times.

Labrys gingerly lifted her shirt up and over her head, groaning as she did so.

"Hey! What are you doing?" Shea caught herself staring at Labrys' chest and turned away.

"Taking a shower to rinse out my hair. You're gonna help me, right? I need someone to make sure I get out all of the blood and debris."

"Understand that you and me—we're over." Shea heard the rustle of Labrys' motorcycle jeans. *What the hell am I doing here?*

Without warning, Labrys' arms wrapped around Shea's chest from behind, pressing their bodies together.

"We don't have to be," Labrys whispered. Her breath tickled the back of Shea's neck.

Shea felt herself get aroused. "Deb, cut it out. I mean it! You wanna take a shower? Do it. But hurry the hell up. Never know when Bonefish is gonna call back."

Labrys slapped Shea on the back. "Geez, I was just kidding around. You're no fun."

A few minutes later the shower started running in the bathroom.

"I shouldn't be here." Shea wandered around the room. Everything from the stained-glass lampshade to the knick-knacks on the floor-to-ceiling bookshelf brought back more memories. Antiquing in Jerome. A road trip to see a Pink Trinkets concert at the Coachella Music Festival. Attending a marriage equality rally at the state capitol in Phoenix. Riding with the Dykes on Bikes in Ironwood's LGBT pride parade.

Shea's phone rang. Her pulse quickened. *Shit, this is it.* "Yeah?" she said in a deadpan voice.

"Hey, baby, it's Jess. I called the shop and Terrance said you weren't there. What's going on?"

"Oh. Hey." A lump formed in Shea's throat. "Just getting . . . uh, things resolved. You know, so it's . . . um, safe to come home."

"I've been worried about you. People are saying there've been some random shootings in the area. That wasn't you, was it?"

The sound of the shower cut off. Shea swallowed hard. "Me? No, not at all. I . . . I'm safe."

"What's wrong? Your voice sounds funny."

"Is that Bonefish?" asked Labrys, walking out of the bathroom, dripping wet.

"Who's with you, Shea? That's not Deb is it?"

Shea's face warmed. "Technically, yes. But it's—"

"Why the hell are you with her?"

"We're getting . . . uh . . . things worked out. Look, I need to hang up. I'm expecting a call."

"Oh really? You send me off to stay with Terrance so you and Deb can play house?"

"Jess, it ain't like that."

Labrys pressed her wet body against Shea's. "Hi, Jessica."

"After all the time we've spent together. I can't believe you'd do me like this." The anger in Jessica's voice turned to hurt.

Shea twisted away from Labrys. "Jess, trust me. I wouldn't do that to you . . . to us. I'm just trying to put all of this craziness to bed. I mean, put it to rest. I'm waiting to hear back from someone. I'll be home soon."

"Fuck your fear of commitment. Fuck your bad-girl mystique. Fuck Iron Goddess. Fuck the Athena Sisterhood. Fuck your obsession with vigilante justice. But most of all, fuck you, Shea Stevens. I'm done being the only one making this relationship work."

The line went dead. Shea's hands shook with anger. She glared at Labrys as the scent of cucumber-melon lotion filled Shea's nostrils. "Thanks a lot for that. Jessica dumped me 'cause she thinks I'm cheating on her."

Labrys shook her head, a mocking expression on her face. "So paranoid. You know, that kind of jealousy isn't good for a relationship. It never would have worked out anyway."

"Just shut up and get dressed." Shea walked away and sat on the living room couch, staring at her phone.

Labrys plopped down on an ottoman opposite her. "Hey, I'm sorry. I was just kidding around. If Jessica's got any brains, she'll take you back. And if she doesn't, well, I'm still available."

"Yeah, thanks, but no thanks. How's your head?"

"Better." Labrys gazed absently at the floor. "Look, thanks for saving my life."

"I didn't do nothing." Shea looked up at her. "You got another helmet?"

"Yeah, an old Bell I haven't worn in a while. Strap always chaffed my chin, but it'll do for now." A tear ran down Labrys' cheek. "I thought I was up for this. But after what happened, I . . . I don't know. Maybe we should just turn this whole thing over to the cops."

"That mighta been an option if I didn't have a shitload of hex in the top case of my bike."

"I'm scared, Havoc." Labrys' trembling hand clasped Shea's. "I never came that close to dying before." She leaned forward and hugged Shea tightly.

Shea held her as a wave of sobs burst forth. "I'm know it's scary. I've been there more times than I can count."

"You're so tough, Shea. I guess that's why I'm drawn to you. I need your strength."

Shea pulled away. "You are strong. I mean, look at you. You're the president of the Athena Sisterhood. You organize protests and fund-raisers. You lobby politicians." Shea put a hand on Labrys' bare arm. It was as soft as she remembered. A longing welled up in Shea. More than a longing. A need. She felt herself leaning toward Labrys' pillowy lips and pulled herself away, shaking away the cobwebs of seduction. "Get some clothes on."

Labrys nodded. "All right."

Shea's phone rang again. The caller ID told her it was Terrance. "What's up, T? I'm kinda expecting a call."

"Chlöe Stansbury wants to stop by the shop at seven tonight to see how the bike's coming."

"T, I can't. I've got something important going on. Besides, the shop closes at six. Can't she come by tomorrow?"

"She insisted on doing it tonight. She paid a lot of money for this bike. Least we can do is accommodate her a little."

"Can't you show it to her?"

"I offered, but since you're the one building it, she wants you."

Shea's grip tightened on the phone. "All right. I'll meet her at the shop. Seven o'clock."

"Appreciate it! Oh, and what the hell's going on between you and Jessica? She called and said she's going to stay with a friend."

"She what? What about Annie?"

"She'll be all right. Elon's out of school for the holiday break. He can keep an eye on her. So you two have a fight or what?"

"Sorta. It's complicated. Tell Elon thanks. I owe you one."

"No, you owe me several. But you can start paying me back by making Ms. Stansbury happy."

"Will do, T."

Shea ended the call and pounded her fists against her head.

"What was that all about?" said Labrys.

"Goddamn client. Insists on stopping by the shop to see the bike I'm building for her."

"What about dealing with Bonefish? We can't do this without you."

"Relax. This shouldn't take long. If Bonefish calls, I'll stall her long enough for us to set up an ambush."

46

Shea was unlocking Iron Goddess' back door when two vehicles pulled into the back lot—Chlöe's beige Mercedes and a dark green Jaguar convertible. Shea waited by the door as Chlöe got out of her car. A tall woman with dark hair and broad shoulders emerged from the Jag—the same woman who had glared at her a couple of doors down from the Tenth Inning. This evening she was dressed in a sport coat over a dark shirt.

"Shea, this is Ms. Elizabeth Schwartz, one of my associates. She and I have a business dinner later, so I asked her along. I hope you don't mind."

"No problem. Come on in." Shea led the two into the service bay and over to where Chlöe's bike rested on a bike stand. "Here it is. We'll be sending off to paint soon."

"Oh my, it looks great." Chlöe pointed to something on the bike. "What's that there?"

Shea bent down to examine what Chlöe was pointing at. "What? The oil pan—"

Too late Shea sensed Schwartz slip in behind her and

slam her head into the bike's gas tank. Before Shea could recover, Schwartz pulled her up in a half nelson.

Chlöe's delighted expression was replaced by a mask of malevolence. "Where's my product?"

Something clicked in Shea's brain. "Bonefish." That would make the Amazon holding her collar Lizzie Black.

"That's right," said Chlöe. "Now where the hell is it?"

"Safe."

Lizzie Black punched Shea in the kidney. Shea's eyes bugged out as she gasped in pain. Even with the motorcycle jacket the blow hurt like hell.

"I don't have time for games." Bonefish nodded at Lizzie Black, who pressed a .38-caliber revolver to Shea's head.

"Why . . . why're you dealing that shit?" Shea took a deep breath, struggling to control the pain. "Ain't you supposed . . . to get people off drugs?"

"I don't need to explain my business decisions. Now where the hell is it?"

Shea caught Lizzie Black with an elbow to the chin, knocking the revolver out of her hand. Shea kicked it away and barely avoided a haymaker barreling down at her head. Shea drove her fist into Lizzie's eye. The towering woman stumbled back.

Shea ducked behind Orphan's banged-up motorcycle, drew her Glock, and fired three shots into Lizzie's chest. The woman doubled over, groaning in pain, and dropped to her knees. A fourth shot and she collapsed on the floor, moaning quietly.

A bullet whizzed past Shea's ear. Bonefish knelt behind the shop's drill press with a small pistol in her hand. A second smacked into the bike's engine, a third punched through the seat, leaving a spray of foam rubber as it exited.

Shea returned fire, but Bonefish was tucked in good

behind the drill press. Two shots hit the base of the machine, a third the rack of tires behind it. "You kill me, you'll never find your drugs."

"Tell me where my product is or I'll kill everyone who works here."

"Not before the Athena Sisterhood tracks you down."

"A bunch of coed bikers? Hardly a concern." Bonefish chuckled. A bullet ripped into the bike's rear tire, as if to emphasize her point. Air hissed out of the deflating tire.

"That's what the Confederate Thunder thought till we burned down their bar." Shea noticed Bonefish's foot sticking out from behind the drill press. Shea took aim. Movement to her left caught her attention.

Shea ducked to avoid a four-foot-tall fire extinguisher hurtling toward her, but the nozzle caught her in the face. Lizzie was on her in an instant, driving her to the ground. The Glock skidded out of reach.

"Where is it?" growled the tall woman.

Shea struggled to escape but Lizzie sat on her chest, wrists pinned to the floor. Four bullet holes in the woman's shirt revealed an armored vest underneath.

"If I tell you," said Shea, "you leave us alone. Iron Goddess. Athena Sisterhood. All of us."

"You're not in a position to dictate terms, Shea Stevens." Bonefish stood over her, pointing Lizzie's revolver at Shea's head. "Where. Is. My. Product?"

Shea hocked a loogie and spit it in Bonefish's face. Shea then rotated her hip and used her knees to flip Lizzie onto Bonefish. While the two women untangled themselves from each other, Shea picked up a steel tailpipe from a rack and slammed it into Lizzie's broad back. Shea swung again aiming for Lizzie's head, but Lizzie whirled around and caught it in her hand.

Shea grappled for control of the tailpipe but Lizzie ripped it away from her and swung.

Pain exploded in Shea's head. She reeled backward. Her mind went hazy. A second blow knocked Shea off her feet.

"Where is it, Shea?"

Lizzie yanked Shea up by the collar. The room felt like it was spinning, making Shea sick to her stomach. Sounds had a weird echo and she was seeing double. "Fuck . . . you." She choked on the blood dripping from her nose back into her throat. Another punch to the gut knocked the wind out of her.

"Top case," Shea wheezed. "Back of my bike."

"See now. That wasn't so hard." Bonefish grinned. She handed the revolver back to Lizzie, her own pistol in her other hand. "Let's go see if you're telling the truth."

They marched Shea into the back parking lot. Snow flurries danced in the yellow glow of the security light. The cold helped Shea to focus as she unlocked the top case on her bike and opened it to reveal the bag of drugs.

"Thanks, Shea. Pleasure doing business with you." Bonefish nodded again to Lizzie, who raised the revolver and pulled the trigger.

Shea felt like she'd been hit in the chest with a sledge-hammer. A second shot hit her under her left arm at the edge of the vest. She gasped, struggling to control the searing pain. She fell to her knees, clinging to her bike for support. Her ears were ringing, her vision blurred.

"Told you not to fuck with me," said Bonefish somewhere in the darkness.

The revolver's warm muzzle pressed against Shea's forehead. "Fuck . . . you."

The gun's hammer clicked. Shea gasped. No gunshot. "Empty."

Shea's smile was rewarded with an explosion of pain as

Lizzie smacked her in the head with the .38. She found herself on her back, clinging to consciousness.

Have to stop the bleeding. She pressed on the wound under her arm, unable to stop shaking from a mixture of shock, cold, and adrenaline. The harder she pressed, the woozier she got. Until she blacked out.

47

"Havoc? Havoc! Can you hear me?" A worried voice called out from the darkness. "Please wake up!"

"Holy cats! She's bleeding," said a deeper voice.

Someone started shaking her. Her body felt numb and yet still hurt somehow. The chill of the winter night felt like a block of ice sitting on her chest, filling her mind with fog and mist.

"Havoc, it's Labrys. Oh Goddess, please be okay!"

"Havoc, can you open your eyes for me?" the voice sounded like Savage.

Shea opened an eye. Savage crouched over her, silhouetted against the lemony glow of the parking lot lights. Labrys and Indigo stood nearby.

"W-w-where . . . ?" Shea's voice sounded like gears grinding. She sat up. A sharp pain in her chest made it hard to breathe. "S-so . . . c-c-cold."

"Let's get you inside, girl," said Savage.

"No, wait!" insisted Labrys. "Don't we risk doing more damage if we move her?"

"Are you crazy?" asked Indigo. "It's fucking snowing. We leave her out here, she's gonna freeze to death."

"Normally, I would agree with Labrys. But her lips are blue. Pulse is weak. Right now, hypothermia's the most pressing issue."

"In-in-inside," croaked Shea.

"We gotcha, girl," replied Savage as she heaved Shea's arm over her shoulder. "Indigo, get on her other side and gently lift her up."

Savage and Indigo raised Shea to her feet. Shea cried out in agony as pain pounded through her body. A rush of vertigo left her nauseated.

"Be careful with her," said Labrys.

"You need us to carry you?" asked Indigo.

"No," Shea gasped as she forced herself to swallow the pain and the urge to vomit. "Inside."

Labrys opened the door. Savage and Indigo helped Shea limp into the brightly lit garage. The intense light made her head hurt worse. The air felt warm on her face, which helped to settle her stomach.

"There." Shea pointed to a chair near the shop's water jet cutting machine.

They lowered her onto the chair. She slumped a little but managed to remain upright.

"You got a coffeemaker in here?" asked Savage.

"Yeah. Showroom. Waiting area." Shea gestured toward the door that led to the office and the showroom. "Down the hall. Turn left."

"Labrys, you mind making us all some coffee?"

"Say, who's giving orders around here? I'm the president. You're just the sergeant at arms."

"I'm also an EMT and this is a medical emergency. So, get your bony ass down that hall, Madame President, and make us some fucking coffee. Unless you want Havoc here to freeze to death."

"You're gonna regret saying that, Savage," called Labrys. Her boot heels clicked a staccato beat across the concrete floor.

Shea couldn't help but smile.

"Let's see where all this blood is coming from, shall we?" Savage pulled off Shea's jacket and the prospect cut, sending sharp jabs of pain from her left underarm. Shea winced but refused to cry out.

"Her shirt's covered in blood," said Indigo. "What the hell happened to you, girl?"

Shea tried to focus, but her mind was clouded with pain and cold. Memories of the fight machine-gunned through her brain. "Shot." She closed her eyes and winced as someone pulled off her shirt.

Indigo gasped. "Someone shot you?"

"Thank goodness you were wearing your vest," said Savage. "So where are you bleeding from?"

Shea's body was jostled as Savage undid the Velcro straps with a ripping-crackle sound and lifted off the vest. Shea opened her eyes. Savage and Indigo were gaping at her, leaving Shea feeling exposed, wearing only her bra. Shea instinctively covered her chest with her uninjured arm and started shivering again.

"Holy cats, girl!" said Indigo. "Them welts are the size of grapefruits. And all that blood. Are the bullets still in her?"

Savage knelt down and examined first the vest, then Shea's chest. "Impact broke the skin on the one in the middle of her chest, but the slug's still in the Kevlar. But this one under her arm."

"Ow, fuck!" The jolt of pain at Savage's touch made her vision go gray for a moment.

"Sorry. Looks like the slug struck the edge of the vest,

penetrated the skin and muscle tissue and out again. Just a through and through. Most of the bleeding's stopped, in part due to the cold. I'd say biggest risk now is infection."

"And c-c-cold." Shea's teeth were chattering now.

"Hang in there. We'll get you warm real soon. You got a first-aid kit around here?"

Shea nodded toward a red box mounted on the opposite wall.

"Excellent." Savage retrieved it, cleaned out Shea's wounds with a bottle of water, and dressed them with antibiotic cream and bandages. "This is just temporary. You should see a doctor."

"Maybe we should call 911," suggested Indigo.

"No!" Labrys reappeared with a cup of coffee. "Don't need the cops involved."

"Then at least take her to the hospital," continued Indigo. "Look at her, she's a mess."

Shea's hands wrapped around the mug as she sipped the coffee. It was bitter, but hot. "No hospital," said Shea. "They'll report it."

Savage exchanged a glance with Indigo. "Well, you're the boss. Just keep an eye on it."

"Sweatshirt." Shea again pointed to the hallway door. "Showroom."

"Oh right. I'll get one for you." Indigo hustled away.

"So, what the hell happened tonight?" asked Labrys. "Who shot you?"

"Client. Chlöe Stansbury." The fog in her mind started to clear. "She's Bonefish."

Labrys' eyes went wide. "Bonefish was here? Who the hell is this bitch? Where do we find her?"

"Runs a rehab. Ironwood."

"Optimus?" asked Savage.

Shea started to nod, but it hurt to do so. "Yeah."

Indigo reappeared with a white sweatshirt bearing a large black Iron Goddess logo on the front. "This oughta help."

"Thanks."

"Why would someone who runs a rehab facility be dealing drugs?" asked Savage as Indigo helped Shea into the sweatshirt.

"Money. Always money." Shea remembered Bonefish holding the stash of drugs. "They got it."

"Got it? Got wha—" Labrys' jaw went slack. "Oh Goddess! They got the drugs back? Shea, how'd you let this happen?"

Shea flipped her the bird, but didn't speak.

"What does this mean?" asked Savage. "Are they still coming after us?"

"Don't know. Possibly." Shea glanced around the garage. "Could come back here. I should call Terrance."

Shea handed the cup to Indigo, pulled out her phone, and called Terrance. It rang four times before he answered it.

"Damn it, Shea! It's one o'clock in the fucking morning. Ain't it enough I'm taking care of your family?"

"T, something happened."

Terrance sighed loudly. "All right, what's going on, girlfriend? We haven't been robbed again, have we?"

"No. But our client . . ." She rubbed her chest, reliving the fight.

"Chlöe Stansbury?" There was concern in his voice. "You didn't piss her off, did you? We need the revenue from this job."

"She tried to kill me."

"She what? Why the hell would she do that?"

"She's the drug dealer. Bought the hex from the Thunder. Recut it with rat poison. Selling it at clubs." The security camera up by the ceiling caught Shea's eye. "All on the security feed."

"Are you okay?"

"I will be. Thanks to the Sisterhood. They found me. Patched me up. Lousy coffee."

"Well thank goodness for them. And the shop? They didn't burn it down, did they?"

"Shop's fine. We should close for now. Bitch is fucking crazy. Don't want no one else hurt."

Terrance sighed. "As much as I hate for us to lose the revenue, I agree. You called the police, right?"

"No."

"Well, why the hell not?"

"It's complicated. Gotta take care of this my way."

"Don't do anything stupid, Shea. You can't help Annie if you get your ass sent back to prison. Or killed."

"I'll be careful. How's Annie?"

"She misses you. Doesn't understand why she can't come home or why Jessica left."

"I didn't cheat on Jess. But haven't been a great girlfriend lately. I'll make it up to her."

"I'll call her in the morning. You gonna be all right?"

"I'm a hard one to kill. Maybe just too stupid to die."

"Watch your back, sister girl. Annie can't afford to lose no one else."

"Always. Talk at ya later." Shea hung up.

Indigo yawned. "So what now?"

"Sleep," said Shea.

"Can you ride?" asked Savage.

Shea tensed her jaw, knowing it would be a painful ride home. "I can manage. I live just a couple miles south."

"I'll go with her," said Labrys.

"No." Last thing Shea wanted was Labrys hovering over her, especially if Jessica called.

"Actually, Shea," said Savage, "I think that'd be a good idea. You shouldn't be alone. Not after what's happened. I'll be at Indigo's. Orphan and Fuego are over at Brillo's. Safety in numbers."

Shea looked wearily from Savage and Indigo to a very hopeful-looking Labrys. "Fine."

48

———

ICY WIND BLEW through the bullet holes in Shea's jacket as she wound through the twisties on the south side of Sycamore Mountain. She was grateful her home was just a few miles from the shop. As battered as her body was, she wasn't sure she could take much riding.

When they reached the house, Shea pulled into the garage and Labrys followed.

"You can't sleep here." Shea emptied the pockets of her jacket, now peppered with bullet holes, and tossed it into a black plastic garbage bin.

Labrys pulled off her helmet. "Why not? I thought we agreed. Safety in numbers?"

"If Jessica saw you here, she'd rip you a new one."

"I think I could take her." A smirk curled the corners of Labrys' mouth.

"That's not the least bit funny."

"I'm kidding. Geez! Besides, I thought you two were broken up."

"She's just pissed. You said yourself she'll come around."

"Either way, we need to stick together for safety's sake."

"You wanna be safe? Go home. Bonefish and Lizzie Black probably know where I live." Shea crossed her arms and winced in pain. "Gah!"

"See? You need me here to protect you."

"And how exactly you gonna do that?"

Labrys pulled her Glock from her saddlebag. "With this."

Shea glowered at her. "Fine. You can stay. But you're sleeping on the couch. And no funny business. Got it?"

Labrys gave her a three-fingered salute. "Scout's honor."

"Great. Now put that thing away before you shoot yourself with it. Or worse, me." Shea closed the garage door and led them inside.

The place felt so empty without Jessica and Annie. *I'm a horrible girlfriend. No wonder she left. I never make time for her. I'm not the least bit romantic. I fucking suck. I'd dump me, too.*

Shea pulled a bedsheet, a comforter, and a pillow from the hall linen closet and handed them to Labrys. "Here. If Ninja bothers you in the night just hiss at her. She'll get the message."

"Thanks. How's the pain?"

"It's pain. It hurts."

Labrys pulled a small white plastic cylinder from her pocket. "Try one of these. It'll help." She unscrewed the cap and deposited a round blue pill in Shea's palm.

"What the hell's this?"

"Percocet. It'll help you sleep."

Shea stared at it. Her head was pounding. Her chest ached. And her underarm still burned. She wasn't going to get any sleep without some help. Still . . . "No thanks." She held it out for Labrys to take back.

"Why the hell not? You've been shot, for Goddess' sake."

"My sister was addicted to that shit. Messed her up good. Got enough problems without turning into a junkie."

"Oh please! A single pill is not going to turn you into a junkie. It'll just help you sleep. You won't get addicted." Labrys pressed Shea's hand closed around the pill.

Labrys' fingers felt so cool, so hauntingly familiar. Her scent once again pulled sensual memories to the surface, memories Shea had worked hard to erase. This was the real drug.

"Fine. Just one." From the freezer, Shea pulled out a bottle of vodka. She took a swig, swallowed the pill, then chased it with another mouthful. "Going to bed now."

"Need any help getting undressed?" Labrys asked with a chuckle.

"Not from you."

In her bedroom, Shea shooed Ninja off her pillow and gingerly wriggled out of her clothes, leaving them in a pile on the floor. Jessica would have insisted she put them in the clothes hamper. But Jessica wasn't there.

As exhausted as she was, when she slipped under the sheets, she couldn't get comfortable. Everything hurt. *How long's this shit take to kick in?* she wondered. Ninja insisted on snuggling up against her, purring loudly and leaving Shea feeling uncomfortably warm, even in the cool room.

What the hell am I gonna do? How am I gonna stop Bone-fish and Lizzie Black without putting anyone else at risk? I don't know where the hell they are.

After what felt like hours, she drifted into a series of bizarre dreams. She found herself pulling off on the side of the road where two cagers were doing something to a body on the side of the road. The cagers, a man and a woman, jumped into their car and fled. Shea rushed to the body to see it was Jessica. Shea's heart leapt as she searched for a pulse.

After Shea had almost given up hope, Jess opened her eyes. "I missed you," she said.

"Missed you, too, babe," said Shea, showering her with tears and kisses.

Suddenly they were no longer on the side of the road, but in bed, kissing, caressing. Jess was sucking on Shea's nipple, a hand between Shea's thighs.

"Oh God, that feels amazing."

"I thought you'd like that." But the voice was wrong. The aroma of tropical flowers and vanilla evoked distant memories.

Shea woke to find Debbie wrapped around her.

Shea gasped and pushed her away. "Deb, what the hell?" Her head swam in a pillowy haze from the Percocet.

"What's wrong? Just a second ago you were into it."

"I . . . you . . ." Shea rubbed her eyes as she separated dream from reality. "I . . . I was dreaming."

"Oh?" A coy smile played across Labrys' face. "So, you were dreaming about me, huh?"

Shea brought up her knees and cradled her head. "Not exactly."

Labrys sat sideways on the bed and rested her hand on Shea's thigh. Warmth radiated from Shea's crotch. Sexual need became a gravitational force urging Shea to respond. But she wanted to remain loyal to Jessica.

Why should I be faithful? Jess dumped me. I'm free to fuck who I want, when I want. And right now, I want Deb.

Still Shea resisted, avoiding her ex-girlfriend's gaze. "Deb, we had a deal. You're sleeping on the couch. Scout's honor, remember?"

"Truth is, they kicked me out of Girl Scouts after Megan Levine's mother caught us making out."

"Gee, what a surprise."

"I know you think I'm a manipulative monster. And

maybe I was back then. But I've changed. Our break-up taught me how selfish I was." Debbie planted a series of kisses starting at Shea's knee, moving up to her lips.

The pull of sexual gravity intensified, drawing Shea relentlessly into free fall. She uncurled her body, opened herself to Debbie's affections. As she did so, the bullet wound on her side burned sharply.

"No, I can't do this. Jessica . . ."

"Jessica isn't here. She abandoned you, remember? But I'm here. *For you*. In *your* time of need."

"But . . ." Shea wrestled with the conflicting emotions, her mind muddled with painkillers, loneliness, and need.

"Shhh . . ." Debbie put a finger to Shea's lips.

Shea looked up. Debbie's eyes glimmered in the dim light. Underneath all the mind games and manipulations, there was that same loneliness and vulnerability Shea was feeling. A longing to connect on multiple levels.

"I missed you," Shea said without thinking about it.

"I never stopped loving you."

Debbie kissed the bandage above Shea's breast. The aching of the bullet wound transformed, intensifying into pleasure as Deb's lips teased Shea's nipples. Shea's back arched. She pulled Deb on top of her, letting their bodies grind together in a rhythm driven by her racing pulse and unlocked memories.

Shea's strong, callused fingers found the familiar places that always drove Deb to ecstasy. Deb gasped as Shea pushed deeper inside her. All anger, guilt, and pain dissolved in a primordial state of bliss and oneness.

When their passions had peaked, Deb collapsed next to Shea on the bed, each of them breathing hard. Shea's pulse raced, her mind numb, as if shorted out with a flood of endorphins.

But as the euphoria faded, guilt once again crept in.

The bullet wound throbbed despite the woozy feeling in her head. Shea wasn't ready to let go of her relationship with Jessica, but now she'd ruined any chance of getting back together. She curled into a fetal position, turning her back on Labrys.

"Hey, come here, lover," said Debbie, nibbling at Shea's ear.

"Stop."

"Uh-oh. Here comes the guilt. You were always so good at beating yourself up."

"I betrayed Jessica."

"Oh please! That bitch broke up with you."

"Don't call her that." Shea faced her Debbie. "What Jessica and I have is special."

"And yet here we are. Couldn't have been that special now, could it?"

"Don't give me any of your pseudo-psychoanalytical bullshit. You have no idea what she and I have."

"Had."

"Get out."

"What?"

Shea stood up and stumbled as the change in position made the room swim. "Get the fuck out of my house!"

"Oh, you'll fuck me, then shame *me* into leaving. Even with that psycho drug dealer on the warpath. We need to stick together, Havoc."

Shea gritted her teeth. "Fine. Go back and sleep on the couch."

Labrys stormed out of the room. "You know, we could have something special if you just got out your head long enough to stop fucking it up."

Shea slammed the bedroom door closed and collapsed onto the bed. Ninja leapt onto Shea's chest. "Get the fuck off me, ya damn cat."

Ninja scurried off the bed and shimmied up the carpeted kitty tower, settling into the circular platform on top.

Shea lay there, her mind racing. *What the fuck'd I do?* She couldn't even picture Jessica's face. Guilt tightened her chest, making it hard to breathe. *I'm such a horrible person.*

Shame-filled thoughts chased each other through her head, desperately searching for a way to make everything all right. But there was no way to do it.

Eventually she drifted back into a troubled sleep filled with dreams of wandering naked and barefoot through a postapocalyptic landscape. Plague-infested rats scurried among decaying bodies and smoldering ruins. A dirty wind howled and rattled through the broken windows of buildings.

A gunshot ripped her out of the nightmare and back into reality.

49

Shea bolted upright, her heart thudding in her chest. Predawn light cast a hazy glow across the bed. She listened, hoping the gunshot was just a part of the nightmare.

"Oh. Oh shit. Oh Goddess," came a voice from outside the bedroom.

Shea opened her nightstand for her Glock. It wasn't there. *Fuck! Where the hell is it?*

She remembered the fight from the night before. Her pistol was somewhere in the Iron Goddess workshop. She dashed to her walk-in closet, keeping the lights off. Her fingers found the small gun safe on the top shelf, tapped in the code from muscle memory, and pulled out a small Smith & Wesson Bodyguard .380.

She was still naked but didn't care. Clothes wouldn't stop a bullet and she didn't have time to put on her Kevlar vest. She had to deal with the threat now. She chambered a round and opened the door as slowly as she could. It creaked, setting her nerves further on edge. No one in the hallway.

From the living room came the clacking of someone

working the slide of a gun. Shea raised the Smith & Wesson, finger hovering above the trigger, and inched along the wall. A string of profanity followed the *ting-ting* of loose bullets falling on the living room floor.

In a surge of adrenaline, Shea rounded the corner and aimed her pistol at the figure sitting on the couch. "Freeze!"

Debbie whipped around, a look of shock and fear on her face. She dropped the Glock she'd been holding and it clattered to the concrete slab floor. "Don't shoot! It's just me."

"What the fuck!" Shea's pulse was pounding in her ears. She lowered the Bodyguard and set it on a nearby table. "Did you just fire your gun in my house?"

"I . . . I didn't mean to. It just went off. By accident."

"By accident?"

"I mean, it was unloaded, and I was dry-firing it to break it down like it says in the manual." Deb picked the Glock off the floor and held up a small booklet. "How could it fire if I'd taken the clip out?"

Heat and anger gripped Shea. "First of all, you moron, it's called a magazine, *not* a clip. Second, you obviously didn't clear the chamber before you pulled the goddamned trigger."

"Clear the what?"

Shea rubbed her temple as she took a deep breath, resisting the fury curling her hands into fists. "Get the fuck out."

"Shea, I am your president."

"Not in my home you're not. You're a mistake. You're my history come back to haunt me. And I want you out of here."

Debbie stood tall, a defiant look on her face. "You gonna make me, tough girl?"

Shea narrowed the distance between them in a heartbeat and aimed the Smith & Wesson at Deb's face. "You really don't wanna test me right now," she growled.

"You're fucking crazy, you know that? Just give me a second to get my shit together."

"I'll give you five. Four . . . three . . ."

Labrys slipped into her shoes and grabbed her purse and coat. "What about my gun?"

Shea laid the Smith & Wesson on the coffee table and picked up the Glock. In a flash, she pulled and locked the slide back, then handed it to Labrys grip first. "That's how you fucking clear the chamber, you twit."

Deb tucked the Glock in her purse. When she reached for the magazine and a box of ammo on the coffee table, Shea pushed them away.

"You can have those back once you take a safety course or two. Last thing we need's you shooting someone by *accident*."

Deb glowered at her. "You're going to regret this, Havoc."

"I already do. Two . . . One." She took a step toward Debbie, fist raised.

"Okay, I'm leaving. Geez Louise!" Labrys stormed out the door and slammed it behind her.

Shea collapsed on the love seat and buried her face in her hands. Ninja hopped onto the coffee table, meowing to be fed.

"Why the fuck did I let her in here, Ninja?"

Ninja batted at something metallic on the table. Shea pushed the cat away and picked up Debbie's silver labrys earrings. *After all that shit, why do you still have a hold over me?*

She walked to the breakfast bar and dropped the earrings in an enameled dish where she and Jessica kept their keys. Next to the dish, a framed photograph lay face-down. She righted it.

The photograph was one Terrance had taken of Shea and Jessica. Cracks in the glass radiated out from a hole that had been punched through the image of Jessica's face. There was a matching hole in wall next to the fridge. "Jesus fucking Christ." She pulled the bottle of vodka out of the freezer and had a long drink.

~

AT NINE FORTY-FIVE THAT MORNING, Shea arrived at Iron Goddess to retrieve her Glock. The Smith & Wesson was tucked in an ankle holster, just in case Bonefish and Lizzie Black made an encore appearance.

To her surprise, Terrance's 1956 industrial green Ford Hauler pickup and Lakota's 1950 Harley Panhead were parked in the parking lot.

Shea walked into the workshop. "Hello?"

A rapping on the office's window drew Shea's attention. Terrance beckoned her with his finger. As Shea crossed the workshop floor, she spotted her Glock on the floor. She holstered it and continued on into the office.

"Morning," she mumbled.

"You all right, girl?" asked Lakota in a mothering voice. She hugged Shea tightly.

"Ow, ow, ow." Shea pulled away, her hand pressing against the bullet wound under her arm.

"Oh, I'm sorry." Lakota took Shea's face in her hand and looked her over. "What in the world happened to you?"

Shea grasped Lakota's hands in her own and pulled them away from her face. "Long story. What are y'all doing here? I thought we agreed to keep the shop closed until this situation is resolved."

"I have a ten o'clock conference call with Renegade Engine Works," explained Lakota. "Took me weeks to set this up."

"And I didn't want her here by herself," added Terrance.

Shea nodded. "Ever the gentleman, eh, T?"

Terrance shrugged. "So Chlöe Stansbury really did this to you?" asked Terrance.

"Her and some Amazon named Lizzie Black."

"Lizzie Black?" Lakota's eyes narrowed. "Built like a WNBA player?"

"And hits like a sledgehammer."

Lakota blanched. "I think I know this person. You got her on video, right?"

"Yeah." Shea pulled up the security feed on her computer and showed Lakota and Terrance.

Lakota covered her mouth. "Shit, I do know her. Terrance and I both do."

"Lakota . . ." growled Terrance.

"How?" Shea looked at one then the other. "How the hell do y'all know her?"

Lakota stared at the floor. "I shouldn't say."

"Lakota, she nearly killed me. She's the reason we're closed. So quit playing games, you two, and tell me where I can find her."

"We know her from Narcotics Anonymous," said Terrance matter-of-factly. "I don't know where she lives. I just see her at meetings. Goes by Lizzie B."

"Lizzie B., huh? Chlöe Stansbury introduced her as Schwartz," said Shea.

Terrance nodded. "Makes sense. Schwartz is derived from the German word meaning *black*."

"Great. Thanks for that lesson in entomology."

"Etymology, actually," said Lakota. "Entomology is the study of bugs."

"Whatever." Shea held up her hands in frustration. "Bottom line, I need to know where I can find this bitch. What meetings she go to?"

"Shea, I'm sorry. But it's anonymous." Terrance frowned.

"Are you fucking kidding me?" Shea clenched her fists. "These people aren't recovering addicts. They're drug dealers. Probably trolling the NA meetings for new customers."

"Be that as it may," insisted Terrance, "I can't break NA traditions."

"Geez, you can really be infuriating sometimes, T."

"What about Ms. Stansbury?" suggested Lakota.

"What *about* her?" Shea felt like she was beating her head against a wall. *Why don't they see how important this is?*

"You know she works at Optimus Rehab," said Lakota. "Call that detective friend of yours."

"Who? Rios?"

"That's her. Tell Rios that Stansbury and Lizzie attacked you last night. Let them handle it."

"She's right," said Terrance. "The cops can put them behind bars without anyone else getting hurt or killed."

"Rios ain't my friend. She's just another one of Buzzkill's drones. They're on the Confederate Thunder's payroll. Monster told me. And even if they weren't, the recording has Bonefish asking *me* where her drugs are. Rios hears that, she's likely to send me back to prison."

Lakota looked concerned. "You had her drugs? Where?"

"In the top case on my bike," mumbled Shea.

A vein on Terrance's teddy bear face throbbed. "You stole illegal drugs from a dealer and brought them here? Are you insane? If the cops found out, they could seize the property."

"Which is why I'm *not* calling Rios."

"Hold on!" said Lakota. "I think I can fix this."

"How?" asked Shea.

"Scoot over." Lakota sat down at Shea's computer. "I'm going to email the video file to myself, okay?"

"Yeah, okay."

Lakota then pulled her laptop out of a computer bag and opened the video file in an editing program. Screenshots of the video spread across the screen. The audio track appeared below it. Lakota made a few clicks and the audio track vanished. "Now I'll send this back to you. Tell Rios the security system malfunctioned and didn't record the audio for some reason."

"Lakota, you're a genius."

"Yeah, so they tell me."

"Now where can I find Lizzie Black?" Shea said.

"Shea, I can't." Lakota winced and looked at Terrance.

"This bitch has murdered several people including my friend Pipes. She nearly killed me."

Lakota's jaw dropped. "She killed Pipes? Terrance, we gotta tell her."

"Fine. Tell her." Terrance huffed.

"She's a regular at a two o'clock meeting at the Lambda Resource Center on Red Tanks Trail in Ironwood, just south of the university."

Shea felt an unexpected burst of strength and energy as she contemplated exacting her revenge. "Thanks."

Terrance shook his head. "Girl, just let the cops handle it. You're in no shape to be playing vigilante. You're beat to shit and you reek of alcohol."

She fixed her gaze on him. "Nothing is gonna stop me from—"

Terrance's phone rang. "Elon? Slow down, son! What's wrong?" His face grew dark with concern. "When d'you see her last? Okay, stay put. We'll find her, okay? Love you, man." He hung up and looked up at Shea. "Annie's missing."

"What? When?"

"Elon's not sure. Not more than thirty minutes ago."

Shea pulled out her phone and dialed Annie's cellphone.

"Aunt Shea, please don't be mad," Annie pleaded.

"Annie! Where are you? Are you hurt?"

"I'm fine. I'm . . . I'm with Gramma Julia."

"Julia?" Shea asked. "Why the hell you with her?"

"Aunt Jessica went away and I got bored at Uncle Terrance's. So, I called Gramma Julia." Her voice cracked with emotion. "And . . . and Grampa Monster's dead. I didn't even get to say g'bye." Annie broke into sobs.

Shea wrestled with a mixture of anger, relief, and empathy. "Sorry about Grampa Monster. I know you were close. I'm just glad you're safe. Is Gramma Julia there with you?"

"Uh-huh."

"Can I speak to her, please?"

There was a rustling as the phone changed hands. "Annie, you go play in your room. Me and Aunt Shea-Shea gotta talk grown-up stuff," said Julia in a weary, cigarette-burned voice. There was a pause, and then, "Morning, Shea."

"Morning? That's all you got to say to me?" Shea clenched her jaw so hard her teeth ached. "You fucking kidnapped my niece!"

"Shealene Eleanor Stevens, I did no such thing. And don't you *dare* talk like that to me! I am in *no* mood. Ya hear me?" Julia said. "I am torn up making arrangements to bury my old man. I won't put up with your smart mouth."

"I'm sorry about Monster. But you had no right to take Annie without permission."

"First of all, Annie called me begging to be picked up after you pawned her off on that colored fella."

Shea's grip on her temper began to slip. "I didn't pawn her off on nobody. Terrance and Elon are family."

"And Annie is *my* family. I've known her her whole life. After Wendy died we ain't hardly seen her at all."

Shea didn't know what to say to that. "I know," was all that came to mind.

"If you needed someone to watch her, darlin', you shoulda called me."

"You?" Shea scoffed. "Maybe if you weren't involved with the Confederate Thunder I'd consider it. But they're why I sent Annie to stay with Terrance in the first place. They've shot at me. They've run members of the Athena Sisterhood off the road. And you want me to trust Annie around these people?"

"Don't you get so high and mighty with me, young lady. Several of my friends are dead because the Sisterhood fire-bombed Bootlegger Bob's."

"The Sisterhood had nothing to do with Bootlegger Bob's."

"Well the cops seem to think differently."

"The cops!" Shea scoffed. "The cops are in the Thunder's pocket. Monster said as much."

"When did he tell you that?"

"Doesn't matter." A chill ran down Shea's spine warning her to watch what she said.

"I heard someone was seen driving away from our house right after Monster allegedly shot himself. Maybe that was you. And maybe it wasn't Monster who pulled the trigger."

"Don't be ridiculous! Why would I shoot Monster?"

"Same reason you were threatening to out him with that photo you sent. Trying to get the Thunder to back off."

Shea was stunned. "You knew?"

"Course I knew. I'm his old lady. He tried to hide it, but I ain't stupid. He just didn't know I knew."

"I didn't kill him, Julia. Why would I? He was dying of cancer. What'd be the point?"

There was a moment of awkward silence. "Bottom line, Julia, Annie's my responsibility."

"And you can have her back when you show you can be responsible for her."

Shea wanted to argue, but with Lizzie Black still on the loose, maybe she was safer with Julia. For the moment, at least. "Fine. Keep her for now. But don't let any members of the club or their associates near her."

After a pause, Julia said, "I can do that."

"Tell me something. If you knew he was gay, why the hell'd you stay with him?"

"Why shouldn't I? He was a good provider, a loving godfather for your sister, and a decent friend to me. What more can a girl want?"

"I can think of a few things. The rest of the club know?"

Julia laughed darkly. "What do you think? They woulda killed him. I'm the keeper of secrets in this family. Monster's secrets. Club secrets. Your mother's secrets. Even your sister's secrets."

"My sister's secrets? What secrets?"

"I swore to keep them to my grave."

"This got anything to do with Annie?"

"Annie's father, if you must know. But since he's outta the picture and Wendy's dead, none of it matters anyhow."

"If it don't matter, then just tell me."

"I gave my word and I aim to keep it."

"Do what you want. Just keep Annie safe for now. I have business to attend to. And when I'm done, Annie comes back home with me."

Shea hung up and took a deep breath.

"Everything all right?" asked Terrance.

"Yeah. Annie's safe." Shea stood up. "I'll forward the video to Detective Rios and let her know that Chlöe Stansbury is the one dealing the hex. Meanwhile, I'm on the hunt for Lizzie Black."

Terrance stood, locked eyes with her and put his hands gingerly on her shoulder. "Watch your back, sister girl."

50

SHEA PULLED into the parking lot of the Lambda Resource Center, armed with both the Glock and the Smith & Wesson. The edge of her Kevlar vest rubbed against the bandage over her wound, but it beat leaving herself vulnerable.

She scanned the area for Lizzie Black. Being as tall as she was, she'd be hard to miss. But as the meeting start time approached, Shea wondered if Lizzie was already inside.

Shea hung her helmet from her right handle bar and followed the scattering of people inside to a meeting room with two dozen chairs set in a circle. Shea took a seat opposite the door so she could spot Lizzie the moment she walked in.

A woman with messy hair and a bony face plopped down next to her. The Optimus Rehab sweatshirt she wore hung loose on her frame. She alternated pulling at her hair and scratching the inside of her elbow. "How's it going?"

"Okay." Shea felt like an intruder. She wasn't a junkie. "You?"

"Grateful for another day clean. This your first time at this meeting?"

"Uh, yeah."

"Welcome. I'm Sabina."

"Shea." She glanced at Sabina, then back at the door.

"You keep staring at the door. Don't worry. We don't bite."

"I'm just checking things out." Shea didn't know what else to say.

"Yeah, I hear ya. I wasn't sure either. They say to give yourself six meetings before you decide."

"Good to know."

"It was all I could do not to bolt outta here my first few times. Only I couldn't 'cause I had to get my sheet signed, which they wouldn't do 'less I stayed the whole meeting. Didn't want to go back to prison, so I white-knuckled through it."

"Just got a lot on my mind."

"What's your drug of choice?"

A ripple of panic ran up Shea's spine. "Uh, well . . ."

"Let me guess—crystal, no wait, prescription painkillers. Am I right?" Sabina sniffed in Shea's direction. "And alcohol, too, I reckon."

"Something like that."

"Heroin's my ride—that and married men." She smirked in a self-deprecating sort of way. "Been clean just over a month now. Some days are a real bitch."

"Okay, we're gonna get started," said a man in an Arizona Cardinals hoodie and a bushy, retro-style hipster beard. "My name is Morgan and I'm an oxy and heroin addict."

"Hi, Morgan," said the rest of the people sitting in the circle.

What am I doing here? She ain't gonna show.

Morgan asked a member of the group to read the twelve steps from a handout. Something about turning things over to God, which Shea didn't believe in. The bit about restoring sanity sounded nice. Someone else read the group's traditions. *Bunch of bureaucratic nonsense,* Shea thought.

Shea started to get up and Sabina pushed her back down in the chair.

"You'll thank me later," the woman whispered.

Shea gritted her teeth as the meeting's main speaker prattled on about his addiction. "Didn't matter what happened, I'd come up with a reason to use. Got a new job? Smoke a little meth to celebrate. Lost that job? Smoke some to feel better. Crash the car? Smoke. Get kicked out of my girlfriend's apartment? At least I got my crank."

Memories of all the times Jessica and Terrance had complained about Shea's drinking started popping up in her head. And now Jess was gone. *But it's not because of my drinking,* she told herself.

"... I realized I could always come up with an excuse to use, no matter what was going on ... ," droned the speaker. "Wasn't until I had no home ..."

She pushed Sabina's hand aside and headed for the door. Lizzie Black wasn't coming. It was stupid to think she would after what happened. She and Bonefish were either holed up somewhere or on the run.

Shea hopped onto her bike and raced south to Sycamore Springs. As the stretches of snow-dusted land-scape flew past, Shea's thoughts strayed to her night with Debbie. Even her guilt wasn't enough to drive out the memory of Deb's soft lips, her intoxicating scent, her nimble, skilled fingers. Shea's body grew painfully aroused, aching to be touched, caressed, filled all over again.

The air horn from an approaching semi caught her

drifting into the oncoming lane. Her heart lurched as she swerved back to her side of the road. Waves of shame reminded her why she had left Debbie—the jealousy, the mind games, the gaslighting. She didn't need all that shit. Debbie or Labrys or whatever the hell she wanted to call herself hadn't changed. She was still the same manipulative control freak she had always been.

Should I quit the Sisterhood? As far as Shea was concerned, she'd fulfilled her obligation to Rios. She'd pointed the detective to the source of the drugs. She had no intention of turning over Orphan. *Let the club deal with her as they see fit. I've got my own life to lead. One that doesn't involve Debbie.*

But the thought of leaving the Athena Sisterhood felt like giving up on something. Something good. Despite being pressured by Rios to join, Shea had fallen in love with these women.

They were there for her when she needed them. If they hadn't shown up, she would have died in the Iron Goddess parking lot. Could she put up with Labrys as a sponsor for a year? It seemed so daunting. Maybe she could talk to Savage about changing sponsors. She wasn't sure if that was possible, but it might be worth a shot.

Shea breezed through Olde Towne Sycamore Springs without so much as a glance at Iron Goddess. She just wanted to get home. The back of her bike slipped sideways a few times on the ice hiding in the tight curves going down Sycamore Mountain. She slowed until she reached the straightaway that led to her neighborhood.

Her heart leapt when she saw Jessica's car parked in their driveway. *Is she back?*

She skidded to a stop in the driveway and rushed to the front door. It was ajar. *What the hell?*

"Jess? You home?"

A muffled cry from their bedroom sent Shea running.

51

DETECTIVE RIOS, FBI Special Agent Obregón, and DEA Agent Cho walked into the main lobby of Optimus Rehabilitative Services, accompanied by three CCSO deputies.

Rios flashed her shield to the receptionist. "Detective Rios. I need to speak to Chlöe Stansbury. Is she here?"

"Yes, is she expecting you?" The woman's expression was a mixture of formal politeness masking a tremor of uncertainty.

"We need to speak to her immediately."

"I'm sorry, but Ms. Stansbury is unavailable at the moment. If you'd like, I can make an appointment for you to come back at a later time."

Rios sighed. *Enough of this nonsense.* She glanced at the woman's nameplate. "Look, Belinda, Agents Obregón, Cho, and I are investigating a series of murders. You wouldn't want to be charged with obstruction, would you? Comes with a rather stiff prison sentence."

Belinda's lower lip trembled. "Um, let me see what I can do." Belinda dialed the phone. "Hi, David, I . . . uh, have some, uh, police officers here. Th-they're looking for Ms.

Stansbury. Yes, I know she gave very specific orders not to be disturbed. B-but they are threatening to arrest me if-if I don't let them see her. Y-yes, thank you."

Belinda hung up and took a deep breath before re-presenting her practiced smile. "Someone will be right up to speak to you." Her voice quavered as she spoke, eyeing Rios's gun.

A moment later, a man in a tailored black suit with emerald-green eyes, coppery hair, and a game-show-host smile strolled into the reception area. "Hello, I'm David Callahan, the center's chief information officer," he said, offering his hand to each of them. "How can I help you all today?"

"Detective Rios," she said shaking his hand. "Where's Chlöe Stansbury?"

"Ms. Stansbury isn't here at the moment, I'm afraid. Is there something that I can help you with?"

"Your receptionist said she *was* here," said Agent Cho, crossing her arms.

He shot her a dirty look. "I'm afraid Belinda was mistaken."

"How can we reach her?" asked Agent Obregón. "She have a cell number?"

"I'm sorry, I'm not authorized to give that information out. What is this in regard to?"

"We're investigating a series of murders," growled Rios, producing a folded piece of paper. "I have a warrant for her arrest."

He crossed his arms, shaking his head. "I'm sorry, but I have strict—"

Rios whirled him around, cuffed him, and pushed him against the receptionist's desk. She leaned down next to his reddened face, pushing up his arms until he yelped in pain.

"I know about your boss' little drug operation, Mr.

Callahan, and the people who've been killed because of it. So, either produce Ms. Stansbury, or I will have my associates here haul you off to jail. Are we clear?"

"All right, she's here! I'll take you to her office."

"Lead the way." Rios pointed to Belinda. "And don't you dare tip her off."

Callahan nodded to Belinda, who unlocked the door. Rios and the others followed him down a long carpeted hallway adorned with framed photographs of the company's board.

They stopped at an office with Stansbury's nameplate beside the door. Rios knocked. Someone inside was talking very heatedly about something, though the words were indistinguishable.

Rios tried the knob but it was locked. She pounded on door. "Ms. Stansbury, open the door! Cortes County Sheriff's Office! We have a warrant."

A gunshot followed by the sound of shattering glass sent a shockwave through those gathered outside the door. Rios drew her sidearm and turned to Obregón. "Go around. Make sure she doesn't get out through the window."

SHEA RUSHED into the bedroom and found the floor lamp had been knocked over. The mirror over Jessica's dresser was shattered. Knickknacks had been scattered across the floor. Jessica lay curled in a ball on the floor. Blood soaked into the carpet around her.

"Jess!" Shea rolled her onto her back.

Jessica cried out in pain. Her belly was slick and dark with blood.

"Oh shit, shit, shit!" Shea pulled up Jessica's shirt, wiped away the blood, and found two gunshot wounds in her abdomen. She grabbed a folded bed sheet from their linen closet and pressed it against the wounds.

Jessica screamed.

"Sorry, baby!" She held the sheet against the wounds while clumsily calling 911 and informing them of the situation.

Jessica mumbled something amid her cries of pain. Shea set the phone down and leaned closer to her. "What'd you say, baby? I didn't hear you."

"Shhh . . . she . . . she shot . . . me."

Hot tears blurred Shea's vision. *Fucking Lizzie Black!* "Forget that bitch. Just hold on, okay? Help's on the way."

"Hurts." Jessica winced and began gasping for breath.

Shea wanted so badly to hold Jessica's face in her hands, to comfort her with a shower of kisses, but she had to keep pressure on the wounds. "Oh, Jess, I love you. I've missed you so much."

"I . . . I luh . . ." Jessica's eyelids drooped.

"No, no, no, no! Don't close your eyes. Stay with me." In the distance an ambulance siren wailed, growing louder as it approached. A second one with a faster rhythm joined the first.

"Hear that? They're coming."

A trickle of blood dripped from underneath the bandage, followed by another. Shea pressed harder, fearing Jessica would cry out. Hoping she would. But Jess made no sound. "Oh God, baby, please hold on!"

Moments later, a familiar voice called, "Hello? Cortes County Emergency."

"In here!" yelled Shea.

Savage and two other EMTs rushed over with their medical kits and a gurney. "Shea? What happened?"

"Jess. She . . . she . . . someone shot her."

Savage kneeled next to her and peeled back the bedsheet. "Okay, stand back. We'll take care of her, okay?"

Shea forced herself up on shaky knees as Savage and her coworkers replaced the sheet with a large pad, set up an IV, and put an oxygen mask on Jessica. The whole situation felt surreal. *This shouldn't be happening. Why'd you come back here, Jess? I told you it wasn't safe.*

"Ma'am?"

Shea looked up to see two uniformed deputies, one a middle-aged white man with a mustache, the other a clean-cut Latino in his thirties. *More fucking cops. They should be out looking for Annie.* She glared at them. "What the fuck you want?"

"Ma'am, I'm Deputy Graham," said the older white cop. "This is Deputy Cruz. Do you live here?"

"I ain't talking to no one but Rios."

Cruz raised an eyebrow. "Detective Rios? I'm afraid she's not here. We have—"

"Then fucking get her here. She's the only one I trust."

The EMTs lifted Jessica onto the gurney. Shea pushed past the deputies. "Where y'all taking her?"

"Cortes General," Savage said as they pushed the gurney through the living room.

"How is she?"

"She's lost a lot of blood. If we can get her to the hospital in time, she's got a chance."

Graham grabbed Shea's arm. "Ma'am, I need to know who you—"

She snarled in the deputy's face. "Shea Stevens. This is my fucking house and that's my fucking girlfriend. I'm following her to the hospital. You wanna stop me, then shoot me."

Graham and Cruz exchanged glances and Graham released her arm. "I'll have Detective Rios meet you at the hospital."

"Yeah, you do that."

52

———

As Shea's motorcycle roared along the highway behind the ambulance, the darkness inside her rose once again, a miasma of guilt, anger, and hopelessness. Her chest felt squeezed as if by a giant hand.

Please don't leave me, Jessica. I don't deserve you, but you shouldn't be the one to pay the price. Why wasn't I there? Why didn't I tell you every minute of the day how much you mean to me? Why did I let myself get distracted by all this biker nonsense? Oh God, please don't die!

As an oncoming semi barreled toward them on the highway, Shea was tempted to swerve into its path. *Rios'll have one less CI to push around.* The bike drifted toward the centerline. The distance between them narrowed. The truck blared its air horn. She ignored it.

A single thought pulled her back into her lane. *What about Annie?*

Who'll take care of her? Julia most likely. And Annie would continue in her mother's and grandmother's footsteps. She'd fall for some asshole outlaw biker who'd treat her as his property.

Just another Confederate Thunder old lady. A life of submission, violence, and drugs.

Shea would not let that happen. She would protect Annie from all that.

The ambulance stopped in the breezeway for the emergency room. Shea parked in the nearby lot and rushed through the automatic doors, pulling off her helmet as she went.

"Jessica . . . Taylor," Shea said to the elderly man sitting behind the information desk. She struggled to catch her breath. "She was brought in . . . by ambulance . . . just a minute ago. I'm . . . I'm her wife." It was a lie, but the guy behind the desk wouldn't know.

"Taylor, you say?" He tapped the information into his computer. "Looks like she's in surgery. I can have the surgeon come out and speak to you when she's finished."

"She's still alive?" Her heart thundered in her chest.

"I presume. She's in surgery."

"Oh, thank God! Yes, please." Shea found a seat in the waiting room, feeling a glimmer of hope cut through the gloom.

Shea called Terrance. He picked up on the first ring. Emotion nearly cut off her air as she tried to speak. "Jessica . . ."

"What? What happened to Jessica?"

"Lizzie Black. She shot her."

"Where are you?"

"Cortes General ER"

"I'm on my way."

"Hey, Havoc." Savage took a seat next to her. Savage's fellow EMTs stood talking to the guy at the information desk, just out of earshot. "You want me to call Labrys and let her know what happened?"

"Not right now." Shea pressed her fists into her temples. "It's all my fault."

"Don't say that. You didn't shoot her."

"Never shoulda gotten involved with this hex business."

"You didn't know this would happen." Savage put her arm around her. "She's gonna pull through this. Dr. Sossaman's the best trauma surgeon in the county."

The other EMTs approached looking impatient.

"Listen, Havoc. I hate to abandon you, but I still have three hours left on my shift. I'll be back as soon as I can, all right?"

Shea nodded. "Thanks for saving her. That's two I owe you."

"Naw, it ain't. You may be just a prospect, but I already consider you my sister. You hang in there, ya hear?"

Shea realized she was shivering as Savage and her team hurried out the ER's automatic doors. A chilly wind blew in, causing Shea's teeth to chatter.

Not since she ran away at fifteen had she felt so alone. *Yeah, go ahead and feel sorry for yourself. Never mind that Jessica is on death's door.*

She buried her head in her hands and wished for the first time in years that she believed in God so that she would have someone or something to pray to.

SHEA WAS NODDING off when someone called her name. Outside, night was falling. She looked up to see Rios standing in front of her. Anger surged through Shea's body. "This is your fault!" she growled. "Jess wouldn'ta been shot if you hadn't forced me to be your snitch."

"Shea, I understand you're angry. But I'm not the one who shot Jessica."

"Lizzie Black mighta pulled the trigger, but you put me and my family in the line of fire."

"You witnessed the shooting?"

"No," Shea said, attempting to stop her hands from shaking. "I found . . . I found Jess in our bedroom. Place was trashed."

"Did she say anything about what happened?"

Shea glowered at Rios. "She said Lizzie shot her."

Rios made notes on a small spiral-bound pad. "I'm working with the FBI and DEA on the Stansbury cases. We're processing the scene now and have a BOLO on Lizzie Black. Ms. Stansbury's already in custody. I'm hoping she'll flip on Ms. Black."

"Whatever."

"Shea, I know what it's like to lose people close to you."

"Oh really?"

"My parents were murdered by the Guatemalan government when I was a child. I lost my sister to heroin. And a few years ago, a drunk driver killed my girlfriend. No matter what happens, you will get through this."

"Your girlfriend? You're gay?"

"I am." Rios sat next to Shea and put a hand on her arm. "Everything I've done has been to protect people and bring criminals to justice. I got you involved with this case because people were dying. The information I had pointed to the Athena Sisterhood. Obviously, I got bad intel."

"And Jessica paid the price."

"Shea, I will do everything I can to make this right." Rios looked Shea in the eyes.

Despite her resentments, Shea could see the honesty and compassion in the detective's eyes.

Dr. Sossaman approached wearing olive-green scrubs. Shea recognized her from the previous times she'd been to the ER. The doctor's short dark curls peeked from underneath a matching surgical cap. Deep-set, hawklike eyes focused on Shea. "Ms. Stevens."

"How's she doing, Doc?"

Dr. Sossaman sat next to Shea, her face unreadable. "Jessica's lost a lot of blood. There was significant damage to her small intestine. The risk of infection is very high. We removed one of the bullets. The other is lodged against her L4 vertebra." Sossaman pointed to her lower back.

"We're assessing how best to remove the remaining bullet without causing further damage to the spinal column. As is, there's a good chance she may be paralyzed below the waist. But miracles do happen, so we'll just have to wait and see."

Shea found it hard to breathe. The guilt felt like a motorcycle lying on her chest. "Is she awake? Can I see her?"

"She's sedated until we get a better picture of the damage. We have her scheduled for a CT scan. It will probably be a few hours before she can have any visitors." Sossaman stood. "We'll do everything we can for her. I promise."

Shea nodded as Sossaman walked away.

"You probably won't be allowed home until we're done processing the scene. That may be awhile yet," said Rios as she stood to leave. "But we *will* bring Lizzie Black and Chlöe Stansbury to justice."

"Whatever." All that mattered was saving Jessica. She rested her elbows on her knees, cradling her head, trying not to feel or think.

Movement by the sliding glass doors caught Shea's attention.

Terrance and Elon walked in, both bundled up against the evening cold. Terrance wrapped Shea in a bear hug.

Shea surrendered to it until the bullet wound under her arm caused her to pull away.

"How's Jessica?" asked Terrance.

Shea shook her head. "Even if she lives, she may never walk again."

"When will you be able to see her?"

"Doc says it could be hours."

"Any luck finding this Lizzie Black woman?"

Shea shook her head. "Cops arrested Stansbury at her office. Lizzie wasn't with her."

"Aunt Shea," said Elon. "I'm sorry I didn't keep a better eye on her."

Shea forced a smile. "It's all right, kid. Annie's safe. That's all that matters."

Terrance pressed his head against Shea's. "Please tell me you'll let the cops handle this."

Shea sighed. Exhaustion and sorrow clung to her. "The idea of trusting this to Rios goes against everything I know. But honestly, I don't know what else to do."

"That's the smartest thing I've heard you say in a while." Terrance stood up. "Come on. Let me take you home."

"I can't go home. FBI's processing the scene for evidence of Jessica's shooter."

"My place then."

"Sounds good. Thanks, T."

"Least I can do, sister girl."

53

———

THE NEXT MORNING Shea pulled on her clothes from the day before and wandered into the Terrance's kitchen. He was sitting at the table, sipping coffee and reading the business section of the newspaper. Her motorcycle jacket was slung over one of the chairs.

"How you holding up?" he asked as he lowered the paper.

"I'm alive." Shea poured herself a cup and sat across from him. "I'll feel better when Lizzie Black is dead."

"Girl, let the cops handle it. They arrested Stansbury, didn't they? They'll get Lizzie, too."

Shea's phone dinged. The screen revealed a text message from Rios. "Fuck!"

"What's wrong?" Terrance arched an eyebrow.

"Stansbury's out on bail. Wonder who they're going to come after next. Lakota? Elon?"

"Shea, don't talk like that."

Memories flashed through her mind of Lizzie Black standing by the door of that shuttered gallery. The large plate glass windows reflecting the downtown square.

Something bothered her about the image. Not something that was there, but something that should have been there but wasn't. And then she had it.

Shea dialed a number. "Labrys? Get ahold of as many of the Sisterhood as you can. Tell 'em to meet me at nine o'clock this morning in the alley behind the Blue Coyote Art Gallery."

"Blue Coyote? They went out of business months ago," said Labrys.

"I know that. Just do it."

"Why?" asked Labrys. "What's going on?"

"I think that's where Bonefish's drug operation is."

"How do you know this?"

"I'll explain later. Just listen to me for once."

"Excuse me, prospect. But I—"

"Fucking do it, Labrys, before Lizzie Black kills someone else."

Shea tossed her phone into her inside jacket pocket. "I'll be back later."

"Shea, I wish you wouldn't do this."

"How many people should I let Bonefish hurt before I take action?" Shea rushed into the guest room, pulled on her boots and the Kevlar vest. She stuffed the Glock in her waistband and the Smith & Wesson in her ankle holster.

When she ran back to the kitchen for her jacket, Terrance stood and wrapped her in a bear hug. "Be careful, girlfriend."

SHEA'S PULSE was firing like a machine gun as her motorcycle swerved around bags of trash and discarded pallets behind the north side shops of Ironwood's square. A couple of doors past the rear entrance to the Tenth Inning,

Shea spotted a metal door painted with the words BLUE COYOTE FINE ART GALLERY—DELIVERIES.

A black creeper van sat parked beside the door. The gallery's name had been scraped off the side, but the outline of the letters remained visible. Shea spotted Labrys' Roadmaster on the other side of the van and pulled up next to her.

Two other bikes thundered into the alley. Shea recognized Savage's Harley Street 750, with Indigo riding on the passenger seat. Fuego rumbled in behind her on her Kawasaki Vulcan with Orphan on the back.

Shea adjusted her Kevlar vest, drew her Glock, and chambered a round. The other women gathered around her, all but Orphan with a gun in hand.

"I'm a little surprised to see you here," Shea said to Indigo. "I thought you were afraid of going to prison."

"I am. But after what happened to Jessica, to Pipes, to Richard, the time for sitting on the bench is over."

"You sure this is the place?" asked Fuego, eyeing the door.

"Pretty sure. I saw Lizzie Black standing beside the front door a few days ago, smoking a cig," Shea explained.

"The gallery's been closed for months," said Savage.

"And yet there's no Realtor signs out front. When's the last time a downtown landlord shut down a place without immediately putting up a sign looking for potential renters?"

Fuego patted the side of the van. "*Órale!* Check this out. This van is spotless. After the weather we've been having, you'd think it'd be filthy just sitting here. Someone's been using it for something."

"Let's quit chatting," said Indigo, "and do this before they all run out the front door."

Labrys pulled her Glock out of a fanny pack holster.

Shea glowered at her. "Put that damn thing away!"

"Excuse me?"

"You shot a fucking hole in my wall the other morning. Right now, you're more a danger to us than Lizzie Black."

Labrys shrugged when the other women gave her curious looks. "What? It was an honest mistake. Could've happened to anyone."

Fuego shifted her weight. "*La Jefa*, all due respect, you're kinda new at this. Maybe you keep yours holstered unless the shit hit the fan."

"For safety's sake," added Savage.

Labrys' mouth formed a thin line of discontent. "Fine." She slipped her Glock back into the fanny pack and zipped it shut. "Satisfied?"

"Yeah," said Shea, relieved at least she wouldn't die from a bullet in the back.

"What about me?" asked Orphan. "I don't have one."

"You know how to shoot?" asked Shea.

"Took a few courses awhile back. Pawned my Springfield a few months ago to pay bills."

"*La Jefa*, why don't you give Orphan yours," suggested Fuego.

"Not a chance," Labrys crossed her arms. "It's mine. I will *not* be left defenseless just because this prospect couldn't handle her finances."

Shea rolled her eyes in frustration and pulled the Smith & Wesson from her ankle holster. "Here." She handed the compact pistol to Orphan. "Just be sure to place your shots. It's small and'll ride up on you if you're not careful."

"Thanks, Havoc."

"So, what's the plan?" asked Indigo, looking a little nervous.

"Two of us should go around front, make sure they don't get away if they're in there. But keep your guns hidden until you absolutely need them. The stores on the square don't open for another hour or two, but there may be early risers wandering around. The less attention we have, the better."

"I'll go." Fuego patted Labrys on the back. "You wanna join me?"

Labrys frowned. "Yeah, I suppose. I'm beginning to wonder who's running this club."

Fuego patted Labrys on the back. "You are, *La Jefa*. We're just here to keep you safe."

When the two of them had sufficient time to get around the building, Shea approached the door. Orphan, Indigo, and Savage circled around her, weapons drawn.

Shea pounded on the door and took aim. Despite the chill, a bead of sweat trickled down the side of her face.

After a few moments with no response, Indigo said, "Maybe no one's home."

Shea tried the door. It was locked.

"I guess we don't get to see what's behind door number one," joked Savage.

"Hold on." Shea holstered her pistol and pulled lock pick set from her jacket's inside pocket. After teasing the tumblers for a couple of minutes, the lock's cylinder turned. She rotated the knob and prayed there wasn't a security system as the door opened. No blaring alarm. No persistent beeping.

"Holy cats!" said Indigo, giving Shea's shoulder a nudge. "Girl's got some skills."

"Benefits of a misspent youth." Shea couldn't help grinning. *Nice to be appreciated.*

Shea stepped inside and found a light switch. The place had a distinct odor that was equal parts burned plastic, cotton candy, and chemical solvent. Along the walls, plastic bins filled metal shelves, each marked with a letter. A large machine dominated the center of the room.

"What the hell is all this?" asked Savage as she examined the bins.

"I know what this is," said Orphan sullenly. She pointed to each category of bin. "K is Special K. P is poppers. E—ecstasy. L—acid. M—weed. They had me selling this stuff at the clubs."

"What's this big machine here?" Shea looked closer and saw a catch tray full of black pills stamped with a pentagram.

"It's for pressing hex into pill form."

Savage unlocked the front door and let Labrys and Fuego inside. Shea rifled through the office until she found what she was looking for.

"*Órale,* this is like a million bucks worth of shit," said Fuego. "What should we do with it?"

"Burn the place down," said Labrys matter-of-factly.

Savage shook her head. "No, the smoke could be toxic. And the fire could spread to the other businesses. When the Horse Thief Tavern caught fire a few years ago, it nearly wiped out the entire south side of the square."

"We take it," said Shea. "Bonefish made bail this morning. I bet she's planning on running. She's not gonna leave all this inventory behind. We load into that van out there and haul it someplace safe. Then I call Bonefish and tell her we'll return it if she gives us Lizzie Black."

"Where will we take it?" asked Indigo.

"Black Rock Mine."

"How we gonna take the van?" asked Fuego. "No, wait. Lemme guess. Havoc here knows how to hot-wire cars."

"I do, actually, but I prefer using these." Shea grinned and held up a set of keys she found in the office.

"Wait a minute," said Orphan. "You're not gonna let Bonefish get away after all she's done?"

"Nope." Shea's smile vanished. "We take her out, too."

54

———

Within an hour, they had the van loaded. Shea handed her motorcycle keys to Indigo. "Her name's Sweet Betsy. Try not to wreck her."

"Long as no one's running me off the road, I'm fine."

Shea hopped into the van and led the other women onto the two-lane highway up to Black Rock Mine. Billowy steel-gray clouds drifted silently under a higher cottony blanket. As the morning waned, the temperature hung just above the freezing mark. Rain would be bad for the motorcycles behind her, but snow or sleet could make the road downright treacherous.

While she struggled to focus on the job at hand, thoughts of Jessica crept in. Her heart ached. She'd lost so many people in her life to violence. Her mother, her sister, Monster, too. She couldn't lose Jessica.

She had tried so hard to escape, to live the life of a standup citizen. But the past wouldn't let her go. It stalked her like a predator, twisting her, until she became a predator herself.

Until now she had only killed out of self-defense, in the

heat of a fight. Never in cold blood. But if everything went according to plan, that would change.

At the mine's security fence, a cold drizzle fell, peppered with bits of sleet. The gate was chained and secured with a combination padlock. Shea stepped out of the van. From the lock pick set, she selected a homemade shim she'd made years earlier from an aluminum can. She inserted it between the shank and the lock and twisted. The lock popped. She tossed it on the side of the road and pushed the gate open. Indigo, who waited on Sweet Betsy just behind the van, gave Shea a thumbs-up as she hopped back in.

The windshield fogged as the loaded vehicle bounced along the road leading to the mine's parking lot. She shivered. Seven years she had served for boosting cars. And yet here she was, driving a stolen van full of illegal drugs, trespassing on county property. It felt like a homecoming of sorts. A world where she knew the rules. A world where she belonged.

She parked the van behind the excavator at the far end of the lot. If Rios or some other county employee showed up at the mine office, the van would be out of sight. She slipped on her motorcycle helmet and gloves and walked up to Indigo, still sitting on Sweet Betsy.

"This is a nice ride," said Indigo with a curt smile. "Can I keep her?"

Shea grinned. "Sorry. Not for sale. But I have others like her."

"I'll keep that in mind." Indigo climbed off the bike. "What now?"

"Soon as I hear back from Bonefish, I'll let everyone know. For now, I'm headed to the hospital. Gotta check on Jessica. "

"Want some company?"

"Yeah, that'd be nice."

Indigo hugged her. "You got it, sister. I'll tell Savage."

AFTER STOPPING by the information desk, Shea found Terrance and Elon sitting in the waiting room for the Intensive Care Unit. Orphan, Indigo, Fuego, and Savage followed her inside. Labrys had a class to teach but promised to listen for Shea's call when Bonefish got in touch.

After introducing everyone, Shea asked, "How is she?"

Terrance pointed to a nearby chair. "Maybe you better sit down."

Shea sat, a tremor of fear rising up her chest. "What's wrong?"

"They took Jess back into surgery to remove the bullet near her spine."

"Did she say anything before they took her into surgery?"

"From what I've been told, they've been keeping her sedated. Didn't want her moving around and risking further injuring the spinal cord." Terrance looked down at the floor. "I hope you don't mind. I told them she's my sister."

"No, that's cool. When will we know some answers?"

"Not sure. She's been in surgery for two hours. Don't know how long something like this takes." Terrance glanced at the other members of the Sisterhood. "Y'all do whatever it is you needed to do?"

Shea shrugged. "Sort of. We're waiting on a phone call."

"Well, the less I know the better."

Shea clasped Terrance's hand as her eyes watered. "Thanks for being here, T. You truly are my brother from another mother."

"Yeah, and you're my sister from another mister." He chucked her on the shoulder, before embracing her in a long hug.

Shea held on longer than she normally would. Terrance felt solid in a way that nothing else in her life did. *How does he manage to stay out of trouble? He's an ex-con same as me. Maybe I should listen to him more often.*

She let go of him. Across the room Orphan bawled silently, while Indigo and Savage sat next to her. Shea found herself walking over.

"Orphan?"

Orphan glanced up, her face wet, red, and puffy. "Havoc, I'm so sorry! If I hadn't gotten involved with Bonefish, this never would have happened to Jessica. You must hate me."

"I don't hate you." It was the truth. "You got in over your head with some bad people. I've been there. More than once. What happened to Jessica and Pipes. Even your boyfriend. It ain't your fault. Blame rests solely on Bonefish and Lizzie Black. And we will make them pay."

Orphan stood and hugged her. "Thanks, Havoc."

Shea's phone rang. "Hello?"

"Well, well, someone's been mighty busy. And here I thought we killed you," said a familiar, authoritative voice.

"Happy to disappoint you, Bonefish. I'm not an easy one to kill. Neither is my girlfriend."

"Girlfriend? I don't know anything about your girlfriend, but I am interested in getting my inventory back. It's time for me to skedaddle. Unfortunately, the feds have seized my bank accounts. So, if you know what's good for you, you'll return what you took."

"You can have your *inventory* back when you give me something I want."

"And what, pray tell, is that, Ms. Stevens?"

"Lizzie Black. You turn her over to us, you can have your drugs."

"Lizzie? Are you insane?"

"Those are the terms. Take 'em or leave 'em."

"Normally I wouldn't be inclined to surrender one of my business associates to a common hoodlum such as yourself. However, circumstances being what they are, I can see my way into making this arrangement."

"Great. Meet me at the Black Rock Mine. Two hours from now."

"Oh dear, that simply will not do. Meet with you and your girl gang out in the middle of nowhere? Do you think I'm stupid? That's a setup if I've ever heard one. Here's my counteroffer. Back of the Blue Coyote Gallery. I think you know where that is. Six o'clock this evening."

Shea considered the suggestion. Going after them on their home turf seemed liked a bad idea, especially with all of the potential witnesses having dinner and drinks around the square. "Now who's setting who up? No deal. The mine. Two hours."

"Well, guess I'll have to hit the road without my merchandise. No worry. Lizzie Black's very capable. She retrieved my product from you last time, she'll do it again. But this time, I'll insist she finish the job. She'll kill you, your girlfriend, and your kid."

Shea tensed her jaw. She sucked at negotiating. That's why Terrance was the business manager and she built the bikes. She couldn't afford to put Annie or Jessica at risk any longer. "Fine. I'll meet you behind the gallery at six. But so help me, if you double-cross me, you'll be sorry."

"Not to worry. I may deal in illicit substances, but I'm an honest businesswoman. I take my customer service very seriously. I'll have Lizzie Black wrapped up like an early Christmas present."

"See that you do."

55

———

SHEA PHONED Labrys shortly after hanging up with Bonefish. The call went straight to voicemail. "Deb, meet us behind the gallery at six. Bring your gun."

For two hours, Shea waited nervously for an update on Jess's condition. But she was still in surgery when Shea and the other Athenas headed to the mine. There had been no call back from Labrys, either.

At five o'clock, they arrived at the mine. The rain and sleet had slacked off to a light misty drizzle. After a brief strategy discussion, they unloaded the van and stashed the tote bins full of drugs under the sluice box of the mine's old wash plant where the ground was dry. Returning the drugs wasn't even a consideration.

"You mind if I ride shotgun with you?" asked Orphan as they prepared to ride to the gallery. Her face was pale, her lips blue. "I'm freezing my ass off out here."

"Fine with me," replied Shea. "Just so you know, we'll be leaving the van at the gallery. It's a liability. Once we've taken care of Bonefish and Lizzie, you're riding on the back of someone's bike."

"At least I'll have a little time to warm up."

They rode in silence most of the way back to Ironwood, which suited Shea just fine. She needed to focus on the task at hand. A surreal calm descended on her, her energy coiled deep within her, ready to strike.

"I've never killed anyone before," said Orphan as they entered the Ironwood city limits. "Have you?"

"Yeah," said Shea, keeping her eye on the road.

"Who?"

"People trying to kill me."

"What's it feel like?" Orphan's voice wavered. "To have killed someone?"

"Empty mostly. Like you've become something you never thought you'd be."

"I don't understand."

"It's crossing a line you can't uncross," said Shea dryly. "Can't explain it more than that."

"Yeah, I think I get your meaning. Just never thought my life would turn out like this."

"Me neither."

A few minutes before six, Shea parked the van twenty feet from the rear of the gallery, the high beams lighting up the back door like a stage. Bonefish waited for them in front of the door, shielding her eyes. Julius and Tony from the Tenth Inning stood on one side of her, while a burly man Shea didn't recognize was on the other. All had guns in their hands. Lizzie Black was nowhere in sight.

Fuego pulled up on the right side of the van, while Indigo and Savage parked on the other. Shea was miffed at Labrys' absence, but not surprised. "Well, guess this is it."

An H3 Hummer roared down the alley from the other direction, while a black Caddy sedan cut off their escape route. The drivers of each vehicle popped out and drew their weapons.

"Oh shit, Havoc," cried Orphan. "It's an ambush."

"Keep cool, Orphan. We may get out of this yet." Shea climbed out of the van. "Where the hell's Lizzie Black?" she yelled to Bonefish and her crew.

"Lizzie's inside. Where's my inventory?"

Shea pounded the side of the van. "Inside. Show me yours, I'll show you mine."

"Fair enough." Bonefish turned to the burly man on her right. "Reese, go fetch Lizzie."

Reese disappeared inside the gallery. Orphan climbed out of the passenger side of the van holding the Smith & Wesson Shea had loaned her. When the gallery door opened, Lizzie emerged with her hands behind her back.

Shea drew her Glock, took aim at Lizzie.

Lizzie dove behind the gallery's metal door, wrists unbound, and fired the revolver she'd been hiding. The van's driver side window shattered. The air erupted with gunfire. Shea jumped into the driver's seat hoping to use the van's engine block for cover.

Orphan screamed and fell, scarlet spreading across her chest.

"Cover me, Indigo!" shouted Savage amid the relentless drumroll of bullets and cries of pain. "Hang on, Orphan!"

Shea turned to Tony and Werner, who were firing from behind a stack of wooden pallets. She dropped them with one shot each.

Bullets punched holes in the van's windshield. Another thunked into the front grill. Steam spewed from the radiator, obscuring Shea's view and filling the air with the reek of antifreeze. Shea caught a glimpse of Bonefish shooting from behind a Dumpster. Shea fired. Bonefish dropped, screaming in agony for someone to help her.

Two gunshots whizzed past Shea. She locked eyes with Lizzie, who was shooting at her, shielded by the gallery's back entrance. Shea squeezed off two rounds but hit only the metal door. When Lizzie didn't return fire immediately, Shea thought her shots had penetrated. No such luck. Lizzie ducked around and fired again.

"Lizzie! Reese! Help me!" screamed Bonefish. "Please!"

Reese dashed out of the building as Lizzie Black unleashed a volley of lead. A couple bullets zipped over Shea's head, while the others peppered the van's engine.

A flash of fire blew past and struck the ground in front of Reese, engulfing him in flames. Shea glanced behind her. In the narrow alley between the gallery and the next building, Labrys stood, throwing a second Molotov cocktail. It arced and exploded near Bonefish, setting her legs ablaze. Bonefish's screams grew primal and incoherent.

Lizzie fired two shots toward Labrys then ran to Bonefish. Shea lined up her shot and fired. Lizzie's head exploded, splattering the nearby Dumpster with gore.

For a moment, the silence of the encroaching night returned except for the dying hiss of the radiator and the screams of the wounded. Shea realized her heart was pounding. *Is it over?*

"Havoc! Savage ¡*Ayudame!*" Fuego reclined on the ground cradling her arm as she called for help.

Indigo ran over to Fuego with a first-aid kit.

"How is she?" asked Shea.

Indigo pointed. "Go help Labrys."

Shea found her ex-girlfriend moaning and clutching the side of her throat. Blood had pooled around her and squirted periodically between her fingers.

Shea was looking for something to use for a compression bandage when she spotted the iconic silver earrings dangling from Labrys' ears. Shea had left them in the key dish by her own front door. *How did Labrys get them back?*

Icy anger filled Shea's heart as she realized the truth. "You fucking bitch. You shot Jessica."

"S-sorry," Labrys choked.

Shea yanked Labrys' hand away from her throat and held it to the ground. Blood gushed in a series of spurts. Labrys' eyes went wide with terror. Shea covered the dying woman's mouth and nose until her lids drooped. The spurting stopped.

Shea's heart thundered in her chest, staring at Labrys' lifeless face. Tears blurred her vision. Shea wiped her face and walked away.

The smell of burned flesh drifted on a faint breeze. Shea shuffled to where Bonefish uttered barely audible cries. "Please. Kill me." Her legs and torso were scorched with second and third-degree burns.

Shea raised her Glock, her finger resting on the trigger. Then stopped. "No. No quick death for you."

She found Indigo wrapping gauze around Fuego's arm. "How is she?"

"Just a graze, fortunately. I got the bleeding to stop." Indigo turned to her. "How's Labrys?"

Shea looked down at the blood coating her hands and arms, then shook her head. "Didn't make it. Is Orphan okay?"

Indigo grimaced. "Savage is with her. Doesn't look good."

Sirens screamed in the distance.

"Shit," said Shea. "We gotta get outta here."

"How?" asked Fuego, wincing. "We're blocked in."

Shea pointed toward the narrow alley that Labrys had walked up. "We should be able to fit through there. Indigo, you take Fuego's bike. VP, you're riding bitch."

Shea ran around the van. Orphan lay in a puddle of

dark liquid, her blood-spattered face looking waxy in the pale glow of a nearby streetlight. "How is she?"

Savage stood and closed her eyes. "She's gone."

Anguish squeezed Shea's heart. "No, there's gotta be something you can do. CPR or something. You're an EMT, for God's sake." Shea felt for a pulse on Orphan's neck and then her wrist. Both were cold and lifeless. She started doing chest compressions until Savage gripped Shea by the shoulders.

"Havoc, stop! There's nothing we can do." The sirens were getting closer. "We need to leave."

Shea sat back on her heels, tears streaming down her cheeks and throat. Shea wiped her face, smearing blood across it in the process. "We can't leave Orphan's body here."

This was her sister all over again. Shot dead in the street by some asshole. It had felt wrong then to leave Wendy's body. It felt equally wrong to leave Orphan, a fellow prospect.

Savage pulled Shea to her feet and out of her head. "We gotta get moving unless you want to be arrested."

Shea took a deep breath and jumped on Sweet Betsy. Police cruisers with blue and red lights flashing charged down both sides of the main alley. Shea slammed the bike into first and followed Indigo and Fuego between the buildings, with Savage hot on her heels.

56

————

In the Iron Goddess restroom, Shea scrubbed furiously at the blood on her hands, arms, face, and chest. Her shirt and bra, both splotched with ruddy brown stains, lay in a heap on the floor. She kept thinking about Labrys. Those fucking earrings glinting in the light. The look of surprise and horror as Shea let her die.

The restroom door squeaked open. "Havoc, you all right?" asked Indigo. "You been in here awhile. Oh, sorry, I didn't realize you were naked." Indigo turned around, shielding her eyes from Shea.

"Labrys shot Jessica."

"What? But you said it was Lizzie."

"Labrys left her earrings at my place the other night. She was wearing them tonight. Musta come by to pick them up and found Jessica there." Shea dried herself off with paper towels and pulled on an Iron Goddess hoodie she'd taken off the rack.

Indigo met her gaze. "Even if that were true, why would Labrys shoot her?"

"Jealousy, I suppose. She also firebombed Bootlegger Bob's."

"Yeah, guess you're right on that count. You think she also bombed that titty bar and the senator's office?"

"Probably. I'll leave that to the cops to figure out." Shea leaned back against the sink. "She's dead now, so it don't matter much anyway."

"Guess this means Fuego's the new prez."

Shea nodded, leading Indigo out of the restroom. "I think she'll be good at it."

They found Savage sitting sidesaddle on a production sport bike in the showroom, staring at the floor.

Indigo kissed her and threw a leg over a nearby V-4 cruiser similar to Sweet Betsy. "Where's Fuego?"

"Gone home," said Savage.

"How's her arm?" asked Shea.

"Got it cleaned out in the men's room. Should heal up okay."

Shea sat on the floor and rubbed her temple, feeling exhausted and empty. "I can't believe Orphan's dead."

"Labrys, too," said Savage.

A brooding silence filled the space. No doubt Rios would suspect Shea and the others were involved in the shootout, but without proof, it was all speculation. They had worn their motorcycle gloves loading, unloading, and driving the van. There'd been no security cameras. And no survivors to tell the tale.

Indigo turned to Shea, putting her hands on the handlebar grips. "I love this bike, Havoc. How much does it go for?"

"Twenty-eight grand."

"Shit, the insurance company wrote me a check for only twenty grand. Cheap motherfuckers!"

Shea stood and straddled the front wheel. With all the

darkness eating at her soul, she felt a shaft of light around Indigo and the other members of the club. "You can have it for twenty."

"Seriously?"

"Terrance'll be pissed, but he'll get over it. We won't be giving back the deposit Bonefish put down on her bike. I'd call it a wash."

"Can I take it tonight?" asked Indigo with a gleam in her eye.

"Sure, why not? Just be careful till we got the paperwork done."

BEFORE LEAVING IRON GODDESS, Shea sent a text to Julia. By the time she pulled up in the hospital parking lot, Julia had responded.

Yes, they will meet with you.

Shea walked into the ICU waiting room. Terrance stood as she entered, his fingers entwined with another man's with tan skin, green eyes, and a narrow face. Shea guessed he was Terrance's boyfriend, Jake. Elon sat in the corner playing a video game.

"How is she, T?"

Terrance released Jake and hugged Shea. "Doc says she's gonna live. With therapy, she may be able to walk again." When he pulled back, his eyes held a concerned look that unsettled Shea. "She doesn't want to see you."

"What?"

"Her folks came up from Phoenix. They're going to be relocating her to a rehab facility down in Scottsdale."

Shea felt as if her world were coming apart. "No, they can't take her. She's my girlfriend."

Terrance cupped Shea's head and their eyes met. "It wasn't Lizzie Black who shot her. It was your ex."

"I know, T. But . . ." Her words got stuck in her throat. "I gotta talk to her." Shea pulled away and rushed down the hallway.

Shea spotted Jessica's name on a whiteboard outside room 347. Rios sat in a chair next to the door. She stood as Shea approached.

"Hold on, Shea. You and I need to talk."

Shea tried to push past her. "I gotta talk to Jessica first." On the other side of the room's large plate glass window, an older African American couple looked up and glared at Shea.

Rios held firm, blocking her way. "Shea, look at me!"

Shea tightened her jaw, but stopped resisting and met Rios' eyes. "What?"

"For starters, she doesn't want to see you right now. Second of all, it wasn't Lizzie Black."

"I know."

"You know?" Rios huffed and pointed to a room off the corridor leading to ICU. "Let's you and me sit and discuss this privately."

They stepped into the nurses' break room. A white table stood in the center, surrounded by four blue plastic chairs. Rios locked the door once they were inside and directed Shea to one of the chairs. "Where've you been for the past few hours?"

"Riding around to clear my head."

"In this weather?"

Shea shrugged. "I ride in any kinda weather. What's it to you?"

"Well, while you were 'riding around' clearing your head, someone turned Downtown Ironwood into a war zone."

Shea looked at her stone faced. She knew enough not to say anything. The only question in her mind was when to call Dragon to serve as her lawyer.

"You have nothing to say about that?" asked Rios, her facing warming with frustration.

"Why would I?"

"A couple of members of the Athena Sisterhood were found dead on the scene."

Images of Orphan's half-lidded eyes tugged at Shea's heart. "Who were they?"

"Sarah Cohen, aka Orphan. And Deborah Raymond, your club's president."

Shea stared at the floor and picked at dried blood in her nail bed. "What do you want me to say?"

"Turns out Ms. Raymond is the one Jessica claims shot her. But somehow you knew that. How?"

"Deb had left some earrings at my place a few nights ago. After Jess was shot, they were gone. I figured either Jessica's attacker stole them or it was Deb."

"Did you also know Ms. Raymond was responsible for the Bootlegger Bob's fire?"

"No." Anger, frustration, and sorrow pummeled her soul. "Anyone else dead?"

"As it happens, Chlöe Stansbury and Elizabeth Schwartz, otherwise known as Lizzie Black."

"Can't say I'm sorry to hear that."

"No, I suppose not. Any ideas what may have happened this evening?"

"Maybe Orphan and Labrys were dealing hex at the clubs for Bonefish. Maybe they got in a fight about money. I'm just guessing, since I wasn't there."

"Funny thing, there weren't any drugs there."

"That right?"

Rios studied Shea for a moment. "Whoever's got them's facing a whole lotta jail time."

"Good to know. Can I see my girlfriend now?"

"If she's willing, yeah. But last I talked to her, she's pretty pissed at you."

"I don't blame her." Shea got up, opened the door, and walked past the ICU nurse's station to the door of Jessica's room.

The man Shea guessed to be Jessica's father stood up. "Miss, I think you need to leave my daughter alone."

"Daddy," said Jess in a weak voice. "It's all right. Let me and Shea talk."

He and Jessica's mother gave Shea a stern look before walking out of the room. Shea sat next to the bed, her eyes welling up with tears, bile burning her throat.

"I'm so sorry. For all of this."

Their eyes met. Jessica had a pained expression on her face. "I know. You're always sorry. But I can't live like this anymore. The hiding. You being gone all the time. When you do show up, you're always bruised or bleeding or worse. This isn't a relationship."

"I . . . I know. But I . . . I love you, Jess. Annie loves you."

"I love you, too." Jess grasped Shea's hand. "I'm scared. I may never even walk again."

"But you don't gotta be scared no more. Lizzie Black's dead. And I'll take care of you."

"Lizzie Black isn't the one that shot me."

Shea looked away. "I know. Deb. I found out it was her." Her hands felt damp, as if still slick with Deb's blood. "She's dead, too."

"I found her earrings in the dish by the door."

Guilt punched Shea in the chest. "After you left, I . . ."

"Shea, don't. I don't want to hear what you and Deb did." Jess knitted her brow. "Did you . . . did you kill her?"

Shea looked up. "I did what I needed to do to. To protect you."

"Shea . . ." Jessica's mouth went slack, her mental calculations reflected in her eyes.

"She's not a threat anymore."

"And the Confederate Thunder? Are they going to stop attacking the Sisterhood?"

"We're meeting with them tomorrow morning to discuss a truce. There's nothing more for you to worry about."

"Shea, I want to believe you. But as much as I truly love you, I just want a quiet life. I know it sounds boring. But I've realized I like boring."

Shea's pulse thundered in her ears. "Please, baby, I can be boring. You'll see."

Jessica held Shea's face in her hand. "You are my bad girl. There's not a boring bone in your body. And that's part of what drew me to you. But . . . this whole roller-coaster ride has been giving me anxiety attacks."

"Anxiety attacks? When?"

"Doesn't matter." Jess sighed. "My dad has a friend who's offering me a job with Home State Insurance down in Tempe."

"Was this his idea?" growled Shea.

"No, it was mine. I'm doing this for me."

"What about Annie?"

"Annie will be fine. She's got you to take care of her."

"She ran away after you left Terrance's."

Jess raised an eyebrow. "Ran away?"

"Well, technically she asked Julia to pick her up."

"But she's safe?"

Shea shrugged. "Yeah, I suppose."

"Then you and Annie can use this time to get to know each other better. Without me in the way."

"I want you in the way," Shea pleaded.

"I've been in the way too long. It's time to grow up, Shea, and be her guardian. More than a guardian. Her parent."

"I can't convince you to stay, can I?"

Jess shook her head. "I have to do this for me. If you love me—"

"I do, babe."

"Then let me go."

The room felt cramped and stuffy, despite the cool air. Shea kissed Jessica's hand. "I'll miss you."

"I'll miss you, too."

Shea shuffled out.

57

Under a bone-chilling sapphire sky, Shea watched the members of the Confederate Thunder Motorcycle Club wind their way down the switchback gravel road that led to the mine's parking lot. Shea guessed their number to be between three and four dozen. The ground trembled with the sound of so many Harley engines.

Around her stood Fuego, Savage, Indigo, and the two dozen or so other members of the Athena Sisterhood, all sporting the club colors. They were horribly outnumbered and outgunned. If this turned violent, they had no chance.

One bike in the middle of the pack caught Shea's attention: Monster's royal blue Screamin' Eagle Fat Boy. Julia was riding two-up with Annie on the back. Shea released the breath she was holding. Things were looking up.

The Thundermen parked in a semicircle, two deep, around the Sisterhood.

"I'm seriously about to pee myself," whispered Indigo. "We get outta this alive, it'll be a miracle."

"We'll be fine," replied Shea.

"Havoc, Savage, come with me," urged Fuego.

Shea gulped. "Why me?"

"This was your idea, prospect." Fuego put an arm around her as they marched slowly toward One-Shot and Mackey, who were dismounting their bikes.

Annie rushed up and hugged Shea. "Missed you, Aunt Shea."

"Missed you, too, Doodlebug."

"I understand you have a business proposal," said One-Shot, pulling off his wraparound Ray-Bans.

"Both clubs have lost people," said Fuego in a strong, unwavering voice. "It's time to end this feud before anyone else gets hurt."

"Why should we?" asked Mackey. "This is our territory."

"Awhile back you sold Bonefish the hex you stole from the Jaguars," said Shea.

"Allegedly," said One-Shot.

Shea locked eyes with him. "We have it now. Not just the hex, but Bonefish's entire inventory. Ex, weed, acid, Special K, poppers, you name it. Worth over a million on the street."

"Where's Bonefish?"

"Dead, along with her crew. That includes Lizzie Black."

"Yeah, right!" Mackey said with a sneer. "Don't forget, Prez, they shot you while trying to rob our cabin. They can't be trusted."

"I'm aware," said One-Shot.

"We're telling the truth," asserted Fuego. "We'll give you Bonefish's entire inventory at no cost. All we ask is you leave us alone. No more running us off the road. No more harassing."

Shea pointed a finger at Mackey. "No more fucking drive-bys."

Fuego put a hand on Shea's shoulder and continued. "No raping or murdering."

"What about y'all?" asked Mackey. "Y'all burned down our goddamn bar. Killed four of our members and three old ladies."

Fuego looked from Mackey to One-Shot. "That was our former prez, Labrys. On her own. None of us knew anything about it."

One-Shot arched an eyebrow and took a step toward Fuego. "Where's this former president of yours?"

"In the county morgue. Lizzie Black killed her last night. I'm the new president. I'm asking for a truce between our clubs. We give you Bonefish's inventory. We retain our independence, but stay out of your affairs."

Mackey scoffed. "Enough of this nonsense, Prez. Let's just waste these bitches and take the drugs for ourselves."

"No, you don't!" Annie grabbed Mackey's Ruger SR22 out of his side holster. Her hands trembled as she pointed it at him.

"Annie," said Shea as calmly as she could. "Put the gun down, sweetie."

"Fucking brat took my gun!" Mackey glowered at her, his fists balled at his side. "Give that back, ya little cunt, before I beat you senseless with it."

Annie took a step back and cocked the hammer. "You wanna kill my Aunt Shea, you're gonna have to go through me."

"Don't!" Shea wrapped her arms around Annie and grabbed hold of the gun, but not before it fired, punching a hole in the heel of Mackey's boot.

Mackey charged, swinging. Shea smacked him upside the head with the Ruger. He fell face first into the gravel. The chatter of guns being drawn and slides pulled filled the air.

Shea looked up at One-Shot, keeping the Ruger trained on Mackey.

Julia pushed her way through the crowd until she stood before One-Shot. "You listen to me, young man. I've knowed you since you was a little squirt. Your mama didn't raise you to treat women and kids this way. Annie is my grandbaby. Shea-Shea's my family, too. She's done good raising Annie after that pig killed Wendy. What these gals are asking ain't unreasonable."

Mackey wiped blood from his temple. "She's just an old lady. She got no voice in this."

One-Shot looked at Julia, then Shea, before lifting Mackey to his feet. He pulled out a knife and offered it handle-first to Mackey. "Mack, go sit on your bike, take the VP patch off your cut, and shut the hell up."

Mackey sulked over to his bike and did as he was told.

Shea was pleasantly shocked. Not only was it the most words she'd heard One-Shot say in one breath, but she couldn't believe he'd slapped Mackey down for once.

One-Shot extended his hand to Fuego. "The terms are acceptable."

Fuego shook his hand. "Pleasure doing business with you. Drugs are over there underneath that mining equipment. Need some help loading them up?"

"I'd appreciate it."

Fifteen minutes later, the Thunder had emptied all the tote bins from the gallery, packing the bags of drugs into the saddlebags and top cases of every one of their bikes.

Julia dropped a small orange-and-black duffel bag emblazoned with the Harley Davidson logo next to Shea's feet. "Annie's change of clothes is in there."

Shea handed her Mackey's Ruger. "Thanks for watching out for her."

"Try to make her visits a little more reg'lar, if you don't mind."

"I can do that." Shea turned to Annie. "You 'bout ready to go?"

"I gotta stay at Terrance's again?"

"Nah, we're going home."

Annie wrapped her arms around Shea's middle.

Once again, the air shuddered with the sound of Confederate Thunder motorcycles, trekking up the gravel road toward the highway.

Shea pulled out her phone and dialed Rios. "They're headed your way and they're flying heavy."

Are Some Secrets Worth Dying For?

Shea Stevens and the Athena Sisterhood Motorcycle Club agree to protect a troubled woman from a state senator who will do anything to conceal a dark secret.

The situation turns deadly when the powerful politician pulls some strings the Sisterhood didn't anticipate. Shea and the Sisterhood are forced to call in old favors to stem the violence and protect the woman and their own.

Will it be enough to keep the high desert streets of rural Arizona from running red with blood?

Author Dharma Kelleher delivers another high-octane, crime thriller where the twists come as fast as the punches. A must-read for fans of gritty crime fiction about strong, diverse women who kick ass in the name of justice.

Blood Sisters *is the third installment in the highly acclaimed* **Shea Stevens Outlaw Biker** *crime fiction series, although each book in the series can be enjoyed as a standalone.*

Curl up with Blood Sisters and join Shea on this thrill-a-minute ride through across rural Arizona's high desert—a story that will keep you turning the pages into the wee hours.

ABOUT THE AUTHOR

Dharma Kelleher writes gritty crime thrillers including the Jinx Ballou Bounty Hunter series and the Shea Stevens Outlaw Biker series.

She is one of the only openly transgender authors in the crime fiction genre. Her action-driven thrillers explore the complexities of social and criminal justice in a world where the legal system favors the privileged.

Dharma is a member of Sisters in Crime, the International Thriller Writers, and the Alliance of Independent Authors.

She lives in Arizona with her wife and a black cat named Mouse. Learn more about Dharma and her work at https://dharmakelleher.com.